THE GOOD FOR NOTHINGS

DANIELLE BANAS

NEW YORK

A Swoon Reads Book
An imprint of Feiwel and Friends and Macmillan Publishing Group, LLC
120 Broadway, New York, NY 10271

Printed in the United States of America by LSC Communications, Harrisonburg, Virginia.

Library of Congress Cataloging-in-Publication Data is available.

ISBN 978-1-250-31125-2 (hardcover) / ISBN 978-1-250-31126-9 (ebook)

Book design by Liz Dresner
First edition, 2020

10 9 8 7 6 5 4 3 2 1

For the dreamers.
And for anyone in need of a crew
to traverse the galaxy with.

Welcome.

1

THE GUARD WAS LAUGHING AT ME.

This was *not* part of the plan.

We'd only just begun and already this heist was heading south. Or this *job*, as my family phrased it. *Heist* sounded too unethical, and after all, the point of a job was to make money—and that's what we were doing. Making money. Whether or not it was legal . . . well, that was inconsequential.

Today's illustrious venue: the Solar Hall in the Grand Treasury of the icy planet Vaotis.

The plan: While my parents and cousins were busy doing what they did best—skulking in the catacombs, preparing to pull off the biggest robbery in Saros family history—I was in the lobby, doing what I absolutely *did not* do best, despite my mother forcing me into the role during a shouting match this morning over breakfast. I was given the arduous task of distracting the head security guard. And I was failing.

Hard.

I often thought of my family's crime empire as belonging to a secret club, and right now, I was dangerously close to having my membership revoked.

"Just hear me out, sir, please. I'm not trying to sell anything, just take a pamphlet."

I shoved a stack of freshly printed flyers at the guard's chest as he loomed over me. All the inhabitants of Vaotis were tall enough to double as skyscrapers, their skin the brownish gray of sludge, thick enough to combat the harsh elements outside the opulent treasury doors. "You may be unaware, but Vaotis is neglecting thousands of innocent creatures *every single day*. We at the A.R.S.E., that is, the Alliance for the Rescue of Slugs and Eels, are giving a home to the homeless, a voice to the voiceless. They make excellent companions, you know, and we are encouraging all citizens to consider adopting one of these cuddly, docile—"

"You're wasting my time is what you're doing," the guard said in garbled Isolat, the common universal dialect. He ripped one of the flyers into a dozen pieces and scattered them at my feet. Irritation sizzled through me. Slugs made me gag. Eels made me cringe. But stars, I had worked *hard* designing those fake posters, too hard to stand idly by and watch them be desecrated.

The guard sighed. "I don't want nothing to do with your *arse*—"

"A.R.S.E.," I retorted.

"Right. That. It's ludicrous. Girl, the last solicitor who couldn't take a hint and leave when they were ordered to mysteriously found that their head had come unattached from their body."

Beeeeep! At the mention of decapitation, a tiny, frightened sound rose up from behind me.

"What is *that*?" The guard's lip curled as he finally noticed the little robot hiding behind my legs. "Is that an EL-102.5? That model is ancient. You'd be better off junking it."

"How dare you!" I drew Elio against me, clapping my hands over his long, floppy ears. His appearance was humanoid from the neck down, but the rest of him resembled an Earthan bunny rabbit, with a bulbous silver head, a black button nose, and huge blue sensors for eyes. He had been a part of my family for decades. Most definitely long enough to make him incredibly sensitive about how outdated his android body was.

I tensed as the guard reached out to poke Elio's dented forehead. "Where did you get that thing, anyway? Definitely not on Vaotis."

"Neptune," I blurted before my mind could catch up with my mouth. "The dark side. At an antique sale last year."

Elio twitched at the word *antique*.

The guard stroked his pointed chin. The dark side of Neptune was a dismal wasteland, not exactly a prime destination for . . . *antiquing*. While he mulled that over, I glanced at the clock hanging on the wall above the doors, wondering when I would receive the comm on my wristband letting me know that my family had made it into the vaults below the treasury. They should have been there by now.

"Wasn't aware they sold bots on Neptune," the guard grunted. He placed one hand lightly on the blaster strapped to his belt, and I felt my pulse quicken. But he only chuckled. "Get out of here, child, while I'm still in a good mood."

"But wait! The A.R.S.E.—"

He turned to go. "I've had enough of your *arse*, girl."

"No, wait! I don't think you understand just how dire the situation is." I hurried after him as he headed for the security desk, which displayed a whole slew of monitors that I *really* didn't want him looking at right now. "We're raising awareness for the Relief of the, uh, Alliance . . . No, wait. The Alliance Rescue for the . . ."

Oh, crap. What did I name this fake organization again?

"Alliance for the Rescue of Slugs and Eels," Elio whispered behind me.

"Yes!" I snapped my fingers. "That! Listen, sir, I know that as a species they may be a little slimy, but they're really quite sweet and desperately in need of your attention. In fact, if you'd just review the pamphlet again, you'll find that arse—"

"I thought it was A.R.S.E.?" Elio whispered urgently.

"Not. Helping," I hissed back at him.

I slammed my hands on the guard's desk just as he started to examine the cameras. "Hey! Listen to me!" I screeched, forcing a group across the lobby to pause and watch the spectacle. The louder I yelled, the more guards would be drawn to the lobby to detain me, and the better chance my family would have of making it in and out of the vault undetected. *Hit 'em when they're not looking*, that's what my mother always said.

But it was one thing to be a nuisance, to be the reason that ten million ritles of gold would successfully vanish into my family's hands without a trace—it was another thing entirely to do the job well.

My hands shook as the guard eyed me up and down before switching his beady gaze to Elio. The aura around the Vaotin flickered in shades of deep mulberry, telltale signs of frustration. My stomach balled into knots; if Elio and I pushed him too far, if we got on his last nerve and he actually had us arrested, we were going to be so screwed.

"Elio." I cleared my throat, glancing at the guard's name tag. "Tell this nice man, uh, *Roo*, all about your experience with A.R.S.E."

But it was official, Roo'd had enough of us.

"Look, strange child, junky android, if you don't walk out those doors right now I'll—"

Beep!

Roo peered down at Elio, who barely came up to his knees.

Beep! Beep! Beeeeeep!

"What is it doing? Is it malfunctioning? I told you it was ancient."

"No, you're making him upset!" I lunged for Elio, just as a wire sparked near his front-end processor and a gear slowly started to turn in his jaw. I could feel him heating up, each of his sensors pulsing with unadulterated rage. Being called ancient for a second time was just enough of an insult to get him really riled.

"Listen here, you mean, ugly gray blob!" Elio yelled in his staticky voice. His processing system was so hot that it was a wonder the paneling wasn't melting off his frame. I winced as I gripped him tighter. Heat seared my palms, adding to the years of scars already etched into my skin. Maybe he really was malfunctioning. Wouldn't be the first time.

"It's a known fact that—*beep*—that androids have one-point-seven trillion times the intelligence level of the average person—*beep*—and—"

"And where is this intelligence?" Roo asked. "So far you have demonstrated none of it."

I let them go at it, twisting my arm out of Roo's line of sight when my wristband vibrated with a comm from my cousin Blair. I scanned the words quickly, positive I was about to develop some kind of stomach ulcer and die a slow and painful death. This was not going well.

Do something drastic, his message said. *There are still half a dozen guards on rotation down here.*

Drastic? If I weren't busy trying to get a stupid guard to join in my completely fabricated cause, then I could have hacked the security system and had them all in and out of the vaults already, but this was the plan they'd wanted to go with. Now I'd really have to take things up a notch.

More social interaction. This was *so* above my pay grade.

"Hey! You there!" I waved to a treasury employee entering the main doors, and to another exiting the lift against the wall. "And you! Say it with me! SAVE. THE. SLUGS. SAVE. THE. SLUGS." My voice echoed around the cavernous lobby as I chanted. "SAVE. THE. SLUGS."

"Save the—*beep*—slugs!" Elio joined in.

I leaped onto the security desk, scaring away a new wave of employees that had just entered the lobby. "You, sir, in the suit! Don't run! Ma'am! Join our cause! Yell it loud and proud! SAVE THE SLUGS!"

Drastic enough for you, Blair?

"That's ENOUGH!" Roo pulled his blaster from his belt like he was unsheathing a sword. He brought his free hand up to his mouth and muttered into an armband, calling for backup to aid in our untimely demise.

Like that was going to happen. I was already jumping back down to the lobby floor, motioning for Elio to come closer.

Roo's large face contorted in rage. A black storm cloud swirled around his entire body—the aura of the majorly pissed off. I knew that one well: my mother showcased it to me all the time.

I almost jumped out of my skin as he charged forward, the light at the end of his blaster glowing like a sun. He blocked our path to the door just as more guards burst into the lobby. Six in all. The vaults were clear.

"You should have left when I told you," Roo said with a sneer as the rest of them surrounded us.

"Well, lucky for you," said Elio, "we're adorably stubborn." He took a protective step in front of me, giving me the perfect opportunity to reach into the satchel hanging from his shoulder.

"No, what you are is one move away from being carted to the waste management sector."

Elio hung his head. His ears drooped as he let out a feeble, teary beep.

"And *you*." Roo rounded on me. "I'm going to need to see some identifica—*hey*!" He leaned closer. "What's wrong with your face?"

"What do you mean what's wrong with my face?" I wasn't winning a Miss Galactica pageant anytime soon, but I wasn't hideous.

"It's . . . It's *flickering*."

"What do you mean it's . . . *Oh no*."

Not caring what he would think, I plunged my hand down my shirt and ripped off the paper-thin contraption stuck to my chest. A visual enhancement device I'd invented a few months prior during a particularly dull evening at home. Even though I swore I had charged the battery this morning, the enhancer had gone dead.

Beside me, Elio whimpered. It looked like we were dead too.

What the guard had seen before had been merely an illusion—a plain, slightly rumpled Earthan girl. Certainly not a member of the Saros crime family with our fluorescent yellow eyes and the pointed ears that most citizens on our planet of Condor possessed. But that disguise had gone right out the window, along with Roo's angry aura. As soon as the cloud around his head pulsed bright orange with curiosity, I knew he was looking at *me*. The real me.

And he knew that I had something to hide.

He pulled the trigger on his blaster.

"DUCK!" I yelled. Elio and I rolled across the lobby floor, barely missing the red burst of energy that soared over our heads. It connected with the wall, leaving a gaping hole in the stone. The treasury's alarm system blared so loud that it felt like a knife in my brain. White lights flashed along the walls, almost blinding. The group of guards closed in, body armor glinting, blasters raised and ready to annihilate.

"Saturn's rings." Elio tottered to his feet. "I think a few of my bolts got knocked loose. Cora, can you check?"

"Sure thing. After we escape imminent danger, I'll get right on that."

"Thank you."

I jumped back up as my wristband buzzed with a second, long-overdue comm from Blair: *When I said "drastic," I didn't mean "make things go boom!"*

It was followed by a third: *Oooh, you're in trouble!*

"Don't move!" The guards were blocking us from all sides. There was only one way out. And as far as I could see, that way was to plow directly through them.

I held up my hands to placate Roo as he pointed his blaster at my forehead. "Sorry, okay? We're sorry. We're leaving."

"In chains," a female guard piped up.

"Well, before we do that, I have to ask . . . do any of you happen to have plans for the rest of the day? Meetings to go to? Net programs to watch?"

"No," grunted Roo. "Why?"

"Oh. Splendid." I dropped my arms and shook out my sleeves, letting a homemade stun grenade fall into each hand. "Because you're about to be unconscious for the next ten to twelve hours."

Then I pulled the grenades' pins with my teeth and lobbed the weapons through the air.

They exploded in a pulse of electric blue light and a bang that shook the building to its foundation. The guards toppled one by one, landing in a tangled heap. The noise was disorienting, but it didn't affect me the way it affected them. The reinforced plugs I'd grabbed from Elio's satchel and shoved into my ears had absorbed most of the sound.

I bolted for the tall doors across the lobby. The blast took them down, but it was the gas that would spill from the grenades within the next ten seconds that would keep them unconscious. I didn't intend to be around to join the party.

Out of the corner of my eye, I caught a glimpse of Elio scurrying toward Roo. The Vaotin was on his knees, wavering, but he hadn't collapsed yet. As soon as he fell, Elio tugged the blaster from his hands.

Across the lobby, more guards appeared. They were just about to shoot when Elio raised his stolen blaster and fired, sending them sprawling as half the ceiling crashed down on their heads.

"Sorry about that!" I called as Elio caught up with me and we slammed through the treasury doors.

The air outside felt like a wall of ice. I pulled up the collar of my coat to ward off the cold, but it didn't help. Snow stung my cheeks, numbing them instantly.

The few guards left standing were giving chase. I could feel their presence even if I couldn't see them through the swirls of snow and sleet; the glow of four warm bodies pulsed like amber lights through the ice.

Elio grabbed my hand and yanked me sharply to the right, his stubby legs working overtime. "Serpentine! Serpentine! We'll be harder to shoot!"

He swung the blaster behind us and pulled the trigger. An explosion and a chorus of screams greeted us as our feet pounded the crowded city streets of Vaotis. "This thing is awesome! I feel so cool. I can't believe you said that you bought me at an antique sale!"

"Can you hold off on being offended for, like, the next ten minutes maybe? We're in a bit of a sticky situation here."

"But, Cora, an *antique sale*?"

"Ten minutes, Elio. Just until we get up into the sky."

We sprinted around the street corner, sending snow flying in our wake. I'd poorly parallel parked my pod ship—our getaway vehicle—at the end of the block, between a row of pubs and a security station, which in hindsight was probably the worst place I could have left the thing. The puny, dented ship was covered in a thick layer of snow, but it had something else lying on it too. As I leaned against a nearby streetlight, catching my breath, Elio plucked a wet piece of paper from my front viewport.

"You got a parking ticket."

"Oh, for the love of—" I swiped the ticket off him, crumpled it, and chucked it in a trash can at the edge of the sidewalk.

"Cora, you can't do that! It's illegal to throw away a parking ticket!" He glanced nervously through the door of the security station, like he expected one of the officers to come out and reprimand us.

I leveled him with a look. "Seriously? You live with a family of criminals and you're worried about me illegally disposing of a parking ticket?"

"But according to article 7B of the Intergalactic Statute of Transportation—"

"Elio!"

"Sorry!" Then there was a soft beep, and he clapped his hands over his mouth so hard that he stumbled back a step.

Somewhere through the snowdrifts I could hear the furious shouts of the guards, followed by a blast that rocked the street corner. They were coming.

Working quickly, I swiped the snow off the ship, then pulled hard on the lever to open the hatch.

It wouldn't budge.

I thrust my hands into my jacket pockets in a desperate search for my key fob to open the pod.

"Cora?" Elio pointed at the viewport. "You locked it inside the pod."

Sure enough, there it was. Thrown haphazardly on top of the control panel.

"*What*? No, no, no!"

Elio brought his fingers to his mouth and started nibbling them, probably concealing the beep that threatened to burst forth.

"This day is getting better and better." Our images had undoubtedly been caught on multiple security monitors since we ran from the treasury, and now the last thing the good people of Vaotis were going to see before we escaped their star-forsaken planet would be me breaking into my own pod ship. Not the most dignified exit.

"We're going to try something." I removed a palm-size disc from my pocket and slapped it on the middle of the hatch.

"Oh, the phaser!" Elio straightened. "You fixed it?"

"Not quite." If the phaser worked the way it was designed to, it would disrupt the molecules in any solid object enough that we would be able to slip easily through. Of the two phasers I'd built, the better one was currently being used by my family to get into the vaults. This one always struggled to work properly no matter how many times I crossed and uncrossed the wires.

Still listening for the sounds of approaching guards, I turned the phaser on. The slush-streaked side of my pod ship glowed, then shuddered, blurring like I was looking through the hatch from underwater. The image flickered for a second, the hatch hardening before turning liquid again.

"Go! Go before it backfires!" I shoved Elio toward the door.

Just as I started to follow, the guards barreled around the corner in an armored transport, snow crunching beneath its wide tire treads. A delivery pod soared off the road to avoid them, crashing into an awning hanging over the front of a diner. Pedestrians ran as smoke filled the street like a low-hanging fog. I couldn't tell if the guards had spotted us yet or not.

I took my first step into the hatch, but the phaser flickered again, short-circuiting. Elio's eyes flared bright with alarm while his hands flew across the control panel, powering up the ship. I tried slogging forward, my muscles tensing and burning as I struggled to push through the hatch. It was only a foot thick. It should have been easy.

A blast of light flew over the ship, exploding into the face of the building behind us. The pod started to solidify around me, and I had a flash of fear that I would get trapped inside, half in and half out of the ship, struggling to breathe until Elio could track my family down and get the other phaser to reverse the damage.

But before my panic had a chance to reach meltdown levels, I felt a hand on my arm, pulling me out of danger as if dragging me through mud. With an earsplitting pop, Elio and I landed in a heap in the bucket seats at the front of the cockpit, and the hatch sealed behind us.

"Up! Go, go, go!" I yelled.

We lifted off, crashing into the parked pod in front of us in the process. The guards shot at us a few more times, but they hadn't accounted for us having an escape pod. In seconds, we were out of range.

A grin pulled at my lips as we hurtled through the atmosphere around Vaotis. We were coming up on the Triangulum Galaxy's only wormhole, our ticket home. Elio pushed forward on the ion thrusters. The wormhole sphere bulged and spun before us like a bubble. And just like any bubble, the wormhole could only exist for a few precious seconds at a time before popping.

The pod ship shuddered as the thrusters ignited. A shiver raced up my spine. Jumping galaxies always put me a little out of sorts. Something about the speed and the pressure made my body feel like a jar of putty.

Double-checking my harness, I watched as white light flared from the widening sphere, obscuring the front viewport. Then, as always, time seemed to slow, and that beautiful rip in the universe opened. Straight as an arrow, the pod ship soared through.

Good riddance, Vaotis. A pleasure you were not.

My harness cut into my shoulders as the ball of energy bent around us and we were launched out the other side at top speed, only slowing once we hit deep space and the peaceful expanse of stars. Every time I saw the view, I could barely breathe. I knew that space was just . . . nothing. A vacuum. But even so, that quiet void brought me more serenity than any planet in the universe.

My smile faded only when Elio adjusted the propulsion controls and switched course, sending us down the five-hour trek toward home. In five hours, I'd have to face what I'd done. I'd drawn *too* much attention. I'd nearly gotten us all killed.

But maybe it wouldn't matter. If they got their hands on the ten million ritles, my family would overlook one mistake.

Fingers shaking, I sent off a quick comm to Blair. *How did it go down there?*

He responded immediately.

We failed.

I gripped the straps of my harness in both fists as an all-consuming dread welled up inside my chest.

His next message simply read: *Your mother is not happy.*

THE DARKNESS ON OUR TINY PLANET MADE IT THE PERFECT locale for crime to flourish. And it was an even better locale for hiding my family's heaps of junk.

Condor's permanent blackout was courtesy of our empress, Verena. During the few minutes of the day that sunlight touched our borders located in the farthest corner of the Andromeda Galaxy, Verena released a dark tint on the dome that warmed our planet, leaving our streets and neighborhoods in dank, dreary blackness. Why she chose to do it, no one knew. She rarely stepped into the public eye, and I'd heard every rumor from she was a monster that would burn in sunlight to she had skeletal deformities and didn't want anyone to see her.

I disagreed on both accounts. I never believed that Verena preferred the dark over the light; I thought she just didn't like change.

I was similar to her in that way.

By the time Elio parked my pod in the filthy alleyway behind our house on the east side of Condor, my nails were bitten to nubs, and I'd worked myself up into a nervous frenzy. Another pod, a far cleaner and fancier one, was parked just in front of us. I didn't have to squint through the shadows to know it belonged to my parents. If they beat me and Elio home, then my mother must have been flying ridiculously fast.

Meaning she was *ridiculously* mad.

Elio and I hurried up the walk to the front door, almost tripping on a pile of trash strewn across the stones. Another day in paradise. Any one of us could have cleaned it up, but every member of my family put an enormous amount of effort into pretending we weren't swimming in stolen gold and priceless artifacts.

The house buzzed with activity when we stepped over the threshold. White lights bounced off the high ceiling in the entryway, giving me an instant headache after the darkness outside. I could hear a few of my cousins arguing from one of the upper hallways, and when I closed the door with a snap, a group of them poked their heads over the banister.

"Cora's home!" Mina yelled, her aura glowing like pink soap bubbles as she threw her hands in the air. She was four years old—and the only person in our house who was ever happy to see me.

Mina waved, then ducked back into her bedroom, four of my other cousins following suit. That left only Blair, who mounted the banister and slid backward from the second floor to the foyer, dismounting with a sloppy grin on his face.

"I can't believe you actually came home. You have bigger balls than me."

"Shut up." I slapped his arm and he swayed before grabbing Elio to steady himself. Elio immediately scooted closer to my side. "Where are my parents?"

"In the kitchen. Probably planning your funeral." His smile widened. He looked strangely happy for someone who wouldn't see a payday this week because of my screwup.

I leaned forward to smell his breath. "Have you been drinking?"

"You insult me, Cora. There are children up there." He pulled a fat pipe out of his pants pocket. "I've been smoking. Just a bit of moon dust."

"You're repulsive."

Blair shrugged and took a long drag of the pipe. "It's perfectly legal . . . just not on this planet. You might want to take a hit before you go into the kitchen and talk to Mommy Dearest." He turned to Elio, saying in a false whisper, "You know, Cora couldn't steal a bag of cash if it had two feet and no clothes and . . . and . . ."

"And was dancing naked in front of me?" I finished. "At least I can finish a sentence, human blunt."

The tips of Blair's ears filled with a dark blush. "Don't hate."

"That stuff is going to rot your brain."

His bright yellow eyes narrowed at both Elio and me. He puffed a cloud of red smoke in our faces before heading up to his room. "At least I'll be rich."

"Always a delightful boy," I muttered once he had locked himself behind his door.

With Blair gone, I had no choice but to continue through the house and confront my parents in the kitchen. Sure, I could hide in my room for a while, but they would find me. And then everything would be a million times worse.

"I feel like we're heading to the gallows," Elio said. His tiny fingers gripped mine and squeezed. "Earthans used to kill people that way. I saw it in a net program."

"Stop worrying. They won't be angry with you."

We crossed the foyer, stepping carefully over several crates of rare geodes that were due to be smuggled to traders on the outer fringes of the galaxy, and continued down the long passage to the kitchen. The hall was always too messy to walk in a straight line. Every few steps we had to dodge boxes and bags and more crates, each one full of objects that my family either stole for our trusted buyers or stole for ourselves with the sole purpose of turning around and selling back to the owners for double or triple what they were worth.

This had been going on for as long as I could remember. Longer even. The stealing, the conning. We hit up every planet and moon in both the Andromeda and Milky Way galaxies. Triangulum was the newest conquest, and it was also proving to be the one that was making us the wealthiest.

When I finally pushed open the kitchen door, I noticed that my parents had assumed their usual positions—backs to me—standing halfway between a table filled with protein pouches and a table covered in "priceless materials."

Many things in this house were considered priceless, but others could be loosely translated to *useless piles of junk*. Case in point: The headdress that my mother snatched right off the brow of the long-ruling Queen Adona of Oprora VII? *Priceless*. A set of Earthan badminton shuttlecocks from 1985? *Junk*.

Cruz and Evelina Saros were hoarders, plain and simple.

"Someone will have to go back to Vaotis and take care of the guards," my father said, tearing into the shiny silver wrapper of a protein pouch. "They saw too much."

"Killing over a dozen guards will draw the kind of attention we've been working so hard to avoid." My mother tilted her head, considering. "But if we really have no choice . . ."

I made a noise halfway between a gasp and a whimper, forcing both Cruz and Evelina's attention my way. I'd never killed anyone, but if those guards died, wouldn't that make me partially responsible? I was the reason today's job had failed, after all.

Evelina yanked out a chair from the elegantly carved ivory dining table. It was a new addition to the kitchen, meaning she had recently stolen it. "Cora. Exactly who we were looking for."

I sank into the chair while Elio cowered behind me, his ears twitching nervously. "I can explain."

"Can you?" A threatening black storm cloud pulsed like a heartbeat around her head. It was almost unbearable to look at her when she was this angry. Just like the rest of the men and women born on Condor, Evelina and I had the same bright yellow eyes, the same pointed ears, the same silver hair that I preferred to tie up, because otherwise it fell in a frizzy mess down my back. We had the same pigmentless, pale skin, an outcome of living in an endless night, but right now hers was flushed pink with fury, and I knew I was about to get it.

"Listen," I said, "I know what happened today looks bad, but—"

"*Looks* bad?" Evelina screeched. "*Looks*? That was the biggest job we've had all year! Not only are we out ten million ritles, not only did you ruin our relationship with our client, but we have to send someone back to Vaotis to clean up your mess. Your face must have been on every security monitor on the planet—the galaxy even! And now that the guards saw that infernal device you made, they'll be on high alert!"

I brushed my fingers over the VED concealed in my pants pocket. "It was fully charged. I don't know what happened."

"You neglected to account for the possibility that it might not work. And then your pod got ticketed. Oh yes, I know about the ticket." She grinned like she'd just won a criminal of the year award. (Though that ceremony wouldn't occur for another six months.) "For all you know, the officer who ticketed you also put a tracker on your ship. What will you do when they come knocking on our door? How will you explain everything that's in this house?" She spread out her arms, showcasing the stolen goods stacked in the corners.

I looked back at Elio to see his eyes wide and fearful. Neither of us had thought there was a possibility that we might be followed.

"There wasn't a tracker on the pod," I said. "I checked." Or I *would* check, just as soon as this conversation was over.

"You didn't check." Evelina bared her teeth in triumph. I imagined them slicing into my jugular. "But your father did. There's nothing there."

She almost looked disappointed.

"See? I didn't completely mess up," I said.

"You were lazy," she snapped. "We taught you better."

"Did you? Because last I checked, you taught me how to hack a computer system and build a blaster from scratch. You never made me a distraction. You never put me in the line of fire. I could have died." I gestured to Elio. "*We* could have died."

Elio shuffled his feet. "I would prefer you leave me out of this."

Evelina pouted, as if she actually cared. But unless my skin was suddenly made of gold, her caring was highly unlikely. "We wouldn't have let you die, Cora. Oh, don't look at me like that, we wouldn't have. And calm down. I can see your aura spreading all over the room."

"Been practicing, have you? Congratulations." Everyone native to Condor had a slight talent for reading auras, but my skills far surpassed anyone else's in my family. It was probably the only thing I was better at than them.

The corner of Cruz's mouth quirked at my sass, but Evelina's nostrils flared. She tapped her long nails across the tabletop. She'd taken to filing them into points recently, making them a deadlier weapon than almost any blaster.

She looked about ready to skewer me with them when the door creaked open and my Nana Rae shuffled through. Seeing Nana was like looking into Evelina's future. Her back was bent like a crowbar, her milky skin soft and full of wrinkles. She dug through the protein pouches, ignoring us completely while she hummed the low notes of the Condor national anthem.

"Evelina, about today—" I started.

She shushed me. "Don't complain while your grandmother is in the room."

"It's not like she can hear us." Despite having bionic implants, Nana Rae always had her ears turned off.

After scooping up half the box of protein pouches, Nana Rae pivoted, swaying a bit under their weight. When she finally noticed the four of us, she gasped, and a few packets fell to the floor.

"Oh!" Her humming started up again, louder now. She paused only long enough between verses to peer out the window and mutter, "It's darker today than it was yesterday."

Evelina stepped forward. "It's the same, Mother. It's always the same."

"No." Another verse of humming. "Definitely darker." Her neck arched as she peered up into Evelina's eyes. "Or perhaps that's because you're in the room, dear."

Elio snickered.

Evelina's golden eyes appeared to be spitting sparks. "Mother, go to bed. Cora will bring those to your room."

Nana Rae heaved her bundle of pouches a bit higher. "I am perfectly capable of getting a meal on my own. What's next? You're going to hand-feed me? I'd like to see you try." She continued to hum as she exited the room, loud and off-key and disruptive enough to hopefully draw all the attention away from me and Elio. I tried sliding quietly out of my chair to creep after her, but Evelina snapped her fingers in my direction, her deathly nails clicking.

"Where are you going? We're not done with you yet," she snarled. "We're holding back two months' pay after what happened this afternoon."

"What?" I looked desperately from her to Cruz, who only shrugged. "No! I need that money."

Elio and I *both* needed that money.

"Cora. Sweetheart." Evelina placed her hands on my cheeks, squeezing slightly. She didn't appear to be mad anymore, which I knew was even worse. She was like a snake, waiting to strike until the time was right. Cruz wasn't any better. Always silent, always standing in her shadow. Why he put up with her, I didn't have a clue.

"I need that money," I repeated pathetically.

"Cora, I know it's hard," she cooed. "I remember when I was your age. Seventeen." She pinched my cheeks a bit harder. "So young. You just want to help, right?" She jerked my head up and down. "Right. You are the future of this family. You need to take on more responsibility, but perhaps you just aren't ready for it."

Her soft words took on an icy sting that I saw coming a mile away.

"Maybe you really are no better than a distraction."

Forget running a crime empire, Evelina Saros had one true talent: she always had an incredible knack for making me feel worthless.

"Do not disappoint me again, Cora." She pinched my cheeks one final time, hard enough that I felt blood rush to the surface. "I'm doing this because I want the world for you. Your mother knows best, do you understand?"

I nodded, but as soon as she let go of my face, I grabbed Elio's hand and bolted from the kitchen. My skin felt like it was crawling. *Mother*. I hadn't called Evelina that since I was a child.

I knew it would be easier to go along with her, to please her. Eventually, this mess of a family business would be mine, and I would have more money than I'd ever need.

But by then . . . it might be too late.

3

"HAVE YOU EVER NOTICED," ELIO ASKED ME, "THAT WHEN Evelina gets really angry, her eyes bug out like a fish?"

"Yeah, you should tell her. I'm sure she would find that incredibly attractive. Not offensive at all."

"I thought the same thing!"

"That's sarcasm, Elio." We turned the corner on the fourth floor and headed up the ramp to level five. The house was a converted apartment complex, each level separated by spiraling ramps of glowing white moonstone. But despite its grandeur, calling the house a home was a stretch. Even though my family filled its halls, we all agreed that the house was just a place to stash our stuff.

"I understand sarcasm quite well, thank you very much," Elio said as we reached the top floor. "You programmed it into my hard drive when you were twelve. I'm a pro now."

"Thank the skies for that. Could you imagine how bored I would be otherwise?"

We entered my bedroom, the only room up here. Elio and I had christened it "The Nest" years ago, considering we were as far above ground as anyone could get in this house. Three of the four walls were made of glass, showcasing the jagged Condor skyline and the winking lights of the manufacturing district that stretched out around us.

My bedroom was about as tidy as the rest of the house. Wires and gears littered the workbench wedged beside my bed. The lamp on my desk illuminated a stack of blueprints for potential gadgets that I'd yet to find time to make, along with a half-built X-ray sensor for Elio that shocked me every time I tried to touch it.

I chucked the broken phaser and the visual enhancer onto the workbench, where they landed on top of the remnants of last night's dinner—fried jellyfish from Condor's central marketplace. Only then did I notice the cuts dotting my hands from falling at the treasury. I'd have to clean them, and then they could join the dozens of scars on my palms and fingertips. An unfortunate side effect of playing with metal and wires. Every once in a while, things decided they wanted to catch fire.

"I think the phaser needs a new molecular generator," I said, digging a screwdriver into the control panel and prying it open. "I definitely don't have enough money to buy one. Do you think we could steal—?" I looked over my shoulder. "Elio?"

Saturn's rings, not again.

Roo had called Elio's beeping at the treasury a malfunction. But the twitching he was doing now—frozen mid-step in the doorway—was the real problem. If the universe were a fair place, then I could say that this was the first time Elio had glitched. But it wasn't. And he had glitched too many times over the last few months for me to count.

"Hang on. I got you, I got you." I maneuvered his body, which felt as heavy as a sack of bricks, across the room and deposited him on my bed. While he lay motionless, I stumbled over to my desk and ripped open one of the drawers, dumping out a tangled pile of wires. A few screws and a stray bolt rolled across my path, but I kicked them under the bed, diving for a thick purple cord, frayed at the edges from years of use.

One end of the cord plugged into the side of my computer, while the other popped into the charging port at the base of Elio's neck.

I picked at an old scar on my palm while the computer ran a

diagnostic test, feeling the contents of my stomach swirl up into the back of my throat as I watched a hologram of Elio's body spin above the screen. A red light pulsed over his head. Same as always. The source of his glitching—and the reason for my current money problems—was hidden deep inside Elio's robotic brain.

I hated thinking about it, because thinking about it made me nauseous, but his memory core was depleting even faster than usual. The computer pinged with his test results. Only 79 percent functioning. Last week it was functioning at 87 percent. The week before: 91 percent.

I dropped my head into my hands.

Elio had always been a bit . . . off. A bit more human than the other bots my parents had owned throughout my childhood. Even for a bot, he was small. When we stood side by side, his dented head barely reached my hip, but that wasn't the only reason he was different.

Elio was originally built to be a servant bot, until something in his programming chip warped. He was *supposed* to be able to cook gourmet meals, but everything he made ended up burnt beyond recognition—except for his cookies, strangely enough. He was also *supposed* to be able to clean an entire house at top speed. But whenever he tried, the rooms ended up messier than before. My parents had attempted to fix him numerous times, but no repairs ever worked. If anything, he got messier. *More* human. Eventually they got tired of trying and gave him to me to play with when I was six or so. Eleven years later and he was still my best friend.

I wasn't going to lose him.

I knew exactly what would fix him—he needed a new body. His was too old, too small, and his memory core had grown too advanced to be compatible. I wiped my hands on my pants before turning to my computer and flipping through pages of data, re-reading everything I already knew.

Elio's brain was too human, and now his body was rejecting him for it.

Heaving a sigh, I tapped a few times on my keyboard, sending a pulse of electricity down the cord straight into the back of his neck. Elio jolted, slamming my bed against the wall. The fan near his front-end processor whirred angrily, but still he didn't wake.

"Come on, you stupid piece of junk, come on!" I pounded the keyboard again, sending more electricity into his charging port. When in doubt, a good insult always roused him. It was like he refused to die out of pure spite.

A third pulse of electricity. Another jolt on my bed.

And then . . .

"*Ouch*!" He pulled the cord out of his port, mouth agape with horror. "I am *not* a stupid piece of junk."

"Welcome back, Elio."

He grimaced and balled up the cord before dropping it back on my desk. "How long was I out this time?"

"A few minutes. Not too terrible," I lied. Right before he disconnected himself from my computer, the capacity in his memory core had jumped back up to 83 percent, but it was likely falling again. He had too much knowledge and not enough space to contain it.

"Can I see?" He scooted next to me, flipping through the data from his diagnostic test. I couldn't read his aura—being mechanical, he didn't have one—but during times like this I really wished that weren't the case.

After a minute, he shut off the computer and busied himself with picking up the wires I'd dropped on the floor. Somehow, he managed to twist them into a ball of knots in five seconds flat.

"My name is Elio," he recited slowly. "My favorite thing to eat is cookies—"

"You can't eat," I reminded him.

"Not yet. Just wait until someone builds me a body that can."

He screwed up his eyes and continued. "My favorite thing to eat is cookies. There are one hundred and ten species of bullfish in the lake on west Condor—"

"One hundred and eleven."

"What? No, there's one hundred and . . ." A pause. "Eleven. Cora, how did I forget that there are *one hundred and eleven* species of bullfish?"

"Relax. That's such a minor fact that it's basically insignificant."

Every time Elio glitched, he temporarily lost a piece of information from his memory core. It could be anything. Something trivial (like the common lillybird migration patterns or which of the one hundred and eleven species of bullfish was most vicious during mating season), or even something critical, like the friendaversary party I'd thrown him every year since I was eight. Or his favorite cookie to bake. Or the worst glitch yet—when he forgot his name for five whole minutes.

I promised myself—and him—that last instance would never occur again. I was no seamstress, but I'd sloppily sewn his name into every article of clothing he owned—because in his quest to be human he'd purchased *two* closets full of Condor's most fashionable outfits—so he wouldn't forget. I'd even sewn it into his underwear.

Especially his underwear.

"If we don't get me a new body, then I'm toast," he said quietly.

"Elio, we'll get you a new body."

If only it were that easy. Stealing a fresh android body was out of the question. I'd never accomplish a heist of that magnitude by myself.

I dug through one of the larger drawers at the bottom of my desk, removing a steel box weighed down by a lock as thick as my fist. I punched in the combination and started counting the money, even though I knew exactly how much there would be: ten thousand gold ritles. My life savings from working for my parents. It was nowhere near the kind of money I would need to buy Elio a new body. And my mother wasn't exactly big on giving me loans.

"I have enough to fix up some of your patches," I told him as he abandoned his attempt to tidy my room and sat back down on the bed.

"I appreciate you trying to make me feel pretty, but they aren't what I'm worried about." He rubbed a hand over the paneling covering the side of his neck. Most of it appeared normal, a bright silver that never once hinted something was amiss. But a large square along his throat was wearing away more and more each day, a hole forming to expose the translucent coating that covered a mess of wires and gears along his man-made spinal column. He had similar patches on his face and arms, and while he found them unsightly, they wouldn't harm him the way his memory core would.

"How much more money do we need?" he asked.

I didn't bother sugarcoating it. "Fifty thousand."

He flinched. "I'm sorry. I know this is hard for you."

"You mean hard for *you*." He always put others before himself. That was the only part of his programming that wasn't faulty. "We'll get the money. Maybe I can find work somewhere else."

But really, where would I go? My marketable skills consisted of lying, stealing, and building things that went *boom*. Not exactly clean-cut qualities.

Elio resumed reciting facts about himself ("*My name is Elio. My favorite thing to eat is cookies . . .*") while I cleaned off my desk, organizing a stack of blueprints and sorting a cup of screws according to size and color. When I reached the bottom of the cup, my fingers hit something smooth.

I almost threw the object in the trash. It was a round piece of moonstone no larger than my thumb, a supposed good luck charm that Evelina gave me when I was a child—before she spent her time reciting all the ways in which I was a disappointment. But oddly enough, I couldn't bear to throw it away.

Next to me, Elio was busy listing all one hundred and eleven species of bullfish, his deep blue eyes glowing, looking far more earnest and far more human than anyone else in this house.

I studied the piece of moonstone again. I didn't know if I could ever get back to the time when Evelina gifted it to me—when I wasn't just her employee but her daughter—but I knew what I could do to satisfy her now. I could give her something very valuable, and in turn she would reinstate my paychecks. Maybe then she really would look at me like I was her child.

Like I was more than just a distraction.

"Hey . . . Cora?" Elio pulled at my sleeve, his voice very small and close to breaking. "If we don't find me another body, it'll be okay."

I shook my head. He didn't understand. He wouldn't be the one who would have to live in this house without their best friend.

"Absolutely not. I'm not letting you disappear. I'll stick your memory core in Evelina's pod ship if I have to."

The corner of his mouth lifted slightly. "I've always thought it would be cool to have wings."

"Well, don't start practicing your liftoff techniques yet. We're going to get that money, I'm going to stop being the family disappointment, and we're going to fix everything."

"But how are we going to *do* that?"

"By beating them to their next mark. We're going to do their work for them." I flashed him my wristband, then started scrolling through my recent comms. I knew there was a message about my family's next job in here somewhere . . .

I jumped up when I finally found it. "Cruz's pod ship heads back to Vaotis in two days. So *we're* leaving tomorrow."

Elio jumped up too, but he had to stand on his toes to get a good look at my comm link. "Back to the treasury? Are you crazy? *Beep*!"

"No. We're not going anywhere near that place." I lowered my wrist to show him the message, complete with a map of the planet. "There's a cemetery in the backcountry that's home to a very royal, very *rich* family."

"*Ohhh* . . . wait." It took a moment, but then my plan seemed to click in his head. "You don't mean . . ."

"I sure do." I tossed an arm around his shoulders. "Elio, how do you feel about grave robbing?"

"Enlighten me, dearest Cora, star of my life, best friend forever, et cetera, et cetera: Why am *I* the one who has to pilfer the dead lady's tomb?"

"Because, dear Elio, my handsome friend, I'll be the one running surveillance."

"That is such a rip-off."

I eased our pod ship into the gravitational pull of Vaotis, shielding my eyes against the frozen white expanse stretching out before us. I often complained about Condor's constant dark, but being in a constant state of cold was, in my opinion, far worse.

I zipped up my heavy jacket as we landed in a deserted country field, and pulled a hat low over my ears while Elio released the air lock on the hatch. Already I could feel tendrils of ice creeping into the cockpit. What I wouldn't give for a wool blanket right now.

"You're also the only one out of the two of us who can't feel changes in temperature," I said. "Plus, you're stealthier because you don't throw off auras for people to read."

"Flatter me a bit more, why don't you?" He pulled on a coat and wrapped a scarf around his mouth, covering most of his patches. "I wanted to run surveillance."

"The last time anyone let you run surveillance, the computer started smoking and then you roasted sugar snaps over the flames."

Elio smacked his jaws together. "They were delicious. Way better than Earthan marshmallows."

"You can't eat!"

"Yet."

He was impossible. And yet, if I failed to save him . . . Well, I couldn't think about it. But I knew that I would miss him. Terribly.

Shaking myself back into action, I tossed Elio a comm for his wrist while I monitored the progression of the sun over the hills. I could just pick out the angular shapes of tombstones and vaults beyond the snowdrifts. The cemetery would be closed now, and once the sun disappeared and I hacked into the security monitors placed outside the gates, we would have no witnesses.

Elio exited the pod—almost tumbling into a pile of snow in the process—and waded through the field and up the hill to the cemetery. He made slow progress, the snow up to his belly, giving me more than enough time to disable the cameras and replace the footage in the servers with a recorded loop from the prior evening.

My fingers flew across the many monitors in the pod ship, never stalling, like a choreographed dance. I was at home in the silence of the ship, with only the lights of my control panel and the soft blue glow of the screens for company.

This was what I should have been doing during the job at the Grand Treasury. *This* was where I excelled. Once Elio and I pulled this robbery off, we would never have to be distractions again.

"I'm guessing all the rich, dead Vaotins and their heaps of gold are buried in the largest crypt?" Elio asked, appearing on the monitor closest to me. Graves filled the space behind him, poking out of the ground like teeth.

I consulted Cruz's notes on my comm link. "Second-largest crypt. Apparently they were trying to throw off all the peasants like us. Oh, and once you get in, do me a big favor and take one of the queen's bones. Cruz has written here that conspiracy theorists claim the bones are full of magic that can open a black hole into another universe or something equally ridiculous."

Elio burst out laughing. "That isn't possible."

"As long as we can sell them to one of the suckers, then I don't really care. I doubt Cruz and Evelina will either."

"All right, then. Bone. Heaps of gold. Priceless gems. Is there anything else you would like me to retrieve for you? The moon, perhaps?"

"I've always wanted someone to get me a comet for my birthday."

"Will do." He gave me a quick salute, then turned his comm so I could see the door of the crypt, which was made of white moonstone, blending in perfectly with the surrounding hills and valleys. A twisting black lock cut across the width of the door like a river. "Can you crack this?"

"Can I?" I scooted forward in my chair to get a closer look, fingertips tingling. "That's approximately six inches of plutonium. Cobalt handle. Magnum D-57 locking mechanism." I grinned. "Might as well have asked me to break open an egg."

Two quick taps on the keypad in front of me and . . . "Done. Give that a try."

He jiggled the handle. The door didn't budge.

"Should I say a magic word? *Open-please-says-a-me*!"

"Try kicking it," I suggested. He did, and the door opened with a creak. "See? Evelina should give me a raise. In you go."

Elio took a few steps into the crypt, the screen on his comm darkening until he was just a shapeless blob on my monitor. "Hey, do you think my new body can have a mustache? I've always wanted a mustache."

"You can have whatever your little synthetic heart desires." I checked the live feeds from the cameras in the cemetery, searching for any possible intruders, but I found none. Well, I might as well get some work done while I waited.

Swiveling in my pilot's chair, I dug through my bag for the faulty pieces of my visual enhancement device. If I fixed it *and* we managed to bring back a good haul . . . then Evelina might actually smile at me today and mean it.

"I think I want a goatee to go with my mustache," Elio prattled on. "And I'd prefer a body that's really tall. Oh—okay, I'm going down a few steps here." His figure bobbed on-screen. "Oh, yikes, a lot of steps. This place is really dark." He flicked on a flashlight built into the palm of his hand. "That's better."

A crackle of static shot through the screen, and Elio's voice and image cut out for a second before reappearing.

"—oor?" was all I heard him say.

"What?"

"I said, 'Can you get the next door?' It looks the same as the last one."

He was deep in the crypt now—or at least that was how it looked. White walls streaked with something black that I *really* hoped was just dirt bracketed a wide archway. No signs of royal dead people, but maybe they would be in the next room.

I unlocked the door with a few quick keystrokes, and Elio headed inside.

The video feed from his comm flickered again. A spark shot out the top of my own comm as the screen went black.

"Elio?"

I could still hear his voice, far off, like he was shouting across a valley. "I found them. They're encased in glass. They look like they're sleeping." He beeped. "Cora . . . they still look alive. They're not alive, right?"

"Formaldehyde," I said, distracted by the black screen on my comm. Was my connection bad, or was his? More importantly, why did it seem like everything I touched lately was malfunctioning at the worst moments?

"Formaldehyde," Elio repeated. "Right. Sorry, I'm nervous. It's creepy down here. Can I come back now?"

"You can as long as you don't come back empty-handed."

"No worries there. This place is full of gold. I think I can open the glass and get one of those bones you wanted too."

"Excellent. Just make sure you . . ." My words died as quickly as the comm link in my hands. As quickly as the monitors on my control panel, which blinked out one . . . by one . . . by one . . .

An icy feeling crept over my shoulders, one I was positive had nothing to do with the unfortunate weather patterns on this awful planet.

"Elio?" I gripped my comm tight enough to break it. The power button was still lit. Maybe I was overreacting. Maybe everything on his end was fine. "Are you still there?"

"Cora?"

I sighed in relief. "Yeah. Hurry up. I want to get home before someone spots us." I stopped any nerves from leaking into my voice. I didn't want to scare him even more.

But he didn't hear me. "Cora? Cora, are you there?"

"I'm here. I—"

"Something down here doesn't feel right. I don't think I'm glitching. It feels like—"

The line went dead.

"Elio!" I shook the comm, resisting the urge to throw it at the wall. "Elio!"

My heart slid into my throat as the power in the pod ship went out with a groan, leaving me in the dark.

Elio.

The dark I could handle. Cold I could not, but I didn't stop to think about it. I pulled down on the emergency release to open the hatch, and then I was racing through the snow, up the hill to the cemetery, my hat blowing off in the harsh winds. Damn my surveillance to the edges of the universe, I shouldn't have let Elio go in there alone.

The crypt had even more stairs than he said, and I stumbled down them in the pitch black, cursing myself for not bringing a flashlight as I shouted Elio's name. When there was no response, I had to pinch myself so I wouldn't panic. Were there guards down here? Something I had so easily overlooked? Evelina was right: I wasn't ready to lead a job like this.

I hit the bottom of the stairs, almost slipping in a puddle. The arch that I'd seen on Elio's comm loomed in shadows cast by a soft light in the room beyond, which glowed inside the glass prism containing the Vaotin queen. The lid of her tomb was pushed open a crack where Elio had attempted to get inside.

I found him collapsed on the dais beneath the tomb.

"Elio!" This didn't appear to be a glitch. He wasn't rigid, frozen in time. He was limp, as if he'd just had enough for the day and powered down. It was exactly what I always imagined would happen if his memory core really did die.

"You're okay. I'll fix you." I refused to let myself panic as I hauled him up. Shifting him underneath my arm, I reached out to the tomb to brace myself.

My fingers dipped through the crack Elio had made, hooking around the ice-cold arm of the dead queen inside.

It happened all at once.

The door to the room slammed, shaking the walls, rattling the heaps of gold and jewels piled in the corners. There was no handle that I could see from the inside. No way out. The temperature plunged well below freezing, so cold that the breath stopped in my lungs.

Water began snaking out of cracks near the ceiling. The air should have been cold enough to freeze it instantly, but it barreled onward, gushing hard enough to cover the floor and creep up the steps to the dais in a matter of seconds.

I took a step back, bumping into the queen's tomb and consequently sending another wave down the walls and across the floor. Elio's body sagged against me. I couldn't keep a hold on him. I couldn't even keep a hold on myself.

My mind went silent as the water climbed higher. Soul-crushing, world-darkening silence. For all that Cruz and Evelina had taught me—how to pick a pocket, how to build a bomb that would destroy half a city—they never thought it was pertinent to teach me how to swim.

I was going to die.

Today. Here. *Now*.

I pulled Elio closer as the water hit the edge of the dais, washing over the toes of my boots. Only then did I feel the lump against his side—the shape of a blaster and a pocket full of some of my most powerful explosives.

Either I could risk the crypt collapsing on top of us, or I could drown in this room. An explosion, at least, seemed like the quicker way to go.

The water rose—*faster, faster, faster*. It covered my ankles, surpassed my knees, my thighs, my hips. A sweet-smelling mist filled the room, similar to Blair's moon dust but far stronger. My skin rippled with tingles, my limbs so weak I could hardly stand. Pulling the trigger on the blaster seemed impossible. A grenade it would be, then.

My vision went black around the edges as I pawed around in Elio's jacket. Just as the water reached my chest, I ripped out the pin of a fat yellow explosive with my teeth and lobbed it at the door.

Before I could hear the bang, my mind darkened completely, and the water rushed over us both.

4

"DO YOU THINK SHE'S DEAD? I'M PUTTING MY MONEY ON dead. Not that I have any money on me at the moment . . ."

Something sharp dug into my side. I tried opening my eyes, but they refused to budge. Somewhere nearby, the voice continued, a high-pitched drone that sounded as if it were drilling a hole into my brain. If I could remember how to operate my arms, then I would have rolled over and punched whatever dared to interrupt my sleep. But I just lay there—wherever *there* was—immobile and cranky, my mouth filled with a sour tang as if I'd licked the inside of a trash can.

"The little one is pretty shiny. If he doesn't wake up, we could harvest some of his parts." The voice laughed, and there was a slapping sound followed by a growl. "Come on, you lump! Help me move them in from the door. Chivalry isn't dead yet. I should—*oh*! You're awake!"

"Cora?" Elio's cold, tiny fingers prodded my cheeks, and my eyes flew open. My muscles were cramped, my body pulsing with sudden terror and the overwhelming desire to both vomit and urinate. Four cinder block walls surrounded us, dripping something that was hopefully water.

"What the—" I stopped abruptly, my throat burning. How much water did I inhale in the crypt? Were we still on Vaotis? Memories of our failed job came rushing back, but they were eclipsed by the sight of Elio sitting on the floor beside me. His ears hung limply around his face, and more holes on his neck had cropped up, exposing half a dozen new patches of wires, but he was *alive*. Somehow we both were.

"Oh, goody. New friends," said the same high voice from before. It belonged to a girl about my age, Earthan maybe, although it was tough to tell in the dim light. She had short purple hair buzzed nearly to her scalp, and the cheery grin she gave us practically made her dark skin glow.

I didn't trust her. Anyone who looked that happy was either a liar or lacking sanity. If she attacked, I knew a quick shot with Elio's blaster would put her down. I reached for it in his jacket, the fabric caked with grime from the queen's crypt, but found his pockets disappointingly empty.

"Oh, they kept your stuff," the girl said. "They always do. You had a couple coins in your pocket, but I took those. Finders keepers. I also took the zipper on your sweater. It looks like it's made of Europium. Is it? I've been itching to touch some for years but never managed it and—"

"Whoa! Can you shut up for *a second*?" In addition to all the other aches in my body, now my head was pounding. And look at that—my zipper really *was* missing.

A sudden noise came from the opposite corner of the room, almost like a laugh, but I couldn't see far enough into the shadows to pick out a body. Maybe I made it up, desperate to talk to anyone other than the girl, who had scooted closer and was talking again.

"My mom calls me Magpie. I'm always swiping things for myself, but it's actually a very misleading name, because according to research, magpies are positively terrified of shiny objects. And I very much like them. Shiny objects, that is." She ran a hand over her scalp before offering to shake. "I'm Wren, by the way. Also known as your welcoming committee."

I just stared at her. The aura around her head shimmered a soft periwinkle blue. Far too calm for being stuck in this freezing, windowless room. She was most definitely out of her mind.

Of the two of us, Elio was the only one who tried to be polite. He pinched Wren's hand between two of his fingers in a halfhearted shake. "I'm Elio. This is Cora."

"Nice to meet you. What are you in for?"

Elio frowned. "I'm not sure what you mean."

Wren grinned. Again. "Grand theft auto? Homicide? No, not homicide. You don't seem like a murderer. She does though." She nodded to me, and I swore I heard another chuckle from the shadows.

Still not seeing anything, I pulled my eyes away from the corner. "We didn't do anything," I said. "Where are we?"

Finally, *finally* Wren's grin faded. "They didn't tell you when they brought you in?"

"We weren't conscious when they brought us in," Elio said, but my ears were ringing. At last everything clicked into place.

If we ever got out of here, Evelina would kill us both: we'd broken a criminal's only rule.

We got caught.

Wren had the grace to look apologetic as she nodded to the door—a block of steel with no handle and no window. Just a faceless slab of metal.

"You're on Andilly. In the Ironside maximum security prison."

Andilly, despite its warm and fuzzy-sounding name, was the planet where all good parents threatened to send their children if they misbehaved. A primitive nation made of sprawling, provincial villages that were constantly locked in some kind of war with each other, Andilly's inhabitants were known to be so violent that not even Evelina wanted to steal from them.

And if their personalities weren't dazzling enough, they also had prison cells that smelled like curdled milk and feet.

We were *trapped* here.

I should have realized it immediately, but it had taken a while for my brain to play catch-up. Wren's baggy red jumpsuit, the dark and dank cinder block walls, the general sense of despair and anger in the air—we had been caught, manhandled onto a ten-hour flight from Vaotis to Andilly, and thrown into the largest penitentiary in the galaxy. And I didn't remember any of it.

The not knowing was what made my skin crawl. Someone must have seen my pod ship land at the cemetery. When I unlocked the door of the crypt for Elio, no alarm had gone off—at least not one my monitors had picked up. It must have happened when he opened the queen's tomb, when that strange vapor had filled the room, seeping into his processing system and my lungs, and knocked us both out.

We're probably cursed now. Doomed to listen to Wren's incessant talking as punishment for our many crimes. For being locked in a cell, the girl sure didn't seem too sad about it.

The worst part of it all, I realized with a twist in my gut, was that our blasters, my inventions, all my hard work, had been left behind in the pod ship. I'd have to build another visual enhancement device from scratch, assuming I ever managed to find the parts again. Or assuming we ever got out of here. No. *We will.* I would live to hear Evelina yell at me again, I would live to hear Nana Rae sing the Condor national anthem off-key, I would live to see Blair's ugly, annoying face. I would not die in this cell.

I looked to my left, where Elio was pretending to politely listen to Wren describe the customs associated with birthdays on Earth. They involved yelling "surprise" at each other in a dark room and then lighting things on fire, and to Elio's credit, he didn't look as frightened by that as I expected him to.

We'll escape, I silently promised Elio as he gave Wren a nervous smile. Because if he continued glitching, I would be useless to him trapped in here. I hadn't committed years of crimes to get locked up now.

"Hey, Wren?" I interrupted her explanation of Earthan slang and didn't feel the least bit sorry about it. "We'll get a trial, right? They can't keep us here without a trial."

She started playing with my stolen zipper. "I doubt that's on anybody's mind right now. The prison is pretty packed at the moment. That's why we're sharing cells. I've been in here for weeks and no one's come to talk to me." She stuffed the zipper under a threadbare blanket. "By the way, what are you being charged with? You never said."

I raised an eyebrow. "Murder."

"Unlikely. I'm pretty sure you have a conscience. You keep looking at your little droid like you're more worried about him than you are about yourself. So maybe you killed someone, but if you did then it was an accident, because I personally don't think you have it in you." She crossed her arms and winked. "That's right, alien-Cora. I'm more than just a loud mouth and a dazzling personality."

I jerked my chin up in an attempt to look threatening. How had she figured all that out without the ability to read auras? "What are you in for, then?"

"Well, since you asked, I guess I'll share. It's a harrowing tale." She rubbed her palms together. "I may or may not have blown up a space station."

Elio beeped. "*May or may not*?"

"Okay, I did. But it was an accident."

"Did you make the explosives?" I asked, an idea forming. She'd hidden my zipper under her blanket; maybe she had more odds and ends I could use to build a device. If I could collect enough, I could blow the cell door clear across the prison.

"I—" Wren started, but the hydraulic hiss of the door had her timidly backing up to block her stash of trinkets.

The door opened fully to reveal a woman in a crisp white guard uniform, her bulky silhouette weighed down beneath blasters on her hips and armor across her shoulders. The only exposed skin on her neck and face was bright red, covered in scales that formed a trail up into her hairline. I'd seen holograms of Andillian people when I was in school. I remembered my teacher anxiously referring to them as "flesh-eating lizards."

I sat up as the guard's tongue darted out, ignoring Elio cowering behind me. "We're innocent," I said adamantly.

Her lips curled back over yellow teeth.

"I demand to talk to whoever brought us here. I swear, when my mother hears about what happened—"

"You tell her, Cora," Elio muttered.

"—she'll rip the front door of this place off, and stars help us all, she'll—"

The guard flung two red jumpsuits and slip-on sneakers over my head, where they landed in the back of the cell. "B'shkrah," she mumbled in a guttural, accented voice. I didn't know much Andillian, but I knew that word. *Brat*.

The insult echoed through the cell as the door hissed closed behind her. The sound of two locks clicking filled the air, followed by her retreating footsteps.

"Wait! Come back!" I pounded my fist against the door, but all I got was a sharp pain in my hand. "What happened to innocent until proven guilty?"

"Cora?" Elio whispered.

"Or our one comm? Don't we get that?"

"Um, Cora? Please stop yelling at the door."

"Why?"

Elio's hand shook as he pointed across the cell to where the jumpsuits had landed. They weren't on the ground any longer. Instead they were balled up in the lap of something very bulky and very . . . alive.

Elio beeped.

The shape stood, slinking out of the shadows like a ghost.

I jumped back. This was the thing that had laughed at me, I was sure of it. But then why hadn't I noticed them? Why hadn't I seen the spike of an aura around them? I may have been losing my touch as a criminal, but I wasn't losing my touch at reading people.

The dim light fell upon our other cellmate. Another citizen from Andilly, bigger and more menacing than the guard. He looked around my age, face hidden underneath a hooked nose and elegant lines of dark tattoos swirling across his forehead. With his red skin and red prison uniform, I couldn't help thinking that he resembled a giant drop of blood.

"Oh. Him." Wren barely looked up from the metal shavings she was sorting into piles on her blanket. "Don't mind him. He's been here longer than I have. I've found that the more you look at him the more nightmares you have, so I try to ignore him."

My stance wavered as he neared me. Several scales along his neck had peeled back, revealing burnt skin and a long rope of scar tissue, like someone had carved into him with a knife.

I tried bringing my arms up as he got closer but froze under his hateful stare. His dark eyes had an odd, liquid shine to them. Almost like an insect.

"Does . . . does he have a name?" Elio squeaked.

Wren shrugged. "No one from Andilly has names. They have numbers. I've just been calling him Anders."

"Anders?" I tried tentatively. He brushed a matted piece of black hair behind his ear, but otherwise he didn't answer me.

"How did you get here? What can you tell me about the guards? I think I can get us out if you—*hey*, where are you going?"

He had dropped the bundle of jumpsuits and shoes at my feet and was lumbering back into the shadows.

"Hey, Big Red! I'm talking to you! How did you do that neat little disappearing trick?"

That got his attention. He glared over his shoulder, hands curling into fists.

"I can read auras. I can't feel yours. It was like you weren't even in the room. Is everyone from Andilly like that or just you?"

Nothing. I might as well have been talking to the wall. He sat back down again, not even a hint of emotion flickering off him.

"See?" Wren said. "Just ignore him, because he'll only ignore you. I'm not sure if he can talk at all, to be honest." She held up a square piece of metal, examining it. "But whatever you do, don't call him Andy. He tried to strangle me the last time I tried."

"Charming." Elio snatched the metal out of Wren's hand, digging a long scratch in the wall behind her head.

"What are you doing?" I asked.

"Counting the days we're here. That way if Big Red rips out my wires in the middle of the night, the universe will know that this is the place I last stood." He shivered. "It already feels like we've been in here for an eternity."

"You've been here for an hour," Wren said. She made a grab for the metal, but Elio danced out of reach.

I removed my soiled jacket and pulled on one of the red jumpsuits the guard had left for us. The arms and legs were too baggy, but at least it was warm. I settled against the nearest wall while Wren continued sorting her treasures, singing a jingle about each one and its metallic components. Anders let loose a low chuckle, the sound ringing out of the darkness like a bell. A drop of water fell from the ceiling and landed with a splat on the tip of my nose.

It was enough to drive even the most placid soul to murder.

5

"SO . . . ," WREN SAID, RUBBING HER PALMS TOGETHER. "ANYONE up for a game of charades?"

There were a few communities of Earthans scattered throughout Condor, but I'd never met any of them, so I had no clue if they were all this annoying, but somehow I didn't think so. It was day two in the cell, and it was also the twentieth time I'd ignored Wren's attempt at conversation. I'd spent the prior night shivering in a ball, listening to Elio's fans whir and Anders shift around in his darkened corner. He still hadn't spoken, but that didn't mean I could let my guard down and sleep. Some primal part of me was convinced that if I closed my eyes, I'd find his fingers clenched around my throat.

"Charades?" Wren asked again, eyes bright. "Come on, it's so boring in here! We have to keep ourselves entertained somehow. Okay, look. Guess who I am." She slouched against the wall, baring her teeth and growling.

"A bear!" Elio shouted. "Wait, do they still have bears on Earth?"

Wren shook her head. "They're extinct. Try again." She scrunched her face up and growled louder. "I'll give you a hint. I'm super mean and I hate everyone's guts."

"Are you my subconscious?" I muttered.

"No, but thank you for participating, Cora. No, guys, look! I'm obviously Anders!"

Across the cell, the real Anders leaned out of the shadows just enough for me to see his scaly face. And he looked like he wanted nothing more than to eat us all.

I hastily looked away from him, pulling my knees up to my chest. "This is absurd," I said to Elio, slipping into lilting Condish. I didn't know how many languages Wren and Anders knew, but I hoped they didn't know mine. I needed some tiny shred of privacy in this place.

"It could be worse," Elio replied.

"Oh, really? How?"

"Well, I mean, we could be dead."

Okay, fair point. But dead or alive, I had a feeling my family wouldn't care that we were gone. On second thought, they probably hadn't even realized we were gone. And even if they had, they'd probably only feel relief.

I hung my head. We needed to get out of here.

Reluctantly, I switched back to common Isolat. "This is absurd," I said again.

"Oh, I don't know," said Wren. She pulled a long piece of metal out from under her blanket and measured it against the side of her forearm. "I have a feeling we're all exactly where we're meant to be."

I bristled. "What is *that* supposed to mean?"

"Nothing. Just . . ." She peered up at the dim lightbulb hanging from the ceiling, her eyes so focused that I wondered if she was trying to have a telepathic conversation with it. "It's just that I think we should get to know each other a little better if we're going to be living here together, you know? For example, I'm a snorer. Feel free to slap me awake if I'm really bothering you."

"Are you sure you want to give me permission to hit you?"

Wren shrugged. "Whatever works."

Elio raised his hand. "Can I share next? I think everyone should know that even though I was built to be a servant bot, I'm downright messy. *But* I bake excellent cookies, and as far as I'm concerned, that's all that really matters."

Wren pointed to him. "This one I like. Anders? Can you top Elio's baking abilities?"

All three of us ducked as Anders lunged out of the shadows, grabbed a handful of Wren's coveted scrap metal, and chucked it at our heads. I covered my face as tiny pieces rained down on the back of my neck. Anders reclined against the wall, looking smug.

"Huh." Wren pulled herself up and started collecting her displaced scrap metal. "He must be more of a chip and dip kind of guy."

Rolling my eyes, I marched over to the door. I brushed my fingers around the sides, the track running along the floor, the points where each of the four cell walls met, searching for weak spots. I found none. Any bit of hope I'd had in my heart since we entered Ironside began to wither and die.

How are we going to get out of here?

"Cora?" Wren called. "I think it's your turn to share."

How am I going to save Elio?

"Cora? C'mon, don't be shy."

How do we get home?

"Cora?"

I rounded on her. "Shut up! Can't you tell I don't want to talk to you? Can't you tell I don't want to be here? Just *shut up*!"

Panicked silver starbursts exploded through her aura, lighting up the cell. Elio let out two quick beeps, then hid his face behind Wren's blanket. And Wren—well, she shouldn't have put out the offer for me to slap her awake, because she was staring at me like I had done just that.

"I . . . um . . . I'm s-sorry," she stammered, taking her blanket back from Elio. After fluffing it up with shaking hands, she lay down and watched me through frightened eyes. "What are you looking at?"

"I'm watching your aura . . ." I held out my hand, marveling at the glittering stars that floated through the air and gathered in clusters on my fingertips. "It's very . . ." Somehow I thought telling her that her fear was pretty to look at was the wrong thing to say. "You know what? Never mind." I slumped down and watched the stars dissolve into the shadows.

Wren glanced around the cell. "Oh, that's right. You said you can see auras." With a yawn, she settled into her blankets. "That must be very helpful. Thank you for sharing."

"I'm not sharing, I'm—"

But what I was doing didn't matter. In under a minute, Wren had fallen asleep. If only I could be so lucky. Instead I had to listen to her snores shake the walls all night long.

The Ironside prison yard was less of a yard and more of a slab of concrete with weeds poking through the cracks. An electric fence hummed around the square, four guard towers standing at attention in each corner, watching the inmates like birds of prey beneath a blood-red Andilly sky. Packed gray soil stretched out from the prison in every direction, broken up only by empty roads and a distant snow-capped mountain range. It was impossible to gauge how far away we were from civilization, but when Elio and I finally escaped this hellhole, it appeared we would have very few places to run.

"So . . . Condor?" Wren gestured to my silver hair. I'd managed to find a piece of twine to tie it up (the air outside was so humid that it felt like I was standing inside an armpit), but a few pieces had escaped and hung in my eyes. "I've never been. What's it like?"

"Dark."

"A truly verbose description." Even after receiving the brunt of my fury last night, she was still determined to chat me up, and I was too exhausted to push her away. She led me through the crowd of inmates to a rusted table across the yard. I'd never seen so many different species in one place before. There were winged people from Avis exercising beside Ucarro women with flippers for feet and sharp green gills sprouting from their necks. A man walked past us in the opposite direction, holding a tray of food. His entire body was covered in so much curly brown fur that I couldn't even make out his face.

"That's Po," Wren said. "He gives one heck of a neck massage. But where was I? Oh, right. My family is originally from London, but we left after Earth's fifth world war. Did you hear about that one? It was a doozy. Anyway, I grew up in a colony on the south side of Mars. I really miss it."

Mars. I'd helped rob their central treasury a total of three times in the last year. Security systems there were so easy to hack that it was almost embarrassing. But I felt like that probably wasn't a fact she would appreciate.

"Why'd you leave?" I asked instead.

"Well, you see, I robbed it blind."

Or maybe that was a fact she already knew.

"And how did that work out for you?"

"Better than expected. I snuck into the president's mansion. Everything was going according to plan until I tried to steal the ferret . . ." She looked at her shoes.

"The *ferret*?"

"Long story. Its collar was worth more than my house. And, I mean, it was fuzzy and had this cute little pink nose. Who could pass that up?"

Uh . . .

"I kind of have an issue," she continued, "with taking things." And to prove her point, she swiped a bread roll off the plate of a passing inmate, her fingers slicing through the air with impressive speed. The guy had eight eyes by my count, and he didn't even notice. That was a rare gift she had.

Wren hopped onto the tabletop and crossed her legs, looking out over the prison yard like she was holding court—even though her cheeks were stuffed with bread. She acted like she was sitting on a throne, not at all fazed by the many people here who could probably destroy her in a blink. I didn't know whether to be impressed or confused.

"Aren't you scared to be here?" I asked her.

She continued scanning the yard, jaw tight. "Of course I am. But I can't show it. They'll eat you alive if you do. And I mean that literally. There's a chick in cell block D with a head shaped like a shark's."

I couldn't help snickering a little.

She glanced down at me. "You're laughing, but you don't like me."

Well, she wasn't wrong. But I didn't like many people anyway. "I just don't understand you. You're in prison and you're . . . I don't know. I guess *cheery* is the best word?"

"I'm a happy human. So what." Her dark eyes hardened. "You could stand to be a bit more pleasant yourself."

I still didn't get it. What did she want? For me to be her prison buddy just because we were sharing a cell? I didn't *do* people skills. I didn't have time for them. I needed to get out of here, steal something expensive enough to appease Evelina, and then use my cut of the profits to buy Elio a new body. *Those* were the priorities. Not friendship.

Wren stuffed the remainder of her bread into her mouth. "I know it might be a challenge for you not to bite my head off this time, but how about you tell me more about these auras you can read."

"Why?"

"Because my mother always told me I'm too curious for my own good. My brother did too, now that I think of it. Just humor me. Can you read the guards over there?" She pointed to a table across the yard, where a fight had broken out. Four guards raised their blasters and were halfheartedly attempting to intervene.

"Depends on if they're doing the same trick Anders did. And I usually have to pick out a specific person, like tuning into a certain net program. I can't read everyone at once."

A violet cloud of excitement spilled off her, perfectly matched to her hair. "Try."

"Fine. Whatever." But I chose an easier mark to start. "Okay, see the man emptying the trash receptacle? He's heartbroken. The guard in the tower just behind us? She's so exhausted she can barely stand up straight. I'm guessing she just worked a double shift." My skin buzzed with energy as I stretched my affinity to the four guards dragging the fighting inmates back inside. "Tired, bored to tears, giddy, oh . . . um, constipated."

"Do me next." Elio appeared at our table, laden with trays of powdered eggs, some kind of smoked meat, and more bread rolls.

"You know you don't have an aura, you little goof. What's with all the food?"

"Couldn't pass it up. I heard it's delicious."

"Robots can eat?" Wren asked.

"*No,*" I said at the same time Elio declared, "I dabble."

With a shrug, Wren snatched another roll off Elio's plate and tore into it with her teeth. Her eyes continued scanning the yard, and while she was distracted, I pulled on Elio's sleeve.

"How are you doing?"

He considered for a moment. "Well, I'm in prison, so . . ."

"That's not what I meant." I lowered my voice to a whisper. "Your glitching. You don't feel anything coming on, do you?"

He nudged his food around his plate. "Eh, my optic sensors are a bit fuzzy, but that's been happening for ages, so don't worry about it."

Don't worry. Right. He could just cease to exist at any moment and I didn't have the means to prevent it. But, hey, no biggie.

"Cora. Friend." Elio took my cheeks in both of his tiny hands. "I'm not going anywhere. *Literally*. We're locked in here." He nodded across the yard, where we watched as a man spurted a plume of fire from his mouth and tried to throw a punch at a fifth guard before being detained. Elio shrugged, unfazed. "Have some bread. I don't know if Wren realized it, but I can't really eat."

"Oh, I realized it all right." With a grunt, Wren swung herself down from the tabletop and settled on the edge of the bench. "Hey, you essentially have a computer inside your head, right? That must come in handy. You don't have any other special talents, do you?"

I felt my guard snap back up as I noticed a curious orange sunburst arc over her head. "You're taking *way* too much of an interest in us. What gives?"

"What? I'm just being friendly."

"No one is *that* friendly."

"I am!" Elio interrupted. He leaned forward, the front of his prison jumpsuit hanging down into his eggs. "Did Cora tell you about the bombs she makes? If you need an explosion, she's your girl."

"Elio," I warned.

"She invented all kinds of things on Condor," he continued. "Of course, only half of them worked . . ."

"*Elio*!"

Call it intuition, but this didn't feel right. Wren was fishing for something. I just wished I knew what.

I watched her chew her meal, a feline grin spreading across her face. What I wouldn't give for a way to force her to tell me the truth. I could read auras, sure, but I couldn't change them. I couldn't make her feel things she didn't feel; I couldn't make her act on the feelings that she had. Right now her aura was a rainbow of colors I could barely keep up with. Auburn and powder blue, violet and sea-foam green. All muddled together in an indiscernible, murky swirl.

"Wren, I'll make a deal with you. I'll give you something that you want, and in exchange you tell me exactly what you're up to. Sound good?"

"What is it you think I want?"

“Acceptance.” Her colors shifted then, and I could see it all over her. The desire to fit in. An Earthan trapped among aliens. “Or, well, I at least promise not to yell at you anymore.”

“That’s the best I’m going to get out of you, isn’t it?”

“Afraid so.”

She huffed out a long breath. Poked at the food in front of her. Shook her head, like she couldn’t believe what she was about to say. “I think . . . Cora, I think I know a way to get us out of here.”

“*WHAT*?” I screeched. The table next to us turned and stared, and I lowered my voice. “*What*?” I demanded in a whisper.

“It’s not going to be easy, but I think—”

Her voice broke off in a scream and a string of curses as, out of nowhere, a neon blue tentacle shot across the table and smacked her in the jaw.

“Hey!” I was instantly on my feet as Wren’s head snapped to the side. Elio dived forward, determined to help her, but a second attack didn’t seem to be what the intruder was after. The tentacle was more than six feet long, attached to the jaw of a woman smirking two tables over, and she used it to deftly lift Elio’s heaping plate of eggs into the air.

I assumed she was going to steal them for herself—because that seemed logical. What I didn’t expect was for the tentacle to twist with a lazy ripple, dumping the food on top of our heads.

“Seriously?” I grimaced as I picked a scalding piece of egg from between my cleavage. Wren grabbed it from me and sent it flying at Tentacle’s head.

“Watch it, Calamari! Try that again and I’ll rip your intestines out through your eyes!”

“That isn’t possible.” The woman started laughing, a few companions at her table joining in.

Wren crossed her arms. “Maybe not for you.”

The woman stood. I wished I had a blaster or a knife to defend us if she came over here, but Wren didn't seem to need my help. She held the woman's gaze, her chin high and defiant, and for a moment I wondered if she actually was capable of pulling off a murder that gruesome.

Finally, the woman took a step forward. Her hair rustled, more tentacles emerging from beneath the silky strands. They slithered toward Wren, skimming her shoulders before flicking her chin. Then they wrenched her to her feet by the throat.

"Earthan child. When's the next match?"

"Tomorrow," Wren answered, her voice rough under the pressure of the tentacles.

"And have you found me a worthy opponent? The last one was too weak. I could have crushed their fragile body in my sleep."

Wren smirked. "Let's just say that your new opponent won't give you that issue."

"They better not." She licked her lips. "I like a challenge." She retracted her tentacles, leaving the column of Wren's throat covered in dark splotches from the suckers. Wren was shaking, gasping desperately for breath. Seeing her start to break after acting so tough all day long made me feel something sharp in my chest that almost, *maybe* could have passed for sympathy.

Or maybe it was just indigestion. These prison eggs were disgusting.

Once the tentacled woman headed for the doors leading back to the cell blocks, her posse tagging along behind her like a bad smell, I turned to Wren. "A match? What match?"

She slumped back down at our table. "She just had to steal my thunder. I was getting to it, I swear. Have you ever played Snaps?"

"What's Snaps?"

"'*What's Snaps*?' she asks. It's a betting game played with gems. It's called Snaps because—"

"Because the winner usually celebrates by breaking the bones of the loser," Elio interrupted. His eyes flickered as he ran a net search. "Created in Andilly in the year 2126, Snaps has since been outlawed in nineteen different galaxies. The average mortality rate of Snaps losers amounts to 64.61 percent, making it the eighth highest cause of death on the planet, right behind—"

"Yeah, yeah, we get it, Elio." I patted him on the shoulder. "Snaps is very violent."

"Only if you lose," Wren added. "And you're looking at Ironside's head Snaps bookie. I rig all the odds. People only lose when I want them to. In the end, it all works in my favor."

"Wait—you're actually making money off this?" *And how do I get in on it?*

Wren shook her head. "Not money. They confiscate all our money here. We trade in gossip. Which brings me to my brilliant escape plan. Drumroll, please . . ." She beat a quick rhythm on the table. "I have a charter ship. The *Starchaser*. It's the largest in this galaxy, thank you very much. I hijacked it from a station near Pluto—"

"The space station you blew up?"

She waved me off. "Accidentally. Point is, the station is dust, but the ship is fully functional. And thanks to all the intel I've gained from our gullible fellow inmates every time they make a bad Snaps bet, I now know that the warden here put it in a docking bay beneath the prison. And thanks to a few more bad bets during last week's Snaps match between Calamari and my old cell neighbor Tito—stars rest his soul—I know the ship's still here because the guards always complain about how much room it takes up. Apparently, they don't have any space to set up their card table." A proud grin split her face in two.

"So how are you going to get the ship back?"

Her grin doubled in size. "*We*," she corrected, "are going to have a little fun with some of the guards. But first we need . . . *him*." She nodded to a weight bench at the edge of the yard. Anders was sitting there, sweat pouring off the scales on his forehead. Everyone in the vicinity was giving him a wide berth, as if he were contagious or something.

"The guards will be less suspicious that he's trying to double-cross them," she said. "Creepy red lizards gotta stick together and whatnot."

"Do you really think he'll help us?" Elio asked.

"Of course, Small Fry. He's the classic broody schoolyard bully. If we watch closely, I bet we'll find out he has a heart of gold." She howled with laughter.

"Can we get back to the plan, please?" I asked. Looking at Anders for too long was giving me a prickly feeling on the back of my neck. He got off the bench and started doing push-ups in the dirt. I swore his dark, pitiless eyes cut a glance to our table, and it made my stomach bunch up like I'd just swallowed a rubber ball. I didn't trust him. I didn't trust anyone except Elio and myself.

"So Anders helps us and then what?" I picked apart a roll until it crumbled in my hands.

Wren took a piece from me and popped it into her mouth. "You come in with your abracadabra aura-manipulating magic and then we're golden."

"It doesn't work like that. I can read the guards enough to avoid running into them if we make a break for the docking bay, but I can't manipulate them. I—"

"Who said anything about reading the *guards*? Listen, Cora, this will work best if you don't know all the details. Element of surprise and all that. Trust me."

"Yeah, I'm pretty sure I called in sick for my trusting lesson in preschool."

Wren studied the prison yard again, the guard towers, the chattering inmates, the rotten stench of old cafeteria food, and steepled her fingers beneath her chin. "Don't worry. If Anders or anyone else interferes, then like I said before, I'll rip their intestines out through their eyes."

"That really isn't possible," Elio said.

"Maybe, maybe not." She reached over me to take Elio's plate. "You done with that? I'm starving."

I sat at the table, eating day-old bread and peppering Wren with questions about her half-baked escape plan (which she deftly dodged) until a horn blared, signaling the end of the lunch hour. As we lined up and were handcuffed and led back to our cells, a realization struck me, sending a sour wave of nausea lashing through my stomach.

Devious little Wren had more in common with Evelina than I ever did.

And, for some reason, it made me kind of jealous.

BACK IN THE MURKY DAMPNESS OF THE CELL, I SLAMMED THE piss bucket down at the foot of Anders's makeshift bed of blankets. "How do you feel about vomiting on command?"

He blinked up at me, frowning. The big guy had his jumpsuit unbuttoned and shoved around his waist, and his bare red torso was streaked with dirt from his outdoor training session. Once again, no aura surrounded his head or beefy shoulders, and I was filled with the overwhelming temptation to smack him, just to make him feel *something*.

I kicked the bucket closer to him. "Do it. You'll thank us later."

"He might kill us later," Elio muttered.

Anders's eyebrows bunched together, making the tattoos on his forehead wiggle. Then he picked up the bucket and launched it at the opposite wall.

Wren ducked out of the splash zone before it could hit her. "Easy there, Andy! This is a clean jumpsuit!"

Anders only growled.

"Hey!" a gruff voice came from the cell beside us. "Shut up over there! I'm trying to sleep!"

I pounded the cinder blocks with my fist. "*You* shut up over there!"

So much for an easy start to the plan. I went to retrieve the bucket, fantasizing about shoving Anders's head into it. Wren tried slapping my hand in a joyous show of camaraderie, but I ignored her.

I dropped the bucket at Anders's feet again. "Get to it. When the guards come to take a head count, you need to look sick." I didn't know if it was a mistake to tell him the truth, but I figured it was the only way to get him to unclamp his jaw a little. He would crack a tooth or something if he didn't loosen up.

Not that I cared.

"We're breaking out of here. And you're going to ruin everything if you don't vomit in the star-forsaken bucket, Andy, so do it."

The darkness in his eyes seemed to recede a little. For a moment it looked like the spark of an aura surrounded his head, like a happy golden halo, but it was gone before I could really be sure of what I was seeing.

Anders grabbed the bucket, turned his back to us, and then the sound of his gagging filled the cell.

"We have about ten minutes," Wren said, taking up her post beside the door. I didn't know how she knew that without a window or a clock to look at. Maybe it was Earthan intuition.

The minutes passed slowly, accompanied by the echo of Anders's retching and the bitter odor of his regurgitated dinner. When we finally heard the guards' footsteps outside the cell, the four of us slumped to the floor, faking exhaustion and despair—complete with a few authentic-looking tears from Wren—just as the door opened with a hiss.

"We had a bit of an issue," Wren said to the guard who poked his head inside. She pointed to the bucket, which Anders had overturned with his foot so that some of the contents spilled out in a puddle.

The guard barely gave it a second glance as he looked us over. He marked something on his comm before shoving the device into his back pocket and turning to leave. My stomach did a nervous flip.

"Wait!" I shouted. The guard whirled around, reaching for his blaster, and I backed against the wall, hoping to appear unassuming.

I nodded at the bucket and Anders. "You're not going to leave us in here all night with that, are you? He might have an infectious disease or something."

The guard holstered his blaster, reaching for the holopanel to close the door.

"Wait! If he is infected, you might have already been exposed to it. Shouldn't you, I don't know, test him or something?"

The guard only frowned. Stars, my stomach felt like something was burrowing in it. If this plan didn't work, then my dinner was definitely going to join Anders's on the floor.

But to my immense relief, the guard took a hesitant step forward, the door sealing shut behind him. *Phase one: complete.*

He wrinkled his nose, then leaned over Anders.

"S'ichas?" he asked. *Sick?* Anders looked up though half-lidded, watery eyes and managed a small nod.

A laugh threatened to escape me. Who would have guessed that the big guy could act?

Groaning, the guard took another step closer to the bucket, making the mistake of putting his back to us. Wren sidled up next to him. Before I had a chance to worry that he might turn and murder her right there, she slipped her fingers into his back pocket, replacing his protruding comm link with a square hunk of cement that she'd smuggled in from the yard.

She tossed the comm backward. Elio caught it just as the guard wheeled around. Wren innocently held up her hands, nodding to the bucket.

"So, what do you think? Are we all going to contract some mystery virus that'll burn our eyes out of our sockets?"

The guard examined the bucket. "Your eyes, no. Your ears . . . perhaps."

"Good to know. It's not like I need those things anyway." She glared over at me, huddled in the corner. Elio had pulled a wire from a compartment on the side of the guard's comm and connected it to a second one that Wren had swiped from the kitchen staff. I was hiding the second comm beneath Wren's blanket, waiting for the two devices to connect.

Just hack into the pass codes for the hangar doors, she'd told me before we started this madness. *How long will that take you? A few seconds?*

Yeah, sure. If the two comms she'd given me were actually compatible and the net access on the kitchen comm wasn't as slow as dirt. I'd broken through the encryption on the pass codes, no problem, but transferring the data—and doing it in a way that the guard would have no idea what happened—well, that was a different issue.

Wren gave me another hurry-the-hell-up look, as if the net connectivity issues in a cinder block prison cell on an isolated, barren planet were somehow *my* fault.

I motioned for her to stall while Elio grabbed the kitchen comm. He held it up to the ceiling, hopping up and down to get a better signal. I snatched it back. He was three feet tall. I appreciated his hustle, but he wasn't helping.

"It's, uh, it's really good to hear that our eyes aren't going to burn out," Wren said warily. The comm finally beeped, the pass codes starting their agonizingly slow download, and the guard turned toward the noise. Wren hastily slid in front of him, beaming.

"You have very nice eyes, you know," she said. "So black and . . . uh . . . shiny. Just like a lump of . . ." She gulped. "Coal."

I would have slapped myself—or better yet, *her*—if my hands weren't occupied. *Coal?* That was the best she could do?

I glanced down at the comm. *DOWNLOAD IN PROGRESS: 41 percent . . . 42 percent . . .*

The guard gave her a shockingly warm smile, which was less of a smile and more of a flash of teeth that looked like they could shred us into itty-bitty pureed pieces. "Really? You think so?" He preened. "You know, I've always said they're my best feature."

Wren nodded enthusiastically. "Oh, yes. *Definitely.*"

57 percent . . . 58 percent . . .

"They're beautiful," she continued. "I'd go so far as to say stunning."

The guard's face darkened. "I am not *beautiful*!" he snarled, spittle flying across the cell.

Wren squeaked. "Beautiful? Did I say beautiful? I obviously meant horrifying and ugly and nightmare-inducing."

"Truly?" He relaxed. "Thank you!"

On the floor, Anders looked like he was fighting back the urge to laugh, and honestly, I was right there with him. But when the guard's gaze swiveled to him, he gripped the bucket and started hacking up something seriously foul into its depths.

Wren stepped closer to the guard. She brought her hand behind her back, wiggling her fingers in an impatient signal. *Keep your pants on. It's not done yet.* I watched the download progress climb, willing the numbers to move faster. *Come on! You can do it.*

89 percent . . . 90 percent . . . 91 percent . . .

"I have always been intrigued by Earth," said the guard. "Maybe you could teach me about it sometime? I do not understand the fruit known as an *orange*. Is the food named after the color, or is the color named after the food?"

97 percent . . . 98 percent . . . 99 percent . . .

"Ah, yes. One of the great mysteries of the universe. If you think that one's intriguing, you'll love to hear more about jumbo shrimp."

"Fascinating! Is it really both large *and* small? At the same time?"

Wren shrugged, innocently folding her hands behind her back. *DOWNLOAD COMPLETE. Finally!* I disconnected the comms, slapped the guard's into Wren's palm, then marveled as she slipped it back into his pocket under the guise of giving him a spine-crushing hug.

"You'll have to wait and see," she murmured, tweaking the end of his nose. Okay, she was laying it on a little thick, but I guess it had the desired effect. The guard looked horrified at the physical contact, and when he stumbled out the door, his back slightly bent under the weight of the bucket of vomit à la Anders dangling from his hand, he didn't even notice that his coveted comm link had exited and reentered his pocket.

"Don't forget!" Wren called after him. "Jumbo shrimp!" She turned to the three of us and cracked a grin. "Phase two: complete."

"I don't know why we couldn't have just knocked him out and run," I grumbled, flipping through the stolen kitchen comm. All the pass codes were here. To the hangar, to the doors of every cell, every office, every guard tower. My heart skipped a beat. I held the key to the entire prison in my hands. The key to Elio's safety. So close. I could feel it . . .

And then Wren plucked the comm from me, and I felt only irritation.

"Too obvious. Plus, there are too many guards lurking between here and the docking bay. If they think we're making a break for it, they'll shut down every access point in this prison. Manual entry only. You wouldn't even be able to hack it. Trust me, I've been planning this for ages."

"Precisely how long is *ages*?" Elio asked with a beep.

"Fine, you got me. I've been planning this for two days, but it *feels* like ages."

Anders snorted.

I agree with you, buddy, I thought grimly.

"Look, we can only escape when the guards aren't looking. And the only time the guards aren't looking is if we draw all of them far away from the cells and the hangar."

"Which is where, exactly?" I asked.

Wren's response was another grin, and that was when I knew I would have been better off remaining silent.

"Welcome to phase three."

"No! Absolutely not!"

"Quiet!" Wren snapped. "She'll hear you!"

I gave a delirious laugh. "I think it's too late for that."

It's funny how sometimes when you wish for something, you end up in a place that's significantly worse than where you started. I had wanted nothing more than to get off Condor, to have a fighting chance at getting Elio a new body. Now, it looked like we were *both* going to die.

I should have let Calamari shove her tentacles down Wren's throat—because I had a hunch she was dangerously close to shoving them down mine.

The morning after we acquired the pass codes from the universe's most gullible guard, I foolishly let Wren lead me through the yard after breakfast. The second we stepped through the doorway and out into the humid air, I knew I should have grilled Wren a bit harder about what exactly the next phase of the newly dubbed *Worst Plan in Existence* would entail. At least then I would have been prepared for the stares and the jeers as we drew nearer to the Snaps table set up in the center of the yard.

When Wren said she'd found Calamari a new opponent, I never guessed she meant *me*.

Anders, sure. He was intimidating enough to play such a violent game. Even Wren, with her feisty, defiant streak. But me? Not gonna lie, I was really attached to my limbs. *Literally*. And I really didn't want to see them get crushed to pieces when I lost.

"They're all betting against you," Wren told me as we pushed through the screaming crowd. "I made sure of it."

"Umm . . . thanks?"

"Don't mention it."

"No, that wasn't a real thank-you. It was—"

"I know what it was. They're going to be furious when you come out of nowhere and actually win. Or that's what I'm counting on anyway." She surreptitiously brushed her fingers over her pocket, where the comm link was hidden. Our pass codes to freedom.

"What if I don't remember the rules?" I took in the sprinkling of gems spread across the Snaps table. There were only two seats. One was empty, and Calamari was sitting in the other, chatting to a woman covered in pearlescent feathers. She turned to smirk at us, tentacles curling into the air around her shoulders like open-mouthed smiles, like they were laughing too, and I would have given almost anything to dump a plate of eggs on *her* head just to knock her down a peg.

"Rules are hardly necessary," said Wren. "Can you bluff?"

"On occasion."

"Okay . . . well, you can read other people's bluffs."

I watched the nervous pale-yellow aura fog off her skin, like she was leaking sunlight. "Obviously."

She nodded, and her nerves faded a little. "Then that's all that matters. You're the only one here who can beat her, so don't mess this up."

"Right." I heaved a breath. "I'm sure it'll be fine, right?"

"Are you asking for a pep talk?" Elio muttered behind me. "Because she looks absolutely terrifying. I've got nothing. *Beep*!"

The crowd pressed in around the yard, circling the table, sending the heat in the air skyrocketing. Someone was beating on one of the tables like a war drum. All I could smell was sweat and more sweat and fear. Of course, that last one was all me.

"I'm sure deep down inside, she's just like us," I said, the lame attempt at a pep talk dying on my lips as Calamari cracked first her knuckles, then her tentacles. "I'm sure she puts her pants on one leg at a time."

"That's rather presumptuous." Wren scowled. "Who says that's how I put my pants on?"

"Well, isn't it?"

"No." She sniffed, affronted. "Sometimes I like to shimmy into them backward just to see how it feels. *Then* I turn them around and put them on one leg at a time."

"I hate you."

"No, you don't. You're pretending to be angry to repress your natural inclination to develop interpersonal relations. Just let the faux irritation go and let the friendship happen, Cora. Don't forget whose ship you'll be flying away on in an hour."

It was a cute speech, but I frowned at her anyway. "I still can't stand you."

Wren and Elio abandoned me as soon as we reached the table, standing across the circle next to Anders, who shuffled away to hide amid a group covered head to toe in sharp rocky spikes. The thick gray folds of their skin obscured his red scales almost instantly.

Gravel crunched and slid beneath my shoes as I pulled out the chair and sat across from Calamari.

A hush fell over the crowd.

Calamari burst out laughing. "You? When the Earth child said she found me a new competitor, I expected someone a bit . . . larger."

"Afraid my bones will be too easy to break? Don't worry, you won't get a chance to find out."

She laughed again. Two of her tentacles darted underneath my chair, sliding around my ankles. With another smirk, she jerked me forward. My chest crashed into the edge of the table. Half the crowd laughed, the other half booed as I struggled to break free of her grip, and somewhere, hidden from view as the crowd surged closer, I heard Elio beep.

Her aggression lit a fire within me, and I scooped half the gems off the table and hid them behind a small partition in front of my seat. There was a board set up between us, with a circle in the middle to make plays. Despite never having played Snaps, I had received a crash course from Wren before she threw me headfirst to my death.

There were fifty gems—twenty for each player, plus ten spares in a bag to pick from if we couldn't make a play. We took turns matching them either by color (red, blue, green, and white) or by shape (squares, circles, triangles, and diamonds). If we didn't have a match—or if we had a match and didn't want the other to know about it—we could pick up. First one to eliminate all their gems except for three won. And the loser would walk away with a few dozen broken bones.

Was the opportunity to board Wren's spaceship worth the potential torture?

Yes, I thought. *If the spaceship even exists, that is*, I realized with a surge of terror.

But Wren wouldn't lie about the ship, would she? She wanted to escape just as badly as I did. Of course there was a ship.

And yet . . . It was so easy to tell a lie. My family was in the business of lying, and I could confidently say the best lies were the ones you believed to be true. They were the ones that you wanted so desperately, they were your first breath of air in the morning and the last before you went to sleep at night. I already believed Wren was a few gears shy of a whole blaster. Maybe her ship wasn't real.

Calamari took it upon herself to lay down the first gem—a blue square. The rock's glow reflected off her tentacles and shimmered against her skin, making it look like she was encrusted with jewels. Most auras looked similar from person to person, but hers showed itself in shades of blue. Right as Calamari made her move, wisps of cobalt rose off her shoulders, clouding the air above our playing table. She thought this was going to be easy. She thought she had already won.

My skin prickled with annoyance. Who cared if she was underestimating me? Who cared if Wren was a little too happy to be sane? Until I knew for certain the ship didn't exist, there was still a chance. A chance to escape. A chance to save my best friend.

I just had to win.

I set down my first gem. Blue triangle.

She made another play. Green triangle.

Red triangle.

Red diamond.

Red circle.

White circle.

I scanned my gems, hidden behind my partition. I'd need to pick up, which might put her at an advantage. But judging by the way the aura above her had turned darker, more anxious, she didn't have another play either. I reached for the velvet bag full of spare gems. Across the circle of spectators, I noticed Wren give me a thumbs-up.

Uncurling my fingers, I looked at what I had chosen. White diamond. That seemed significant. I just wished I remembered the rules better to know why.

And then . . . *The white diamond is the highest color and shape combination you can get,* Wren had told me on the way to the yard. *If you both get down to three gems in the same round, whoever has the best combination is named the winner.*

I could have set the white diamond down as my next play, but I had a feeling I would be better off keeping it. Pouting in fake disappointment, I pushed the gem to the side with my others and picked up a second time. Calamari grinned in triumph.

"Not doing very well?" Her tentacles found my ankles again and squeezed. The crowd cheered, and I noticed some rush over to Wren to place more bets.

I shrugged. "It's still early. I can turn things around."

Calamari tsked. "You would be surprised just how fast these games move."

Then she used her tentacle to slam another gem on the table.

She was right. After that, I barely had enough time to breathe as the game moved around me. Colors and shapes blurred together, clashing with the growing cloud of Calamari's triumphant aura. Inmates cheered. Even some of the Ironside guards stomped their feet as the pile of spare gems began to dwindle. I had twelve remaining behind my partition. And if I was counting correctly, Calamari only had ten.

I made another play. Green diamond. Calamari was forced to pick up. The crowd erupted in anger.

Her aura flickered, grew more confident.

Crap.

We each laid down two more before she was forced to pick up again. I was in the lead, but only for a moment before I picked up twice more. The bag of spares was empty, and she had one up on me.

I saw Wren grimace. Elio nibbled on his fingertips. Anders was noticeably absent.

After four more rounds, she was still winning. Then, something miraculous happened. She studied the table, tentacles coiling, then stretching like springs about to snap, and her aura took a nosedive. Frosty blue tendrils of fury rushed toward my throat, but her face remained completely serene. The biggest lie if I'd ever seen one.

"I can't make a play," she said calmly.

My breath hitched. "Do I win?"

"Of course not." She rolled her eyes. "You get to lay down two."

But, as I examined my pile of gems, I found that I could only lay down one. A red square.

And that made us even. Six gems to six.

The crowd around us pushed forward once again. Their sweaty bodies were flush against my back, their smelly breathing heavy in my ears. The temperature surged, and above us the Andilly sky seemed to grow even redder, as if it were overheated too.

Calamari set down another gem. Green square.

Green diamond.

Blue diamond.

Cupping my hands around the gems I had left, I looked for my best option. If Calamari could read auras, I knew she would see mine plummet. I found that I had only one move.

My coveted white diamond.

Wincing, I set it in the center of the table, and the crowd cheered. They jumped forward, knocking into my chair, and my chest slammed against the table. Behind Calamari, Wren's hands were clasped over her mouth. More inmates were trying to make bets with her, but she waved them off. Elio was beeping, and I wanted to tell him that it would be okay. I wanted to yell at Wren that this was a stupid plan to begin with, that there had to be better ways to escape Ironside. Calamari's tentacles slithered across the ground, winding around my legs, my hips, locking me in place against the table.

She set down one final gem. A red diamond. I had a red circle, and then we were both left with three.

A tie.

"Before we reveal," Calamari drawled, "and before I inevitably kill you, I'll offer you a trade. Switch places with your Earthan friend, and I'll let you walk away. Refuse . . . and I'll crush you both when I win."

"You're that confident your hand is better than mine?"

She relaxed back in her chair. "I am."

I cut a glance to Wren. Her jaw had gone slack, beads of sweat dripping down her chin. She really thought I was going to give her up. And I guess I hadn't given her a reason to believe otherwise, but I needed her. And she needed me too. So did Elio.

Elio. I found his eyes as he was jostled by the restless crowd. I just hoped he had enough sense to run when this plan went up in flames.

Looking back at Calamari, I shook my head, sealing my fate. "No deal."

A bored sigh left her mouth. Her tentacles gleamed in the sunlight. She pushed away her partition to reveal her final three gems.

Two green diamonds. One blue triangle.

Not a bad combination, according to Wren. Diamonds were the highest shape, but green and blue were the second and third highest colors. I didn't even bother acting surprised. Despite Calamari's calm façade, I'd read her aura loud and clear. For the last three rounds, I'd known she was far less confident than she was letting on.

I pushed aside my own partition. Even though I'd given up the highest white diamond, I had something nearly as good. And sometimes, *nearly* was just enough to win.

Three green diamonds winked in the sunlight.

"No!" Calamari jumped to her feet, shoving the table away from us into the crowd. "I don't lose!"

Around us, spectators yelled furiously, pushing and searching for Wren, who had vanished as soon as I revealed my winning gems. My stomach lurched. Where was she? Where was Elio? Calamari was closing in on me, her eyes as hard as ice chips, her tentacles winding around my torso, *squeezing, squeezing, squeezing*. It didn't matter that I won. She was going to break me anyway.

The crowd grew deafening. The ground rumbled underneath the beat of their angry footsteps. Calamari bared her teeth, tightened her hold, and I started to feel something in my spine *pop*—

And then a heaping pile of eggs and meat smacked into Calamari's face and slipped down the front of her jumpsuit.

"*What*?" Slowly, she turned . . . and noticed Wren standing on the fringes of the crowd, armed with trays from the cafeteria. "What did you *do*?"

Wren shrugged. And that was when I unequivocally knew she had lost her marbles.

Because no sane person would ever scoop their hand into a bowl of mushed-up mystery meat and fling it at their enemy, yelling, "FOOD FIGHT!"

The meat got lodged in Calamari's hair, some of it slipping down her cheek, leaving a muddy streak on her skin. Wren flung three more globs of meat into the crowd, pelting two inmates and one guard. That was all it took. The spectators either dived for cover or rushed to grab their own ammunition as, all around us, food went flying into tables and faces and fences like we were in the middle of a war zone.

The guards tried to quell the inmates, but they were caught up in the frenzy too. One man took a moldy hunk of bread to the face. Another woman slipped on a stream of vegetable pods and landed face-first in a pile of mushed-up fruit.

What the—? This was Wren's big plan? This was the element of surprise she neglected to mention? I couldn't deny it was effective. Calamari had grown so distracted by the onslaught that her tentacles had started to loosen their grip on me. Reaching for my chair, I beat them away, and the suckers detached from my skin with a sickening squelch. I ducked under the arm of a passing inmate as he aimed a glob of eggs at my face, and rolled behind a table that had been flipped on its side as a shield.

I found Elio hiding behind it, shaking.

My first fear was that he was glitching, but no. "The food! It's being wasted!" With a shrill *beep-beep-beeeep*, he scooped up handfuls of dirty vegetables and clutched them to his chest like they were precious pearls.

"Elio!" I snapped my fingers to draw his attention. "Leave it! Where's Wren?"

"Cora!" Wren dived behind the table with us, an aura of exhilaration brightening her face. "Great idea, right?"

The Snaps game and the dozens of bad bets were long forgotten. An inmate with glittering gold skin aimed a handful of meat at a second woman with smooth black antennae on her forehead. The meat trailed through the air like a comet's tail, hitting its mark with a thud. Antennae Girl giggled and chucked a handful back.

"Come on! This is our chance!" Wren grabbed my shoulder as more guards spilled into the yard. They were caught up in the fight and were quickly distracted, jobs forgotten. Wren rolled out from behind the table as the crowd swelled and more food went flying.

I hurried to follow but was cut off by another inmate jumping through the air to avoid being hit by a bag of bread rolls. He crashed into my hip, and I slammed into the ground, my knees aching with the brunt of the fall. The man didn't even apologize. He picked up a roll with his long trunk and launched it across the yard.

"Oh, no! Excuse *me*! I'll just get out of your way next time!" I gave him a mock curtsy as he crawled behind a table before turning to Wren. "Okay, let's—"

She was gone.

Spinning in a circle, I searched through the chaos. No. She wasn't gone, I was just missing her somehow. Didn't all Earthan kids play hide-and-seek?

But as my heart rate accelerated, I knew I was lying to myself. She wasn't going to fight her way back through this mess to retrieve us. She had the pass codes, her way to the docking bay was clear. She had no need for us anymore. If she really intended to bring me and Elio onboard, she would have made sure we were with her before she ran.

Anger flared in my chest, deep and burning. I wished I had a blaster handy. I suddenly had a passionate need to destroy something.

Dodging another flailing inmate being sprayed with a vat of milk from the kitchens, I ducked behind the table again. A woman tried crowding in beside me, but I elbowed her out of the way. Wren or no Wren, I just had to make it to the docking bay before she did, hack the pass codes again, and then Elio and I would have her coveted ship all to ourselves.

Easy-peasy.

"New plan. Get up." I tugged Elio's hand, but he didn't budge. I looked down and— "*No.* Not now. Not *now.*"

He was glitching, twitching silently on the ground. With the horde of bodies surrounding us, it was impossible for me to find a good angle to lift him up. Even if I managed it, I knew I wouldn't be able to carry him more than several yards.

Maybe I was imagining it, but I swore I could hear the engines of Wren's spaceship firing up, leaving us trapped on Andilly forever.

Suddenly, an unfamiliar voice intruded on my pity party, tentative but with an undercurrent of laughter. "Your friend appears comatose."

"He's not comatose." I grunted as I tried to lift him. "He's glitching. He—*Andy*?"

The big guy leaned against the table, examining a comm link that he must have taken from a guard. His hair was dusted with crumbs, and the leathery red skin of his cheeks was streaked with some kind of pink jelly.

His upper lip curled. "Don't call me that."

"Don't call you—wait, can we back up a millennium? You *talk*?"

His voice was rough as sand, his accent a staccato rhythm, like he was chewing up each of his consonants and spitting them out after finding the taste unsavory. But the fact remained that he was still *talking*. Why he had decided to play Silent But Deadly earlier I didn't know.

"You're truly observant." He looked up from his stolen comm in disgust. "For your information, I also walk, eat, and expel gas from various orifices, most of which I'd rather not disclose while in present company. I promise, I'm multitalented." He even had the gall to wink.

Idiot. "Leave me alone. I'm in the middle of a crisis." I tried to lift Elio again, to no avail. Around us, the food fight was starting to die down. I didn't know how many guards were out here, but I preferred they didn't catch up with us.

"You look like you require assistance," Anders said.

"What I require is a way to stop Elio from dying."

That dropped the smirk off his red face. "He's dying?"

"He could." It was possible for him to bounce back from a glitch on his own, but he hadn't done so in weeks. I always had to shock him back into action. And without a computer system to do it, who knew how many of his memories would be gone by the time he came around.

If he came around.

"We should help him, then," Anders said. "He is timid, but . . . what's the word? Precious?"

"He didn't give you permission to compliment him like that." I gestured to his body. "Just pick him up. If you can."

"I'm insulted." Easily, Anders swung Elio over one shoulder, gripping the back of his legs to hold him steady. "Where's the Earthan?"

"Wren? She ditched us."

Anders growled. "Typical."

"I have to get to her ship. If it's still here. I need to plug Elio into the control panel. It's the only way . . ." I trailed off, throat catching.

Anders looked massively uncomfortable with my sudden show of emotion. "Understood." He faked a cough. "I doubt the ship left. You would hear it if she launched. Trust me, I've been a prisoner long enough to know."

"And how exactly did you end up a prisoner here?" Knowing the inhabitants of Andilly, he probably murdered somebody and then used their bones as a toothpick.

"I don't ask you deeply personal questions, Cora. Now move. I'm right behind you."

Stars, he was bossy. But I listened anyway, not because I cared about him in the slightest, but because I cared about Elio. I hadn't failed him yet. And I certainly wouldn't start today.

Holding Anders's stolen comm in front of me like a map, I followed a blueprint of Ironside as we crept cautiously past the cells and through the dusty gray halls, entering a corridor across from an even grayer and dustier med bay. Vials and syringes littered the floor, showing the path the room's inhabitants had taken during their run to join the food fight outside. Streaks of something black were crusted on the countertops, and a tang of iron filled the air. *Blood*. I suddenly regretted every bite of my breakfast.

"Dumbwaiter?" Anders suggested, pointing out two rusty doors at the end of the hall beside a storage unit. I directed the comm at the lift, hoping to infiltrate the computer system and see what floor it journeyed to last. Maybe Wren had come this way as well. But my search brought back only disappointment: the dumbwaiter hadn't been used in over four months.

"No way. I'm not getting stuck in there. We're taking the ramp down." I headed for a narrower door in the corner, but Anders cut me off.

"Who's helping you transport your friend? You should accommodate my generosity and take the simpler way down."

"Who talks like that? *Accommodate my generosity*." I checked the ramp, which spiraled down to the smallest of the three docking bays. Not large enough to contain a spaceship, but it was a start. "I don't need your help. Roll Elio down the ramp for all I care."

"I'm calling your bluff. You like this robot so much that you might start kissing it." He shuddered.

"Elio's family. Are you purposely trying to be annoying? I know you said you had multiple talents, but I didn't think that—" I froze. "Someone's coming."

"What?"

Wrenching open the door to the ramp, I ushered him inside. Footsteps sounded in the corridor, followed by the low buzz of a blaster powering up. Through a crack in the door, I spotted a bright orange cloud drifting through the air—the aura of a curious Ironside guard.

"He's coming this way," said Anders, his breath hot on the back of my neck. It smelled like he hadn't brushed his teeth in months.

The guard was getting closer, his aura thickening. We could run to the floor below before he spotted us if we moved right now.

"What are you doing? Come on," I hissed, trying to wave Anders forward. He instead lowered Elio to the ground, gently leaning him against the wall, then turned toward the door.

"Anders."

The guard had reached us. His blaster hummed from the opposite side of the door, just a foot away, but it was his aura that really let me know he was so close. Like a cloud of orange syrup. I was gagging on it.

The door opened.

The guard looked at both of us, stunned. He appeared even younger than me, and although he had his blaster raised and ready to fire, I judged by his wide eyes that he didn't truly expect to use it.

Before he could move, Anders lunged for him. I failed to repress a scream as the nails of Anders's right hand lengthened into thick black claws. He was *horrifying*, eyes wild, mouth snarling. I screamed again as his claws plunged toward the guard's chest, tearing open the front of his uniform like it was made of paper, ready to rip through skin and bone and—

He stopped short.

"Anders?" I tried hesitantly.

The guard's eyes bugged out of his skull as Anders slowly curled his hand into a fist. His fingers flashed between nails and claws while he shook his head, like he was trying to dislodge something trapped inside his skull. As dramatic and life-threatening as the entire situation was, I really didn't have time to watch Anders struggle with himself—or whatever was going on in his giant lizard brain. I had a ship to catch. More importantly, I had a droid to save.

Raising my comm, I got ready to bring it crashing into the back of Anders's head, but before I could follow through, his fist shot forward. He smashed the guard's stomach, then his head. The boy wheezed as he tumbled to the ground. But after a moment, he grew still.

The orange cloud of his aura snuffed out like a candlewick.

Even though I hadn't done anything, I fought to catch my breath. "I guess there's some truth to those flesh-eating-lizard rumors after all."

Anders shrugged as the animal claws receded into his fingertips. He picked Elio back up. "I told you I'm multitalented. I also wanted a new blaster. Grab his for me, would you?"

"You . . . didn't kill him, right?" I wanted to pull Elio away from him, out of his monster grip, but I picked up the guard's blaster instead. The handle was still warm.

"He's unconscious, not dead. I'm not . . ." He licked his lips. "I'm not that heartless." His voice held no emotion, but as I followed him down the ramp, I caught him wiping his hand off on his jumpsuit. Like he was willing away the memory of what just happened.

Interesting.

The docking bay at the bottom of the ramp was empty except for dust motes floating in the air. A rolling steel door gleamed from the opposite end of the long room, probably the cleanest thing in this entire prison. It would take me a minute, but I could tap into the pass codes to unlock it so we could run, but then what? We had one comm, one blaster, and one malfunctioning android, none of which would hold up against the citizens of Andilly. Anders was probably the most pleasant of them all, and I'd just witnessed him beat a man unconscious.

So we continued on. A short hallway led from one bay to the next. The second was empty, but the third bay . . . *yes*. There it was. A hulking mass covered in a ragged tarp filled nearly all of the circular room. The *Starchaser*. My heart swelled so big that it took up all the space inside my body. Already I could picture us breaking through the atmosphere and flying into deep space. *Free*.

I hurried forward, but Anders held me back, black claws curling around my shoulder. "Carefully. In case someone is—"

Without warning, Elio let out a wail. He flopped off Anders's shoulder, hitting the ground before jerking up like he'd been run through with a lightning bolt. His ears fell across his eyes as he beeped so fast that it sounded like just one long scream coming from his mouth. I had the sudden urge to shush him, but I was so happy he was okay that I pushed the feeling down.

He blinked up, first at me, then Anders. "What is *that*? Where are we?"

"That's Andy," I said. "You'll remember in a second. As for where, it doesn't matter, because we're leaving."

"Not quite yet," a voice rang out from the other side of the bay.

A shadow rippled beside the *Starchaser* at the same time the doors behind us shut with a metallic snap.

"I knew it," Anders muttered with an indignant huff.

A dozen guards approached us from all sides, appearing out of the corners like phantoms, while the tarp fluttered on the ship and a ramp lowered from the hull.

Wren.

A guard dragged her out of the ship, depositing her on the floor in front of us. A seam in her jumpsuit was ripped at the shoulder, and a bruise was beginning to bloom around her eye, the same bright purple as her hair. I raised my stolen blaster, but I was unsure whether I was better off aiming at her or her captor.

The guard aimed his own blaster at Wren's head. "Lower your weapon or your friend's brains will be splattered all over the walls."

That was a disgusting visual, but my arm didn't budge. After she left us to rot, Wren and I were far from exchanging friendship bracelets.

The bodies behind us crept closer. I felt the brush of a knife along my spine. Elio whimpered. As usual, Anders was uselessly stoic.

"How about this?" the guard tried again. He looked older than the others, with a deep scar across his forehead and left eyelid. "Lower the weapon and maybe I won't kill you. And after that, perhaps if I feel like it, I can arrange for you to set foot on this ship after all."

Could he really promise that? A hand slammed down on my shoulder, rattling my bones. I felt the cold pressure of a blaster barrel press against the back of my neck.

"If I were you," the old guard said with a cold smile, "I would say thank you."

"I—" But I was cut off by the guard behind me. I looked over my shoulder just in time to see her bring the barrel of her gun speeding toward my head. And then I did lower my weapon.

My entire body collapsed to the floor.

7

THE PRISON REALLY COULD HAVE BENEFITED FROM SOME redecoration.

While I was out cold, the guards had apparently cuffed my hands behind my back and then dragged the four of us out of the docking bay and into an office on the floor below. It was filled with a desk covered in papers, a gruesome display of shrunken heads lined up in jars against the wall, and four wobbly iron chairs, which the guards had shackled us to. The room smelled strongly of mold and contained precisely two colors: gray, and grayer.

"That was a valiant escape attempt," the old guard said. He slammed the office door, leaving the others in the hall, and then sat, propping one shiny boot on the edge of the desk like he owned it. Maybe he did.

"It almost seemed too . . . simple," he continued. "You encountered only one guard on your way to the bays, one who didn't put up much of a fight. Then you reached the ship to find your friend there first. Although, how she made it on her own, nearly undetected, seems almost too good to be true, despite the little distraction you orchestrated." He turned to Wren, trapped in the chair beside me, and grinned. His bright white teeth didn't match the burnt red scales spread across his skin.

Wren frowned back. *How did he know Anders and I crossed paths with a guard on our way through the prison?* The uncertainty of it all made my stomach twist into knots. There was only one explanation.

"Have you been spying on us?" I demanded. The guard Anders hit was definitely still out cold. There was no one left who could have tattled on us.

The man dug through a drawer in his desk, taking his sweet time doing so. He eventually found what he was looking for—a sharp bone—and used it to pick between his two front teeth.

"You're almost as perceptive as I thought you might be," he said, folding his hands beneath his chin. "Cora Saros."

I stiffened. He knew my name. And if he knew my name, he knew of my family.

I was as good as dead.

Out of the corner of my eye, I saw Wren's head whip toward me, her mouth hanging open. *Great*. A budding thief like her—she was probably a big fan.

"You are Cora Saros, aren't you?" the man asked.

"I . . ." I caught Elio's eye, and he shrugged. "On a good day."

"And what kind of day is today?"

"Honestly, not that great."

The man leaned back in his chair. "I wouldn't be too sure about that yet."

Whatever that meant. "How do you know my name?"

"I know every inmate's name. It's my job. I'm the warden at Ironside." He placed the bone on the surface of the desk, lining it up perfectly with a row of pens and a pocketknife. "You may call me Warden, or you may call me Sir."

Anders snorted. I glanced at him, but his eyes were searing into the sharp bone on the warden's desk.

The warden didn't seem to notice. "You asked if I was spying on you, Cora Saros. I confess, it was no mistake that you were able to acquire the pass codes to the hangar or journey through the entire prison without encountering any obstacles. Nor was it a mistake that your friend was able to board her ship today before I stopped her.

I could have had all four of you killed instantly, but instead I told my guards to step back. You nearly succeeded, because I *allowed* you to. I wanted to see what you were capable of. Miss Saros, when I was told that a pod ship registered under your name had been found on Vaotis and that you were being brought in, I truthfully couldn't believe my luck. You are *exactly* what I've been waiting for."

"I'm really not sure what you mean."

Wren snorted. "I think he's implying that you're the Chosen One."

"I've seen that net drama!" Elio shouted. He kicked his legs, little feet swinging almost a foot above the floor as his chair wobbled from side to side.

The warden pounded his fist on the desk. "Silence! I can have you dragged back to your cell immediately, and believe me I will not make the remainder of your stay at Ironside pleasant—"

"It was pleasant before?" Wren muttered.

"However, if you wish to be useful, then I will—"

"Useful?" This time it was Anders who spoke up. "Funny how you always make that sound like an honor when what you really mean is that we're here to be *used*. Bent to your will, then discarded and left alone in a cell to rot—"

"He *talks*?" Wren gasped.

"A bit too much, it seems," Elio said.

The warden stood forcefully, sending his chair crashing to the ground. In an instant he was in front of us, his nails transforming into claws, just as Anders's had. He grabbed Anders's face and dug them into his cheeks, ripping up his scales, causing a trickle of blood to drip onto the collar of his filthy jumpsuit.

Anders only smiled. "You haven't changed at all. Have you, Father?"

Father? I leaned toward Elio. "Please tell me that's how citizens greet their leaders on Andilly."

"Nope," Elio replied. "Don't think so."

Oh, great skies above. The warden kept his own son locked in a cell? Talk about daddy issues.

"You are no son of mine," the warden hissed, releasing his grip on Anders's face.

Wren piped up. "Except that's what people always say when they *are* talking about their son—*oh!* No thank you, Sir. I don't want your claws inside my face." She tried to shrink away as the warden neared, claws dripping blood. But he surprised us all by letting them retract inside his nails before returning to his seat.

He picked up the bone again. "Any more questions?"

"Just a million," I said. "First, what is going on? You let us hack the pass codes. You let us reach the docking bay. You know who my family is. What is it you think *I* can do for *you*?"

"The better question is what do I think *we* can do for *each other*?" The warden's eyes took on a greedy twinkle. Anders made a sound like he was gagging.

"Have you ever heard of the Four Keys of Teolia?" the warden asked. When we all shook our heads, he didn't seem surprised. "She was the first empress on the planet that is her namesake. Legends claim that upon the eve of her death, she was gifted an elixir made by her palace aide, a woman whom she had been in love with for quite some time. The elixir was meant to grant Teolia the gift of immortality. But before her aide had a chance to administer it, Teolia was brutally murdered in her sleep."

"You look strangely happy about that," I pointed out.

"Indeed," said the warden. "Because the elixir was never drunk by Teolia, her aide had no use for it. She certainly never planned to drink it herself, preferring to die of old age so she could be with her true love once again. So she shut away the elixir in a chest, which could only be opened by four different keys inserted into four different locks simultaneously. Then she shipped the chest and each of the keys to five different corners of five different galaxies, hopeful that no one would ever find them and no one would ever be killed over such an extraordinary gift ever again."

"That's a nice bedtime story," Wren said. "But I'm not sure what you're getting at."

"Oh, it's more than a bedtime story. For I happen to have one of the keys right here."

He opened another desk drawer, producing a key nearly as long as my forearm. The shaft was shaped like a hook, interspersed with multicolored gemstones and orange spots of rust. The warden held it at eye level, practically drooling.

"I confiscated this from an inmate who was arrested last year. He claimed to have found it on a moon of Jupiter, one of Teolia's favorite planets. He never managed to locate the others. Unfortunately, he suffered a tragic accident in his cell soon after his arrival. Never in all my years have I seen a man's spine broken into so many pieces."

"You had him killed," Wren said.

The warden pressed a hand to his heart. "I did no such thing!" But he was smirking. "Regardless, I loathe the thought of having competition."

"Competition?" I asked. "You're trying to become immortal?" Because if that wasn't the ultimate villain objective of the century, then I didn't know what was.

"Perhaps. Or better yet, I can sell the elixir and reap the profits. No one knows about that more than a Saros, right, Cora? If anyone can locate the most valuable treasure in the entire universe, it's Evelina Saros's daughter. You can even bring your little droid and Earthan friend with you." He frowned at Anders, but then his gaze skipped back to me. Did that mean that Anders had to stay here? All alone? I didn't particularly like him, but if we were getting out of here, he could be useful to us. The guy was *massive*. If nothing else, he could offer us protection.

I nodded at Anders. "He comes too," I told the warden.

He chuckled. "Absolutely not."

"What are you doing?" Anders muttered to me.

"Helping you." Like he helped carry Elio. He didn't need to do that; he could have ditched us. But he didn't.

"He comes too," I told the warden again.

"And I told you *no*."

"I'll make a deal with you. You let him come—you let *all of us* out of here—and we'll bring the treasure back to you faster. Say . . . three keys, two weeks?"

The warden tapped his fingers on the desk, each one forming a black claw where his nail met the wood. I was reminded of Evelina's own pointed fingernails. An intimidation tactic, but I was anything but scared. My blood was on fire; my head pounded. Evelina and Cruz should have noticed that Elio and I were gone by now, but the warden hadn't mentioned anyone contacting Ironside to plead my innocence or bribe him for my release.

Of course they didn't care. Considering we were such a *distraction*.

My chained hands curled into fists behind my back.

"Fine. Bring back three keys *and* the chest. Two weeks." The warden stood and approached me. He reached out, the claw on his middle finger digging underneath my chin. I felt blood drip down my throat. "If you succeed, I'll see to it that your criminal records are expunged and you'll never set foot in Ironside again. Of course, if you fail . . ." He licked his lips with a quick swipe of his tongue, as if savoring our misery. "If you fail, you'll be incarcerated until the end of your lives, which could possibly be a very long time or a very short time. It's tough to tell. There are plenty of hungry prisoners in Ironside."

"*I'm* hungry," Wren grumbled. "This has been a very long meeting."

The warden flexed his claws again.

"What's the catch?" Anders interrupted.

"Sorry?"

"The catch. Either we succeed and walk free, or we fail and our situation is the same as before? No punishment? That doesn't seem like you at all."

A dark, furious aura flickered around the warden's head, but it was gone almost immediately. So, he was capable of the same invisibility trick as Anders. Must run in the family.

"No catch." A muscle ticked in his jaw. "Might be a bit different than you're used to."

Anders pulled at his chains, but they didn't budge. "Just a bit. You're lying to my face this time instead of going behind my back."

Wren, Elio, and I exchanged glances. We were definitely intruding on something here. But all I could think about was the elixir the warden spoke so highly of. Eternal life. The value of that kind of prize would be . . . *astronomical.*

I couldn't pass this opportunity up.

"We'll do it." I sat up straight in my chair. Or as straight as the chains would allow. "We'll take the job. We'll be back in two weeks."

"You don't know what you're agreeing to," Anders snarled.

"Sure I do. You're the one not comprehending. Find keys, get elixir, get free. Fail and we're back to having slumber parties in our cell." I glared at the warden. "Does that about cover it?"

"That about covers it," he said.

"Great. So let's get started." My fingers itched, eager to get those keys and feel the weight of the elixir in my hands. *Stars*, I was turning into my mother.

But I knew I would do anything to find that treasure, short of murder. No, maybe even that, if it came down to it, although the thought made me squirm. Whatever kept the treasure chest out of the warden's hands and in my own.

Because *finally*, praise to all the galaxies, I'd found the haul that might reinstate Evelina's faith in me. The haul that might save Elio.

I just had to steal it for myself first.

"Well," Wren said. "He was a treat."

Ten minutes later, we were armed with blasters and comm links, sporting gashes on the backs of our necks where two of the warden's guards had inserted tracking devices deep under our skin. I couldn't think of a good way to remove them without causing damage to my spinal cord. Infuriating things. The warden insisted he couldn't afford to have us running off on him while we were gallivanting about the universe, which made sense, but the grin on his red face when he said it made me think that the trackers were less about security and more about exercising control over his prisoners at any opportunity. They were a reminder that even though we were leaving Ironside, we weren't free.

Not yet.

Anders wouldn't stop grumbling about the warden under his breath as we headed to the docking bay and Wren's ship, the lights in the hallway flickering and buzzing above us. I was shocked that he agreed to come with us, though Wren's zest for life, my annoyance at almost everything, and Elio's frequent beeping had to be better than anything waiting for him back in our cell. Assuming he could keep his claws to himself, maybe we would all get through this job in one piece.

He shot Wren a look so filthy that I had to avert my eyes. "Ah yes," he said. "I forgot your planet enjoys sarcasm."

"Who doesn't? And look, I'm the absolute last person who would ever volunteer to stay trapped on this rock, but how do we even know this treasure is real? The inmate who gave the warden that key could have just been blowing smoke up his butt."

Anders's look of hatred changed to stunned disbelief. "Why would he blow smoke up the warden's butt? What would that accomplish? Wouldn't it just tickle?"

Wren slapped a hand to her forehead. "Oh, stars above."

"It's an Earthan expression," I told him. "It means telling someone what they want to hear."

"But you didn't answer my question. Wouldn't it tickle?"

"It's not literal!" Wren groaned. "There's no smoke! And speaking of no one answering questions, you didn't answer mine. How do we know this magic elixir even exists? He could be sending us on a wild goose chase—"

"We're chasing keys, not geese," said Anders.

"*Oh my*—look. All I'm saying is that we could bring back your superstitious fanboy father a bottle of fancy perfume and call it eternal life. He wouldn't know the difference. Actually, maybe we should do that. It would save us a ton of time."

"The treasure is real," I said. I kept my gaze straight ahead as we walked down the corridor, but I felt Wren's attention swing in my direction.

"You have proof?"

"No, but . . ." But it couldn't be anything *other* than real. I had too much at stake.

Over the years, I had helped my family rob queens and dignitaries; we'd crept inside crypts and bank vaults, touched jewels as large as pod ships and as small as pinheads. I'd brushed my hands over hundreds of millions of ritles. Nothing was too much. Nothing was out of the question. If all those treasures existed in this universe, then why couldn't the elixir?

"According to my net search," Elio interrupted, "there is approximately a 0.8372 percent chance that the treasure is real."

"And what is the percentage of us buying a bottle of perfume for under twenty ritles?"

"Don't answer that," I told Elio. He beeped, then started running to keep up with us when Wren picked up the pace. "We're going to find the keys *and* the elixir," I told her.

"If you say so. I'm just considering myself your getaway driver. But I'm also a glutton for gossip, and I would *love* to know what's up with Andy and his oh-so-loving daddy."

I turned to Anders. "Me too. What *is* up with you guys?"

Anders ground his teeth so loud that the noise raised the hair on my forearms. "I don't answer stupid questions."

"I actually thought it was a pretty good question," Wren said.

"I don't talk to Earthans either. You infuriate me."

"But—"

"Be silent! I can't think with your fruitless babbling." He scrubbed the back of a hand across the tattoos on his forehead as we approached Wren's ship, still covered by the shabby tarp. Four guards were standing across the room beside the service entrance, the barrels of their blasters resting comfortably against their shoulders. Upon seeing us, they huffed in boredom, but then they busied themselves with raising the door. A humid gust of air entered the docking bay, scattering dust at my feet.

My head spun at the guards' reaction. They weren't eager to attack us anymore, not since we agreed to assist the warden. This felt like an alternate universe, but it was one I thought I could quickly get used to.

"Okay, here we are. Feel free to *ooh* and *ahh* to your heart's content." Wren grasped the tarp in both hands, fingers twitching with anticipation. Her aura sparked from gold to bright red to neon green and back to gold again before I could properly read it. But she was ecstatic. I could tell that much.

The air in the bay seemed to still as she tugged the tarp free. It billowed and then settled in a heap at our feet, revealing in all its glory Wren's legendary, grand—

Oh.

Well . . . I thought it was a ship. I was pretty sure it was. About 89 percent sure. Maybe.

Possibly 88 percent.

"It looks like a turtle with wings," Elio whined.

"I have seen scabs on the bottom of my feet that are more appealing," said Anders.

"Cut it out, Andy! It's not that bad!"

Not that bad was subjective. *The largest ship in the galaxy?* By whose measurements? It was fifty times larger than my pod ship, sure, though it was still smaller than any self-respecting charter ship that I'd ever seen. Not only that, but it was *old*. I circled the ship slowly, taking inventory of all the damage.

The round body was covered in a thick layer of rust, which masked *some* of the dents covering the hull. Viewports on each of the four floors had hefty cracks, the one in front of the cockpit most of all. A jagged, diagonal slice that pained me just by looking at it. Next up were the flaps that had come loose along the wings, creating fist-size holes in the paneling. Those were followed by a weird egg-y smell wafting from the ramp leading to the starboard cargo hold, like maybe something had died inside and Wren had forgotten to clean it up. And then there was the landing gear, hanging on by only a hope and prayer, causing the parked ship to sit crooked and sad and—*oh, Saturn's rings, am I really going to board this death trap?*

The answer to that was, unfortunately, yes. For Elio, I would do it.

"This is the *Starchaser*?" I asked. "More like *Starcrawler*."

"*Starturtle*," Elio added. "I'm calling it the *Starturtle*."

"*Stardead*," said Anders. "It is definitely deceased."

Wren looked appalled. "What is wrong with you three?"

"Many things," I said. "I can provide a list at your request, but I promise it won't be anywhere near as long as the list of things wrong with this ship. Is it even flyable?"

"Yes! It passed its inspection last year. Come on, it looks way nicer on the inside." She gestured toward the ramp and whatever horrors lurked inside the cargo hold. "I painted the cockpit after I stole it. The color is called Whispering Peach."

"Are you sure it's not called Dead Salmon?" I muttered, my nose wrinkling at whatever that smell was, and stepped inside the ship.

The cargo hold reminded me a lot of Ironside. Gloomy and gray, it was packed tightly with cardboard boxes and plastic crates. Wren waved toward a closed door in the corner. "The laboratory is that way."

"You have a laboratory?" I said, heart soaring. Before we left, the warden bragged about all my belongings he'd confiscated from my pod ship on Vaotis and then sold on the black market. My VED, my broken phaser, my personal comm link. If I wanted any of them back, I'd have to build them myself. For a second time. From scratch. Using whatever meager supplies I could find on Wren's ship.

Now that I'd actually *seen* the ship, I had a feeling that even asking for meager supplies would be like asking for a moon, but it was still worth a try.

"If you can manage to find anything in there, then you're welcome to use it," Wren said. "It's a storage nightmare right now." Our footsteps echoed off the metal grates on the floor as she led us past the laboratory door to a small lift in the corner. We crowded in—Wren and Elio up front, me and Anders in the rear. I felt the heat of his body on my back as we ascended, his infuriating, aura-less presence making me fidget. I couldn't relax properly until we stopped, the gears in the lift grinding and clunking, and exited into the cockpit.

Whispering Peach. Huh.

The room was really more of a dull orange, like staring directly into a setting sun. The lights on the control panel blinked in a rainbow, broken up by radar displays and cameras showing various rooms in the ship—all dark at the moment. Wren plopped down in the leather captain's chair, patting the seat beside her.

"Who wants to be my co-pilot?"

Immediately, Anders pivoted and stormed out of the cockpit. I whirled around, catching his shadow turning the corner before he disappeared completely.

"Where are you going?" Elio yelled after him.

"Bed," he growled back. A door slammed somewhere in the distance.

Wren's smile fell just a fraction. "Cora? Co-pilot?"

"That depends." I leaned against the armrest of the empty chair, looking through the viewport. The warden's guards were waving us toward the service door and the bleak backcountry of Andilly beyond. Wren flicked a few switches and pulled up on a lever near her feet. The *Starchaser* hummed, an animal coming out of hibernation, before lifting off the ground with a jerk that had Elio and me stumbling forward.

The landing gear and the cargo ramp retracted with a groan, and then we were clearing the prison walls. *Free*. For now, anyway. At least we were leaving Ironside, and we weren't doing it in body bags.

Wren edged the ship forward, out of the prison's no-fly zone and toward the mountains, her face the picture of ease as she studied the control panel. I'd only ever flown my pod ship, and this looked infinitely more complex. More lights and screens and the humming of voices through the comm link that was connected to Andilly's control tower. Wren switched the voices off as we picked up speed, thrusting the cockpit into silence.

"You were saying?" She raised an eyebrow at me.

"I was saying that me being your co-pilot depends on whether or not I can trust you. Don't think you can use me to help you start a riot in the prison yard and then ditch us right when we try to make a break for the hangar. That's not how things work around here." Or that wasn't how things worked for *me*, anyway. But until Elio and I got our hands on the elixir, that fact was irrelevant.

Wren's long fingers stilled, hovering over the ship's controls. "I—I wasn't going to leave Ironside without you. I was powering up the ship first, and then . . ."

"And then?" I prompted. "You were going to leave. You can admit it, you know. You're no better than the rest of us. Not me. Or Elio. Or Anders. You come across so sweet, but I think that's all an act. Maybe you aren't as good of a person as you think you are. It's okay," I added quickly when she lifted a hand to protest. "Maybe I'm not either."

"Cora," Elio warned, nervously biting his fingers. He never handled conflict well.

The aura surrounding Wren flashed red, like the first spark of a fire. *Anger*. And somewhere underneath—*determination*.

Her gaze fell back to the control panel, and the ship continued out of the no-fly zone, gaining altitude. "So your mother is really Evelina Saros?"

"I'm stealing this line from Anders: I don't answer stupid questions."

"Why? Because you don't want to talk about her?"

"I don't want to talk about her in the same way you don't want to talk about trying to abandon us in Ironside."

Wren gripped down hard on the throttle, making the ship lurch. "Fair enough. But you should know that I've been studying your family for months. That heist you guys did at the treasury on Mars last year? *Bravo*. Only . . ." She wiggled her fingers, and I was reminded of her innate ability to steal anything within reach. "I think I could have done it better."

"Is that so?"

She nodded. "Maybe one day I'll be good enough to join your crew."

What? Did she think it was a picnic being part of my family? With Evelina's criticisms and Cruz's refusal to go against the grain and be on my side instead of his wife's for once in his life? With Blair's insults, and the house that was packed full of people and junk but somehow always felt so empty? Would she, after enduring all that, still want to please those people? To prove to them—and herself—that she was more than just an inconvenience?

Probably not. The only person broken enough to do that was me.

"You can fly this thing, right?" I asked. Truthfully, even if she told me she was going to careen us into the mountains, I wouldn't have batted an eye. I needed to get out of this cockpit. I needed to go somewhere quiet, where I could think about the nearly impossible task before me. And what would happen if I failed.

Maybe you really are no better than a distraction.

Wren looked a little crestfallen as I stepped toward the door. "Yeah, it has an autopilot feature. I didn't know where we wanted to head first, so I was just going to get us out of Andilly's atmosphere and then orbit for a—"

"Yeah, great. That sounds great." Was it hot in here? Why was it so hot in here? "I'm going to find a change of clothes, maybe take a shower. Anything to get the stink of Ironside off me. Elio will keep you company. Right, Elio?"

I didn't give him a chance to answer. I stepped back, ignoring the look he gave me—like I'd just kicked a puppy—and raced from the cockpit, my mother's disgust still ringing in my ears.

BY THE TIME I LOCATED A FUNCTIONING SHOWER IN THE residential quarters on the topmost floor of the ship and found new clothes—scuffed brown boots and an olive-green flight suit—I had extinguished all traces of Evelina's voice from my head. But as soon as I took a seat on the lumpy bed in an abandoned cabin and dared to take a glance out the porthole above my head, she was back.

These days, the sound of her voice always brought on sweaty palms and a racing heart, but it hadn't always been like that. There was a time, when I was young, that she would joke and play with me. The lines around her mouth had been from laughing back then, not frowning. I think I was the respite she needed after a long day of work. But then I grew older. She taught me how to shoot a blaster, how to build my first flash bomb. And then she'd made the decision that I was old enough to work alongside her. A decision that I'd had no say in.

If I was old enough to work with my family and share in the profits, then it went without saying that I was old enough to fail with them too. Or I guess fail *without* them, like I was now.

I knew without a shred of doubt that if Elio and I didn't find the Four Keys of Teolia, if we ended up trapped in Ironside again, no one would come for us. Not Blair, not Cruz. Certainly not Evelina. In their mind, we were failures the second we got caught on Vaotis. And my family didn't help failures.

And yet . . . they were all I had. They annoyed me to no end. They were impulsive and rude and condescending, but . . . if I lost them, and then if I lost Elio too . . .

Who would I be?

I grabbed a plaid blanket off the bed, a possession of a former *Starchaser* crew member, and wiped my sweaty hands all over it. Turning away from the depths of outer space, I took a good look at the cabin for perhaps the first time since entering it. Evelina would have hated this ship. There was no glitz, no glowing traces of moonstone like in our house. The cabin, like all the hallways I'd traveled through so far, was a combination of gunmetal gray walls, neon green uplighting, and dozens of exposed rusty pipes. The cabin at least had a few more flashes of color than the rest of the ship. Posters of Earthan men and women modeling skimpy outfits covered the wall across from the bed. Swimming attire, if I remembered correctly. A map of Earth was tacked up beside the photos, with large circles drawn in red ink around various tropical nations on the planet. Whoever lived in this room before me must've had a thing for warm climates.

"Cora?"

The door to the cabin opened with a swish, and Elio scurried through. He took a look around, eyes lingering in interest on the map of Earth, and then climbed up on the bed beside me. "I like your outfit," he said. "It's very ship-mechanic chic."

"Thanks?"

"At least you look cleaner than Anders."

"You talked to Anders?"

"Well . . ." Elio tapped a finger on his chin. "*Talked to* is relative. Wren asked me to find him to make sure he wasn't dead or anything, so I did. But then he yelled at me for waking him up and shut the door in my face. I'm hoping he took a shower after that. My optic sensors may be on the fritz, but I still know filthy when I see it."

"Oh. Yeah, he's . . . unique?"

Elio laughed, a single squeak. "*I'm* unique. *He's* grumpy. You're both alike in that way."

"What's that supposed to mean?"

He picked at a cracked spot of paint on his hand. "Just that I think you hurt Wren's feelings when you said you wouldn't be her co-pilot. And then when you criticized her ship. Maybe rein in the insults a bit?"

"Please, I can read her emotions. I'd know if she were insulted." I thought for a second. The memory of the sad ocean-blue aura surrounding her head when I'd left the cockpit made my heart twist. "Yeah, she's insulted. Crap."

But it wasn't like I was here to be her buddy. Especially not after she tried to leave Ironside without us. *Powering up the ship*, she'd said. Yeah, and Anders was in his room composing a love ballad at this very moment. I wasn't born yesterday.

Although . . . maybe it wouldn't hurt to befriend her. Befriend them both, actually. If my plan worked, and we really intended to take the keys and the treasure chest in the end . . .

"It will be easier if they trust us," I said. I recited my plan to Elio and his eyes glowed, a round of beeps echoing through the cabin.

He almost fell off the bed. "You want to give the treasure to Evelina and use the money to buy me a new body?" He looked like he couldn't believe what he was hearing, which was a definite possibility, if his auditory processors were glitching.

"Do you think it's a good idea?"

"Well . . . won't it hurt Wren and Anders? Don't they need the treasure too? I don't want to hurt anybody."

"No, they'll be fine." *Maybe*. "I swear. Have I ever lied to you?"

"Of course not."

"Of course not," I repeated. "Just promise you'll help me make friends with them." The only way I could steal from them was if they trusted us completely.

"Okay . . ." He sounded unsure. "I love making friends . . ."

I nodded enthusiastically. "Exactly."

"And I really do want that new body. With the mustache!"

"Of course. A *huge* mustache. You're going to look *amazing*."

"And you promise Wren and Anders won't get hurt?"

I couldn't promise anything. Elio needed a new body, and Evelina needed the entirety of this treasure in order for me to get it for him.

I hesitated, but he didn't notice. "I'll protect them. They'll be . . . fine."

It was obvious Elio wanted his second chance at life more than he wanted to think twice about the lie I was feeding him. "Well . . . all right!" He jumped off the bed. "Actually, this is a *great* plan. Think about the possibilities! I mean the *literal* possibilities! I just ran all thirty-five thousand, seven hundred eighty-nine of them through my processing system and determined that giving the treasure to Evelina is by far the easiest way to get me a body."

"What's the hardest way?"

"It involves a hot air balloon and crash landing on Earth. Trust me, you don't want to know the rest. Are you hungry? I'm hungry. Wren said the galley is stocked with Earthan food, so I'm making snacks."

"You can't eat them."

"But I can pretend to smell them, and sometimes that's just as good. Come down whenever you're ready. And *be nice*." He pointed a finger at me as he headed for the door, a newfound spring filling his short robotic strides.

"Yes, boss," I called after him. Picking up a flat pillow from the bed, I gave it a joking toss at his head. He batted it to the ground and kept walking.

Only once the *Starchaser* cleared the atmosphere above Andilly and drifted into a steady orbit around one of its four moons did I exit my room and attempt to find the galley. Millions of stars winked at me as I passed a long row of portholes lining the central corridor. If we actually managed to pull this job off, right after I bought Elio his new body, I was going to buy one of those stars and name it after myself. Just because I could.

The galley was housed in a windowless space directly above the cargo hold, its location only revealed by the smell of chocolate wafting down the hall. The chocolate smell was soon followed by the sound of breaking glass, and then I knew without a doubt I was in the right spot. I just hoped that today none of the shards got trapped in Elio's cooking. Now was not the time to get ten stitches in my tongue. *Again.*

A face full of flour greeted me the second I stepped around the doorframe. I wiped at my burning eyes, watching the blurry form of Elio hurry to grab a pan out of the oven before his cookies started to burn. Wren was seated on a stool at a round table in the corner, wearing a flight suit that matched my own, licking raw batter from her thumb.

"Don't tell me you left Anders in charge of flying the ship," I said, grabbing for a towel to wipe my face.

"Incoming!" Elio yelled right before a glob of cookie dough flew through the air, landing with a splat against a cabinet.

Wren offered me her bowl of batter. "Anders isn't flying anything. The ship's locked in orbit right now. By the way, your little robot is a whiz in the kitchen."

"Only with desserts. Don't try his real meals. I promise you'll get food poisoning."

"Hey!" Elio protested. He rushed back to the oven when a curl of smoke started to snake into the air.

"Last year I tried his lasagna and ended up with a mouthful of glass. He didn't even cook it in a glass dish. I'm still trying to figure out how that happened."

"Oh stars!" Wren dissolved into a fit of laughter. "I swear I'm not laughing at you . . . but actually, I am. I'm so sorry."

"Yeah, well." I picked at the cookie dough she slid in front of me. Like a . . . peace offering, maybe? Okay, then. Might as well start dialing up the friendship charm.

"So, Wren? Hey, I'm really sorry for what I said about your ship. You're right. It's not that bad."

How was *that* for an apology? I'd never had many friends, and consequently never had to make many apologies.

But Wren grinned like I'd just handed her a shooting star. "Thanks, Cora! See, I told you. She grows on everyone."

"Like a fungus," Anders said from the doorway. He stumbled into the galley, gripping the countertop. His red skin had a touch of green to it.

"Excellent. The party's here." Wren pushed the bowl toward him. "Want some cookie dough?"

Anders's lip curled to new heights. It was rather impressive.

"I don't eat . . . that. Sorry," he added when Elio's face fell.

"No worries," he said. "I can make you something else. What do you like?"

"I . . ." He looked around the room, lost. His gaze lingered on the open pantry door, filled with a sparse supply of canned foods and dried packaged fruits, before his dark eyes glinted hopefully. "Do you have pon?"

"*Porn?*"

"No! *Pon.* It's meat, but . . . sorry, I don't know the word in your language. Bloody?"

"Raw?" Elio asked. "Um . . . I can try, but I do best with chocolate. Any sugary substance, really."

"Raw meat," Wren muttered. "Of course that's what he eats."

"Maybe I'll eat *you*," Anders replied under his breath.

Wren popped a hunk of cookie dough in her mouth, feigning

politeness. "Sorry, didn't catch that. Did you say that you have something against Earthans? Did your prison warden father instill that belief in you?"

"Enough!" He slammed a fist on the counter, claws slicing through his fingertips. Elio dropped the pan of freshly baked cookies he was holding, beeping.

Anders stepped forward, oddly unsteady on his feet. "I told you before," he said, teeth flashing, "I don't talk to Earthans. You hide behind your weapons and your words, destroying everything. Well, we'll happily destroy you first."

"Holy—" I pushed my chair away from him.

Wren didn't even flinch. "Wow, look at you talking to me. See, that wasn't so hard, was it?"

Flustered, Anders raked his fingers through his messy bundle of hair. One of his claws got caught in a giant knot and he retracted them instantly, grumbling something in his language that definitely sounded like a curse word.

"Fine," he said. "I will try to be civil if you never mention my father again."

Wren shrugged, not protesting—but also not *not* protesting. For once we were on the same page, equally curious about the warden and his estranged relationship with his enigmatic son.

Anders frowned, giving us all this weird look like he was disappointed about something, and if I could read his aura like a normal person's, then I would've known for sure that's what it was. I guess I could have tried asking, but it seemed like being civil toward him would ruin all the progress I'd made with Wren. I didn't know how to befriend them both.

Another one of my plans, already swirling down the drain.

"I'm going back to bed," Anders finally muttered.

"Nighty night!" Wren waved, not looking at all upset to see him go.

The galley door slid shut behind him. I assumed he would head to his bedroom immediately, dead set on sequestering himself until further notice, but he shocked us all when his footsteps stilled in the corridor with a squeak. A door banged open somewhere nearby, and then the unmistakable sounds of vomiting and a toilet flushing filled the air.

"Oh *stars*!" Wren failed to suppress a fit of giggles. "Big bad Andy gets flight sick? Of all the people!"

Another toilet flush, following by a second verse of puking and a chorus of groans. It was probably the saddest song in the galaxy tonight.

Elio grimaced at me from across the galley. He likely wanted to comfort Anders. Being helpful was ingrained in his programming, after all, but he remained where he was, washing a cookie pan in the sink with steady strokes of a sopping wet sponge.

On second thought, maybe Elio should have comforted him. It would have gone a long way toward aiding my friendship cause.

With a harsh sigh, Wren stood and announced that she was returning to the cockpit, leaving her mostly empty bowl of cookie dough for me to finish. As she passed by me on her way to the door, I was hit with a face full of possibly one of the most depressing auras I'd ever seen. A deep violet, punctured by inky black holes that dripped into the air and formed ribbons that bound around her chest. They contracted, squeezing. Wren's breath seemed to still in her lungs. But then she exhaled through her nose, and the ribbons vanished in a puff of smoke.

"There goes my hope of us braiding each other's hair and telling scary ghost stories," she said with a weak smile. "This is going to be the most fun trip ever."

ANDERS'S CABIN WAS RIGHT DOWN THE HALL FROM MINE, and lucky me, I had the pleasure of listening to him vomit all night long.

When I stumbled into the galley the next morning, running on two hours of sleep and a heap of treasure-hunting adrenaline, I immediately came face to face with my new archnemesis. Anders was hunched over the table, shaking as the ship's old engines shuddered beneath us, his eyes tightly closed.

The bright side was that he wasn't puking. After last night, I doubted he had anything left in his stomach to puke.

"Coffee?" Elio presented him with a mug of dark brown liquid that only smelled vaguely burnt. "Wren doesn't have creamer. Sorry."

"I don't know what that is anyway." He rubbed his temples.

Grabbing the pot from Elio, I poured myself a cup into a chipped tumbler and took a seat.

As I watched Anders sniff at the coffee, I realized that, with the exception of raw meat, I had little clue about his diet. Most people from Condor ate a diet similar to Earthans', having lived among them for the last few decades, but all planets' inhabitants were different. Some ate enough to feed ten or twenty, while others concocted syrupy drinks full of vitamins and minerals found in deep space and had little need for solid food.

The floor vibrated as the engines turned over, causing Anders to moan and clutch his stomach.

"Whatever you do, don't puke again," I said.

Another groan.

"What do you eat anyway?"

Anders looked up at me blearily. "Meat, mostly. Or grains. Anything high in fiber."

"Do you think you'd like oatmeal?"

"I'll make you some!" Elio rummaged through the pantry. "I promise I won't burn it."

"You can eat it," Anders muttered to me over the clang of Elio's pots and pans. "I won't keep it down. Stars, I hate flying. It's a result of humanity's selfish desire to seek more than what they already have in front of them."

"*Or,*" I said, "maybe it's a result of humanity's innate desire to seek something greater. To learn. To better themselves."

Anders snorted. "It's definitely not."

I studied the tattoos arching over his eyebrows, curling in tight spirals. Getting those must have hurt something awful. "Be honest with me," I said. "What's the real reason you don't like Earth?"

"It's not that I don't like it. I . . ." He sighed, looking half his massive size. "It's personal."

His change in demeanor shocked me. All his former anger from last night had vanished as quickly as the claws on his fingertips, and I wondered briefly if he'd had the same idea I had. Befriend now, betray later. Anders and Wren weren't idiots. If I had ulterior motives, they could easily craft a similar plan.

I watched as Anders hunched over his knees, gripping his stomach. Or maybe he was still too sick to resume yesterday's angry Earth rant.

"Hey, I've been thinking . . ." (For the record, I hadn't; it just popped into my head.) "It's okay if we keep calling you Anders, right? You don't hate that, do you?"

I didn't care about his feelings—I just wanted him to believe that I was nice.

He shrugged. "Anders is fine. Andy is less fine, but what do people usually say? Is the phrase *whatever*?"

"Look at you integrating into modern society. Your planet is archaic, by the way. Tell me, do you battle wildlife for fun?"

"Fun? The Andilly sea bear is a prime food source. You're just jealous that we're more resourceful than the good people of Condor." He started to do something that looked like a smile, but then he gripped his stomach tighter. "No net programs rotting our brains."

"I'm surprised you even know what a net program *is*." Then I remembered an Andilly fun fact Wren shared during the first hour in our cell. "So everyone on your planet has numbers instead of names?"

He nodded. "It's efficient."

"It's so . . . cold." And I knew cold. I'd witnessed *and* been the target of plenty of Evelina's insults. "What number are you?"

He recited in one long breath: "Four million, eight hundred and thirty-two thousand, five hundred and sixty-six."

"Yeah. Calling you Andy is way quicker."

A hint of a genuine smile actually peeked through his grimace that time.

I knew I was treading on choppy waters, but for some reason I pressed on. Blame it on my lack of sleep. "Your father never called you anything else?"

And the smile disappeared. Shocker.

"Right, sorry. You said not to talk about him. But . . ." Here was a chance to connect with him. To befriend. And the pleasant surprise was, I didn't even have to lie to do it. "I know how it feels to not get along with your family. I know it's lonely."

And there it was. Behold Cora Saros ripping her heart out of her chest and sticking it on a silver platter for the entire universe to see. The things I did to acquire endless fortune. *Sharing emotions*. Nothing was more criminal than that.

"Really?" Anders looked unsure. "You do?"

"I do."

I had to look down at the table because, stars, this was embarrassing, and that was when I saw it. His hand, long knobby fingers with yellowed but neatly trimmed nails, inching across the table. *Closer*.

He definitely wasn't reaching for a napkin. His hand was seeking out my own, and whether or not it was some kind of deception on his part, it freaked me the heck out.

Just then, Wren burst into the galley. "Good morning, fellow treasure hunters!"

His hand stilled. The nervous roaring inferno inside me extinguished instantly, replaced by the relief of a soaking cold sweat.

Wren busied herself with making a bowl of cereal for breakfast, sliding up next to Elio. They bumped their hips together, then he tapped his left elbow against her left, his right against her right, they spun around, and then finished by whooping and slamming knuckles. *What in the* . . . They had a secret handshake *already*? Elio was too sociable for his own good.

Anders watched Wren, puzzled, as she shoved a spoon in her mouth. "Is that the food known as oatmeal?"

"Cornflakes," Wren mumbled, mouth full. "I wanted the frosted kind, but I'm low on ritles and couldn't afford the splurge. When we stop for supplies, I'm stealing some."

"Heads up!" Elio grinned, slamming a steaming bowl down in front of Anders. "*This* is oatmeal."

"Why is this one fuming when hers is not?"

"Well, that's the beauty of Earthan foods. Some are hot. Some are cold. And some are . . . both."

"Like sandwiches," Wren said. "Skies, I'm starving!" Spoon sticking out of the corner of her mouth, she rooted through the refrigerator and pulled free a plate of bread topped with some kind of floppy brown meat, which she shoved into the humming microwave above the stove. "It tastes better warm," she told Anders when she caught him sniffing the air hopefully.

Standing on shaky legs, Anders slowly made his way to the fridge to investigate for himself. Gingerly, he tugged open the freezer door and pulled out a round tub of . . .

"*Ice cream*!" I practically sighed the words. Double chocolate chunk ice cream. Years ago, Cruz brought some back from the Earthan colony on Mars, and I ate so much I was sick for two days. Evelina took it away from me after that. Probably finished the rest herself.

Anders tried taking the coveted tub to the microwave, but Wren leaped in front of him and snatched it away. "No! Not that one! We don't heat that one! It needs to be cold."

"But you said . . ." He shook his head, helplessly pointing to a circle of dough that Elio was busy ladling with red sauce. *Pizza*. It had been years since I was allowed to have that too.

"Most people eat that one hot, but certain weirdos prefer it cold," Wren said.

"Oh, for Neptune's sake! I hate all of you." But his insult held none of its usual venom. "I'll be in my room." He grabbed Elio's entire pizza and rushed from the galley.

"I wasn't finished with that!" Elio shouted after him. "Hey, do you think we should tell him that the pizza has raw anchovies on it?"

I stared at him blankly.

"Anchovies are little stinky fishies—"

"Oh stars, yeah, we should tell him." I bolted from the galley, but

I'd barely cleared the bend in the corridor when I was met with the familiar sound of Anders's retching coming from a nearby washroom.

Here was the thing: as a criminal, as Evelina Saros's daughter, I should have turned right around and left him to his misery. We had a treasure to find, and he was dragging us down. But as a friend . . . as the girl who sat across the table from him and tried not to flinch while his hand crept closer—whatever that had been about—I knew I couldn't abandon him, not after I'd bargained for him to come with us. As much as I hated to admit it, we were a team. Or we had to appear as one anyway.

The only food I had on me was a ration packet that I'd swiped from the galley counter. Dehydrated potatoes infused with vitamin C. Not the best meal, but when he finished being sick he would definitely be starving, and it was better than nothing.

I pulled the packet from the front pouch of my flight suit and slid it under the crack at the bottom of the door. Anders groaned before another round of vomiting echoed through the corridor.

Maybe he would have been better off with the ice cream.

"He's weak," Wren said when I returned to the galley. Elio was admiring a spread of jellied toast that he'd arranged alphabetically by color across the table. "I'm pretty sure that on certain planets the leaders choose to eat the weak."

"He just needs something to settle his stomach," I said.

"You're defending him?"

"No! I just . . ." I just knew I had to make this work. To make sure everyone got along so they would eventually let their guards down. But once again it seemed like taking a step toward Anders was a step away from Wren. I needed to figure out a happy medium, but right now that was just as invisible as Anders's nonexistent aura, which was a sharp contrast to the smoky clouds of guilt spilling off Wren's shoulders.

"Sorry," she said. "I guess I'm just hangry."

"Hangry?"

"Hungry-angry. Elio, be a dear and toss me some toast. Toast is my life."

He scooped up three plates. "Do you want peach jelly, grape, or boysenberry?"

"Surprise me."

He spun in a circle, beeping excitedly as he presented her with a slice of (slightly burnt) toast dripping peach jelly. He offered me the boysenberry, and I picked at a bit of the crust, pleasantly surprised to find that it didn't taste nearly as bitter as usual. Elio watched with rapt attention as I chewed—wait, was that a hair?—swallowed—yep, that was *definitely* a hair—and gave him a shaky thumbs-up.

"Yes!" He rushed back to the counter to make more. I didn't have the heart to tell him to stop. He looked happier aboard the *Starchaser* than I'd ever seen him at home under Evelina's eye. He didn't look like he was about to glitch anytime soon, even though nearly twenty-four hours had passed since his last. His recent record was four days glitch-free, but I wasn't trying to push his already bad luck.

"So what's the plan?" I asked, watching Wren bite into a second slice of toast and knock it back with a swig of milk. "The warden didn't exactly give us a map. How are we supposed to know where to go first?"

Wren shook her head. "And you call yourself a criminal mastermind." (I'd never called myself that a day in my life.) "First stop is to get Andy stomach meds. I need to land at the nearest outpost to refuel anyway, so we can grab them there. And I need to get a few repairs done on the engine. Not sure if you've noticed, but this ship, though charming, is a little old."

No, really?

But instead of throwing another insult her way, I thought of Elio and the new body that would save his memory core. I shrugged and smiled. "I can do the repairs. I'm good with mechanics."

Wren looked unsure. "I thought you were good with bombs? The last thing we want is this ship blowing up."

The *Starchaser* was already one loose lug nut away from falling to pieces, no bomb required, but I kept my mouth shut about it.

"Can you fix the coolant chamber?" she asked. "It's sort of, well, not cooling anything, so the engine likes to make this wheezy-sneezy noise like it has a head cold. It's kind of concerning. And the tertiary molecular containment filter keeps clunking. That's a little shady. And the flight stabilizer is tilting portside whenever I accelerate. Oh! And if you have a moment, the pipes underneath the level two toilet next to the med bay are backing up."

"I don't do plumbing repairs. The rest I can fix with a spark plug and a few rolls of tape."

"Really?"

"Sure." I mean, *maybe*, but I wasn't going to admit to her that I didn't have the slightest clue about charter ship engines. Whatever. Elio would download a blueprint. It would be fine.

Wren clearly didn't believe me, but it looked like she too was trying out the shut-up-and-let-it-go method. "Okay, fine. Wonderful. I'll let you know when we're about to land. It gets bumpy, which won't be good for Andy's stomach."

The galley door slid open automatically as she approached it. "Elio, fill her in on where we're heading after the outpost." She looked up at me, beaming. "He came up with this all by himself. Whether or not this treasure is real, I'm convinced that together we will accomplish great things. Great, but possibly not legal, things." And then she was gone.

"Well, well, well." I ran my knuckles across the top of Elio's head. "Looks like someone made a friend." If I joked about it, hopefully he wouldn't realize I felt a little slighted that he told Wren some vital piece of treasure hunting information before he'd shared it with me.

I tried to clear my mind. Jealousy would ruin everything. *Befriend now, betray later*. I needed to get it together.

So I sat in silence, choking down another piece of toast, and listened to Elio talk. Apparently, there was a plethora of information about the Four Keys of Teolia spread across the net if you knew the right places to look. Dark, shady corners of cyberspace filled with conspiracy theorists and those who had long since succumbed to treasure hunting fever. The only information the warden had given us was that one of Jupiter's moons had been the location of the first key—Teolia's favorite planet, a place she adored. And so Elio delved deeper into his research, noticing the same name of the same planet spoken again and again by all the fanatics on all the net sites: Cadrolla.

It was rumored that Teolia had adopted pets on Cadrolla in the spiraling Whirlpool Galaxy during her adolescent years, which wasn't shocking considering the planet's tropical climate and sprawling jungles were home to a host of questionable creatures. Most were outfitted with claws and horns that could turn a fully intact body to ribbons of flesh before an attacker knew what hit them. Others were cuddly but bulged full of poisons so rare and vile that not even Elio could name them.

And then there was the flora. The shrubs that dripped acidic substances and the weeds that used their vines to strangle passersby without provocation. There were the streams that reversed their currents on a whim, sucking everything within reach to a watery grave. The loosely packed earth that caved in at the slightest movement, sending each living creature in the vicinity to a premature death.

Teolia must have been a warrior to step foot on that planet and leave alive. Either that or she had no fear.

If we were looking for a pattern between the keys' locations, Cadrolla was a prime suspect. Elio stated it had been a place she visited frequently, each time bringing home another furry terror plucked from between the jungle vines to unleash on her enemies. According to Elio, many of the theorists on the net believed one of the keys was hidden in the ruins at the top of the planet's tallest mountain, though no one could say for sure. Everyone who claimed they were off to seek the key had never returned to the net to post about their experience. Likely because they had been ingested by something not very friendly that lived in the jungle.

"Cadrolla is barely the size of east Condor. The key shouldn't be that hard to find," Elio explained, scrubbing at the plates covered with toast and jelly. One of them slipped, crashing at his feet. "Whoops."

I helped him pick up the broken shards. "Assuming we don't get eaten." Not to mention the oxygen levels on Cadrolla were dangerously low. If Wren didn't have sufficient oxygen masks on board, maybe I could construct some. It would give me a good excuse to poke around the *Starchaser*'s laboratory, maybe even start rebuilding some of my old gadgets.

"Everything will be fine, Cora," Elio said. He leaned in to hug me, but his body was so small that his arms only reached my thighs. "And then we'll be one step closer to home."

Where we will accomplish great, but possibly not legal, things.

I didn't know if searching for a key on a jungle mountaintop filled with poisonous critters and oodles of killer vegetation was classified as *legal*, but it certainly wasn't classified as *sane*.

And yet, I had been making a habit lately of doing things that were considered not quite sane.

Elio grinned, nestling his head against my legs, beeping softly. Hopefully. But I noticed with a pang of sadness that he was refraining from beeping too loud—hoping too much.

Sighing, I hugged him back.

Might as well keep my insanity streak alive.

10

IT RAINED DURING OUR ENTIRE STOP AT THE FUELING OUT-post, which I considered a disheartening omen for the trip ahead. Winds whipped, sending debris pinging off the *Starchaser*'s hull, adding more dents to its already impressive collection. The cargo hold flooded with four inches of water, and Elio and I spent the majority of the afternoon scooping it out using gritty pots and pans that we dug from a cabinet in the galley. I recoiled every time the murky water rushed over my skin, seeping between my fingers. I was standing in the *Starchaser*, but in my mind I was locked in the crypt in Vaotis, floodwaters swallowing me whole. I was eight again, flailing in the inground pool in the backyard of Cruz and Evelina's house while they deemed me an unfit swimmer and left me to drag myself out of the water, coughing up chlorine.

Eventually, Anders took over for me, tossing water out onto the tarmac while he cursed Wren in his native language for landing the ship in the middle of the only storm the desert outpost had seen all year. She had conveniently disappeared as soon as we started mopping up the ship, and we hadn't seen her since.

The only consolation during our otherwise dismal day was that Anders had finally stopped regurgitating his meals. The pills Wren had stolen for him from the outpost's general store before she ditched us had curbed that problem pretty quickly. A small victory, but a victory nonetheless.

Late in the evening, just as the roar of the storm receded to a dull drizzle and the clouds parted slightly, allowing the moon's glow to shine over the wet tarmac, Wren returned to the *Starchaser*, lugging two bulging bags of food behind her.

"What is that smell?" Anders asked as Wren dropped the bags at her feet. I poked my head out of the engine room just in time to see a heavy can roll out of the larger bag and slosh through the remaining water on the cargo hold floor. I ducked back down the ladder, landing with a thud beside the engine. My spark plug and tape idea was going swimmingly. As in, some of the water from the cargo hold had dripped on top of the panels above the engine and I would be stuck *swimming* down here if we didn't drain it. Elio ducked inside the engine room, tossing me a towel and a schematic of the molecular containment filter before disappearing again.

I heard Anders's angry growl from the floor above. "Whatever that is, it smells *foul*. I have very sensitive olfactory receptors. I can't be in the same room as that."

"It's just canned ham. Eat up, kiddos. I was only able to steal from the expired stash."

"I've never tried canned ham before," Elio said.

"That's because you can't eat!" I called up from the engine room. A moment later, Wren appeared at the top of the ladder and held out a hand to me.

"About done?"

I gave the filter one final twist with a screwdriver, then kicked the main control panel until it let out a contented purr. Honestly, it was shocking how many mechanical issues could be solved with a simple kick. I just wished that applied to life issues too.

I took Wren's hand and let her pull me back up. "Yeah, it's done, but the room is going to flood if we don't do something about it. Then we'll really be in trouble."

She tugged off her boots, turning them upside down to drain

them. "I'll take care of it. It is pretty swampy in here. What have you guys been doing all day?"

A growl of epic proportions escaped Anders's mouth, making the crates in the corners of the hold vibrate. If I could see his aura, I knew it would look just like mine. Inky clouds spilling off both of us, moving toward Wren's throat to choke her.

Eyes blazing, Anders turned and splashed toward the lift. "I'll be in my room."

"But what about the water?" Wren asked.

"Wren, I am finding myself terribly hungry, and if I stay in this room any longer I might not be able to fight the desire to eat something. Believe me, the first item on my menu will not be canned ham. Does that make sense?"

"I—"

"He means you," Elio finished somewhat unhelpfully.

"Oh please. Anders, if you tried to eat me, I would strangle you from the inside out."

The lift doors slid shut, obscuring the points of Anders's bared teeth and the promise of death spilling from his eyes.

Wren couldn't have been less affected. "The ship is fueled, the engines aren't totally flooded yet, and Andy is grumpier than usual. Everything seems in order. Onward to Cadrolla!"

Cadrolla was a three-day journey, fueled primarily by Wren's sass and Anders's brooding. I didn't see much of either of them, having sequestered myself in the *Starchaser*'s laboratory to hammer out a design for oxygen masks. I was enjoying the respite from their arguing, the peace and quiet that came from sitting at a workbench, wrapping wires between my fingers and listening to Elio recite recipes for foods he couldn't eat. But of course, nothing lasted forever. I shrieked and nearly burned my hand off with a soldering iron when Anders stormed into the room and dropped down on the stool beside me.

"Canned ham is disgusting. Do you agree or disagree?"

"I'm firmly neutral," I said.

"How can you be neutral? It's abominable. I can't stand it being in the same room as me."

"What a coincidence. Neither can I." I looked pointedly at him, then internally slapped myself. I was supposed to be *nice*. But I couldn't concentrate on my work with the wheezing sound of his breaths permeating the lab. Andy was a mouth-breather, and I was *so* not having it.

"Can you turn your head the other way? I don't want your spittle getting lodged in my brand-new oxygen masks, please and thank you."

Huffing, Anders grudgingly stood and circled the lab while I worked. Frosted glass desks and a cluster of gleaming machinery were surrounded by sterile white walls and built-in shelves jammed full with books—some crammed in vertically, others horizontally and diagonally—filling every available inch. Most were written in languages that I didn't understand, not that it mattered much. I couldn't remember the last time I'd even touched a book, let alone read one. The invention of comm links had rendered physical reading material obsolete decades ago.

Studying the shelves, Anders grabbed a book at random and flipped it open. The spine cracked, a puff of dust filled the lab, and the *Starchaser*'s filtration system hissed manically as it struggled to purify the air around us. Coughing, Anders shoved it back on the shelf and resumed his seat beside me.

"I'll breathe through my nose this time," he promised.

Or you could just go away. *Whichever*.

Stars, I was terrible at this friendship charade.

"Why are you overhauling the oxygen masks?" He rolled the

sleeves of his flight suit up to his elbows with sharp, precise folds. A line of symbols crawled across the insides of his wrists, octagonal runes that were just as dark and intricate as the tattoos on his forehead. I might have gone so far as to call them beautiful—you know, if they had been on literally anyone else's body.

When he caught me staring, Anders quickly pulled his sleeves back down. "They're Andilly military." He looked at his hands like they were hideous. "They're branded into our flesh by our lo'zoka—our general—if we can make it back to base camp after surviving in the mountains for forty days without food or water rations. That's the last phase of our initiation."

"I didn't know you were in the military."

"Obviously. I didn't tell you. I was in for a while . . ." He fingered the edge of his sleeve. "Until I wasn't."

More specifically, until he did whatever thing he'd done that landed him trapped in a cell in Ironside, I assumed.

"I'd prefer not to talk about it," he said.

"Fine. We can talk about the oxygen masks instead. Whoever used these didn't take care of them at all. They have tears in the lining, the valves are cracking. We won't last three minutes on Cadrolla with these."

Anders picked up one of the three masks on the workbench, digging a dirty fingernail into the hose trailing from the front. "You know how to fix them?"

"I want to do more than just fix them. First off, I want to make the face shield larger to cover our eyes. Elio said there are a lot of potential irritants on Cadrolla that might affect our retinas, so I'm trying to add a film to counteract against ultraviolet radiation, and I even thought about a night-vision feature, but I'm seriously lacking in materials and . . ." I swallowed. "What are you staring at?"

"What do you mean?" He pulled the broken oxygen mask over his head to hide the freaky growing smirk he was giving me. He was fighting to rein it in, but even through the dirty silicone of the mask I could see his sharp teeth glinting.

"You're . . . smiling," I said. "It's creepy."

"You're an inventor. It's impressive."

"I mean, I try . . ." The first thing I'd done upon entering the lab was dig through every desk drawer and storage crate, searching for materials to rebuild all the gadgets I'd lost when the warden seized my pod ship. I'd managed to collect my weight in screws and scrap metal, but even with a blowtorch it would take much more than those pitiful supplies to re-create my phaser and visual enhancer. Perfecting the oxygen masks was my only project for now.

After giving me another disturbing smile, Anders slipped off the mask and dropped it on my workbench. "Even still," he said before heading back to the ship's upper levels. "It's very impressive."

I didn't want his kindness—if that's what it could be called. For all I knew, he was trying to stroke my ego for his own gain. But I wouldn't soon forget the nugget of information he'd shared, a fact about himself he'd likely thought insignificant. Anders had received professional combat training from the most violent planet on this side of the universe. He was even tougher than I initially thought.

When the time came, and the keys and the treasure were finally in reach, he wouldn't be as easily outsmarted as I'd originally hoped.

Anders joined me in the lab the following two days, his hulking shadow a constant presence in a swivel chair beside the bookcases. At first I thought he'd only come down to read. Maybe I even dared to hope my plan was working, that he was starting to think of me as a friend and he'd come to offer me company. But no. Anders was predictable, though it was in an entirely different manner: he could always be counted upon to complain about Earthans. *Loudly*.

"Cora, I don't get it. They all make such strange sounds. Like this morning, Wren expelled a gust of air from her nose at a frighteningly high speed. Correct me if I'm wrong, but I believe on Earth it is referred to as a *sneeze*. It was adorable, yet repulsive."

"Did you have a point? Because all I hear is *blah, blah, blah . . .*" Hastily, I shoved an errant lock of hair from my ponytail behind my ear before reaching for a pair of pliers and giving the oxygen masks a few final tweaks. I loosened one of the screws just a bit, which proved to be way too much when it shot across the room, narrowly missing Anders's head, and struck the window separating the main lab from the auxiliary observation bay.

A spiderweb of cracks spread across the glass.

"Oops."

Anders didn't notice I'd almost decapitated him. "Not only that, but I know she ate the plate of beef tips in the refrigeration unit that I specifically labeled with *my* name—"

Actually, *I* ate the beef tips. But I wasn't about to tell *him* that.

"—and when I left the galley she was pressing her lips together and making this screeching *noise*—"

"Was it a whistle?"

"A . . . whiffle?"

"No." I laughed. "*Whistle.*" I tried to show him, but it didn't work very well.

"Yes, but . . . it doesn't seem like it serves a purpose."

"Not really. It's mostly for entertainment."

"We don't have much of that on my planet." His raspy voice took on a confused edge, and he cocked his head. "So she puts her lips together . . . and makes random noises . . . for fun?"

"They're not random noises," I said. "They're supposed to be a tune. Music."

He grimaced. "She is not very good at it."

I found myself laughing again as I hunched over the workbench, giving the masks another twist with my pliers. "Don't you think you're obsessing over her a little bit?"

He paced in front of the shelves, tying up his hair with a long string of rubber that he'd dug from the trash can. But he soon tore it out, combing his fingers through the oily strands. "What? Of course not. I do not like her or hate her enough to obsess. The way I feel about Wren is the way I feel about you, for example. I do not particularly want to talk to you, but also your existence does not make me want to paint portraits on the corridor walls using nothing but your blood."

Saturn's rings. "Anders, has anyone ever told you that you're excellent at flattery?"

He frowned. "No?"

"Good. Here, see if this works." I tossed him the largest of the three oxygen masks I'd modified. He'd only come to the lab to whine, but he might as well make himself useful while he was here.

The face shield hissed as the edges molded to his skin, the hard shell creating a dome from his eyes to his mouth. Anders's chest heaved with deep inhales, making the front of the mask fog with the heat of his breath.

Nodding, he released the suction with the press of a button. "It's possible that this won't be a complete disaster after all."

"Such a glowing compliment of Cora's craftsmanship," Elio's voice chimed from the door. He tottered into the lab, unable to help himself from cleaning up the mess of hoses and valves that I'd left strewn across the floor. But in a minute he'd picked up more than he could carry, and the bundle in his arms toppled to the ground. "Never mind. I'll get those later. In more important news, Wren said we're about to land."

11

FROM THE SKIES ABOVE, CADROLLA LOOKED LIKE THE perfect tropical paradise: acres of lush jungles, leaves speckled in shades of green and purple and blue, crystalline water lapping at miles of deserted coastline. But on the ground, I knew it was a different story.

"If anything tries to attack you, scream that you have diarrhea," Elio told us while we secured our oxygen masks in the corner of the cargo hold. "No one messes with someone who has diarrhea."

"How would you know?" Wren asked.

"I watch a lot of net programs."

Oxygen in place, the four of us crossed the air lock, and Wren entered the code to open the exterior doors. They slid apart with a hiss, revealing a white sun shining through a neon blue sky. Sweat beaded along my neck. It was nearly as humid here as on Andilly.

Wren looked back longingly at the ship as we traipsed across Cadrolla's pink sand beaches. "She'll be safe, won't she? Like . . . you think it's okay that we're just leaving her here?"

"Odds are she'll be fine," said Elio. "Of course there are also odds that something will creep onboard, commandeer her, fly her away, and then we'll all be stranded here until we die, *but* . . . the odds are higher that she'll be fine."

"Well, when you put it like that, how could I ever be concerned?"

"I do understand sarcasm, you know. Come on. This way." He

held his comm out in front of him, showing us a well-worn path leading up a steady incline. "This is the quickest trail to the summit."

"You're certain?" Anders asked. He held a glowing blaster at his shoulder, another at his hip.

"If you have a better idea," Wren said, "we'd all love to hear it."

"I'm just double-checking. I don't know about you, but I'd like to be in and out of here before nightfall."

"Well, we aren't making any progress standing around, so . . ." Wren ushered Elio forward a few steps. She was looking over his shoulder, studying the map on his comm that glowed with four red dots marking our position, and so she didn't notice the vine slowly snaking out of a shrub on the side of the path. It slithered across the dirt, leaves elongating like fingers as it reached out to wrap around her ankle.

Just before it made contact, I jumped forward and stomped on it with my heel. Wren jolted in surprise, and the vine shot back into its home, hissing angrily.

"What the—?" Wren whirled around, searching for more creeping vines. I joined her, noticing instantly that both sides of the path were covered in identical thorny bushes, each with a cluster of vines undulating at their roots. Upon closer inspection, I realized the soil surrounding every shrub was soaked—dyed ruby red.

Blood. These plants drank *blood*.

"*Vampiris liana*," Elio recited, marking something on his comm. "According to the map I found on the net, the trail is covered with them until halfway up the mountain."

"Oh goody. All this for a treasure that might not even be real." Wren kicked a clump of dirt at the nearest man-eating shrub, hopping out of the way when its vines darted forward to attack again.

"Look alive," Anders said, pushing in front of us to lead. "It would be such a shame if someone were to lose a toe."

"Sarcasm doesn't suit you," Wren muttered. Her voice sounded muffled behind her face shield, but Anders understood her fine.

"On the contrary, it's not Andilly nature to make jokes." He glanced at me. I swore I saw him wink.

Wren ignored him, pointing instead at a wooden sign stuck into the ground on the side of the path. "Look."

The base of the sign was surrounded by various articles of clothing, from muddy socks, to shoes, to a ripped and bloodied raincoat, which gleamed in the sun. *Fresh.* Come to think of it, the blood underneath the shrubs looked fresh too.

Someone had come through not long before us, though we hadn't spotted any other ships on the beach when we landed. But that didn't matter now. What mattered was that it looked like this person, whoever they had been, didn't make it very far.

Wren read the writing on the sign. Two words spelled out in blocky letters, painted with smears of blood that had long since turned brown and flaky: STAY AWAY!

"Well. That's lovely." She stepped back. "I think we should listen to it."

"If only we had that choice," I said.

Anders didn't look the least bit frightened. He noted our position, then drew a large X in the dirt with his blaster before continuing onward. "Follow me." He drew another X a few yards up. Our breadcrumb trail to find our way back. "Stay quiet and keep up. I'm not a slow walker."

I headed after him, listening to Elio and Wren's footsteps as they fell behind us. The plants along the dusty path writhed as we passed them, almost like they were whispering to each other—warning whatever existed farther up the mountain that we were coming.

Unhooking my blaster from my belt, I powered it up and let it rest comfortably against my shoulder. I had a feeling I was going to need it.

It turned out the *vampiris liana* was the friendliest shrub we encountered on our way up the mountain. A similar-looking plant, which Elio identified as *orchastris hemitomon*, sang hypnotic notes as we hurried past it. We tried plugging our ears, but the music pervaded the air anyway, sinking into our brains despite our attempts to avoid it. Drowsiness spread through my limbs as we rounded a bend near a stream, and without even realizing what I was doing, I found myself on the ground, struggling to keep my eyes open while Wren and Anders collapsed beside me.

The ground was so soft; a clump of moss formed a pillow beneath my cheek as the music relaxed every inch of my body. I was so tired. The stream bubbled nearby, the perfect harmony to the song spreading over the mountain. Maybe I could take a dip in it. Even a single drop of water would surely feel refreshing. And after all, I was *so tired* . . .

The light of a blaster shot over my head, burning the cluster of *orchastris hemitomon* instantly. Elio stood behind the blaster's barrel, the only one out of the four of us who was immune to the plant's effects.

A burst of anger sizzled through me as we dusted ourselves off and continued up the mountain. If I had touched that water, I would have drowned. Elio had told me ahead of time what Cadrolla was capable of, and I'd still nearly let myself fall victim. Without his help, we would all be dead before this treasure hunt even began.

After passing through a field sprouting wispy orange feathers (which didn't try to kill us but released some kind of perfume that left Wren sneezing for half an hour), we reached a stone wall stretching into the jungle canopy, covered with pink and yellow fruits shaped like teardrops. Unable to hold himself back from anything edible, Elio reached for one of the lowest hanging ones, eyes gleaming with childlike glee.

"Elio, don't!" Wren and I yelled at the same time. He couldn't be poisoned, but I had a hunch poison wasn't the worst that could happen on this planet.

"Why not?" Elio asked. Thick brown goop dripped from a crack in the fruit's hard shell, puddling at his feet.

"Because—if it's not already obvious—it might devour you," said Anders, pointing out a row of jagged teeth peeking through a seam in the shell. Beeping, Elio hopped back. The fruit growled like it was sorry to see him go.

"Oh!" he gasped. "My mistake! I just get *so excited* around food."

"Same," Wren agreed.

I took a tentative step toward the wall of mysterious fruit, making sure to keep well out of reach of their teeth. Maybe there was a way to capture them for use as a weapon. The pod Elio had tried to touch growled again. Then it split open along the vine, spilling a few more drops of brown goo. They bubbled upon hitting the jungle floor, and then, to my astonishment, they started to *grow*. In less than a minute, half a dozen new fruits were rolling along the ground, vines flailing, teeth gnashing.

Elio beeped. "I saw a net drama once about people-eating plants. Trust me, it didn't end well for the people."

"Good to know," I said. The four of us backed into each other, forming a tight circle as more fruits hit the ground. One splattered on impact, the brown stuff inside hitting the knees of Wren's pants. She shrieked behind her oxygen mask as the material fell away, leaving an angry red blotch on her dark skin.

Acid. The fruits were spewing some type of acid. *Great*. Poison, at least, would have been less painful.

Anders obliterated three of the fruit pods with his blaster, sending brown goop flying. He didn't flinch as a spot landed on the side of his neck, forming another burn to add to his collection. I cursed when a glob hit my forearm, nearly causing me to drop my blaster. Elio grabbed a knife from the pack on his shoulders, flinging it and spearing the pod at his feet. The pod opened, wailing, but then it quickly wilted and rolled into the safety of a nearby shrub.

What a little genius. Blasting the pods apart caused the slime inside to spread, multiplying them. But a less flashy measure of destroying them would stop them for good.

"Drop your blaster!" I yelled to Anders. He hesitated as I slid a rusty butcher's knife from the galley out of my own pack, stabbing two of the pods rolling toward our feet. They sputtered as they died, only shooting out a small drop of slime that burned my wrist. Anders and I kicked them into the underbrush.

Wren looked up from stabbing her own pod into submission. Her clothes were singed and smoking, her face shield covered in beads of sweat. With a shaky hand, she pointed to the dense jungle in front of us.

My breath hitched. I no longer felt the burns covering my skin.

The trees were moving. Parting.

We had company.

The fruit pods seemed to shiver as the ground vibrated under the weight of incoming footsteps. Elio's hands moved to cover his gaping mouth, and I noticed new wire patches dotting his already corroded forearms. Not even being robotic could spare him from the acid's wrath.

Another footstep. The fruit wall shook. A few pods plummeted to the ground, screaming, and a tree just north of our path cracked and tumbled to the jungle floor. To hell with the knives. The four of us raised our blasters instead.

I tried to ignore the nagging thought in the back of my mind, the one that told me Wren was right: we had no proof that Teolia's key was even stashed on this mountain. It could be gone, collected by someone else years ago. It could have never been here to begin with. And now we were facing the dangers on this planet for nothing, nothing, *nothing*.

I had agreed to this. I let the warden give us this job. If we died here, if Elio died here, murdered by whatever was creeping toward us, that would be on me.

From the depths of the shadows, a spindly figure emerged. My first instinct was to call it a human, but that wasn't correct. It had pale, pinkish skin dotted with wispy hairs, but it also had thick claws on its hands and feet and a round, upturned snout. A tail writhed behind its body, tipped with a tuft of black fur and a crusty glob of mud.

What kind of horror show was this planet putting on?

The creature stooped down a few yards away, pawing at the fruit hiding beneath the bushes. The pods squealed in terror, but they were silenced when the monster bit into their shells. It chewed, jaw working furiously, then swallowed and licked its lips. A drop of acid dribbled down its chin.

Wren nudged me. "It just ate—"

"I know." If the creature could chow down on a mouthful of acid without breaking a sweat, then what in all the stars would it do to us?

"It looks sort of like a pig," said Elio. "Man. A pig man."

Wren wrinkled her nose. "I think it looks like Anders."

Anders muttered something unintelligible.

"Play nice, children." I wedged myself between them, raising my blaster higher. It was low on power already, despite my having barely used it. Lousy piece of junk. The light at the end of the barrel flickered before the blue glow faded entirely. Dead. How pathetic.

The monster stepped closer, snorting and sniffing out the air for a fresh food source.

Us.

I thought fast. "*Bang*!" I shouted, pointing my useless blaster at the treetops, hoping to distract the snorting menace. I pulled back theatrically on the trigger, shifting my weight from toes to heels, really getting into it. "Plug your ears, everyone. This is going to get loud. *Bang*! *Bang*!"

"What in all the stars . . . ?" Wren muttered.

"Shoo!" I waved the blaster in the direction of the pig creature, barely holding back a gag when it snorted and sent thick green mucus flying at my face shield. This was just like the time my family held some diplomats' children hostage on the planet Viicury. Well, kind of. I had been responsible for occupying the nursery containing the infants, who, despite having ten glittering eyes apiece, were far cuter than this creature. There had been just as much mucus, though.

At least the monster was distracted. It hardly noticed when Elio powered up his blaster with a grinding buzz and aimed right between the creature's eyes.

"NO! STOP!"

His finger flinched on the trigger.

The shout had come from Anders. Until now, I was convinced he didn't care about any living organism except himself, so I definitely thought I was hallucinating when he put himself between Elio and the beast, holding up his hands while it continued to snort.

"You can't shoot it," he said, eyes wild behind his mask. "It's endangered. It responds best to gentle encouragement."

"What *is* it?" Wren asked.

"A porci." He smiled fondly at the pig man. Of course Anders would have a soft spot for a beast that guzzled acid like water and spewed fountains of mucus. "We had one when I was in the military. The wild ones are a little rough, but they can be trained. They're excellent trackers."

The porci snorted again, flinging a glob of mucus at the side of Anders's head. He cursed but didn't stand down.

"Key?" He twisted his hand like he was trying to unlock an invisible door. "Do you know where we can find the key?"

The porci took a step closer, pawing at the dirt.

"It thinks you're trying to beckon it." I shoved Anders's hand to his side. "Stop it."

"Be calm, Cora. It knows exactly what I'm saying. It's smart."

Wren scoffed. "I'd argue that those fruit pods were pretty smart to try to incapacitate us with their jelly insides. Or the shrub that wanted to drain me like a tropical drink."

"Hush. Your voice is making him agitated."

"He doesn't look agitated. He looks hungry."

"Fine, I lied. Your voice is making *me* agitated. Settle down."

I studied the creature, which was drooling saliva from its fangs onto a boulder at its feet. To me, it looked hungry *and* agitated.

"Easy now." Anders walked toward it, hand outstretched. If he wanted to lose a finger, then that was his issue. I kept my butcher knife handy just in case the porci turned on us.

But it didn't. It let Anders place a gentle hand on its head, stubby snout scrunched up contentedly, and sighed. Then something truly alarming happened: Anders leaned close enough to touch his face shield to the porci's snout and . . . he started to *sing*.

Wren's jaw dropped. "Oh dear God . . ."

Elio ate the performance up, swaying while Anders's deep voice carried up the mountain path. A few sour notes rang out, but most were clear, their low timbre echoing around us. He was singing in his native language, so I barely knew the words, but that didn't matter to the porci. It edged closer, tucking its head into the crook of Anders's neck like it was nothing more than a house pet. I just hoped it wouldn't try to follow us back to the ship.

Wren scowled at the two of them; the porci looked like it was close to falling asleep on Anders's shoulder. "If I didn't think we needed them, then I'd say we ditch them and keep the treasure all for ourselves."

"I thought you didn't believe in the treasure," I said.

She shrugged, silent. Would Wren try to leave us when everything was said and done? Surely she wouldn't. She wasn't me.

After another minute, Anders finally shut up and pulled his head away from the porci. "It will lead us to the key now."

"Fantastic." I followed the beast as it shoved aside a few leaves and scampered up the trail. "You have the voice of an angel, just so you know."

"I feel like you're making a joke."

"A joke? Me? I don't even know what a joke is." I edged to the side of the path as Wren charged past, carrying Elio on her back.

Anders brought up the rear. His steps were so silent (thanks, Andilly military) that if I didn't know he was behind me, I would have jumped sky high when his hand darted out, claws gleaming, and clenched around my neck. The wind was momentarily knocked out of me when he dragged me back, slamming my body against his chest.

"Never," he growled in my ear, "speak of my singing again. Because if you do, I will rip out your vocal cords, mince them, and delight in drinking them through a bendy straw."

I fought to catch my breath. "There's the Andy I know and fear."

His grip around my neck was loose enough for me to talk, so I knew he didn't really want to hurt me. He hadn't even restrained my arms, which I took full advantage of by driving my elbow back, nailing him with one of the only self-defense moves I knew: strike to the solar plexus.

Anders doubled over, releasing his hold on my neck. And that was how I *really* knew he never intended to harm me. If he wanted, he could have had me crushed under his boot in five seconds flat. Maybe even three.

I stepped over him, leaving him crouching in the dirt. "By the way," I added, "if the porci changes its mind and gets hungry, I'm volunteering you to be its first snack."

12

DUSK WAS CREEPING IN BY THE TIME WE REACHED THE summit, wispy pink clouds streaking the sky. We encountered no other obstacles on the journey. It seemed like everything on Cadrolla feared the porci, but I couldn't shake the prickle at the back of my neck, the warning that we needed to get off this planet as soon as possible. We were supposed to be gone before nightfall. I already wasn't fond of Cadrolla's daylight creatures. The nighttime creatures—*stars*, I couldn't even imagine what those must be like.

The porci was the only one of us who didn't seem the least bit anxious. The star-forsaken thing was disgustingly joyful as it bounded from shrub to shrub, digging up dirt and shoving its snout into holes to search for food. Wren removed a protein pouch from her pack and chucked it at the porci's head just to get it to calm down. After the creature tore into the package, inhaling the powder inside with such enthusiasm that it dissolved into a coughing fit, Anders tapped it on its bony shoulder and gestured around the mountain peak.

"Well? We're not taking a moonlit stroll for fun. We're looking for a key, remember?"

The porci nodded, ears flapping, then put its snout to the ground again. It spun in a circle once, twice, then finally picked its head up and pointed with one long finger to an opening in the rock face. It was tough to see in the shadows, but it looked like there was a gravel path sloping down into the depths of the mountain.

A tomb. Just like on Vaotis.

Elio and I locked inside, floodwaters rising.

My heart rammed against my breastbone as the violent hiss of oxygen filled my mask, struggling to save me. No, it wouldn't happen again. I wouldn't drown, even if there was water down there. I had oxygen this time. I wasn't defenseless.

I let out a small yelp when I felt the tentative pressure of a hand on my back. *Wren*.

"You coming?" The others were already ahead of us, disappearing into the cave. Elio was last, and he looked back for a second, tilting his head in question before the darkness swallowed him up.

And then it was just me and Wren and the whisper of the jungle that spread out below us, the dark leaves blending into the velvet sky until the planet was nothing more than a sea of blackness spreading out for eternity. If I didn't know any better, I would have thought we had been dropped right into outer space again. The only things missing were the stars.

Wren cleared her throat. "If you're claustrophobic, deep breaths help. Luckily you already have oxygen on you."

"I'm not claustrophobic."

"Then what?"

I wished I could brush her off, grit my teeth, and follow the others, because it wasn't any of her business. But if I wanted to continue following my grand master plan, I had to make it her business.

"I don't do well with water," I confessed. "And the last time I went underground like this . . . there was water and . . ." And even I knew how pathetic I sounded, afraid of something that I couldn't even see yet.

But Wren didn't look at me like I was pathetic, like Evelina would have. Instead she simply linked her arm through my mine.

"I'm afraid of birds," she said matter-of-factly. "I suspect it's the flapping noise they make, but I also hate when they fly close enough to buzz me. So there. Now we know each other's dirty little secrets."

Yeah. Not quite.

But before I could argue, Wren dragged me forward, doing either the friendliest or most vindictive thing she could have done in the situation. She stood at my side as we entered the cave, following the sloping floor down into the black hole. She didn't let go of my arm, not when the porci's snort broke the silence, making me jolt in fear. Not when the steady *drip, drip, drip* of water trickled from the stalactites, hitting the cave floor and us along with it. She refused to let me run.

Maybe she really was trying to kill me. It would be to her benefit, after all.

The porci led us around twisting corners, the path growing so narrow that we eventually had to walk single file. I struggled to keep track of the turns we took. Left, right, right again at a fork, through a path of stalagmites and across a rocky bridge over a (blessedly) shallow stream. Maybe a few more lefts after that, but honestly it felt like we were walking in circles. With each step we took, the temperature dropped, until I was shivering in my flight suit.

"Are we there yet?" Elio whined.

As if in reply, there came a noise from around the next bend. It started off as a delicate humming but culminated in a powerful rushing as my unsteady footsteps brought me closer. The sound was static in my head, jangling my bones, filling my nerves with an electric charge so powerful that I could barely stand. Wren was still gripping me, leading us all toward the sound of water cascading down rocks inside the cave. I dug my heels into the ground but was met with a slick patch of gravel offering little resistance.

"It's fine, Cora," she said. "You're fine."

Yeah, right. The waterfall pounding into the pit below us was one issue, but the thick streams of water hovering over our heads were another impossible problem entirely. Bands of water twisted through the air like ribbons, glistening where moonlight filtered in from gaps in the rocks way, way, *way* at the peak of the mountain. How far had we traveled underground? Half a mile? A mile?

At the bottom of a short stone ramp, the water from the falls lapped at the shoreline, spreading out to form a dark lake inside the base of the mountain. And in the middle, where the current appeared to be fiercest, waves smashed against a pedestal, cracked and worn away by the tide.

But it was the thing on top of the pedestal that caught our attention, causing Wren to grin, Elio and Anders to sigh, and me to whimper like an injured animal: the key, made of copper, studded with diamonds, gleaming beneath the lid of a glass case no larger than the palm of my hand.

No wonder no one had ever managed to retrieve it. There was no way out to the post that I could see except to swim. The violent undertow from the waterfall could kill any human instantly. And if that didn't manage to do the job, there were always the ribbons above us, wiggling like snakes. I imagined one darting down my throat, drowning me, and my knees went weak again.

Somehow, I managed to pull myself together long enough to speak. "What an adorable setup. So who wants to venture inside the pit of despair first?"

Elio looked over at me, well aware of the Cora-is-terrified-of-water issue. "We don't have to do this—"

"Of course we do," Wren interrupted. "The warden wasn't crazy after all."

"No, he's definitely still crazy," Anders said. He looked toward the porci, claws out. "This is *it*? There's no easier way to the key?"

The porci merely shrugged. It swiped Wren's pack from her shoulders, digging through until it located her bag of protein pouches, then ran from the cave, kicking up dust in its wake.

Abandoning us.

Anders stared after it, seething. "*B'shkrah*! Useless creature. If I ever see it again, I'm going to skin it and turn it into a stew."

"*Beep-beep*! Now what do we do?" Elio asked.

None of us had an answer to that, proving once and for all that we truly were the worst group of misfits to carry out the warden's treasure hunting scheme. But we were *so close*. I could feel the key's energy pulsing around me, like it carried its own aura, although its colors were lost in the cloud of mist spilling from the waterfall.

"There's a skiff." Anders motioned to the ramp leading down to the water's edge, where a little wooden boat poked out of a clump of reeds. "Follow me. Carefully."

He seemed more than happy to be our self-appointed leader, which was fine with me. What was not fine was how close we were getting to the water. I held on to Elio's arm as we shuffled down the slick ramp onto a shore covered in mossy pebbles. With a beep, he ejected a few suction cups on the bottom of his feet to keep from slipping.

"It looks rotted," Wren said as she tugged the boat out of the reeds. Anders bent down to examine the water lapping at his boots. "It'll be a miracle if it doesn't fall apart right under us." She nudged the skiff with her toe, and we both frowned as a piece of the hull broke off. "Lovely. I'm assuming you don't want to paddle out with me."

"I'd rather not," I replied. "But if you need me to . . ."

She waved me off, tugging an equally rotted oar from the depths of the skiff. "Nonsense. I'll be fine alone. Stealing a priceless artifact is practically a day at the beach for me and—"

A bloodcurdling wail cut through the cavern.

"What was *that*?"

We turned to Anders, crouched at the shoreline, fingers in the water. His jaw hung open in silent alarm while the noise rang out around us, as if the air in the mountain was shrieking in pain. A ghost, maybe? I didn't think I believed in ghosts.

While the screams continued, the waterfall pounded harder, a furious drumbeat. It shook the ground beneath my boots, like something was crawling up from the depths of the underworld to devour us. Waves rose higher, nearly obscuring the pedestal and the key at its center. My heart stuttered. *Please don't fall.* If the key got knocked to the bottom of the lake, then we'd never find it.

I looked frantically to Elio. Then Wren. Then Anders, who slowly stood, pulling his hand from the lake. As soon as his fingers cleared the surface, the waves receded. The strange screams subsided to an echo, and then nothing at all.

"That was interesting," he yelled to us over the rush of the falls.

"Let's just get the key before it happens again." I helped Wren push the bow of the skiff into the water. Elio scrambled to climb in after her.

"Someone should come with you," he said. "I can't drown, so it may as well be me."

Her eyes swept over his metal plating, looking unconvinced. "Can you swim?"

"I can't drown," he repeated as if that were the same thing. He tossed a small bundle from his pack at my chest. "Cora, friend. Hold my chocolate fudge. I'm going in."

"Where did you get this?" The fudge felt as hard as a brick. "You can't eat this."

"I made it!"

"Of course," I muttered, but he had already pushed the skiff off shore. Part of me wanted to make him stay on land, but I knew it was pointless. Elio was capable of making his own decisions, and Wren might need another hand.

"Is he waterproof?" Anders asked me while we watched Elio and

Wren paddle against the tide. They were only several yards out, but they were already soaked. I flinched when a particularly large wave nearly capsized the skiff, sending a spray of water in their faces. Reaching into his pack, Elio extracted a pair of goggles and snapped them over his eye sensors.

"Mostly," I replied. The goggles were more for effect than anything. Elio always did like to play the part.

Anders paced the shoreline. "This will work. I know this will work."

"Positive affirmations. Always a good idea." Though my stomach was twisting just as violently as the ribbons of water above our heads. My heart stilled as two of them swooped down toward the skiff, curling over Wren and Elio. But they only doused them with a stream of dirty water before retreating higher into the cave.

"*Please*," I whispered under my breath. "*Please work*."

They made it a quarter of the way across the lake, encroaching on half in good time, though they had to paddle harder over the crest of every wave. I accidentally bit down on my tongue when the skiff toppled off an eight-foot surge, plunging into the lake and sending a spray of water in every direction. As they struggled, Anders continued to pace. The constant motion made me want to strangle him.

When they got halfway there, I started to relax. The ribbons continually spun above us, ever-present phantoms, but they hadn't attacked again. Ahead of the skiff, the key gleamed beneath its little glass box. Beckoning.

Thirty yards to go.

"Come on," I pleaded. "You can do it. You can do it."

Fifteen yards.

Even Anders stopped pacing, too transfixed by the sight before us to move.

As the skiff closed in on the pedestal, a wave behind it started to rise.

I clapped a hand over my mouth. The water was curling toward the boat in the opposite direction of the tide. *Impossible*. Then again, so were the ribbons above us, swirling faster. They condensed, forming globes of water that spun before lengthening again, changing shape. Forming . . . was that a human? No, two humans . . .

Elio noticed them at the same time I did. Nearly sixty yards away and I could see the fear cloud his eyes as if he were standing right next to me.

I gasped as the water took the form of Cruz and Evelina.

The resemblance was uncanny, even though these versions of my mother and father weren't made of flesh and blood. The figure of Evelina glanced toward the shore, looking at me for just a moment, and the resentment in her eyes was spot-on.

But they weren't here for me. Elio crouched down in the skiff, shielding his head while Cruz and Evelina floated closer. He was more afraid of them than I was, and when the water around Cruz's hand swirled and re-formed into a wrench, Elio nearly lost it. He'd told me numerous times of the attempts Cruz and Evelina had made to rewire him, to dismantle their broken servant robot and program him into something deemed more acceptable. It had happened when I was too young to remember, but Elio was far too smart to ever forget.

I shouted his name over the waterfall's roar as Evelina nodded to Cruz and their figures crowded in. I didn't know what kind of impossible magic this was. How did the water know Elio's worst fear?

I could hear his helpless beeping all the way from the shore, and when Cruz raised the wrench over his head, Elio dived for cover. Wren batted at the figures with her oar, but they didn't retreat.

The skiff tilted.

The figures exploded, flooding the small boat instantly.

"No!" I took two steps into the lake, water surpassing my ankles. I couldn't make myself go any farther before nausea overcame me.

The boat capsized, Wren clinging to it with Elio on her back. Cruz and Evelina were gone, but the wave that had been creeping higher finally crashed down. Elio flailed. Wren screamed as they were both shoved under the surface.

I grabbed Anders's arm. "What do we do?" Out in the lake, Wren's head broke through the surface. More ribbons of water curled around her face before bursting into hundreds of tiny birds, each with the head of a young boy I didn't recognize. But Wren seemed to. She sobbed as they flocked her. Elio tried paddling to help her, but he was just as soon thrown underwater again.

"We need to get to the key," Anders said. "We need to use them as a distraction."

"We need to *save* them!" I took another tentative step into the lake. What kind of horrors would the water hold for me? Then again, I was already experiencing my worst fears in real time. There was water and there was Elio, in more danger than I could ever imagine. No illusions necessary.

Anders pulled me to a stop, and that's when I remembered the screams the first time he'd come in contact with the lake. So that made him afraid of what, exactly? Loud noises?

"Whatever you're thinking, I guarantee it's incorrect." He crossed his arms over his chest like a shield, but not before a bit of residual fear leaked through the aura he tried so hard to push down.

He yanked his defenses back up, and the crimson cloud around his head vanished in a puff of smoke. "Don't do that," he growled.

"Do what?"

"Read my emotions."

"It's hard not to. Are you actually admitting that you have emotions?"

Another growl. "Of course I do. This is a stupid conversation to have right now."

Obviously. But my default setting in these kinds of situations was humor. The waves were intensifying, shaking the mountain walls each time they crashed down. Beyond the crest of a wave, I noticed Elio clinging to the side of the capsized skiff. Wren was swimming fiercely in the direction of the pedestal and the key, swatting at more birds and trying to keep afloat.

Anders nodded at the rocks to the side of the waterfall while he shucked off his boots. "Do you see that ledge up there?"

"You mean the one that's the width of a toothpick?"

"That's the one. Climb it."

"Excuse me?"

He removed his flight suit, leaving him in only his oxygen mask and underwear. His red skin prickled with goose bumps as he walked into the lake up to his knees. "Go up the ramp, back the way we came. The ledge should be almost ground level there. Shuffle around the outside wall and it'll bring you right to the waterfall."

"Yeah, because that's exactly where I want to go."

"It will bring you right above the *key*," he stressed. "If Wren can reach the pedestal, she might be able to hand it to you. Maybe she'll be able to climb up too."

I inspected the ledge that he pointed out, squinting across the inside of the mountain. The thing was so narrow, and even worse, it looked like the rocks around it had very few handholds to grasp.

"If Wren or I fall, it's a thirty-foot drop," I said.

"My advice is not to fall. I'm getting Elio out. Hurry." Then he dived. His dark head of hair popped up ten yards out, and more of those deep, anguished screams—whatever mysterious fear that was—filled the cave.

"'*My advice is not to fall,*'" I mimicked while I slipped up the ramp to the main floor above the pit. "Sure, why don't I just land a spaceship on a sun while I'm at it?" I found a long braided rope coiled in a cluster of shadows at the very end of the ledge. It was soaked through with water, but I didn't want to think about the person who might have used it last. Obviously they didn't succeed, or the key wouldn't still be here.

I gulped as I took my first step onto the ledge and looked down into the pit.

Okay, bad idea. Ignore the water, ignore the screams. I needed to think of something peaceful. Piloting my pod ship was kind of peaceful when I wasn't flying to escape a job gone wrong. All right. Need something more peaceful than that. *Inventing*. That was nice. The sure weight of the tools in my hands, the holographic blueprints humming on the computer at my side.

Then again, my inventions rarely seemed to function properly . . .

Stars, this isn't working. I adjusted the coil of rope on my shoulder as I shuffled forward. The ledge was barely wider than my foot, covered in a slippery layer of moss. All the handholds I could see were in awkward locations. Either I had to scoot down to grab them (nearly slipping to my death) or stretch up too high (also nearly slipping to my death).

More than halfway around the wall, the ledge widened a few inches, and I paused just long enough to loop the end of the rope around my waist and knot it, in case I could use it to pull Wren to safety.

Just like with all my inventions, I had a feeling this was not going to end well.

"Cora!"

I chanced a quick glance down, gripping a crack in the wall near my knees when I almost lost my balance. Wren had reached the pedestal and was clinging to it.

I let out a scream of delight when I noticed the box containing the key clutched in her hand.

"Toss it!" I heard Anders yell. I saw a flash of silver as his head and Elio's head vanished beneath the waves.

"I can't toss it," Wren called up to me. "Help me!"

I could tell from my position on the ledge that the water level was rising. The mountain knew that we got what we came for. Wren screamed as a wave crashed into her, threatening to knock her from the pedestal. Another one hit the wall just below me, sending a spray of water against my legs.

I crept along the length of the ledge. *Slowly. So, so slowly*. Wren said something else, but by the time I reached the side of the falls I couldn't hear her. I couldn't even hear my heart beating in my ears, but I could feel it pounding in my chest.

Holding on to the rock wall for dear life, I tossed the end of the rope down, where it dangled above Wren's head. All she had to do was swim a few yards to the wall and climb.

The suspicion on her face and in her aura said it all. She didn't think I could support her weight. And maybe I couldn't. I had two good rocks I could wedge my feet between to brace myself and one above my head I could grasp, but I didn't know how long they would hold me. I was going to fall. I knew it. Into the water, where I would be sucked under, unable to surface. Eventually my oxygen would run out, and that would be the end of me.

Below my knees, the rope went taut.

I turned my face to the wall, double-checked that the knot around my waist was secure. *Please, please,* please *don't let the rope snap. Please don't let us fall.*

A wave hit my back, slamming me face-first into the wall. The rope swung wildly. My feet started to slip, and I squeezed my eyes shut. I didn't want to see us fall. I didn't want to know how much farther she still had to climb, because, stars, I didn't think I could hold on anymore. My legs were aching, my fingers were bloody, nails ripped away where they dug into the rocks. My mask was running out of oxygen. I could tell by the sparse puffs of air hitting my cheeks, like it was spitting at me.

We were both going to die.

Maybe . . . maybe it would be best to leave her. I could untie the rope, let her fall, and then I could escape. If she died, Elio and I would have one less person standing in our way to the treasure.

No. No, no, no. Gripping the wall with more determination than before, I despised myself for even thinking like that. That was the kind of thought Evelina would have.

Just when I thought I couldn't bear it, just when my feet slipped farther back and my heels teetered on the edge of the ledge, I felt the rope give a little, and a soaking wet weight slammed into my back. I hit the wall, nearly falling again.

"Go!" I read Wren's lips over the roar of the water. "I have the key! Run!" Another wave—the tallest one yet—was rising above the pedestal, ribbons of water trailing from it like fingers trying to grasp us.

It was pure luck that neither of us fell as we shuffled all the way along the ledge while the wave continued to grow. By the time we reached the main platform of the pit, my legs were like jelly. I fantasized about collapsing on the spot and sleeping for eternity, but I didn't have that luxury. Anders was dragging a beeping Elio in our direction, jabbing his thumb to indicate the monster wave, which had reached its full height above the walls and was starting to quiver.

Yeah, Andy. As if I didn't already notice the one-thousandth thing today that's trying to kill us.

We ran just as the water fell.

I was lost in the twisting catacombs, but Anders had no trouble remembering the way. He led us—Elio on his back, me and Wren exhausted and stumbling behind him—around corners, through the stalactites and stalagmites, across the bridge spanning the shallow stream, and out into the blissfully warm Cadrolla evening air. The wave lapped at our heels, chasing us, but by the time we exited hell and reached the mouth of the cave, the water had dwindled to a harmless trickle. The mountain groaned, ground shaking, and then the little bit of water that followed us outside was sucked back into the cave.

Wren patted me on the shoulder. “I think I understand,” she gasped between breaths, “why you hate water so much.”

“Do you have the key?” I managed to choke out.

She held up the glittering box. “Everyone have all their limbs?”

I nodded. So did Anders. I looked to a patch of grass beneath a bush where Elio had fallen after we burst from the cave.

A terrifying coldness spread through my limbs.

It was worse than the water in the lake, worse than thinking I was breaths away from death.

I didn’t care anymore whether my oxygen was running out.

Under the silver glow of the moon, Elio twitched silently on the ground.

Glitching.

13

"MOVE! GO! *GO*!" I YELLED WHEN THE AIR LOCK HISSED, doors opening into the *Starchaser*'s cargo hold. I barreled into the lift, stabbing my thumb against the button for cockpit access. Wren darted in after me, followed by Anders, a glitching Elio balanced across his shoulders.

Anders had carried him all the way down from the top of the mountain, running to keep pace with me while I'd sprinted through the jungle, and he hadn't complained once. But now that we had stopped moving, I could finally see exhaustion forming wrinkles around his eyes. The four of us had almost died out there. And now, one of us could very well die in here if I didn't do something to prevent it.

"Ignite the engines!" I ordered Wren as soon as the lift doors slid open onto the bridge. "Then I need you to reroute the ship's auxiliary power to control panel A. Anything we can spare. Power from the backup generator, hot water pump, electricity from the refrigeration units. Any lights outside this room, shut them off, redirect them here so that I can pump them into Elio. Now, a cable. I need a cable . . ." I wrenched open drawers along the walls, ripping out the contents and spilling anything that I deemed useless on the floor. I tore off my oxygen mask and let it join the mess.

The cockpit floor rumbled as the engines beneath us whirred to life. Wren looked over the back of her captain's chair, holding a thick three-pronged cable.

"Will this work? It has a universal connector. Power reroutes are above my pay grade though. My skills are limited to that of getaway driver and friendly interplanetary kleptomaniac. Maintenance is more *your* strength, isn't it?"

"I'm not leaving Elio." I snatched the cable from her. "Anders, lay him across the co-pilot's chair. Roll him onto his back. Yeah, just like that." I ushered Wren out of her chair, then inserted one prong of the cable into the power circuit on the control panel, one into the outbound drive on my comm link, and the third into Elio's charging port.

"Wren, *please*. Go down into the engine room. You just have to flip a breaker. I'll walk you through it. Unless you want this ship to explode into a fiery ball of death instead."

She hesitated. Bit her lip. Then she glanced down at Elio, still and quiet. "Fine. Give me a minute."

I wanted to snap that I didn't think we had a minute, but she was gone too soon. My fingers twitched anxiously as I made a few adjustments on the control panel. The lights overhead surged, then dimmed. Outside the cockpit, the ship's usual daily hums and vibrations fell silent, while the engines groaned louder.

I was prolonging reading Elio's diagnostic scan on my comm, because I already knew what it would say. *Failing*. His memory core was failing, its capacity probably plunging lower than it ever had in the hour it took to run down the mountain. It was a mystery to me why none of Cadrolla's creatures had tried to attack us. Had they left us alone because we found the key? Had the powers that guarded it inside the pit followed us out and guarded us too, now that we had it?

It was a miracle Elio's body hadn't already given up after such a long glitch. I reached for his limp hand, looping my little finger around his. He shouldn't have been so human, but he was. Another miracle. I looked behind me, where Anders was keeping vigil against the wall. We were alive. The key was here. This planet was full of miracles tonight.

Surely one more wouldn't be too much to ask.

"Okay, I'm down here. What am I doing?" Wren called over the comm system. "Please don't tell me this is going to blow up my ship."

"Not if you do it right. Yellow lever, second panel to the left of the door. Do you see it?"

I heard her gulp. "Yeah . . ."

"Pull it out from the wall, then push it up toward the ceiling. In three . . . two . . ."

"Wait, wait! I'm not ready!"

"One!"

I flicked a switch next to a row of dark monitors, cutting all internal communications. All electricity that wasn't absolutely necessary to operate the ship was now wired into the control panel beneath my fingertips. The metal surface grew hot with power. A row of green lights blinked in time with my rapid heartbeat. *Go, go, go.*

Against my better judgment, I looked at Elio's diagnostic scan.

Memory Core: 27 percent functioning

23 percent functioning

17 percent

8 percent

I peered over my shoulder again to Anders. "Plug your ears."

Then I slammed my palm onto the screen of my comm link.

A sound like a small bomb going off came from the engines. With flames shooting from the control panel, I sent every watt of electricity that the *Starchaser* possessed directly into Elio's brain.

"My . . . my name is Elio. I like . . . I like . . ." He pulled a blanket tight around his shoulders as he curled up on my bed. "I can't remember what I like right now. I just wish I could sleep."

I shut my cabin door and joined him on the bed. The universal time clock on the wall said that it was well into the early hours of the morning. Ordinarily, I would have hit the mattress and passed out instantly, but at the moment there was no chance of me making my mind shut down. With every blink I saw my hand pressed against my comm link, sending not one, not two, but *three* giant pulses of electricity from the ship into Elio to jump-start his memory core. I saw Elio flopping in the co-pilot's chair, unresponsive, as if he were already gone. I saw Wren, sniffling as she returned from the engine room and gripped Elio's hand. She collapsed in her pilot's chair, and even though she didn't meet my eyes, I noticed hers were red and puffy. I saw Anders picking him up gently once he finally started to stir, cradling his tiny breaking body while he brought him up to the residential quarters to rest.

No one was celebrating finding Teolia's key. No one had said much of anything since the engines rumbled and Wren declared over the intercom that we were clear for takeoff. Just before her voice cut out, I heard her start to blow her nose.

After Elio regained consciousness, his memory core's capacity had climbed all the way to 54 percent. It plunged again for a minute, but now it was back on the rise. I checked the results of his latest scan on my comm. *Memory Core: 62 percent.*

Not great. But good enough for now.

Through the porthole above the bed, I watched Cadrolla grow smaller and smaller behind us, the little planet a marbled swirl of bright blues, vibrant greens, and muted pinks. Beautiful and unassuming—that is, until you got too close.

Without meaning to, I pressed my thumb against the back of my neck, touching the lumpy tracking chip that the warden had given us before we left Ironside. A reminder of his omnipresence. Was he watching us right now, monitoring us? Did he know we almost died?

At the foot of the bed, Elio pushed himself up onto his knees and pressed his palms to the porthole glass.

"One," he counted. "Two. Three."

"If you're counting the stars, you're going to be there a while."

He refused to turn away from the depths of space. "Maybe not. We don't know how much longer I have left."

"*Don't.*" I squeezed my nails into my palms until the pain of it distracted me from my anger. "Don't say things like that. You're going to be fine."

"That's nice of you to say, Carla, but—"

His mouth snapped shut. Across the room, the air filtration system whirred, filling the cabin with a weak breeze that smelled like wet cardboard. Finally, it cut off with a clunk, and a painful silence flooded the bedroom.

"My name," I whispered, "is Cora."

"I knew that," Elio said hurriedly.

"Did you?" My voice grew high and tight with panic. "Do you even remember where we were today? Teolia's key?" I prompted when he said nothing.

"The . . . key . . . ?"

"For the treasure. To pay Evelina back. To get you a new body." I hopped off the bed, scrolling through his diagnostic tests on my comm. "You're getting worse. You're forgetting more, and it isn't coming back."

"But it will. It always does. Look, I remember now. There was a—a pig, right? And . . . and water! You hate water!" He stood on the bed, beeping desperately.

I'd never been so happy to hear anyone talk about my greatest fear. "Fine. But that doesn't change the fact that that was the longest glitch you've ever had." I swiped my fingers across my dirty comm screen, searching the net. We had two more keys to find. We needed a plan, and we needed one fast. There had to be something useful on all those message boards Elio had read through. Some hint, some clue . . .

"Cora." Elio's tinny voice came from beside me. I looked down, noticing his floppy ears wiggle slightly before falling still. "Maybe . . . it isn't worth it."

"What isn't worth it?"

"The keys. The treasure."

"No, you're still not remembering correctly. You—"

"I remember enough. You could have gotten hurt. And Wren. And Anders. You all can die easier than I can."

"So? If we don't get the keys, we end up back in Ironside, probably forever. Whether we use them to help you or not, we don't have a choice but to keep pushing on." I located the message boards Elio had scoured and started scrolling. Pages and pages, thousands of threads. This would take me days to sort through. "I'd really appreciate it if you could get back on board."

He didn't reply, just turned on his little heel and climbed back onto the bed with his face pressed to the porthole. Fine. He could be angry all he wanted; I was just doing what was best for the both of us, and he was too busy being noble to see it.

"Hey," I said quietly. "Do you remember when I was little and we had campouts in my room? We'd pretend to roast sugar snaps over your flashlight because we didn't want to risk starting a real fire and—"

"Waking Evelina up," he finished. Still, he didn't look at me. "How could I forget? Actually, that's a poor choice of words." He laughed, one tiny beep that sounded more like a sob. "Things were easier back then."

I patted him on the head before walking to the door. "I'll be right back. I lost your fudge on Cadrolla, but I'm going to the galley to see if Wren has ingredients to make you a milkshake to smell. Chocolate, okay?"

Finally, he turned around. "With a cherry on top?"

"Of course. See? You're back to your old self already. I knew you'd be fine."

But for how long? Elio deserved a good life, full of milkshakes and friends, one where he didn't constantly have to worry about disappearing. He deserved so much more than I could give him.

No matter what, I vowed I would get those keys. I would take that treasure to Cruz and Evelina, even if I had to pry it from Anders's and Wren's cold, dead—

"Wren!"

She hip-checked me just as my cabin door slid shut. I thrust out my hands to brace myself as I was pitched against the corridor wall, cold metal biting into my palms.

"Oh, Cora! Sorry! I was just coming to see you. How's Elio?"

"Fine. He's fine." I massaged a point on my wrist where I'd bent it funny. "I mean, all things considered. He's resting now. He'll recover."

I hoped.

"Good. Great, actually." Wren glanced at my cabin door like she thought Elio might open it and waddle out. A startling realization struck me: Wren really *did* think she and Elio were friends.

After another hopeful glance at the door, she cleared her throat. "I also wanted to tell you that all systems are back to functioning as designed. And if you're wondering why a quarter of my left eyebrow is missing, that's because of the explosion that *you* caused in the engine room." But she was grinning as she said it, pointing out a bald patch on the outer corner of her eye. "I think I can turn the look into a new fashion trend."

"No offense, but I don't think I'll be joining you on that one."

"None taken." She laughed. "You want to come down to the rec room with me? I'm going to marathon some reruns of *Matchmakers Anonymous*. I'm a sucker for bad reality dating shows."

"Thanks, but I told Elio I'd get him a milkshake. To smell," I clarified when she lifted her non-burnt eyebrow.

"I thought he couldn't smell."

"He thinks he can. Honestly, it's easier to let him believe it."

"Okey-dokey, then. I'll see you later." Reaching forward, she adjusted a button on my flight suit I'd accidentally put into the wrong hole. "Get some rest. You look like death."

"Wow. Thanks."

"Just saying. Oh! We need to have a meeting with Anders. Figure out where to fly next."

"Already working on it, but yeah, I'll find him."

"Splendid." The low lights cast shadows on her shoulders while she walked away, projecting onto the grimy walls of the ship. For a moment, she looked like she had wings; in the gloom of the corridor, her silhouette had stretched into a bird preparing to take flight.

And speaking of birds . . .

"Wren, wait!"

She spun around.

"Um . . ." I didn't want to think about the birds, because then I'd have to think about the water. "How are *you* doing?"

She looked at me like I had just announced plans to marry the porci.

"The birds," I said. "In the cave. They had faces. For a second, it looked like you recognized them and I thought that maybe . . . you'd want to talk about it?"

Wren crossed her arms. Spun around again. "I don't," she called over her shoulder as she walked away.

Excuse me? "Wren, hang on a second."

But her footsteps just sped up. Around the corner of the residential quarters, past a maintenance closet with the door hanging off its hinges. She skirted around it and booked it toward the ramp spiraling down to the rec room.

I caught her arm before she could get too far ahead. "Hey. Look, I'm sorry. I'm just trying to be nice."

She pulled out of my grip, huffing. Her lip was trembling. Just like in the cockpit after Elio glitched, she looked like she was about to cry.

"Good night, Cora," she said hoarsely.

I could see her aura brightening the corridor. Terror, exhaustion, sadness. All bad things. And yet I didn't stop. Tonight I had been chased, drenched, burned, almost lost my best friend. I was so mentally and physically exhausted that something inside of me snapped. I couldn't keep my stupid mouth shut.

"Good night? That's it? You know, for someone who keeps preaching honesty and teamwork, you sure don't follow through."

She pivoted. An aqua flash lit up the air around us as her sadness multiplied. "I said good night, Cora."

"At least tell me you put the key in a safe place. Where is it?"

Yes, I was one hundred percent fishing for information. A twinge of regret pained my chest when I thought about how much I would still have to deceive her, but I pushed it down, just like I pushed all that electricity into Elio not an hour before. I had a job to do. Friendship—or whatever Wren and I had cultivated in the depths of that cave on Cadrolla—wasn't important.

Panic as chilling as tendrils of ice filled the corridor. "Oh. I—yes. It's very safe. *Obviously*." Her voice sped up. "I, uh, I contacted the warden while you were in your cabin with Elio to tell him about the key, and he demanded that we keep it hidden at all times. So that's where it is. Hidden, you know?" Her gaze flicked up to the ceiling. "At all times."

"*Right*. And where exactly is it hiding at all times? I would find it and ask it, because I'm sure it would give me a more detailed answer than you are, but as you so eloquently pointed out, it's hiding. At all times."

"Um . . . yeah . . . It's . . . you know. Just in my . . . room?"

"In your room?"

"Yep," Wren said. "My cabin's a mess, so it's a good spot for something to stay . . . hidden."

"At all times. So you've said."

"Yeah . . ." Her eyes shifted down the corridor. The lights around us buzzed, their green glow reflecting off our skin, making Wren look like she was about to puke. "Are you, um, are you really sure you don't want to watch *Matchmakers Anonymous* with me? Elio can come too."

Shifty eyes, stammering, no consistency in speech. She was clearly hiding something. I could choose to be a good "friend" and trust that whatever she was concealing wasn't that big of a deal, but I wasn't that kind.

I wasn't even really her friend.

"Actually, that sounds really nice," I told her. "Thanks. Let me go grab his milkshake and we'll be right down."

I watched her walk toward the rec room, footsteps quick, shoulders hunched, until the outline of her body was obscured by the shadows.

"Or not," I said to the dead, recycled air. I stood against the wall for a few minutes, replaying our weird conversation and hoping that *maybe* it would sound more normal as the time ticked on. No such luck. Still weird. Still up to something.

"You know . . . ," came an amused voice from behind me. "Staring into space is often thought of as the first sign of madness on my planet."

"You don't say." Turning, I was greeted by the always bizarre sight of Anders grinning. I nodded to the nearest row of portholes lining the ship's exterior wall, where stars glinted millions of miles away like shattered glass. "Looks like we're screwed, then."

"I'm not sure I understand."

"You said 'staring into space,' and space is right outside the window and . . . you know what? It was a bad joke. Not important. What are you eating?"

He pulled out a little ball hidden inside his cheek. An orange hunk of candy attached to a stick.

"Lollipops?" I made a grab for it, but he stuck it back in his mouth. "You like *Earthan* lollipops?"

"No," he sputtered. "*No*. I *don't*. It was the only thing in the galley. Wren ate everything else."

"C'mon, Andy, admit it. You like sweets from Earth."

A flash of disgust crossed his face, but still he bit the sucker in half, chewed, and swallowed. The sharp aroma of oranges filled the space between us. "Don't you *dare* tell anyone."

"As much as I'd love to embarrass you, you're in the clear. I'm dealing with more important issues at the moment."

"Like?"

"Like . . ." I tracked the distance between us and the wide, spiral ramp leading down to the rec room. There were no doors at the top or the bottom, but as long as Wren had the volume cranked up on the net screen there was little chance of us being overheard.

"I think Wren's hiding something."

"Interesting." Anders dug into his pocket, producing two more lollipops. He didn't offer me one; he shoved both into his mouth instead. "What makes you say that?"

"I was asking her what she did with Teolia's key and she started stuttering and got all weird about it. Said that she talked to the warden and he wants it kept hidden at all times. She just kept repeating that *over and over*, and then there was this whole thing with the birds and—okay, what?"

He tilted his head. "*What*, what?"

"You're looking at me all squinty-eyed."

"Because I'm thinking."

"You look constipated, but please, think away."

Anders tapped his palm against the wall, a rough beat that had no rhythm to it, only force. The pipes lining the corridor shook as he pounded away. I leaned against the wall beside him, feeling the vibrations rattle along my spine. I pulled my hair up into the highest, tightest ponytail I could manage. Maybe the rush of blood to my scalp would help me think better. Was Wren being honest when she told me the location of the key? Why would she get so nervous if she were telling the truth?

Unless she wasn't telling the whole truth.

Maybe she and I were more similar than I cared to admit.

Next to my head, Anders's fist clenched.

"She wasn't in contact with the warden," he said through his teeth.

"How do you know?"

"Because *I* was in contact with the warden."

My eyes went wide. "You—?"

"Don't go jumping down my throat. We share DNA and I needed to inform him about the key. I'll have you know, he didn't even say thank you. Not that I was expecting it."

"So Wren lied?"

"Most likely." His tapping started again. "You can't be surprised. She's a self-proclaimed thief. I'm sure she has some ulterior motive."

Ulterior motive. How ironic.

"I'm a thief too," I reminded him. "Elio's a thief. *You're*—well, I don't know what you are."

"Charming? Cuddly? I also have three toes on my left foot. Now isn't the time to list my shortcomings, Cora."

"Wait—*three toes*?"

"Not. The. Time." He pushed off the wall. "I'll keep an eye on Wren. Don't worry about it."

Don't worry, he said. But of course, whenever you try *not* to do something, you exponentially increase your desire *to* do it. And so I worried.

If Wren was keeping secrets, it affected me the same as it affected him. Was there a reason he wanted me to forget about it?

"Do you have some kind of plan I need to know about?" I pressed.

He crunched his candy, sharp teeth grinding. "Not yet. Just know that I don't fully trust her. I can't say that I fully trust anyone. Except perhaps Elio." He shrugged. "Hard not to."

"You don't trust me?" I asked, incredulous. "I'm Elio's best friend."

Anders's eyes searched mine for a long moment, until I wanted to squirm beneath his dark gaze. He braced a hand on a pipe next to my head, leaning close, looming over me until his breath fanned across my cheeks. Now that I was really thinking about it, he didn't have *horrible* eyes to look at. As far as eyes went, that is. They softened at the corners, and I felt a rush of heat flood my stomach, drowning the last little bit of sense that I had left. I was overcome with the alarming desire to do something really absurd. Something like maybe, *possibly* take a step closer . . .

But just as my legs inched forward, he stepped back. "I haven't decided about you yet. I'll see you in the morning, Cora."

I watched him leave, passing beneath a row of flickering lights and cutting the corner at a brisk pace, away from the cabins and toward the cockpit. My gaze swung from the spot where he disappeared to the heavy metal door of Wren's cabin. Back and forth. And then again.

Well. I *had* said I was a thief. So a thief I would be. If Teolia's key really was in there, I would find it.

Wren hadn't even bothered to lock her room. One quick wave of my hand in front of the motion sensor next to the doorframe, and I was in.

She had been right about the mess. Actually, *mess* was putting it mildly. A Wren tornado had blown through the tiny cabin, leaving behind strewn heaps of bedding and crumpled, dirty flight suits. I plucked an inside-out sock from on top of her desk lamp, then thought better and replaced it. She couldn't notice that I'd been snooping.

Her cabin was nearly identical in size to mine, but the clutter made it feel even more cramped. With the floor covered in her clothes and shoes and undergarments, I had infinitely fewer places to stand.

While I contemplated how best to proceed, another one of Evelina's lessons flashed in my mind unsolicited: *clutter is a trap*.

Everyone knew rooms were easier to ransack when they were clean. Everything could be easily returned to its rightful place. Messes were more specific. Controlled chaos. And the slob in question always knew if their possessions had been tampered with. They noticed if a pile of clothes suddenly moved two feet to the right. Or if a shoe had been turned ninety degrees in the other direction. Oftentimes the owner of the mess orchestrated it that way on purpose. It was their own cheap alarm system.

I picked my way through the clutter, holding out my arms for balance. Wren wasn't as clever as she thought. The core of the mess centered around her bed, which jutted out from the wall instead of running parallel, like mine. I tiptoed between a pile of undershirts and a stack of old Earthan music records. Likely stolen, knowing the room's owner.

Without displacing her possessions, I knelt at the foot of the bed, lifting first the sheets and then the mattress.

I had to give her points for creativity. She had ripped a hole in the box spring and buried the key and its case deep inside. Most people simply wedged the loot under the mattress and called it a day.

I plucked the box out, heart stalling when the bed squeaked. The key caught the light, winking at me through the glass lid. *Hello, precious.*

I knew I wouldn't have much time. I quickly tiptoed back the way

I had come, careful to leave everything undisturbed. The second my feet left the cabin floor and crossed into the corridor, I ran for the laboratory. All the scrap metal I'd collected would finally come in handy.

Bursting through the door, I snapped on a pair of goggles and fired up the blowtorch wedged under the workbench. I monitored the clock as I melted down the metal into approximately the same shape and weight as Teolia's key, adding a mixture of dyes and acids found in the drawers to adjust the key to the correct color—the flawless pinkish-orange of sunset. I had no way to replicate the diamonds studding the length of the shaft, so I sliced up a few pieces of glass, hoping Wren would be too busy in the coming days to look close enough and notice the difference.

The numbers on the clock glowed a threatening red above the workbench. I'd been down here nearly an hour. Cursing, I tossed my supplies into a storage crate and hid them with a pile of corroded wires. Then I raced back to Wren's cabin.

Please don't be here. Please still be in the rec room. Because if she opened the door when I knocked, the only halfway decent excuse I could come up with for darkening her doorstep was, "*Can I borrow a tampon?*" and I *really* didn't have the energy to go there tonight.

But the cabin was just as deserted (and messy) as before. I crept past her piles of clothes, around the stack of records, to the bed frame. I dropped my fake, manufactured key into the glass case and returned it to Wren's box spring hiding spot, Teolia's real key burning a hole in the breast pocket of my flight suit. In under a minute, I was in and out.

I entered my own cabin in another minute. Elio looked up from my bed, scooting over once I collapsed on the mattress with my boots still on. For some reason, my breaths were coming out in quick pants, even though I had been practically crawling while in Wren's room. What in all the stars? I was a professional criminal; robbing an Earthan girl wasn't supposed to make me nervous.

"Cora," Elio chirped. He crawled up beside my head and poked me until I looked at him. "I do not see, nor do I smell, a milkshake."

"Sorry." I dipped my fingers into my pocket, brushing over Teolia's key in all its luminescent glory. *For Elio.* I was doing this for Elio. "Next time I promise I won't come back empty-handed."

14

I SLEPT UNTIL THE EARLY AFTERNOON. AFTER SEVEN HOURS of cold sweats mixed with intermittent nightmares—during each of which I drowned in faster, more horrifying ways—I shrugged on a fresh flight suit and stumbled into the galley.

Wren stood purposefully when I walked in, as if she'd been waiting for me. My mouth went dry, positive she was about to demand to know who had torn through her room, but she didn't give me any clue that she knew the real key was no longer in her possession. Instead she handed me a mug of coffee with a smile and loudly declared, "We're taking a field trip."

"Where?" Elio asked. He looked far more alert this morning, bouncing in his seat, blue eyes wide. I reminded myself to check his diagnostic scans later, but for now I relished his enthusiasm. For now, at least, he was okay.

Wren chugged her own mug of coffee, wiping her mouth with the back of her hand. "The Fuzzy Lizard."

"Is that another Earthan food that's bound to make me vomit?" Anders asked. He sat at the table, polishing his blaster with the sleeve of his flight suit. He caught my eye for a brief moment, then promptly arched his neck, hocked up a wad of phlegm, and spit it directly onto the barrel. *Yum.* He continued polishing, ignorant of our open-mouthed stares of revulsion.

"The Fuzzy Lizard," Wren said, holding back a gag, "is a tavern on the Tunerth outpost near Mars. Tunerth's a one-and-done kind of place. They sell groceries, toiletries, clothes—which I desperately need because the warden's goons stole all of my good leather jackets when they first seized my ship, and if I have to keep wearing *olive green*"—she plucked the front of her flight suit—"then I'm going to barf. It clashes with my hair."

"I think it looks fine," I said, like I was an authority on fashion. Which I definitely wasn't.

Wren rolled her eyes. "Well, I don't. But *most importantly* . . ." She smacked her hand on the table for emphasis. "They sell booze. And after the week we've had, I could use a friendly visit from my buddy Jack Daniels."

"That's not another treasure hunter you're bringing onboard, is it?" I asked.

"If it is, I will shoot him dead. I hate competition," Anders said, eyes glued to his blaster while he rewired something in the stock.

"Funny. Your creepy father said the same thing," said Wren. "No, but come to think of it, I did date a guy named Jack once. We met at a shopping plaza on Mars. I stole his watch off his wrist and gave it to my dad as a birthday present."

"And he dated you after that?" I asked.

She rolled her eyes. "He didn't know. What do you think I am, an amateur?"

Anders looked up from the table. "An amateur, no. A not-nice person, yes."

"Excuse me, I'm *very* nice!" she retorted. "My dad *loves* that watch. He said it was the best present he got all year, and until someone tells me that making him happy was wrong, I'm going to operate under the assumption that my methods were right."

Anders harrumphed. "Like it was right for you to blow up a space station?"

"It got us this beautiful ship, didn't it?"

"Your way of thinking is . . . very skewed."

"Oh, boo-hoo."

As entertaining as watching them argue was, I knew I needed to intervene. "Okay, okay. The Fuzzy Lizard?"

Wren hopped up onto the counter, crossing her legs like a pretzel. "We're out of supplies. We still have two keys left to find. I guarantee the warden isn't pleased—"

At that exact moment, one of the wires Anders was holding sparked and caught fire. Cursing, he put the small flame out with the dregs from his coffee, but not before he met my gaze and quirked a bushy eyebrow.

"You guarantee it, do you?" But his suspicious tone seemed to fly right over her head.

"It doesn't take a genius. We're five days into our two-week time limit and we haven't made that much progress. After we leave Tunerth, we need to pick a new direction. The first two keys were on Jupiter and Cadrolla—Teolia's favorite places. Those can't be the only planets she loved. What about the planet Teolia? It was named after her."

"But the treasure and all four keys were shipped far away from there ages ago," I said. I swirled the last few drops of my coffee around in my mug, then gulped them down. "For all we know, the last two keys got sucked into a black hole."

"That's unlikely. But if it turns out we have to dive into one to save our souls, then trust me, I promise I'll scrounge up the perfect outfit. Elio, any ideas?"

His ears drooped, and so did my adrenaline high. "In the time it took you to ask that, my internal interface scanned thirty-four million, eight hundred thousand, seventy-two net sites. I found nothing useful."

"So we chart a course for Tunerth," I said. "Figure out the rest as we go along. It'll be good to get out into civilization anyway.

Eavesdrop a bit. We might learn something helpful." Because the alternative was to sit here and pore over more message boards on the net. I'd spent an hour looking through them before falling asleep this morning and all I'd managed to find was that Teolia's favorite dessert was once rumored to be a coconut-covered eel. Apparently, it had been a delicacy on her planet hundreds of years ago. On Condor, eating eel often promised a one-way trip to the toilet.

Point was, I hadn't figured out anything useful on my own. So, in true Saros family fashion, I needed to steal my information from someone else.

It didn't take much to make Wren's day. All I had to do was offer to sit in the cockpit with her as she prepared to jump the *Starchaser* into the wormhole connecting the edge of Cadrolla's Whirlpool Galaxy to the center of the Milky Way Galaxy and the Tunerth outpost. She was itching for a proper co-pilot, and I played my part well, fastening the thick straps of my harness over my shoulders before switching on the internal comm and requesting that everyone on the ship buckle up.

"Wormhole due to open in twenty seconds, according to this schedule." Wren swiped her comm link, transferring the document to my own. I studied the timetable against the ancient analog clock that she had glued to the control panel in front of her seat. Another stolen item, no doubt.

"Engine valves open." She tapped something on one of the many screens before her. "Igniting the thrusters." She gripped her right hand around a wide lever parallel to her chair, her left hand edging the yaw mechanism two degrees portside.

"Go two more degrees," I said, studying the blinking radar display in front of me.

Wren looked over. "You think?"

I gave her my best attempt at a lighthearted grin. "Why have a co-pilot if you aren't going to listen to her?"

"Hmm . . . okay." She made the adjustments with the yaw, the *Starchaser* turning just as the wormhole flickered to life on the radar. She tapped a series of multicolored pedals at her feet. The wormhole opened wide, a sea of light ready to swallow us whole.

Inertia slammed me against my harness as we zipped inside. The bridge of the wormhole lengthened, shortened, then spat us out, leaving me with a pounding headache. I moved to unlatch my harness after it was over, but Wren immediately shrieked and clenched her controls. Out of nowhere, the outermost edge of the Milky Way Galaxy's asteroid belt appeared in our viewport. Cursing up a storm, Wren rolled us to our starboard side to avoid a collision.

"I swear the wormhole let me out in a different spot the last time I was here," she grunted apologetically. The comm system exploded with a stream of irritated shouts from Anders, accompanied by a few nervous beeps from Elio. I tapped the control panel, silencing them both.

"Don't be sorry," I told her. "You're good at this. Piloting." And sure, I was trying to butter her up, but I did mean it. My pod ship was a breeze to fly compared to this beast.

Wren didn't look over at me when she asked, "Good enough that your mother might want to hire a thief who can operate a charter ship?"

She was *still* angling for that? Stars above.

"I'm not sure you want that position, but yeah, I could put in a good word for you once all this is over." *Lies. Dirty, filthy lies.* When this was over, I'd never see her again.

"Really? You'd do that for me?" In her excitement, she accidentally jerked the throttle, nearly knocking the ship into half a dozen asteroids.

“Of course.” I let my gaze fall to the radar display. Tunerth and the Fuzzy Lizard would be appearing in the viewport in under ten minutes, but that wasn’t what I was looking at. I was far more concerned with trying to make sense of Wren. Was this the reason she was acting so strange last night? Had she bragged about a fictitious conversation with the warden to impress me into giving her a glowing job referral? If so, it hadn’t worked. She hadn’t been the confident criminal I’d met in Ironside. She had seemed almost . . . shy.

Maybe grilling her about those birds had thrown her off her game. And that was yet another mystery I didn’t have time to solve.

“I wish I still had my thievery chest onboard,” Wren said. “The warden’s guards took it after they arrested me.”

“Your thievery chest? Is that like a shrine or something?”

She sighed. “Sort of. It was filled with bits and pieces of all the things I’ve stolen over the years. Money, jewelry, packs of gum . . .”

“Gum?”

“I was five,” she said with a shrug. “I didn’t have much to work with.”

“So it was like a résumé?”

“Basically.” She edged the ship around another cluster of asteroids, gently this time. “I always thought it might impress your mother.”

Not many things impressed Evelina, but I didn’t tell her that. Just one more person who was trying to appease the head of the Saros family. We were all groveling for the satisfaction of a boss who I knew would never reciprocate. She would take, take, take until she drained us dry. And we would let her. Because she held all the power.

“I’m compiling a new one,” Wren went on. “So far all that’s in it are a few old records and one of the shrunken heads from the warden’s office.”

I shivered, remembering the jars lining his walls. “When did you take *that*?”

She beamed. *Ah*. There was the cockiness I'd missed from Ironside.

"When none of you were looking," she said.

"Smooth."

She pretended to preen. "I try. I just wish I had more things to put in it. You should've seen all the stuff that I used to have hidden in my cabin."

"Oh." I choked back a laugh while pretending to study the outpost that had just appeared as a tiny dot on the edge of the ship's radar. "I can only imagine."

She hummed in thought. "Elio said he doesn't clean, correct?"

"Yeah. Why?"

"Just wondering . . ." She shot me another grin over the console between us. But for some reason this one seemed even cockier and far less friendly than the last. "I just noticed that my room seemed a little . . . *tidier* this morning."

"Oh?" She was lying. I hadn't moved a thing.

Had I?

My heart started to hammer. *A sock*. I'd touched a *sock*. But I put it back. There was no way she noticed.

Wren shrugged, engaging the landing gear as Tunerth's outpost moved to take up the majority of our viewport. The first of two double doors in the protective dome surrounding the craggy moon slid back. The *Starchaser* entered, and Wren activated the comm to announce our identities to the control tower. After obtaining a landing clearance, she entered the second door into Tunerth's atmosphere and got in line behind a boxy delivery ship, waiting for a fueling bay to open up.

"Maybe it was just my imagination," she conceded innocently. I didn't reply. I'd gone rigid in my seat, too preoccupied with all the mistakes I might have made that were shredding my nerves like tissue paper. "Maybe the lights are just brighter today and it *looked* tidier." She reached over to give my arm a friendly squeeze. I swore her nails dug into my skin for a beat too long. "Never mind, Cora."

Right. *Never mind.*

Wren landed beside the delivery ship with ease, and the cargo ramp groaned as it started to unfold. My legs barely supported my weight as I stood and rushed from the cockpit, leaving its potential dangers lurking in the captain's chair.

Either she was on to me, or I was too paranoid for my own good.

I GRABBED ELIO'S ARM THE SECOND MY FEET HIT THE tarmac. "Pretend you're me. If you had a really huge problem, what would you do about it?"

Elio's squeaky voice took on an even squeakier tone. He flapped his arms around his head. "Oh no, look at me! I'm Cora. My family is dreadfully self-absorbed except for my best friend, Elio. If I have a problem, he'll help me steal something to fix it and then we can—"

"What are you doing?"

"Role playing." The high-pitched whir of his fans slowly died down. "You said pretend to be you."

"Cut the sass. You know that's not what I meant."

"Fine. Our lives are already one huge problem though. You realize that, right? But since you asked, when I'm stressed, I *love* to eat bread."

"Elio, you know you can't—"

"And honey," he added with a beep.

"Never mind," I huffed. Maybe I was overreacting. No matter what Wren thought she knew about me, she would never find the real key. It was looped on a long chain around my neck, buried beneath layers of undershirts and two flight suits. The only way she could get her hands on it was if she dug through the clothes on my body while I was sleeping.

On second thought . . . maybe it would be best to keep my eyes open for the next week and a half. Until after this charade had ended. Yeah. Definitely couldn't risk sleep.

That wouldn't be a problem at all, right?

I peered into the dark hole of the cargo hold. Wren had exited before Elio and me, and was making her way toward a line of waiting pod ships ready to transport passengers into town. I hadn't spotted Anders anywhere.

"Are you coming?" Wren called. "I want to put the ramp up."

"Yeah. Sorry." Maybe I'd missed him? The outpost was small, but it seemed crowded today—mostly with Earthans and Martians, although I noticed a few winged women from Avis holding hands and a pair of fathers from Condor shepherding their children across the nearest intersection. A long gravel road separated the landing bays from the town, which was only a few streets made of brick-and-mortar businesses intermixed with food carts and stalls selling colorful, handmade items. There wasn't any vegetation on the outpost that I could find, just a water tower looming behind the shops. It didn't seem like the people who lived here had much, but all the groups that passed me as I left the tarmac were smiling from ear to ear.

Except, of course, Anders.

Because I still didn't see him.

"Maybe he fell asleep?" Elio suggested. I just stared at him. I was pretty sure Anders slept with one eye open. (Maybe both.) He was unlikely to miss the landing.

My eyes made one last sweep of the tarmac, looking into the shadows surrounding every ship. The sun was setting, floodlights illuminating the landing bays and the surrounding streets. If there was a grumpy Andilly warrior creeping around out here, I didn't see him.

I turned away from the *Starchaser* as the ramp folded into the hull with a clang. Looked like he would have to eat whatever snacks we brought back to the ship without complaint.

I'd just taken my first step toward town when a tall figure cut in front of me. Instinctively, I reached for my blaster before remembering that I'd left it in my cabin to recharge.

"Looking for someone?" the boy asked.

"*Andy*?" His name was out of my mouth before I could stop it, but no—that wasn't right. It was his voice, his same rough accent, his same black eyes. He wore the same green flight suit as he had earlier, paired with a zippered sweatshirt with the hood pulled up, but his face was . . . very much *not* Andy.

"I know, I know." He grabbed my arm and started tugging me at a steady clip across the tarmac. "You don't have to say it. I'm ugly."

"You're—an *Earthan*." I pulled to a stop. Elio, who was following too closely, crashed into my legs and fell to the ground. "Why do you look like an Earthan? *How* do you look like an Earthan?"

Anders—or the boy I thought might be Anders—ran a hand through a mop of dark, unruly hair. Usually it was impossible for me to read his aura, but now it exploded off him, a kaleidoscope of navy blue misery mixed with ruby red fury, covered with iron gray bars that told me he was trying (and failing) to make himself go completely numb.

He held out a hand between us, and his skin flashed from tan to its usual scaly red to tan again before he stuffed his fist in the pocket of his sweatshirt.

"Shape-shifting," I said, connecting the dots. Parts of his face still looked like him—his hooked nose, the angry set of his jaw, the old scar that wrapped around his neck. But he had leaner muscles now, his teeth were no longer sharp, and his stance had grown stooped. He looked so innocent and *human* that even I thought I could pick a fight with him and win.

"Stop staring," he grumbled, looking at his feet.

"You're a shape-shifter," I repeated. "Don't you think that's information we should have known?"

"I thought it was obvious." He made one of his fingers grow into a long claw before retracting it.

"Yeah, but this . . ." I gestured to his body. "Is a little extreme."

"You're cute now," Elio piped up.

"Quiet. I'm hideous."

He *wasn't* hideous. He was gawky, certainly, but he sort of had this understated sweetness now that he didn't come off like he wanted to devour anyone who looked at him the wrong way. It wasn't bad, but still it somehow felt . . . *wrong*. This boy standing in front of us wasn't the boy who had smiled at me from behind the broken oxygen mask in the *Starchaser*'s laboratory, who had complimented my inventions and scowled at Wren's sneezing and fearlessly battled the creatures of Cadrolla. This Earthan boy wasn't my Andy—I mean *our* Andy.

I frowned. *Ours*. Not *mine*.

What was I thinking? Without his red scales, he looked every bit a demon in disguise. What I needed to be focusing on was this unassuming skill of his and all the ways we could use it to get to the next of Teolia's keys. Anders was *my* nothing. Except for my means to an end.

Gravel crunched on the tarmac and suddenly Wren was next to us. "Anders?" she asked hesitantly. He nodded.

She burst out laughing. Groups across the tarmac turned to watch as she doubled over, wiping tears from her eyes. It took a full minute for her cackling to subside.

"Justice is sweet," she said, studying his Earthan disguise. "Anders, you look . . ." Another round of cackles. "Yeah. That's all I got. What's with the new face?"

Anders took off for the closest street lined with pod ships and merchant booths. "I figured we didn't want to draw attention to ourselves. Earthans are unassuming. So I'm pretending to be one for your sakes. My kind isn't typically welcome on planets other than our own. The residents usually think we're there to murder them, which oftentimes we are."

"Andilly does have quite the reputation," I said.

He nodded. We passed a row of tents selling jeweled gauntlets, which Wren stopped to admire (or, more likely, steal). While we waited for her to rejoin us, Elio took the opportunity to pepper Anders with questions. In the next few minutes, I learned that he could transform into humanoid species only; Elio was a little disappointed when Anders told him he couldn't turn himself into Elio's favorite Earthan creature—a three-toed sloth.

"But it would be so cool if the *Starchaser* could have a mascot!" Elio said. Anders looked like he wanted to hit something, but seeing as Elio was far too earnest to hurt, he settled for grinding his knuckles into his palm instead.

Our group split up after that. Elio waddled away to find Wren, and I headed off the main road to a bench near a crowded café. Twinkling fairy lights made out of winged insects hung over the outside patio, and the sounds of laughter and tinkling china filled the air. Anders tentatively joined me, sitting as far away as possible while pulling his hood lower over his eyes, as if he were ashamed to be seen like this.

"Stop fidgeting," I said. Nervous bolts of chartreuse crackled around his head as he crossed his legs and then his arms. Then he uncrossed them both and slumped down until his head was almost level with the back of the bench. "Full disclosure, I'm reading your emotions right now."

"I know." He tapped his foot at a brisk pace. "I can't hold them back when I shift. It takes too much energy to do both. Sorry if they're blinding."

"They aren't worse than anyone else's," I said. His lips curved into a tiny, almost embarrassed smile. Pair it with his new face and he looked more alarmingly approachable than ever, although his aura continued to spark and pop.

A group of legitimate Earthans passed our bench on the way to the café door. Their eyes skipped right over me, put off by the points of my ears and the unnerving yellow of my irises that marked me as decidedly *other*, but they lingered on Anders, giving him friendly nods before disappearing inside.

"Maybe you should pose as an Earthan all the time," I teased once we were alone. "Look how quickly you're making friends."

He glowered. "I hate this. You have no idea how strange it is being in another body. Like my skin is too tight."

"You're also chattier."

"I'm uncomfortable. I'm trying to get my mind off it."

"You're shorter too."

He sat up straight, face twisting as if he just ate something particularly sour. He scooted over to me until we were sitting hip to hip.

Even as an Earthan, his head was still half a foot above mine. "Now you're just being mean."

"*Me*? Mean? I didn't think that would bother you, he who has the stoicism and personality of a brick wall."

He inclined his head toward me. A thick lock of hair fell across one eye. "Am I a fancy, new brick wall at least?"

I leaned back. "Was that a *joke*? You become Earthan and you suddenly make jokes?"

"I was under the impression that people enjoyed them. It's meant to create a bonding moment."

I gagged. "Not particularly interested in bonding with you in any form, thanks."

He edged back to his empty corner of the bench, pouting. "Right. That's good, because I feel the same way. *Bonding*. Blegh." He stuck out his tongue. "If I could abstain from any social contact for the rest of my life, it might be too soon."

"Exactly. That's why my best friend is a robot." Of course, neither of us seemed to have the same views on the ship last night. He had been all up in my personal space, a breath away from touching me. Now, I met his gaze underneath the shadow of his hood, and his lips curled at the edges, dark eyes sparkling with barely concealed laughter. He remembered too.

We had almost died together. Like it or not, we had already created a bonding moment.

Brushing wavy strands of hair from his forehead, Anders sighed and scooted to the middle of the bench. When I showed no indication of moving, he huffed and patted the space beside him. "Maybe we should learn to be more social?" he suggested.

"Yeah, sure." I nudged his shoulder. "When we're dead."

He smiled at me then, a shock to my system after I'd shot him down so easily. His smile was so startlingly open and honest and hopeful that the only response I could think of was to grin back until my cheeks hurt. His aura streamed off him in waves, glimmering bright and mixing with the fairy lights on the patio. Like a treasure trove. An oasis in the sun.

It was in that moment I realized how much I preferred his true face. Looking at that one, at least, I remembered who and what I was up against. This one made me want to trust him too damn much.

"Oy! You two!" Wren strutted down the sidewalk toward us, accompanied by Elio. Two giant bundles of clothes were clutched in their arms. Elio's was so large that he could barely see over it, and he sighed in relief once they deposited the items into our laps. Tactical pants for Anders, fleece-lined leggings for me, and shirts and water-resistant jackets for both of us.

"We stocked up on snacks too," Wren said. "Hope you like cheese puffs, because that's all we could find."

"To my limited Earthan knowledge, cheese is not puffy," said Anders.

Wren and I both snorted. "You're an adorable little alien." She must have found his new face as trusting as I did, because she reached out to pinch his cheeks. She jumped back when he snapped his teeth like a caged animal.

"Try that again," he dared.

"No thanks, I'm good."

Anders stood from the bench, holding up his new clothes. Then he—*what in all the stars?*—started to *strip off* his sweatshirt and flight suit and change his outfit right there on the sidewalk.

"You can't do that out here!" I jumped up to block him as a group of passersby wolf-whistled, but that only put me way too close to his naked chest. Maybe Andillians walked around all the time in the buff in the military, but I didn't want to make it obvious to the entire outpost that he didn't belong.

A second group heading into the café pulled out their comm links to film the spectacle.

"Can't do what?" Anders tossed his old clothes in the nearest trash receptacle before buttoning his fly and shrugging on his jacket, which was a tad too big on his leaner Earthan frame. "Wren, these are fine quality. Tell me you didn't steal them."

"It's like you don't know me at all. And it's only stealing if they *see you* take something. Otherwise, their item of great value is simply . . . *misplaced.*"

"Stars, you could run for office on my planet with that outlook," he replied.

"Maybe I should. My face would look fantastic on a giant stack of money. C'mon, follow me." She led our party down the street, away from Anders's new fans. "So we've got food, new clothes, next is gossip. The tavern's just around the corner. By the way—Andykins," she called over her shoulder. "Nice abs. They don't make up for your crappy personality, but still. Nice abs."

We weaved through the crowd, which seemed to get denser as the sky grew darker. Cheers rang out and glass bottles clinked as we came upon the Fuzzy Lizard and pushed through the front doors.

The room was shaped like a flying saucer, its two levels separated by a glittering quartz ramp furnished with leather-padded handrails. Brass chandeliers and wide net screens hung from the ceiling.

No matter how many planets I'd visited over the years while working with my family, I'd realized pretty quickly that all taverns required four items in order to function properly (besides an abundance of liquor): junk food fried in so much grease you could bathe an army in it; a mysterious musty odor that leeched onto your clothes and remained there for approximately three to five business days; a dozen bar fights that started and ended for seemingly no real reason at all; and drunks. Lots of friendly, close-talking drunks.

The Fuzzy Lizard had a healthy dose of all of the above. Our group weaved between mismatched metal stools surrounding high top tables as we dodged flying bottles and chose a cluster of empty seats at the far end of the bar nearest the bathrooms. Cue the funky, musty odor.

"Just a sec. I'll get us some cash," said Wren. She ducked underneath the arm of a cyclops singing off-key karaoke and approached a group of Earthan girls returning from the toilets.

I'd done a fair amount of pickpocketing in my day, yielding varying results, and I could admit that her technique was superb. She clamped a hand over her mouth, eyes widening in just the right amount of I'm-going-to-hurl terror, and bumped the tallest girl's arm as they crossed in opposite directions. Even while faking sick, Wren was all lithe, quick movements, her footsteps as silent as the crushing vacuum of space. I didn't see her fingers wrap around the clutch that stuck out from the girl's coat pocket, but when I noticed Wren's own jacket hang with a similar weight, I knew the transfer had occurred. The girl stumbled back a few paces before being steadied by one of her friends, and Wren apologized—enough to be polite, but not enough to be memorable after the group walked away. They joined a rowdy crowd at a long table in an alcove across the tavern, Wren's mark instantly laughing about something the boy next to her said, her hands crawling up his shoulders. As intended, Wren and the stolen clutch were now the furthest things from her mind.

Good enough that your mother might want to hire a thief that can operate a charter ship? she had asked onboard the *Starchaser*. Just the thought of it made my breath hitch. Evelina would dote on Wren in a way that she'd never doted on me, but now that I saw Wren in action, I knew she could do far better than working for my family's crime empire. One day, with enough experience, Wren could lead her own.

After extracting a handful of folded bills from the depths of the purse, Wren threw the rest of the girl's possessions in the trash can beside the bathrooms. "Here," she said, forking over the money to Anders. "Buy yourselves something tasty."

"Good trick," he said.

"Oh, that? A baby could do it."

"Not necessarily," said Elio. "Cora only has a twenty-nine-point-three percent success rate with pickpocketing."

"Thank you, Elio—*oof*!" I cried when he shimmied onto my lap to see over the bar top, elbowing my boob in the process. "Why yes, of course you can use me as your own personal booster seat."

"Much thanks."

Wren looked around to make sure no one was watching, then reached over the bar and grabbed two pewter tankards. She shot me a sly wink before shoving them into a paisley carpetbag. At the rate she was going today, we would need to commandeer a second ship just to carry all her ill-gotten goods.

"I need a drink," I muttered. I called out to the bartender, a bald alien with two heads—one wearing a dopey grin, the other a belligerent scowl that rivaled Anders's own—each with mottled gray skin and a gold hoop earring pierced through the nostrils. Nodding, he brought us four bubbling tankards full of some kind of muddy liquid that he deemed "the house special."

"What is this?" I asked. My eyes watered as smoke curled out of the cups. The bartender's grumpier head narrowed its eyes, while the more pleasant one gave us a grin full of chipped yellow teeth.

"Swamp juice!" he declared proudly.

"Bottoms up!" Wren lifted her cup in a toast. The rest of us followed suit, Elio faking it.

The swamp juice had the consistency of rocket fuel and tasted like it too. After taking only one small sip, I found myself unable to breathe, hacking up a lung while the alcohol burned a trail down my throat. Elio pounded his fists into my back to try to revive me.

"What *was* that?" I croaked. My entire body suddenly felt like it was being held together by rubber bands.

"You heard him," Wren said. "Swamp juice." She took a sip, pinkie up. "You don't have to drink it, but at least pretend to act a little drunk. People are more susceptible to confessing secrets to the intoxicated, especially when they think they're too out of it to remember. Act adorably drunk and someone is bound to trust us enough to spill something about the treasure."

Anders frowned. "That's . . . actually not a horrible idea. Oh stars—I can't believe I just complimented *you*. I need another drink." He gulped down the rest of his swamp juice like a champ and signaled for the bartender.

When he came over, left head still scowling, right head still grinning, I decided to test Wren's theory. "Hey there! This is a great drink. Splendid. Best I've ever had, in fact."

"You're laying it on too thick," Elio whispered in my ear.

"Anywho. We're just stopping by on our way to Teolia." I lifted my cup to my lips, pretending to sway a little. "Heard of it?"

"No," grunted the left head, unamused.

"Really? I've been told it's quite the *treasure* of the universe. I'm surprised you've never *hunted* for it on the map."

Right Head let out a girlish giggle. Left Head looked like he wanted to drown me in one of the kegs behind the bar. "I'm charging you double for aggravating me." He shot me daggers before moving to serve a group at the other end of the tavern.

Laughing, Wren swiped another tankard and stuffed it in her bag. "I'll give you an F for effort. And I just realized we're basically the start of a seriously bad joke. *An Earthan, two aliens, and a robot walk into a bar . . .*"

I rolled my eyes. "Scratch that. Maybe I do need another drink." I waved at the friendly right head when it spun in our direction.

F for effort. Yeah, right. I'd show her.

And that's how one tiny sip of swamp juice turned into many, *many* bad decisions. One drink was strong enough; by the time I reached my fourth, my vision was so blurry and I was giggling so hard that Elio had to prop me against Anders's shoulder to keep me from taking a tumble and cracking my head on the floor.

The others weren't doing much better. Wren held her liquor easier than I did, but she still drunkenly challenged a group of Martians to a dance-off, which she won by doing a back flip into a split that ripped her pants.

Then there was Anders. After drink number three, he discovered he could use his endearing Earthan face to interrogate our fellow bar patrons, because no one found him the least bit intimidating when he looked so wholesome. But still, useful information was tough to come by. We made our way around the tavern, and I laughed and drank and tried not to fall on my face on the sticky floor while Anders dropped subtle comments about Teolia's keys. A few people mentioned Cadrolla, and one elderly gentleman showed us a long silver scar he received on his pelvis after diving off a cliff on the planet Teolia during a vacation last year. But no one had anything useful to offer when it came to the treasure.

When the old wooden clock on the wall chimed at the top of the hour, we gave up and returned to the bar, drowning our sorrows in more swamp juice. I'd grown accustomed to its acidic taste. I barely even gagged when I threw back my next shot.

The room spun, and I laid my head down on my arms. "Let's just sleep through the rest of our lives, Andy. When we get thrown back in Ironside, that's all we'll be doing anyway."

"You're a sad drunk," Anders observed.

"No, I'm not." And yet I wiped at the tears that had gathered in the corners of my eyes. He was being so mean. That's what he was. A mean drunk. A stupid drunk.

A burst of something hot and dangerous swelled in my stomach when he leaned his shoulder against mine. Or maybe that hot and dangerous feeling was only the swamp juice gurgling through my intestines. He was even closer than we had been on the ship last night, and even though we'd been drinking all evening, his breath was as sweet as spun sugar. Like one of those orange lollipops he enjoyed so much. Reaching toward me, he twined a silver curl of my hair around his little finger.

A . . . *cute* drunk. Maybe that's what he was.

If so, then I was in serious trouble.

"You know," I breathed, barely audible over the raucous laughter in the bar. "You're not the *worst* person I've ever met."

His shoulders shook with laughter. "I hope there's a compliment hidden in there somewhere."

"Duh." In my inebriated state, I steadied myself against him, and my hand just kind of . . . *accidentally* happened to fall on top of his. "Anders? Hey, Anders?"

"Hey, Cora?"

I studied the bow of his full pink lips, the small cleft in his chin. His onyx stare was so intense, his Earthan face a little *too* aesthetically pleasing. The real Anders wasn't that pretty to look at, but he was smart and he was strong. He was kind, at least to me. Those things held more value than the skin he wore.

Anders's smile blurred, doubling, then tripling before coming back into focus again.

"Anders? I think . . . I think that if you weren't who you are and I wasn't who I am, there's a chance we might have actually been friends."

"I'm . . . not sure what that means."

What it meant was that I was far too drunk to be having such a serious conversation. I was straddling a dangerous line between keeping up with this charade and confessing my intentions once and for all.

Giving my head a little shake, I mentally pulled myself away from the edge of the precipice. Anders didn't need to know all of this was a farce, a scheme I had cooked up, an elaborate lie.

He didn't need to know that whatever minuscule bit of camaraderie we had cultivated was a game I desperately wanted to make real.

And not just between me and him. Between me and Wren. Between all of us. I had done a fine job of convincing myself that I didn't need their friendship, but . . . maybe I did need them. A lot.

Problem was—I needed to save Elio too.

It was impossible to get everything fair and square. That was a lesson Evelina had taught me a long time ago.

But she had also taught me to simply *take* whatever I wanted. And I wasn't in the right state of mind to make rational decisions and do otherwise. I was lying to Anders and to myself, but I curled my fingers around the hot skin at the back of his neck anyway and tilted his head down. A pink flash of his aura lit up the bar as he skimmed his hands along my arms. He held my fingers in his own, so gently—as if we weren't two felons, but just a boy and a girl. As if we weren't searching for an impossible treasure. As if our lives weren't at stake.

Raising my lips to his, I closed my eyes . . .

Buzz!

"What the—?"

Buzz!

My comm link, vibrating against the edge of the bar top. Anders and I sprang apart, and I instinctively wiped the back of my hand across my mouth, even though we hadn't done anything. I wasn't sober before, but I sure felt sober now.

I accepted the call, and to my horror the warden's scarred, red face filled my screen.

Anders ducked. "Don't tell him I'm here!"

"You have a tracking chip in your neck, idiot. He knows exactly where you are."

"Oh. Right, sorry. Still a little tispy."

"Tipsy," I corrected.

"That too."

"Are you quite finished?" asked the warden. He was seated in his office, and the familiar row of shrunken heads filled the wall behind him—although the display looked slightly uneven on the left side, thanks to Wren and her little bout of thievery.

"Hello there, Sir." I waved. "Warden. Sir Warden. Is there, uh, is there something we can do for you?"

He picked up a knife on his desk, spit on the blade, and began wiping it dry. Like father, like son. "Miss Saros, I find myself growing bored."

"I suggest a crossword puzzle, then, Sir."

His eyes flicked up at the lens, and even though I was just watching him on my screen, I still felt the heat of his fury deep in my bones. "I find your humor revolting. I also thought that you would have more news for me by now."

"But—Anders said he commed you last night."

"Who?"

I pointed next to me. "Your son?"

"I don't have a son, I have a spawn—"

"Always a pleasure to see you too," Anders muttered.

"—he mentioned that you located one of the keys, which is all well and good, but I expected better. I expected the job to be further along by now."

"It hasn't even been a week!" I protested. "You gave us two. You never said we had to be finished early."

"I never asked to be blessed with such striking good looks either, and yet here we are." He combed the blade of his knife through his tangled black hair.

"Is he serious?" I whispered to Anders.

"Andillians don't make jokes."

"Except you."

"I'm special." Reaching over the bar top, he grabbed a bottle at random and poured himself a shot. "And still mildly intoxicated."

The warden stabbed his knife into his desk. The hilt swung like a pendulum. "Back to the task at hand. I am bored, Miss Saros. I am afraid you aren't living up to your family's reputation."

My teeth clenched so hard my jaw popped. "*Excuse* me?"

"You're excused. I must admit, I anticipated something a bit flashier. That is your family's forte, it seems. Explosions, perhaps? Maybe a nice death-defying escape? Even the outbreak you orchestrated in my prison was more harrowing than what you have demonstrated in this hunt so far."

"Did you happen to catch the part where we almost drowned in a cave on Cadrolla? Because I did. I'd call that pretty harrowing, wouldn't you, Anders?"

Anders slumped in his bar stool, refusing to speak. I shouldn't have expected him to. The warden wouldn't listen to Anders anyway. Just like Evelina barely listened to me.

The warden fingered his knife, a repulsive look of longing in his eyes. "I require those keys, Miss Saros. It seems like you need more motivation, and I need more entertainment. A good laugh is so hard to come by around here." He sighed so theatrically that I wished I could reach through the screen and slap him. "Here is what I propose: I've assembled a team of my own guards. They fly out of Andilly in, oh, I don't know, an hour. Maybe two. They'll know exactly where to find you. If you can manage to secure the remaining two keys and the treasure chest before they can, I'll honor our agreement and expunge your criminal records. However, if you fail, then I dare say your old cell is getting quite cold with no inhabitants . . ."

"We get the picture," Anders growled.

"Excellent. You know how much I hate explaining things twice."

Anders's fist clenched. A piece of the bar top broke off with a crack, causing the bartender's grumpy head to scowl in our direction.

I held my comm link in a death grip. How was it that this man, who knew next to nothing about me, figured out all the ways to push me over the edge? He wanted me to live up to the Saros reputation? Fine. I would *exceed* their reputation. He wanted explosions? Mayhem? We could do that. We could do better than that. We could blow the other team's ship right out of the sky. I wouldn't even feel sorry.

"One more thing, Miss Saros, before I disconnect," said the warden. "I don't trust that this little competition alone will motivate you. To ensure that you all cooperate, I have one more announcement."

"Which is?" Anders said.

"It loses its fun if I share it with you. I recommend you turn to the nearest net screen. It might inspire you to move a bit . . . faster. Until we speak again." He disconnected with a beep.

"Wait!" I shook my comm, but it was no use. He was gone. "What was he talking about? Is he always so cryptic?"

But Anders ignored me. He buried his head in his palms while muttering a sharp string of curses, loud enough that I could still hear them over the clinking of the glasses around the tavern. His skin flashed from tan to pale pink to dark red and back to tan, like a net program he couldn't tune to the correct frequency. He was losing control. Desperate to bring him back to himself, I yanked his hands down and slapped him across the face.

His eyes flashed with murder. "Do that again and I'll bite your hand off."

"That's an empty threat and you know it. What's our game plan here?"

"Game plan?" He slammed his empty shot glass on the bar. "There is no game plan! He completely—what's the phrase you use on your sophisticated planet? Screwed the pooch?"

"I don't think anyone has ever said that on any planet. *Ever*. Do you mean 'screwed us over'?"

"I don't care what I mean. We can't hunt the treasure when someone else is hunting *us*. He's making this into a game. I knew he would do something like this." A hint of black formed at his fingertips, but he pushed his claws away, keeping his disguise intact. "I told you, Cora. I told you not to take this job with him!"

"Like we had a choice!"

He didn't hear me. "This is what he does. He ruins lives. Mine. My mother's."

"Your . . . mother?"

He plowed on. "Nothing he does ends well for anyone except himself. He's watching our every move." He pressed a finger against the back of his neck. "The second he sees where we're going, his team will follow. All of his guards are ex-military. They went through the same training I did, and knowing the warden, he'll send at least half a dozen."

I gulped. Anders times six?

"Make no mistake, if they don't outright murder us when they get here, they'll find another way to overpower us. They'll get to the keys first."

"Maybe not," I said. "He told us he had another announcement. Something that will make us move faster—" I turned to the net screen mounted on the wall above the bar when it let out a high-pitched wail of warning. Four more screens hanging around the tavern did the same, their displays rimmed in a ribbon of red, black letters scrolling along the glass and casting shadows on the walls. A single bold word caught my attention: BOUNTY.

Four photos flashed underneath.

Our photos.

The tavern went quiet as the warden's voice filled the room, explaining how we had escaped Ironside and were last seen in Tunerth. How we were considered armed and extremely dangerous. Nothing I could disagree with, although the photographs on the net screens told a different story. There was an old school photo of me from about five years ago—my hair in messy pigtails, lips smeared with gloss that I'd probably stolen from Evelina's makeup kit. I looked happy and innocuous, even though I'd already started working for Cruz and Evelina at that time.

Next to me was Elio. His picture was taken from a security camera inside the Vaotis Grand Treasury. He was cowering behind my legs, mid-beep, eyes glowing. Beside him was Anders, dressed in burgundy military regalia, medals adorning his shoulders. The last photo was Wren's mugshot from Ironside. In true Wren fashion, she was winking at the camera.

We looked like the weirdest group of criminals ever.

And to top it off, the warden was offering a lucky group *fifty thousand ritles* to bring us back to him.

"This is not good," I whispered as the implications sank in. Not only was the warden's team of guards chasing us, now the entire galaxy—no, probably the entire *universe*—would be out to get us too.

I jumped when my comm buzzed against my arm. A message from the warden:

I'll retract the bounty when you bring me the keys. Run fast, Miss Saros.

"Not good at all," I said again.

"*Psst*! You two!"

Elio was creeping down the hall from the bathrooms, Wren at his back, her hands protectively gripping her carpetbag. "*Psst*! Hey-ey-ey!" Elio hissed again, slurring his words. "I'm t-trying to b-be inconspicuous by not using your names since we are wanted criminals and instead refer-*erring* to you in the general sense of 'you people' or 'y'all' or 'yinz.' Which would you per—uh—p-prefer?"

"Why are you talking like that?" I demanded. "You aren't drunk."

"I'm pretending." He shrugged. "I like to fit in."

"We have a problem," Wren said. "There's a crowd gathered outside talking about the *Starchaser*. I think someone saw us land."

"How big of a crowd?" I asked. "Can we get past them and lift off?"

Anders tapped my shoulder. "I think the better question," he began warily, "is can we get out of this bar?"

"What do you mean?" My gaze fell to his hand, startled to see the familiar claws gleaming at his fingertips. His skin was red again, scaly, his muscles tense and ready to spring. His disguise had vanished, and with it the drunken swirl of an aura that had existed around his head up until a moment ago. He was on the offensive now. And when I looked over my shoulder at the tavern floor, I realized why.

The Fuzzy Lizard had gone completely still.

The heat of hundreds of eyes seared into my skin. It felt like a spotlight had blown the roof wide open and was shining down upon us, illuminating the truth of our identities for everyone to see.

We were standing on the universe's biggest stage as, one by one, the entire bar stood and stared with greedy recognition in our direction.

16

"RUN!"

I didn't think twice before vaulting over the bar. "Come on! Move!" The others obeyed, their panicked cries drowned out by an uproar as the crowd in the tavern followed suit, chasing us down.

My destination was the door behind the bar leading into the kitchen. Criminal pro tip: every kitchen has a low-key escape route. A simple iron door, a loading dock, a doggy door . . . I learned that last one during a fancy dinner party heist when I was fourteen. My shoulders almost couldn't squeeze through the doggy door then, and I prayed that the Fuzzy Lizard's kitchen wouldn't have one too, because, stars, I knew I couldn't squeeze through one now.

"If anyone has any other ideas besides running like hell, please enlighten me, because I'm just winging it!" I shoved aside two cooks, sending pots of scalding water sloshing to the floor. A burst of fire and smoke shot up from one of the stoves against the wall. I jumped to avoid it, darting around an island covered in chopped vegetables. Just before I pulled open the back door—a regular door, thank the stars—I noticed Elio halt in front of the food. His mouth fell open, fingers stretching forward . . .

Anders hoisted him up without ceremony and tossed him over his shoulder.

"Wait! I wanted a hot pepper!"

"Wren will steal one for you if we live through the night."

The four of us burst into an alleyway behind the building, taking to the streets. The shouts of our pursuers followed like a buzzing cloud of insects. The swarm was growing; everyone we passed seemed to recognize us. A symphony of pounding footsteps crashed along the pavement.

In less than a minute, we reached the end of the block, coming up on more merchant tents that dwindled after fifty yards, leaving room for strips of row houses. There was nowhere good to hide. Everyone was watching us, and I knew that somewhere, somehow, the warden was watching too. Whether he had spies on the outpost or he had hacked into a local security monitor, I could sense his presence as easily as I could sense the hundreds of greedy jade auras fogging the streets.

To my left, I saw Anders pull his blaster from the inside pocket of his new, stolen jacket. He aimed a blind shot over his shoulder, over Elio's head. There was an explosion, the sound of bricks tumbling onto the pavement, and then a few blessed moments of silence as a haze of smoke spread across the crowd.

"This way. Hurry, while they're distracted." Anders grabbed us and thrust us into an alleyway filled with garbage. We emerged on the other side, in the shadow of a pedestrian bridge spanning the width of the street. The buildings were shorter off the main drag, dirtier, with cracks in the windows and chipped paint on the doors. I looked behind us. We'd lost the mob in the commotion, but my heart sank when I realized how much farther we had traveled from the landing bays and the *Starchaser*.

There was nowhere else to run. Nowhere we could—

"Cora!"

I spun around. "What?" I demanded to Wren.

Puzzled, she looked over her shoulder. "I beg your pardon?"

"Did you just say my name?"

"No . . ." She furrowed her eyebrows.

"Cora!"

I heard it again. Right in the back of my head. Felt the hook in my gut dragging me forward.

"Cora!"

"Come on!" I told them. "This way." I sprinted down a side street, not even checking to see if they were following. All the while the voice was there, chanting my name, louder with every step. It probably wasn't the smartest idea to go running toward a disembodied voice, but my feet wouldn't slow, no matter how hard I tried.

"Where are we going?" Elio called.

"Cora, we're not getting any closer to the ship," said Wren.

"I know, but we need to get off these streets." I stopped at the corner, shivering as a tingle spread through my limbs. The voice called to me one more time, an echo in my head. And then everything fell still.

"What *in all the stars* was that about?" Wren caught up to me, panting.

"I'm not sure you'd believe me if I told you," I said, helping Elio slide down from Anders's shoulder. I eyed a cellar hatch at the edge of the sidewalk. Somehow, deep in my bones, I felt the call to open it. It was locked, but I knew better than anyone that every lock could be picked.

Anders pointed out a fire escape wrapped around the nearest building. "We'll get a better vantage point up there. Higher ground."

"Yeah, until your father's friends find us and fire a missile at our heads," I said.

"Well, I've always imagined dying with a serene view."

"How interesting," came a new voice. "I thought Andillians didn't make jokes."

We all jumped. Anders aimed his blaster in the direction of the cellar hatch, which had swung open toward us. Elio flicked his wrists, unleashing two serrated knives hidden in his jacket sleeves. Wren raised her carpetbag, and I knew it was heavy enough with stolen objects to knock out any enemy with a single swing.

Though the new enemy—if that's really what she was—was so emaciated that a hit from the carpetbag might have been enough to kill her. I looked down, meeting the green eyes of a young Earthan girl peering up out of the cellar door. Despite having an arsenal of weapons pointed in her direction, she didn't seem frightened at all.

With a grunt that seemed too loud for a kid so small, she shoved the hatch open all the way. A concrete ramp disappeared down into a dark, yawning hole. "Unless you're interested in adding 'death by angry mob' to your résumés," she said, "feel free to follow me."

With only a few wary glances at each other, we followed the girl underground. The hatch slammed shut behind us, darkening the room except for the dull blue glow at the end of Anders's blaster. Through the shadows encroaching on us, I could just make out the edges of dozens of wooden shelves lining the walls of the square bunker, each one covered in boxes and twisted heaps of metal. I angled my body toward the closest shelf, eying up a long, rusty pole. If the girl turned on us, that would be my go-to weapon.

The girl stood on tiptoe to retrieve a pack of matches from a shelf, then used them to ignite a lantern in the middle of the room. We groaned at the sudden burst of light, but when my eyes adjusted, it was no longer the young girl staring back at me from across the cellar floor.

The new figure's green, crepe-y skin was mostly covered by a long shawl, but I could see her face well enough. And she was grinning at us with a mouthful of rotted, black fangs.

I dived for one of Elio's knives, reaching for the rusty pole with my other hand. Even though the creature before us had a mouth, where there should have been a nose and eyes, there was . . . nothing. Just more wrinkled skin.

"Come now," said the creature in a breathy voice. The same voice that had been *in my head.* The voice that had drawn me here. "I don't bite. Often."

Anders held his blaster at the ready. "Make one move and I will detach your skull from your body. Don't think I'll hesitate."

I felt Elio shaking behind my legs. "What *is* she? She doesn't have a face. Is anyone else seeing that she doesn't have a face?"

I took a small step back. "Thanks, Elio. I would have completely missed that if it weren't for you."

The figure opened her mouth. "I have been many things to many people. A friend . . ." Her body contorted, and then I was looking at clones of all four of us standing across the room. My double winked at me. Anders took a shot at them, but they scattered into clouds of mist and re-formed into the faceless figure once again.

"I have been a lover . . ." The creature's body turned into two shadows caressing each other in the lantern light. "An enemy." She plucked a few strands of gray hair from her head and dropped them to the floor, where they curled into the bodies of four yellow pythons that slithered around our legs. We lashed out with our weapons, but the snakes were too quick, wrapping around us, pinning our arms to our torsos.

"Anders," snapped Wren. "This is an excellent opportunity for you to do some kind of fancy shape-shifting trick too."

He writhed. "I'm focusing on breathing at the moment. Try again later."

"We're going to die." Elio beeped. "We're all going to die."

I couldn't move my arms, but I had limited control over my fingers, which were quickly going numb. I turned the pole in my hand just slightly, aiming for the tail of the python lying on the floor in front of my feet. Putting all the energy into it that I had left, I drilled the piece of metal into the skin of the snake.

The python shrieked. As did the faceless figure, who crumpled to the floor just as all four reptiles vanished in a puff of smoke. Anders aimed his blaster again, but right before he pulled the trigger, the figure lifted her head. Her face was no longer green and wrinkled and eyeless. She had transformed into the scrawny Earthan girl again, shivering into her shawl despite the lantern's heat.

"What. Are. You?" demanded Anders.

The girl pushed herself to her feet. "I have existed for so long that not even I remember. I am simply whatever I am needed to be." Her features melted back into the faceless creature with the round mouth full of teeth. This was her true form, I guessed.

"I summoned you to my home. I sensed that you needed a place to hide, and I knew only an innocent face that you could trust would lure you here." She shuffled over to a row of shelves. How she knew where to step without eyes, I wasn't sure. "So that was what I became. And now I sense that you are in need of something more . . . valuable? I can help there too."

"What do you mean?" I asked.

"You are in search of a treasure chest, correct?"

Wren gasped. "You have one of the keys here?"

The creature shook her head. "I do not. Although I do have a clue." She rummaged around in one of the boxes, extracting a silver cube the size of my fist. "You will have to decipher it. And you, Cora Saros . . ." She turned to me, and my breath caught. "I sense that you are eager to pick through my possessions."

Warily, I took a step toward the shelves lining the edges of the bunker. There was scrap metal galore, far more than what I'd found in the *Starchaser*'s lab. Wires and microchips and a chest full of tubes of liquid mercury. It was tough to be certain without digging through all the shelves, but I suspected there were enough materials to build a few mediocre bombs, a few stun grenades. I was apprehensive of hoping that there might be enough supplies to rebuild my old phaser and visual enhancement device, but my mind was still whirling with the possibilities. We needed to get off Tunerth without getting caught. If I had the correct tools, I could make that happen.

Elio tugged on my sleeve. "Cora, you're drooling."

"Sorry." I turned back to the creature. If I was really nice to her, then maybe she would help us. "Do you have a name? Is there anything we can call you?"

The creature smiled. At least that's what I thought it was. There were certainly a lot of teeth involved. "Mieku," she said.

"Great. Mieku, we would love to take a look at the cube you have there. And if you don't mind me poking around your shelves, that would be wonderful. We need to get off this outpost as soon as possible and—"

"I understand what you seek." Mieku licked her lips. "I can see into your hearts, into your minds. I see all that you have hidden from each other."

Oh boy. I stared straight ahead, forcing back the embarrassed flush that seemed determined to creep up my neck. On either side of me, I felt Wren and Elio shift uncomfortably, but neither said a word. Anders locked his jaw and stood with his back straight, as always.

Mieku's grin widened. "As you wish, I will keep that knowledge to myself. Since my birth, it has been my duty to provide any service that is required of me."

Wren reached forward. "Cool. So . . . the cube?"

"Will be yours. As will any supplies you deem necessary. For a price."

"Excellent!" Wren started digging through her bag. "If there is one language I speak, it's money."

"I don't want your money," said Mieku.

"What scary green alien doesn't want money? *Everyone* wants money."

Mieku rolled the cube in one hand before hiding it in the folds of her shawl. I wanted to lunge for it, but the memory of the python wrapped around my chest kept me rooted to the spot. "I deal in something far more valuable than money," she said.

"Food?" Elio suggested.

Mieku laughed, though it sounded more like a cough. "Life."

"Great," said Wren. "So we made it all this way to die."

"Of course not." She held a hand to her heart. "Do you think I am a monster?"

Well . . .

Mieku stepped closer. "I am interested in conserving life; therefore, I will only take a bit. And my senses tell me that there is one of you here who has just the right amount to give." She took one more languorous step across the cellar. Then, to my immense horror, she bent down.

"Hello, Elio. It is a pleasure to meet you."

17

"NO!" I JUMPED IN FRONT OF ELIO, KNOCKING HIM BACK against Anders's legs. "You can't touch him. You want life? Take it from the rest of us. Take it from Wren!"

"Do not take it from Wren!" Wren yelled back.

"No treasure is given freely," Mieku said, straightening up. "Each one steals something precious in return."

"Well, in that case, we don't need you." I stomped toward the ramp leading out of the cellar. "We appreciate you trying to help, but we'll get off this outpost another way. We'll find the keys another way."

"Cora!" Anders shouted.

"No!" I was halfway up the ramp. The hatch gleamed like a beacon at the top. "Do not make a bargain with that thing. Come on, we can find a way back to the ship. I'll find some scrap metal, build us some bombs to use as distractions and—"

"Cora."

I halted. This time it was Elio's voice, feeble. But when I turned around he was standing with his hands on his hips, determination written into each of his wires, each corroded metal panel.

"I think we should do this."

"What?" I bounded back down the ramp and clutched his arm. "Are you insane?"

"Maybe. But I want to help. Mieku won't take everything." His expression fell as he glanced at the faceless alien hovering behind him. "W-will you?"

"I will try not to. It is not my intention to cause you harm."

"Well, that's exactly what you would be doing!" I said. "His memory core is already malfunctioning."

"I understand the situation."

"Do you? Then take me instead. Take the life from me instead!" My voice cracked. All my energy, all my life force or whatever Mieku believed in, was ready to leap from me and devour the creature whole for even suggesting that Elio sacrifice himself more than he already had.

"Cora, breathe." Anders was at my side, his fingers twitching like he wanted to comfort me, but he didn't know how.

"They can't have him," I stressed. I couldn't lose Elio. Not yet. I hadn't prepared myself to say goodbye yet. "Take someone else."

Mieku shook her head. A strange mist hung in the air between her and Elio. If I listened closely, the mist almost sounded like it was whispering Elio's name. "I will try not to kill him, but he is the one I want. He is the only way I will give you what you seek." She licked her rotted lips. "I told you I was not a monster, Cora Saros, but I never said I was kind."

"Do it," Elio said before I had a chance to speak. He thrust his chin in the air. "If this is the only way we can get home, then I can take it." He reached out, the tips of his fingers brushing the back of my hand. "And if something happens, you'll fix me, Cora. You always do."

Oh, Elio. Sweet, stupid, brave Elio. I loved him dearly.

He had too much faith in me.

Next to Mieku, the cloud of mist grew denser, twirling like a cyclone. At the creature's command, it darted forward, down Elio's throat. Wren jumped when his body hit the ground with a metallic clang. I held back my terror for Elio's well-being, focusing only on my hatred for the monster standing before us. If that thing killed Elio, I didn't care how many pythons tried to strangle me—I would rip Mieku limb from limb.

"It's okay," Elio said. "It just tickles the wires in my tummy a little—*beep*!"

Mieku's long fingers pawed around in the folds of her shawl before pulling out the cube and tossing it to Anders. "As promised." With a nod to me, she gestured toward the towering shelves. "Make yourself at home."

I'd never worked so fast. I ripped down scraps of metal and arranged them on the floor while the mist thickened, forming a bridge between Elio and Mieku. The creature claimed she could provide any service that was required of her, and I supposed that little talent extended to the bunker as well. I found all my usual tinkering supplies on the shelves, from diamond-edge tools to nuts and bolts in various sizes to my favorite three-pronged, four-millimeter cable. But for all the strange powers that Mieku possessed, it seemed like a cruel twist of fate that the thing I truly sought could not simply be plucked from a magic shelf. I needed all of us to leave this outpost alive, though unless I got myself in gear and worked harder, that wasn't going to happen.

A cluster of pythons slithered around our feet, a warning should we try to attack Mieku, but they didn't touch us, and frankly I was too busy to care. I located a blowtorch hidden inside a tool chest and fired it up, dodging sparks.

I managed to knock out two VEDs in about an hour—they were only advanced versions of holograms, using light beams to cycle through a variety of photos to obscure the wearer's appearance. Simple stuff. We would need disguises to make it back to the landing bays and the *Starchaser*. I started on the phaser next. That one would prove much harder. Molecular manipulation wasn't something I could accomplish under duress.

"How do you feel, Elio?" I asked gently.

He beeped. "I'm . . . sleepy."

"Don't close your eyes." I threw a glare at Mieku. "Didn't you take enough?"

"Not yet." She curled her fingers into a fist. The cloud of mist, which I suspected was the power from Elio's memory core, intensified.

"Anders?" I called. "What's in the cube?"

He grunted from across the bunker. "Wren and I are looking at it."

"It's a poem," Wren answered. "And not a very good one."

"A poem?" I stripped two yellow wires before twisting them and cutting off the ends. "How quaint."

I worked through the night. I didn't stop to eat, I didn't stop to sleep, I barely stopped to breathe. I had tunnel vision for Elio, who grew weaker as the minutes ticked into hours. He had fallen to the floor, lying on his side, his eyes flickering in slow, blue pulses that lit up the bunker. Every so often I would catch his eye, and he would offer up a weak smile. But then his gaze would slide out of focus and the only response I could come up with was to grab my blowtorch and light a damn piece of metal on fire, not caring how many burns I accrued on my hands in the process.

Time felt stagnant. But as Elio grew more lethargic, it was also moving entirely too fast.

When dawn started to creep over the streets outside the cellar door, I was delirious from exhaustion and had managed to craft two VEDs, one halfway decent phaser, and about a dozen grenades and minor bombs. I pushed myself to my feet, my hands covered with burns and nicks, just as the final bit of the mist cloud was sucked from Elio's body into Mieku. Rushing across the bunker, I helped Elio up. He was still sentient, but he couldn't stand on his own.

"Safe travels." Mieku ran her tongue over her jagged teeth before transforming once again into the tiny Earthan girl. I wasn't imagining it when I noticed her eyes looked brighter this time around, her cheeks filled with a rosy tint of energy stolen from Elio's memory core.

"I have one thing to say to you," Wren told Mieku. She raised her fist and, with a glare, saluted the creature with her middle finger. "That's it."

Wren and I strapped the enhancers to our chests, taking on the appearance of two slouching, elderly Martians, while Anders once again adopted his Earthan disguise. I pushed Mieku and the hellish bunker from my mind as we traversed the mostly empty streets, passing food carts and shops not yet open for the day, back to the landing bays. The faceless alien had been vile, but she had given us the means we needed to craft a plan and escape. Once we got back to the *Starchaser*, I would hook Elio up to the control panel to recharge, and all would be well again.

"This is either madness or absolute genius," Anders said as he met back up with us, now two grenades lighter than he'd been ten minutes ago.

"Since when is there a difference?" Wren asked. She shepherded Elio, his head and shoulders hidden by a blanket that I'd stolen from the cellar, down the sidewalk. "Cora, is this really going to work?"

I'd given them a run-through of the plan I'd devised while in the throes of sleep deprivation, but I made no guarantees it was a good one. "If these leeches are still hunting us, then they'll be waiting at the landing bays. We need to make them run back into town."

"And so your solution is to *blow up* the landing bays? I swear, if you destroy my ship—"

"Stun grenades aren't destructive. But the initial blast will make the mob think they are. The ones who don't fall down disoriented will run back into town, away from the bays. That's when we make our move."

"And it's also when I make mine." Anders patted a small lump in his jacket pocket. The quickest and most colorful explosive I'd ever crafted. At the next intersection, he veered off toward a cobbled side street leading to the water tower at the edge of town. "Wish me luck?"

"Don't die," I told him.

He shrugged. "Good enough."

Wren and I hurried on, propping Elio's tiny but heavy body between us. Every minute or so he would beep, but he was otherwise silent.

"Did you and Anders figure out the clue in the cube?" I whispered to Wren, averting my eyes as a group with corkscrew horns passed us in the opposite direction. But they didn't spare us a glance. Our disguises were solid.

Wren snorted. "Hardly. It's a nursery rhyme. I'll show you when we get back to the ship."

We stopped in the shadow of a run-down consignment shop a block from the landing bays. Just as I suspected, a crowd now dominated the tarmac. It looked like the patrons from the Fuzzy Lizard had gathered their friends—and their friends' friends—all desperate to collect the bounty. Ships were parked this way and that, squeezed two or three deep in the stalls. Waiting for us.

As intended, the warden's message had reached every corner of the universe. Well, that was fine. More people to witness the show we were about to give them.

Across the tarmac, a man with flaming red hair—their leader, it seemed—weaved through the masses, firing them up. He screamed that we needed to be brought to justice, and the crowd was all too happy to echo his cries. The horde of bodies rippled like a wave across the bays, the dented hull of the *Starchaser* looming in the center.

If the mob wanted to be authentic, then they should have dug up some torches and pitchforks to greet us with. You know, really make the effort to appear hospitable.

"Whazgoinon?" Elio garbled, leaning heavily against me.

I stroked his ears. "Don't worry. We're safe. Just trust me."

He snuggled closer. "'Course I trust you . . . Carla."

Carla. My heart hammered. We needed to move. Now.

The shouts across the tarmac grew fiercer, the crowd spewing a number of derogatory comments about us as they called for our demise. Anders, the barbarian. Wren, a thief, a liar, a traitor to her planet. Elio, just a pile of wires, not even worthy of a name. And me, a con artist, a gutter rat.

A distraction. Evelina's voice filled my head. I pushed it away, spinning my new phaser in the palm of my free hand. "I really hope this thing works."

Wren raised an eyebrow. "And if it doesn't?"

"We run like hell." I pulled out my comm, tapped the screen once, twice, and . . .

BOOM!

Somewhere in the throng, the first grenade that Anders had planted went off. The ground vibrated. A blast of light and a plume of smoke filled the air at the northern end of the bays, five ships down from ours.

"Move!" I shoved Wren in the back. Operation Escape-Tunerth-Without-Dying was a go.

We shuffled out of the shadows, dodging dozens of bodies as we dragged Elio across the tarmac. Some had collapsed, knocked unconscious. Others were dazed and wavering, their gazes vacant after the sudden exposure to such a bright flare of light. My enhancer pulled sharply against my chest as I yanked Elio around the port of a bullet-shaped pod ship, out of the path of a man stumbling toward us with his eyes shut tight. He tripped over another man's legs and sprawled across the ground.

Those who hadn't been rendered incapacitated from the blast sprinted for town, egged on by Wren. "The bad guys are coming! The bad guys are coming!" she shrieked as a group ran past us. "Save yourselves!"

"You're enjoying this way too much," I said. We shoved plugs into our ears right before I tapped my comm again, and then . . .

BOOM!

More shrieks rent the air as the mob ran for cover. Wren and I jerked Elio out of their path, and we rolled across the tarmac, kicking up gravel. My chin hit the ground with a crack. Wren groaned beside me, clutching her wrist.

Looking up, I noticed the small black eye of a security monitor shining from the pole of a nearby floodlight. I gave the tech a sneer, paired with my best attempt at the stink eye, just in case the warden was watching on the other side.

There. How's that for entertainment?

Around us, ships whirred to life and took off for the exit hatch in Tunerth's outer dome. We rolled back the other way, narrowly missing a spurt of flames as an engine backfired beside us. As planned, the landing bays were emptying out, leaving our path to the *Starchaser* clearer than before, but there were still a handful of people scattered across the tarmac, sheltered beneath hulls of ships and inside the doors of the fueling station.

Their frightened auras rumbled across the outpost in clouds of citrine, leaving the air crackling with spikes of electricity. The force of it was so strong, seeping into my skin as it dribbled out of theirs, that I doubled over, my breath stolen. Wren grabbed my arm and pulled me forward. The *Starchaser* was so close now that I could count the cracks lining each porthole.

Great fissures spread across the cement at the sound of another explosion. At the end of the landing bay, a cargo ship detonated. We hit the tarmac, covering our heads as flaming debris rained through the air. Rainbows of oil ran like rivers over the slick ground, beautiful but terrifying in the midst of the chaos.

It took me a moment to realize what was happening as I propped myself up on my elbows, my thoughts muddled. What *was* that? The plan I engineered only involved two blasts. And the grenades I detonated created light and noise only, not destruction. Which meant . . .

That hadn't been one of my grenades.

"Duck!" Wren leaped on top of Elio at the sound of three more ships going up in smoke. Whoever had come armed with their own bombs was getting closer.

Okay. It was *way* past time to get off this rock.

I slapped the phaser on the underside of the *Starchaser*'s cargo hold. We couldn't risk opening the ramp. It would take too long and provide too much opportunity for someone to stow away inside.

I powered on the phaser, quietly cheering as a row of red lights lit up along the top. A rusty panel on the underside of the hull blurred and gave way to the inside of the cargo hold just as a volley of blaster fire lit up the air.

"Elio first." I lifted the left side of his sluggish body toward the gap the phaser had created. The panel rippled, like a mirror turned liquid. Wren rushed to grab Elio's other side.

"Oh stars," she grunted under his weight. "What is this little guy made of? Lead?"

Sweating and swearing, we raised him above our heads. We had him halfway into the hole when the light from a dozen blasters soared over us. With a resounding *bang*, they connected with the side of our ship, punching holes in the wings and the hull, sending sharp hunks of metal flying at our heads. Wren and I lost our footing. We crashed down hard, Elio landing on top of us.

Sitting up, I rubbed at my head. Where was Anders? He should have been back by now. I was shocked and embarrassed to find my chest tight with something that felt a lot like worry.

"Wren!" I pulled at her sleeve. She had been hit, though I didn't know with what. Ships were going up in flames left and right across the bays, so there was an awful lot to choose from. She was unconscious, but still breathing.

Her VED had detached from her chest and deactivated in the fall. So had mine. Grabbing both, I chucked them up into the cargo hold. Our true faces were visible now, but ideally not for much longer. Wren's purple hair was streaked with blood from a cut near her temple. Between us, Elio's eyes flickered like strobe lights. Glitching. Again.

How would I lift all of us into the ship?

Behind us, a column of smoke and fire twisted, engulfing the entirety of Tunerth, turning it to ash. Anders was in there somewhere. I couldn't get us all into the ship without his help, but if I stayed and waited for him . . .

He might never come out.

Muscles burning, I dragged Elio toward the cargo hold. I balanced him against my hip, but that was as far as I could lift him.

Tears stung my eyes. We were trapped here, doomed. The warden had won.

"Cora!"

I spun around. Skies above, I hadn't been so happy to see the big red jerk in, well . . . *ever.*

Anders vaulted over a pile of smoldering metal and rubber, arms pumping as he charged across the landing bay. He tackled me just as a round of blaster fire glanced off the side of the ship, not three feet from the top of my head.

"Nice to see you're not dead," I wheezed, his elbow digging into my sternum.

He stood, pulling me up. "It's nice to see that I'm not dead too."

"No, this is the part where you say, 'It's splendid that you're still alive, Cora. For whatever would I do without you?'"

"Mmmph." He fiddled with his comm, and then the hulking water tower across the outpost released four blasts of shimmery gold sparks. Fireworks that I'd crafted and that he had set up around the base. The first burst formed a perfect outline of Anders's head. The next three formed Elio, Wren, and finally, me.

Not to brag, but it was the best dynamite artwork I'd ever done.

The fireworks were meant to be another distraction, a grand finale while we escaped the outpost, but now, with the fire and fiasco surrounding us, I doubted anyone even noticed.

Until a fifth, surprise blast rocked the water tower.

Slack-jawed, Anders and I turned to each other.

"That . . . wasn't supposed to happen," he said. "Was it?"

I shook my head, breathless, fearful. "Nope."

18

THE TOWER CREAKED, QUAKING ON THE HORIZON. ALL AT once, the top erupted. A geyser shot into the air, rushing into town, flooding the streets as people ran for cover. The deluge put out the fires, but not even the roar of the water could eclipse the screams.

"I think now would be a good time to leave," I said. The water was slowing as it reached the landing bays, but there was still enough to cause some damage. *Great*. Because that last explosion had been paired with the outlines of our faces, the entire universe was going to think we were responsible. I'd meant for the fireworks to be funny. Now someone would use them to frame us for all the destruction that had been caused, and I had a hunch who it would be: the same man who had sent a group of guards to track us and bomb the landing bays.

We were going to be blamed for all of this. *More* people would be hunting us. *More* would want us dead. And the warden would be even more entertained.

I located the nearest security monitor and flashed a very crude hand gesture, hoping he was watching.

As the water continued to flow, Anders hoisted Wren and Elio into the cargo hold. He offered me a leg up before climbing in after me. I deactivated the phaser, solidifying the metal panels and returning the ship to its former state.

We crammed into the lift and rushed to the cockpit. Anders tenderly placed Elio and Wren on the floor, strapping them both down. Elio was still glitching, and Wren was still unconscious.

I tapped the side of her face, hoping to wake her. Even if I could, she was probably concussed. Not in any shape to operate a spacecraft. Then again, neither was I. The *Starchaser* wasn't my pod ship. The size of the control panel alone could eat my pod ship's for breakfast.

"We need to move. *Now*. You need to fly this thing." Anders hopped into the co-pilot's chair. More blaster fire lit up the tarmac, slamming into the front viewport.

"Excuse me?" Maybe I hadn't heard him right over the crackling flames and rumbling engines. I couldn't fly a charter ship.

"You'll have to fly it," he repeated.

"I don't know how to fly this thing!" I yelled, hysterical. "When did I ever say I knew how to fly this thing?"

His eyes went wide with terror. "I just assumed—"

"Why can't *you* fly it? You were in the military!"

"Yes. But I shot things. It was someone else's job to fly!"

"Oh, Saturn's rings." I took in the dozens of holes speckled along the hull. Would this thing even fly? I didn't have time to make any repairs, but what was the worst that could happen? Death? We were already close enough to that.

I glanced out the viewport. Dozens of ships that had escaped the bombing hovered in Tunerth's atmosphere directly above us, attempting to barricade us in. To collect the bounty on our heads.

Not going to happen.

"Well. It's worth a try," I muttered, approaching Wren's buttery leather captain's chair. I hadn't noticed it before, but she had doodled on the armrests in purple ink, random shapes and names of people that I didn't recognize. One said *Marcus* in looping script. A boyfriend? Not that it mattered. But I was nervous, and I was stalling.

Sitting in her seat without permission felt like crossing an invisible line. Of all the ways that I'd planned on betraying her, somehow this seemed like the worst.

I sat anyway.

My sweaty hands formed a death grip on the controls. Left hand on the yaw, right hand on the thrusters, feet on the rudder pedals. Just like I'd seen Wren do.

The engines fired. We jerked off the ground way too fast, tilting to our starboard side without meaning to. We shot directly into the crowd of ships above us, which scattered as we catapulted toward the exit hatch.

"Oh stars, oh stars, oh stars . . ." Anders clenched his armrests.

"Put your harness on, Andy!" I tried to right the ship, but I overcompensated and sent us soaring in the opposite direction, through a cloud of smoke above the center of the outpost.

"The exit hatch is the other way," Anders pointed out unhelpfully.

"Don't be a backseat driver!"

"Well, this is a bit of a dire situation . . ." Outside the viewport, the ships had formed a cluster. They realized I was a poor flyer. They were going to force us back to the ground. Out of the corner of my eye, I noticed the tail of a sleek silver ship painted with a twelve-pointed star. Anders sucked in a breath.

"That's an Andilly military ship. The warden is taking no chances."

"Well, neither are we. How do I get this thing in a higher gear?"

"Blue lever?" he suggested.

"I thought you couldn't fly." I pulled the lever and jammed my feet down on the corresponding blue pedal. We shot forward, toward the exit. Inertia slammed me into my seat. I released a giddy yelp.

"I can't," he replied. "Blue is my favorite color. It was a lucky guess. I just as easily could have killed us."

"I'm loving your optimism, Anders, but we aren't dying today." I was starting to get the hang of this. Blue lever and pedal to move up a gear, yellow to move down. Pink spun the ship all the way around in a counterclockwise circle, green put us into a barrel roll. The thruster and the yaw were the same as my pod ship's. So was the radar display, which was quickly filling up with dozens of tiny blips as more and more ships flew closer to Tunerth—and to us.

"I'm going to be sick!" Anders clutched his mouth.

"If you throw up now, I will murder you," I growled.

We turned on our side, zipping between two larger charter ships as I raced for the exit hatch. Instantly, they turned and gave chase. Another ship tried cutting us off, but I slammed the yellow lever and pedal, dropping a gear, and ducked underneath it. Then blue again as we accelerated, flying higher, dodging the light from more blasters.

"I don't like this," Anders muttered. "I don't like this, I don't like this—"

"Wimp," I grumbled as we came up on the exit hatch. I didn't know if it would open for us, or if it had been locked down. I would crash right through it if I had to.

But by some miracle it *did* open. Both the inner and the outer doors. We cleared Tunerth's dome and hit open space with half an armada trailing behind us.

"We need to find a wormhole." My fingers flew over the controls. "If we time it right, it'll close and no one will be able to follow."

Anders studied the blinking radar display while I rolled the ship portside to dodge a screaming missile. *Oh, yippee. Somebody brought the big guns.*

"Our best wormhole option opens in forty-five seconds. It closes point-five-one seconds later."

Saturn's rings. I'd never made a jump that fast.

"Where does it lead?"

Another missile. Starboard side. It crossed the path of a third one and they exploded. I changed gears, cut the thrusters, and the *Starchaser* dropped like a rock to avoid the blast.

Unfortunately, half of the ships following us did the same.

"Rebrone," said Anders. "Desert planet. Triangulum Galaxy."

"Ugh, I hate that galaxy. But fine, yes, guide me there."

Anders swiped the screen in front of his seat, sending coordinates over to my radar display.

I'd barely had a chance to glance at them when something smashed into our stern, sending us spinning. Nose over tail over nose over—*oh great*. Andy really was going to barf now.

As I fought to right the ship, my eyes darted over the monitors on the control panel. It wasn't a missile that hit us; if it had, we'd be dead. What was it, then? What was it—*there*! A small, fuzzy monitor above my fuel gauge showed the Andilly combat ship, weapons lining the hull. Trained on us.

"They won't shoot, will they?" But just as the words left my lips, blaster fire slammed into the stern. The *Starchaser* let out a groan, and the lights and screens around us flickered.

"Shoot back!" said Anders.

"With what? The imaginary missile launcher that I keep stashed in my pocket? This is a charter ship, Andy, not a fighter jet. It doesn't have guns!"

The military craft crashed into our portside wing. I watched on the monitors as more light beams battered the hull. Oh man, Wren was *not* going to be happy when she woke up.

Another power surge flashed through the cockpit.

"I think they hit something vital," Anders said.

"You think?"

"Engine power is dropping!" he yelled, pointing at the screens. "Forty-seven percent and falling on the main engine. The auxiliary isn't far behind. Can you fix it?"

"I don't know if you noticed, but I'm a little busy right now." The monitors were confirming my worst fears. Dodging ships was putting too much pressure on the engines. If they went down, eventually we'd be dragged back into Tunerth's gravitational pull, and then, with nothing holding us in the air . . . a crash would be inevitable.

My hands slipped on the controls.

Not today. We would not die today.

I cranked the yaw to starboard just as several more ships and a cluster of asteroids cropped up in the viewport.

"How much longer until the wormhole opens?" I demanded, willing my voice not to crack.

A brief expression crossed Anders's face. Fear, maybe? Without an aura, I couldn't be sure. "Twenty-nine seconds."

"I can't keep this up. They're chasing us in circles!"

"What if . . . ?" He studied the radar. "What if we head for a different wormhole?"

"What do you mean?"

He tapped the screens, brow furrowed, one hand clamped over his mouth while I forced the ship to duck and roll. "Ten seconds. Twelve degrees portside. It's coming up in two kilometers."

"Where does it lead?"

"Monocerotis."

A frustrated scream ripped from my throat. "You mean the *black hole*?"

"We'll be fine. Just trust me. Can you do that?"

Trust him. Could I? A week ago, I would have said without a shred of doubt that I absolutely could *not*. And yet now . . . after everything . . .

Either I risked the black hole, or the engines failed and we died anyway. Trust or no trust, we were out of options and short on time.

Off in the distance, the wormhole shimmered into view.

Two more missiles soared past the viewport. One connected with another ship, exploding in a ball of fire. The second flew off into oblivion.

Trust me.

"This isn't some elaborate plan to kill me, is it?"

Anders snorted. "If that were the case, I would have let the porci eat you back on Cadrolla." He reached over and took hold of the throttle. "I'll take care of this. You just pull up on my command. I believe this is called teamwork, yes? Ready?"

"Not in the slightest."

"Good. Let's do it."

I was squeezing the controls so tightly I felt they would be permanently etched into my skin. The ball of the wormhole grew brighter. The ships behind us roared louder.

"Three!" Anders slammed the throttle forward. "Two!"

But we were getting too close. The light emanating from the wormhole had taken over the entire viewport. There was no way we could dodge it. We would get sucked inside. Me and Anders . . . Wren and Elio, who wouldn't even be awake to see the end . . .

"One!" Anders shouted. "Now, Cora! Now!"

Screaming my throat raw, I jammed the gears three notches, pitching the *Starchaser* up at a vertical angle. We arched above the wormhole, just centimeters away from entering its grasp. The string of ships behind us hadn't anticipated a change in direction so suddenly. They zipped inside, one by one. Freighters and private cruisers, never to be seen again. Only the Andilly combat ship had the sense to pull up, veering into the path of an asteroid belt. Though instead of circling back to attack again, the ship righted itself and quickly soared off into the blue-black depths of space.

Beneath us, the wormhole snapped shut.

My hands shook against the controls. My heartbeat drummed heavily in my ears.

Anders broke the silence. "Did . . . you . . . *see that*?" A smile cut across his face as he leaned forward to look at me over the console. I couldn't answer him. I was in shock. Every time I blinked, I saw the flash of light obliterating the ships.

There was no way any of them could have escaped a black hole. We doomed them. And I knew I shouldn't have cared; they were doing the same to us. But still. We doomed them.

Slowly, I spun the ship around and headed for the wormhole to Rebronc and the Triangulum Galaxy.

Anders wouldn't shut up. How unlike him. "Cora, did you *see* that? Did you? For once I'm almost sad Wren is indisposed. She would have loved that!"

"Do you think?" I managed a quick glance over my shoulder, then wished I hadn't. Elio was still glitching. Wren was still unconscious, her chest moving with quick pants, hair sodden with blood. "What we just did was horrifying and reckless and . . . *stars*. You're right. She would have loved it."

"As I stated." He extended his hand, palm facing outward. "Hey. Is this called a five high?"

"High five." Hand still twitching with residual terror, I slapped mine against his. "But I applaud your eff—"

An alarm blared from the control panel, a deafening reminder that the engines were still failing.

Oh. Right.

We were coming up on the new wormhole fast. A turquoise swirl of light the size of a pinprick, bulging larger in preparation to open. We only had a few seconds left before making the jump.

If the engines could even handle a jump.

We both swore as the control panel lit up red with a string of warning messages. The alarm grew louder, followed by a disturbingly pleasant automated voice.

"Primary Engine System: OFFLINE. Secondary Engine System: SHUTTING DOWN in eleven seconds . . . Ten seconds . . . Nine . . ."

Gulping, I looked over to Anders. His grin had vanished, his face a warrior's mask of calm. But I noticed his claws had come out, slicing into his armrests.

"Say, Cora?" His voice started out steady, but then it started to shake. The *entire ship* started to shake. "I think you might need to fly a little faster."

"Right." My own voice didn't have the strength to surpass a whisper. "Faster. Right."

"Six seconds . . . Five . . ."

I punched down on every single lever, switch, and knob at my disposal. *Faster, faster. Please go faster.* The thrusters whined. The eye of the wormhole was right in front of us, growing wider, the door to the next galaxy opening with a—

Something smashed into our auxiliary engine.

"*What in the stars*?" Anders yelled. The impact sent us into a screaming tailspin toward the wormhole. Outside the viewport, twin flames flared from the engine columns. Anders tried grabbing the controls to steady the ship, but it was no use. The engines were shot. The light of the wormhole wrapped around us, dragging us backward to the other side.

Right before we disappeared, I noticed the shadow of a new pod ship hovering just outside the wormhole's grasp. Whether it had fired something at our engines or simply rammed into us, I didn't know, but it made no move to chase us now. Unusual. Even more unusual—the pod ship was unmarked except for a crescent-shaped dent on the front bumper.

My breath turned to ice in my lungs. As much as I tried forgetting about it, I recognized that dent.

I'd made it, two months ago, while parking the pod in front of a streetlight behind my house. And now it was here.

Evelina's ship was here.

"Keep us out of Rebrone's gravitational pull!" Anders shouted as the wormhole spit us out.

Too late. The desert planet hung directly below us, far too close for comfort. We were moving fast, faster than I'd ever jumped galaxies before. With both engines down, there was no stopping us. We were coming in hot.

We torpedoed through Rebrone's atmosphere. Even though we were seconds away from a fiery death, I couldn't stop myself from thinking: *Evelina came. Evelina found you.*

I hadn't heard from her in over a week. But, of course, it only took one announcement of the bounty on our heads for her to finally show.

And then she attacked us.

I wished I could say I was shocked.

All around us, flames engulfed the ship. Next to me, Anders's head was ducked, hands clasped. He was murmuring something that sounded like a prayer.

I took one last look back at Wren and Elio. I couldn't fail them. I couldn't fail *us*.

I studied the altitude gauge above the radar display, needle hovering deep in the red zone. Then I yelled to Anders, "Release the antigravity stabilizer!"

He just looked at me. "The *what*?"

"The parachute!" I screeched. "The yellow valve! *Twist the yellow valve*!"

"Oh. Well, next time just say that."

He deployed the chute. I yanked up hard on the controls, gears groaning beneath us, but it was useless. Like everything else on this shoddy ship, the parachute was too old to function properly.

Below us, the planet's land mass was rising up, eager to crush us in its jaws.

Just before impact, I felt a sudden weight in the palm of my hand. Anders's fingers, threading through mine. Squeezing. He sucked in a breath.

Sand filled the viewport.

We hit the ground hard.

19

I NEVER REALIZED HOW STICKY BLOOD WAS UNTIL I WAS covered in it.

I felt it everywhere. Streaked along my neck, crusted in my eyelashes, a few spots stuck to the tip of my nose. Rubbing my hand over my skin, I opened my eyes just a fraction. The fluorescent lights of the *Starchaser*'s med bay shone down on me. I tried sitting up, but my head swam painfully, and I slumped back down. The med bay was nothing more than a glorified supply closet with a cot shoved in the corner, but it was still here. Still standing. Meaning the ship was standing too.

We made it.

"Don't jump up on my account," a low voice laughed from the sink beside the door. Anders was there, running a torn strip of cloth underneath the water. He squeezed out the excess and came to kneel at the side of the cot.

Looking past him, I noticed the cabinets on the walls had been thrown open, supplies strewn across the floor. Scissors and bandages and broken glass vials filled with multicolored pills. They must have been knocked down during the landing. Actually, *crash* was a more apt term.

Oh, no. *The key*. I gripped my chest, faking a coughing fit. *Thank the stars*. It was still there, the metal chain and Teolia's key still pressed into my skin. Still safe. Relief surged through me, and I let my body relax into the cot.

"We're alive." I winced when Anders applied the cloth to my forehead, wiping away the blood. "Are we *all* alive?"

"Barely, but yes," he muttered. "Stop twitching. You're going to aggravate that concussion of yours."

"Concussion?" Oh, right. Achy head. That made sense.

"I'm assuming that's what happened. You hit your head hard on the control panel when we landed. And then you puked." His eyes narrowed. "All over my boots."

Heat filled my cheeks. "Sorry? I don't remember any of that."

"I thought not. Just don't do it again." He winked. "I'm quite fond of these boots."

When he stood to rinse out the rag, it became apparent that I wasn't the only one who was injured. His gait leaned to the side, right foot dragging as he limped across the med bay. He had removed his jacket and only wore a thin undershirt that had been ripped in several places, spots of dried blood staining the white fabric brown.

He crouched back down beside me. His face and neck were covered with scrapes. I shuddered when I saw that a large patch of scales along his jaw had been pulled up and were now dangling by just a hairbreadth of skin.

Before he could protest, I snatched the rag from him and started mopping up the blood that had dribbled down to his chin. Two leathery red scales fell to the floor.

"How . . . How did we not die?"

"We hit a particularly fluffy sand dune," he said. "You should see the outside of the ship. She's a mess, the engines are a mess, but the fires went out. The electricity stayed on. Divine intervention, if you believe in that sort of thing."

"Do you?"

Anders shrugged. "We're mildly religious on Andilly."

"What does 'mildly religious' mean?"

"A lot of talk about the importance of treating others with mercy, but that usually manifests in ways like . . . oh I don't know, murdering citizens quickly as opposed to torturing them. You've seen what my planet is like." He took my hand in a gentle grip, pulling the cloth away.

Oh no. With the rag in my hand, I'd felt like I was fulfilling a duty. If I was helping him clean up, then I was too preoccupied to notice how close his face had gotten to mine. Or the sweat on his skin, or the stray eyelash that had fallen and was stuck to his cheek. Until now, I hadn't noticed that the ship's usual humming had ceased. There was just the sound of our breaths, and the overwhelming joy of still finding ourselves alive after being so certain we were about to die.

It was funny, actually. On Tunerth, I'd thought I preferred Anders's true face over his Earthan disguise. I was wrong.

I hated them both.

I hated them both, because . . . no matter his appearance, I liked him.

I was completely sober this time, and I could still confidently say that . . . I liked him.

Stars above, this was *bad*.

Anders wet the rag again and started cleaning off a stripe of blood on the palm of my hand. He kneaded the pads of my fingers, scraped underneath the nails, until all evidence from the crash had washed away. Something about the intensity and care with which he worked felt more intimate than if he had grabbed my face and planted a kiss on me.

This was *horrible*.

When he finished, he looked up and gave me a smile and a goofy little shrug. For the first time since I woke, I noticed something strange.

"You're not holding back your aura anymore."

Relief, a frothy minty green, spilled off his shoulders. He tossed the dirty rag in the sink, then sank back on his haunches.

"It was just a stupid military tactic they taught me. Good for stealth, bad for . . . I don't know. Life, I suppose. I've been thinking that maybe keeping everything bottled up all the time isn't worth it anymore."

"Funny. I've been thinking the same." Only it didn't matter if my secrets and lies were worth it or not. I would keep doing all the wrong things for all the right reasons—or *my* right reasons. It was the Saros family way. "Is it bad to admit that I kind of like that you're finally going soft?"

The swirl of colors around him vanished. "I'm not—Cora, I'm not *soft*."

I laughed. "You have a gentle soul. Deep down inside, you're a giant teddy bear."

"Silence! I . . . I'm *not*—"

"Relax." I reached out to touch his shoulder. "I'm kidding."

He sputtered. "Good. Because I am a warrior. I am not . . . a bear."

"Whatever you say, Andy."

"I do say. Besides, I'm too exhausted to put effort into containing it at the moment." A bit of color leaked into the air around his shoulders. "You keep calling me Andy," he observed. "Why?"

"Oh." I felt my cheeks flush. "Sorry. It slipped out. I won't do it again."

"No, don't worry. I don't . . ." He licked his lips. "I guess I don't hate it as much as I did before. It almost makes me feel . . . nice. Like . . . how an orange lollipop makes me feel nice." He pulled two of the candies out of his pocket and waved them tantalizingly in front of my nose. "Want one?"

"Sure."

"Too bad." He stuck both in his mouth. "I already touched them, so they're mine now. Anyway, what was I saying? Oh, yes. It is a good feeling. I'm pretty sure. A feeling of belonging. It makes me . . . not want to think about dismembering bodies."

I choked on a laugh. "So . . . happy?"

"Well, there's always an element of satisfaction in a good dismemberment—"

"*Anders.*"

"Fine. Yes, Cora. I believe the term you're looking for is *happy.*" Then something shifted in his eyes, like a frightened animal caught in the underbrush, and he jumped up. "We should put salve on your cuts." He sifted through the mess of tubes and bottles on the floor. "You definitely need salve."

"*You're* definitely changing the subject, but okay." I tried to make sense of his sudden refusal to look my way. Was he *scared*? Of *me*? No one was ever scared of me.

"I asked if everyone was alive and you said 'barely.' What's that supposed to mean? How's Elio?"

He tossed me a tube of salve. "No concern for Wren? I'll make sure I tell her about that later. She'll be disappointed."

"I appreciate your newfound love of humor, but I'm starting to think I liked you better when you were predictable."

"Really? I thought you didn't like me at all." His lips curled, as if he knew the stupid, infuriating truth.

"Shut up, Andy. How is everyone?"

He deflated with a sigh. "Wren is fine. She seems to have a concussion too. Nothing she can't come back from."

"And Elio?"

Another sigh. He started picking up the first aid supplies, arranging them by size along the counter. "Wren is fine," he repeated.

"Anders." Against my better judgment, I pushed myself up. My head spun, like someone was firing a blaster inside my skull. Anders rushed over to steady me, but I didn't care. I didn't like whatever game he was playing. "How. Is. Elio."

Beep!

I jumped. "Elio!" He stood just inside the doorway, battered but *whole*. Not glitching. I couldn't believe he had managed to snap himself out of it after all the damage Mieku had caused.

Pulling away from Anders, I flung myself at him, enveloping him in the galaxy's largest hug. Elio's little hands wrapped around me, squeezing back.

Beep!

"You're okay! I mean, you *are* okay, aren't you?" I looked him up and down, just to make sure that he really, truly was all there. Anders cleared his throat behind me.

"Cora? A moment, if you don't mind?"

Beep-beep!

"Just a second. His bolts get knocked loose sometimes when he falls. With such a violent crash, I really should check . . ." I spun Elio around and pulled up the hem of his jacket to get a better look. Other than his usual wire patches, everything appeared normal.

Beep-bop!

"Where's my comm link?" I asked Anders. "I need to run a diagnostic scan on him—oh! Careful, Elio!" He had attempted to start cleaning the med bay, but he quickly tripped over a roll of bandages and tumbled to the ground.

"Cora . . ." Anders stepped forward as I helped Elio up. His claws were out again, and he chewed on the end of one nervously, eyes roving the room. "There's something you should know . . ."

"Andy, just spit it out already. Elio probably wants to go make a milkshake or some fudge or something. Right, Elio?"

Boop-beep!

At the edge of my vision, I noticed Anders wince.

Something was . . . not right. My brain was operating on half speed due to the concussion and the joy of reuniting with Elio, but it finally dawned on me that, for as chatty as Elio usually was, I was the only one doing any of the talking.

"Elio?" I knelt down in front of him. "Say something."

The sensors in his eyes widened. He clamped his ears over his face, and his hands over that. He shook his head and—*no no NO!* Every time he glitched, he forgot something, but never like this. I never thought it could be this bad.

I felt Anders kneel down beside us, his hand on my back. I shook him off.

"He hasn't said a word since we landed."

I nodded, holding back tears while Elio continued to beep. Mechanical, nonsensical sounds from my little robot who had once been so human.

"That's because he doesn't remember how to talk."

I wanted to run through the desert and bury myself inside one of the millions of sand dunes rolling outside the *Starchaser*'s doors.

Rebrone was full of them. Hills and valleys, broken up by the odd village. Looking out the porthole in the rec room, I watched heat sizzle off the sand. If I shifted my head the right way, I could see a lake two dunes away. But then I moved, and it vanished like the joke it was.

The inside of the ship was almost too hot to breathe in. The air circulation unit was still operational, but it didn't work well enough to combat the planet's extreme temperatures, and I'd need more than a few rolls of tape to fix it. My shirt stuck to my back in a puddle of sweat. My lips were dry and cracking.

But I had to stay for Elio. Maybe his faith in my abilities was misguided, but I still believed that if I could just get my hands on a fresh robotic body with a fresh memory core, I could put him back the way he was. I had to at least *try*.

And a repaired Elio couldn't come soon enough, because his new efficiency was weirding me out. Since the glitch he seemed determined to scrub and tidy up the ship, and as far as I could tell he hadn't even tried smelling the food in the galley once. When he wasn't attempting to be productive, he stood idly by, silent except for the occasional beep, observant. The humanity that Cruz and Evelina had tried to desperately rewire from his body had nearly dwindled away. He was the perfect servant robot.

"You do remember me, don't you?" I'd asked him almost immediately after we left the med bay. Elio had hurried to find my comm link and wrote out on the touch screen: ***C*** (although he accidentally drew it backward). Then ***O-R-A***.

"At least you know that much," I said as he proudly held the comm above his head. "Hang on a little longer, okay? This is just a bump in the road. Maybe a big bump . . ." A *really* big bump, considering our engines were shot, but I put on a brave face for him. "We can still fix this. Nothing is going to change, all right?"

He tilted his head, as if he could see right through my pathetic attempt at a pep talk. Then he beeped and, upon spotting the mess of overturned chairs and couches in the rec room, busied himself with trying to heave them back into their upright positions.

"Is there a reason you haven't stolen him a new memory core?" Wren asked me. We were meeting in the rec room to discuss the clue in the cube Mieku had given us. We were just waiting for Anders, who was stuck in a comm call with his father. My fists clenched, nails biting into my palms, just thinking about that man. When Elio had given me my comm back, I'd noticed the warden had sent me a message. One word: *Better*.

It was so pleasing to know that surviving multiple explosions on Tunerth, a chase through two wormholes, and a fiery crash hadn't bored him to tears. Impressing him was as strenuous as impressing Evelina.

And where was she now? She was hunting us too, and just like the warden's Andilly guards, I knew it would only be a matter of time before they all tracked us down.

"I can't just steal a new memory core," I told Wren. "They're manufactured on demand. It takes weeks to build a new android, longer for advanced models, and I plan on getting him the highest quality memory core and body possible so that this doesn't happen again."

"Well, fine." She lounged upside down on the chair beside me. Elio beeped in the corner, too preoccupied with picking up shards of glass from the broken net screen to notice we were talking about him. "Put in an order, then. Or I will, if you want."

"With what money?"

She scoffed. "What money? I can get us money. Between the two of us, *we* can get us money."

Of course, getting the money was all part of my plan, but I couldn't tell her that.

"Even if we get the money, any order we put in is going to be tracked directly to this ship. In case you're too concussed to remember, the entire universe has seen our faces. They've seen Elio's face. And we can't even run from them." I pressed my face to the porthole, watching waves of heat rise off the sand. It was going to take me ages to walk to the nearest village and search for materials to repair our engines. Until then, we were grounded.

The floor shook as Anders stomped down the ramp into the rec room. His comm had a web of cracks across the glass, most of which hadn't come from the crash, if I had to take a guess.

"I hate him." His claws were out, looking thicker and darker than I'd ever seen them. "He just spent twenty minutes bragging about the number of civilian ships scouring the galaxy around Tunerth, looking for us. As if we'd actually head back. As if there's anything to head back to."

Guilt clawed down my throat and made a home in the pit of my stomach. Those people on the outpost hadn't deserved what had happened there.

Wren flipped right side up in her chair. "Does he know where we landed?"

"Not yet." Anders briefly touched his neck where the tracking chip was embedded. "But he will soon. We need to move fast. Don't waste your breath talking about my father. Let's talk about that cursed cube." He flopped down on the couch—directly next to me. So close that the toe of his boot nudged mine while he settled himself.

Wren pulled the cube out of her pants pocket. She ran her finger over a groove on the top, and all the sides unfolded with a click, forming a sheet of metal covered in embossed lines of rich, gilded script.

"Anders, why don't you read it?" she said. "You enjoy poetry, don't you?"

He frowned. "No."

I nudged his shoulder. "He does have quite the gentle soul."

Beep! Elio said from across the room.

"See?" I said. "Elio agrees."

Anders hunched his shoulders and leaned close enough to me to mutter, "I thought the gentle soul thing was just between the two of us."

Wren cleared her throat, raising an eyebrow. "Sharing is caring, Andykins. Here, Cora, you read it. You haven't seen it yet." She flung the metal sheet like a saucer, and it spun and landed in my lap.

The edges were sharp enough to slice through my skin. I picked it up gingerly, pinching it between my index fingers and thumbs, and then read aloud the clue that Mieku had given us:

Find me near the thick of gasses.
You'll See me where the water passes.
Look Within a source of heat.
I am a place to rest Your feet.
Spirals, cliffs, the Darkness brings.
I come only when the full moon sings.

"Huh," I said once I had read it through twice. "You know, I don't think I'm a fan of poetry either."

Beep-beep! Elio took the sheet from me, twisting it this way and that. I hoped he was running some kind of net search on it—if he was still capable of that sort of thing. After a minute, he shrugged, handed the poem back to me, and returned to tidying up the rec room.

"Random words are capitalized." Anders read them aloud. "*See Within Your Darkness*. Could that be significant?"

"Who knows." I studied the poem. "It could be trying to distract us." The best cons made you look in one direction when something important was really happening in the other. And what had this entire hunt been, if not a big con organized by the warden to imprison us once again?

"Let's go line by line," said Wren. "'Find me near the thick of gasses.' So to me, that's a hint that Teolia had a serious issue with lactose intolerance."

Anders wrinkled his nose. "I highly doubt that's it."

"Excuse me, were you alive hundreds of years ago? Were you her best buddy? I don't think so."

"Were *you*?" he retorted.

"Okay, okay." I held up a hand to quiet them. "Mieku said this was a clue to find the keys, not Teolia's corpse. So we would find a *key* near the thick of gasses. We would see *another* key where the water passes. Or maybe not another key. There are only four keys, but there are more than four lines of clues."

Wren leaned forward in her seat. "So which clues go with which key? We already found a key in the water on Cadrolla. That's one down."

"The warden said the first key came from Jupiter's moon," said Anders. "That satisfies the gaseous line."

"The next line is a heat source." I scanned the poem again. "A . . .

sun?" Maybe it was too simple a suggestion. But weren't the simplest things the most effective?

Wren scowled. "I am *not* flying this ship into a sun."

Anders rolled his eyes, a shockingly Earthan gesture. "You're not flying this ship *anywhere*. We're stuck here." He drummed his fingers across his chin. "But hypothetically, if we were to fly into a sun, which one would we choose? Any are fair game."

"That's not helpful," I said. Although he wasn't necessarily incorrect. If the warden was to be believed, the keys had been shipped to four different galaxies, the chest to a fifth. We already knocked out Milky Way and Whirlpool, which left . . . way too many to even think about.

I looked at the poem again. "All right, let's come back to that. Next line. Place to rest your feet. A chair?" I counted out the options on my fingertips. "A couch? A bed?"

Wren looked at me skeptically. "Who puts a bed on the sun?"

"I don't know! Give me a better option."

"Maybe it's not such a specific place," said Anders, pursing his lips. "Maybe it could be found anywhere. Like . . ." I didn't think he knew he was doing it, but he started tracing the tattoos on his forehead with his thumb, massaging circles into his skin. I despised myself a little for thinking of his hands rubbing the same circles along my fingers in the med bay only a few hours ago. "What about . . . a bed of sunshine?"

Wren snorted. "That's way too peppy. Aren't you the violent one?"

"Of course I am." And to prove it, he dug ten holes into his seat cushion with his claws. "I'm trying to help."

"Well, then maybe you can work a bit harder to decipher these clues. You know, since you have such a gentle soul when it comes to poetry."

"Can everyone stop talking about my soul? My soul would eat your soul for breakfast any day of the week!"

"Yeah, sure." Wren flashed him a good-natured grin. "Bring it, Andy."

I left them to bicker, approaching Elio still cleaning in the corner. He had managed to collect most of the glass shards, and he was using them to build a miniature fort, complete with a few small pieces of stuffing from the couch cushions for flags and doors. That gave me a tiny glimmer of hope. No respectable servant bot would ever be caught playing in a pile of clutter.

Elio may have been unable to talk, but a part of him was still tucked away in there. Somewhere.

"Have you been listening?" I asked. He nodded. "Any suggestions?"

Elio's eyes flickered, and then he motioned for me to hand him my comm. He started typing a message, which took quite a while in his new deficient state, while Wren and Anders continued to toss ideas around.

"Molecules of material being pulled into a black hole collide with enough intensity to heat up to hundreds of millions of degrees," said Anders. "Heat source. There you go."

"Yeah, and the next clue," replied Wren, "is a place to rest your feet. Because if we fly into a black hole we'll all be *dead*, genius. It's an eternal resting place."

"I thought you wanted to fly into a black hole. Didn't you say you have the perfect outfit for it?"

"Aw, Andy!" Wren squealed. "You *do* listen to me!"

Next to me, Elio poked at my comm, typing one slow letter at a time. Anders's and Wren's brainstorming session was reaching new levels of ridiculous.

"Andilly!" Wren jumped up on her seat. "That's one of the hottest planets I've ever set foot on."

"Why yes." Anders swept his long hair behind his shoulders. "I am familiar with that Earthan slang. We are rather attractive."

"Not *you*, Big Red. The temperature. Do you know how many gallons of perspiration I secreted while I was stuck there? I'll give you a hint, it wasn't as many as you did, because you stank up the entire cell!"

I looked over Elio's shoulder. "Are you done yet? I have a feeling they're going to start throwing things next."

Elio nodded and, with a beep, handed me back my comm. He'd typed out two sentences, riddled with misspellings. The first: *Look owut the windoe.* The second: *Whut wood u do withowut me?*

The answer was probably get thrown back into Ironside for all eternity, because when I looked out the porthole, taking in the dunes rising and falling like steps across the desert, I was filled with a sudden desire to demand the warden lock me back up on the grounds of pure dumbass-ery. It couldn't really be that simple, could it?

But the simplest things are the most effective, I thought again.

"Wren. Anders." I headed back to the couch, dragging Elio with me. "Elio would like us all to take a good, long look outside and then slap ourselves for being complete idiots."

"As long as I get to slap Anders," said Wren. She peered out the porthole. "I see sand."

"And what else?"

"Waves rising off the sand. Heat waves. Heat—*oh*. Yeah, we're dumb. I blame dehydration."

Elio stole my comm again. *Silly hoomuns*, he typed out.

Anders frowned. "But what are the odds that we happened to land so close to a key?"

"You tell me," I said. "How many desert planets are in the universe?"

"Not many," he conceded. "We know there are villages nearby.

A resting place, as the clue states, though I don't know how we'll determine which is the correct one. Rebrone is home to dozens."

"But we can work on that. This all fits. We're in a different galaxy than the other keys, the planet is a heat source . . ."

"But what about the final clue?" Wren held the poem in front of her like a map. "Cliffs, darkness, full moon?"

Elio pulled himself up onto the couch, beeping, flapping his arms. He pointed from his chest to mine and back to his. He didn't need to write out a typo-filled message this time, because I knew exactly what he meant. A fourth planet, a fourth galaxy, one we had explored thousands of times while hunting for all types of illegal treasure on my family's orders.

It was fitting, really. The final key had left the care of one empress just to make a home with another.

"Verena," I said, her name like a sigh on my lips. "The key is with Verena."

Wren frowned. "Are we supposed to know who or what that is?"

I'd just opened my mouth to reply when Anders cut me off. "She's the empress on Cora's planet. Condor. A planet that, coincidentally, is *dark* all the time." He looked at me, all cocky and proud. "See, I'm worldly. Thank the Andilly military."

Wren tipped her head toward him. "Thank you, Andilly military."

Beep! Elio echoed.

"Verena lives in a cliffside compound." I paced the rec room, tracing the spires and arches of the glittering structure in my mind. The mansion had been built into the side of a mountain, almost looked like it had *grown* into the side of a mountain, rocks tapering into iron supports and platinum-rimmed glass—blaster-proof, rigged with sensors and alarms galore, as any good criminal knew full well. Condor's darkness always appeared heightened around Verena's fortress, black fog circling the towers and doorways, as if she was determined to keep all the citizens out. Which she was, of course. Except for one day out of the year: Condor's annual New Moon celebration.

Our planet's largest party, held during the first month of the year, was the only time Verena's home was open to the public—or at least those who were fortunate enough to garner a coveted invitation to her aristocratic gala. And it was happening in three days.

"How do we get invited?" Wren asked when I gave them the lowdown on the event. As if my family, thugs and thieves, had ever been invited to such a high-profile function. Anyone who had heard of our reputation would know we would rob the mansion dry the second we stepped through the front doors. In fact, three years ago, Evelina had tried to do just that. She had been one priceless vase away from getting caught. She grudgingly hadn't attempted entry into Verena's compound since.

Maybe . . . it was time to change that.

"Invitations are always scarce," I told them. "But I think with a few shape-shifting tricks, we'll be able to get in." I nudged Anders in the shoulder and he nodded, resolute.

"What about the chest and the elixir though?" Wren asked. "The warden said it's in a different galaxy than the keys."

"It could have moved," said Anders. "Someone could have found it and given it to Verena, just like Teolia's aide gave it to her."

"Or if it's not with Verena, we might be able to find a clue with her telling us where to go next," I said. "But we need to focus on the key here first. Assuming there is a key here. And we're still grounded." I looked around at the sad, wrecked ship, then met Elio's eager eyes. With one short, happy beep, he threw his arms into the air in triumph. I could almost hear his squeaky voice, declaring that we needed snacks to celebrate such a momentous step forward in our journey. I held out a hand to him.

"Soon," I promised. "Soon we'll be home. Soon you'll be safe."

WE WERE STILL SITTING IN THE REC ROOM, MUNCHING ON cheese puffs and orange lollipops that Anders had been reluctant to share, mapping out our itinerary for locating the final keys, when Wren leaned back into the couch and kicked her feet up on the armrests.

"There's still one thing I'm a little fuzzy on." She licked the tip of a cheesy dust-stained finger. "When we were in Mieku's bunker, she said that she could see everything we hid from each other. So . . . was she just trying to intimidate us to go along with her creepy, tortured alien vibe, or is there really something going on here that someone isn't sharing?"

And so, of course (because this would only happen to me) at that moment, a cheese puff chose to get lodged in my throat, throwing me into a coughing fit. As if I could be any more obvious. Thank you for the betrayal, cheese puff.

Anders pounded my back, hard enough that a spray of cheese dust covered my lap. "I think we could ask you the same question, Wren. What haven't you told us?"

"Andy, you can't answer a question with a question."

"I believe I just did. Look, we could go back and forth on this all day, but frankly we don't have that much time on our hands." Then, instead of staring at her with his usual disdain and suspicion, he gave her an encouraging smile. *What in all the stars?* Either he had been body snatched, or Elio had forced him into watching one of his favorite good cop/bad cop net dramas when I hadn't been looking.

In the heat of the rec room, Wren's cool composure melted away, and she started wriggling in her seat. "I don't want you to hate me. I know we haven't known each other long, but . . . I really do like hanging out with you guys."

"We like hanging out with you too," I forced myself to say. I knew it was the line I was supposed to feed her, a line to gain her trust, but there was a part of me that really did mean it.

Wren sucked in a deep breath. "Maybe it doesn't matter. Maybe we'll end up dead at the end of this or we'll end up back in prison, but you should know that I *did* intend to abandon you in Ironside when we tried to escape. You were never supposed to get on this ship with me."

"Well, it's a good thing we did," I told her. "Who else could have possibly crash landed so gracefully?" I swept out my arms to indicate the broken net screen and torn upholstery surrounding us.

Wren shook her head adamantly. "There's more. Cora, you asked me about the birds from the cave on Cadrolla. The ones with human faces . . ." *Her greatest fear*. But then she hiccupped, and the strangest thing happened. Wren—strong, perky, giggly Wren—crumpled completely and started to sob.

Watching such a brave girl deflate so suddenly . . . It was one of the saddest things I had ever seen.

"Do you want a lollipop?" Anders asked hesitantly. His eyes were so wide with terror I thought they might fall out of his head. Guys were never good at dealing with crying girls, I realized, no matter which planet they were born on.

He patted his pockets, then searched the cushions behind him. "Wait. Where did my lollipops go?"

Wren stopped crying just long enough to hold up a plastic bag. "Right here," her voice wobbled.

"How did you . . . ?" Anders patted his pockets again, looked to her, patted his pockets a third time. He squinted in confusion and, if I wasn't mistaken—which I usually wasn't when it came to emotions—admiration. "They were over here two minutes ago. How did you do that?"

She wiped her nose on the back of her hand. "Just because I'm sad doesn't mean I'm useless." She took a handful of candy for herself, then gave him the rest before heaving another gasping sigh. "I'm sorry. I didn't mean to cry like that."

Elio reached forward to take her hand in both of his. *Beep*.

Wren sniffled. "Thanks. Uh, so yeah. That was awkward. Anyway, the birds. I freaked because . . . each one of them somehow had my brother's face."

"Your brother?" I asked.

Wren nodded. "Marcus. He disappeared a few years ago. My parents thought he ran away, but I think he was taken. He's three years younger than me, but he's always been a good pilot, better than me. Maybe someone wanted him for his talent. I don't know. After he vanished, I started stealing more than usual. I wanted to get a ship and search for him. That's how I ended up with the *Starchaser*.

"Cora, the reason I keep asking about your mother is because I was hoping that if I could join your family's team, maybe I could meet the right people and learn something about what happened to my brother. I mean, no one knows more about shady criminal activity than actual shady criminals, right? No offense, of course."

"None taken." I twisted my hands in my lap while Wren dabbed at the corners of her eyes. *Marcus*. The name I had seen scrawled into the armrest of her captain's chair. Her brother. I'd never guessed, had never even thought to. It hadn't crossed my mind that Wren might have someone out there she was trying to save, just like I was trying to save Elio. Now I wished she'd never told me. Knowing what she was after would only bring more pain—because I would choose Elio over her. My family over hers. Always.

"I'm sorry," said Wren. "I was feeling guilty about using you to get to your mother. That's why when we came back from Cadrolla, I hid the key in my cabin. I thought that if it got back to the warden that I was taking initiative to protect it, then maybe he would reward me and help me get Marcus back. That was stupid too. He doesn't care about us at all."

Anders scoffed. "Finally, everyone understands. But why did you say you commed him after we got the key?"

Wren shrugged. "I guess I wanted you guys to think I was taking initiative too."

Stars, I wished we'd never gone down into Mieku's bunker. Not just because the creature had harmed Elio, but because I was quickly discovering I was better off not knowing what was really going on in Wren's head. She had been trying to impress us. She said she liked hanging out with us. She wanted a star-forsaken friendship, and that was the absolute last thing I could give her.

And yet I still found myself saying, "We'll help you get your brother back." The words were a lie, and they felt like one too. Like bile rising up my throat, choking me.

Beep, agreed Elio, patting Wren's arm. Except he probably really did want to help her.

Clearing her throat, Wren drew herself up straight and wiped away the last remaining tears shining in her eyes. "Well, that got heavy. I think someone else needs to share their deep, dark secret. Anders?"

He jolted, his aura tensing with a spark that raised the hair on my arms. "I'm not a good person," he said through his teeth. "It's important you understand that."

"What an adorable coincidence," I said. "Neither are we."

"No, but I'm really—I—Cora, I've *killed people.*"

"I could have guessed that."

"Right. But you don't know *how many* people." He looked up at the ceiling, shaking his head.

"Go ahead and cry," Wren coaxed. "It's okay, Andy. It's how we deal with our oh-so-dramatic pasts."

"No, thank you. I prefer to shove mine in a metaphorical closet like any respectable person and forget it ever happened."

Wren swiped the lollipop bag from him again. "Ugh. *Men*. Even when they're aliens, they're all the same—"

"I've killed innocent refugees," he interrupted, and she fell silent.

"You've what?" she and I both whispered at the same time.

Anders wouldn't even look at us. "When I was in the military. Andilly doesn't respond well to outsiders. Years after Earth's fifth world war, refugees came to my planet. Some were protected, hidden illegally. Others . . . well . . ." He flinched, and I had a feeling why. Things didn't end well for the Earthans.

"My mother was one of many who organized groups to illegally harbor the refugees. I told her not to do it. I was already committing treason by knowing what she was up to and not reporting her. Things might have ended differently if I had."

"She's your mother," Wren said softly. "You care about her." I watched Anders as he seemed to think that over. If I were in his shoes, I didn't know if I would have protected Evelina or not.

"On Andilly, parents are not close with their offspring," said Anders. "I knew my father because, before he became Ironside's warden, he was a general in Andilly's army, but my mother only raised me until my twelfth birthday. It is customary for children to become the property of the government after that. I tried to visit her though, whenever I had a chance. I remember she would make me the most delicious meals. She would teach me how to cook, and she would hum songs the whole time. She had such a beautiful voice."

He started humming a little himself, lost in the memory until he frowned and shook his head to bring himself back. "My mother was kind," he said with a note of sadness. "Most on my planet are not, but she was."

Just then it hit me that the entire time Anders had been talking, he'd only referred to his mother as a *was*, not an *is*. Which meant . . .

"Someone found out she was protecting the Earthans. I think it was my father, but I don't know for sure. I do know that she meant nothing to him. On Andilly, we do not marry. I don't think they knew each other well. The only thing they had in common was me.

"We received orders to break down her door, destroy her house. A dozen soldiers were there. My father was there." His eyes took on a haunted look, as black as the storm raging inside them. "The kitchen where we cooked, where she sang. My childhood bedroom. The cellar where the Earthans were hiding in the dark . . . we set fire to it. I thought my father was going to leave them in there to suffocate on the smoke, but he had them pulled out. My mother too. And then he ordered me to kill them all."

Wren gasped. Elio beeped. I found myself unable to breathe, my hate for the warden catching in the back of my throat. I understood ruthlessness all too well, but what he had done had been pure, unfiltered evil.

"I refused," Anders continued. "It was more than enough to have me killed too, but that would have been too kind. He called another general, and they drugged me with a serum that was being developed in the army laboratories. It puts you in a hypnotic state, makes you susceptible to suggestion. My father ordered me to kill them a second time, and that time . . ." His voice finally caught, cracking and breaking and barely a whisper as he forced his lips to part and say, "That time I listened. And then we went to another refugee site. And another. And another. And when the drugs finally wore off, I remembered everything. The feel of the blaster in my hand, the look on my mother's face. So naturally, I tried killing my father too."

"I wish you had succeeded," I said.

"Me too. I was dishonorably discharged after that. I thought for sure he was going to have me executed, but instead I ended up in Ironside. Shortly after, he took over as the warden so he could watch over me and gloat. I shouldn't have expected anything less.

"I hate my father. I hate myself for what I did. You can't understand how guilty I feel *all the time.*" He wiped his nose, turning to Wren. "If it ever seemed like I hate you, I don't. But every time I look at one of your kind, I go back to that night, and the only way I can think to protect you from myself is to push you away. Because if I don't, eventually you'll all find out what a monster I am." He looked at the floor. "I don't want to hurt anyone again. Those screams that you heard in the cave on Cadrolla? They were mine—when I realized the horror of what I had done."

I swallowed down the massive lump in my throat. "*Anders.*" But what else could I say except that? I felt his fingers brush the back of my hand, feather light, so quickly I almost wasn't sure they had been there at all. Maybe I didn't have to say anything. Maybe just being here for him was enough.

"So, Cora?" He gave me a sad, half smile. "Do you think you can tell a worse story than me?"

Worse as in violent? No. But I could tell them a worse story in other ways. At least Wren and Anders had shared their big secrets and still came out looking noble. I would have none of that. The words "noble" and "Saros" didn't even exist in the same universe.

"I really don't have a sad story." I worried my bottom lip between my teeth. "You both know everything there is to know about me and Elio and our family. The only other thing is that . . . well . . ." I glanced at Wren. "I snooped through your cabin the other day, looking for the key, because I didn't believe you when you said it was safe. But I didn't find it." I didn't have to fake a guilty face, because that was the only emotion I could feel. A monstrous wave of it, like in the cave in Cadrolla, grasping at my chest.

I was not a good person.

But I knew that already.

If they thought my attempt to spill my guts was pathetic (and it was, compared to theirs), they had the good sense not to say anything about it.

"I figured." Wren nodded. "It's okay though. It made it through the crash. It was stuffed under my bed, but I decided to keep it a little closer from now on." She showed me a chain around her neck, the key dangling from the end, almost identical to the chain around mine.

That key is a fake. Please don't believe me, please see through the lie, please confront me about it.

But she did nothing. Anders did nothing except nudge me in the shoulder and whisper, "I guess you're a kinder person than we are, Cora Saros."

Please don't believe me. I'm not who you think I am. I'm just a distraction. This is all just a distraction. Please, please, please.

Wren clapped her hands together. "So two things are going on here. First of all: this was a huge bonding moment for us. And second of all: it's probably the start of a long-lasting friendship, and every long-lasting friendship involves matching tattoos. What do you guys want to get? I'm putting in a vote for Anders's favorite orange lollipop."

"Does being friends mean that I can't insult your stupid ideas ever again?" Anders asked. "Because I've never had a friend, so I can't be sure."

"No, no, Andykins. Being friends means you're allowed to insult each other *more*."

"Oh, really?" He perked up immensely. "Well, in that case, Wren, let me tell you where you can stick your lollipop . . ."

I drowned them out, their voices eclipsed by my guilt. *Friendship*. I had succeeded. I'd won their trust. I should have been grinning from ear to ear, doing a victory dance, screaming so loud that Evelina and Cruz and Blair could hear me all the way on Condor, *something*. I should have been *happy*.

But I wasn't.

They trusted me now, but they wouldn't trust me for much longer.

This was the only way to save Elio. If we gave the keys to the warden, there was no guarantee he wouldn't lock us back up—or straight up murder us for fun. Even if he kept his word and released us from his clutches, I doubted he would give us reward money to go along with our freedom, and if we tried hiding the treasure for ourselves and disappearing, he would track us down. We would never be safe.

No, giving it to Evelina was the best option. She could deal with hiding it or selling it. She could even find someone to remove the tracker from my neck. If I made her happy, she would keep me and Elio safe. Without her protection, without her steady paychecks, what would I have?

You would have Wren and Anders, a small voice whispered in my head. *You would have people who care about you.*

But Elio. He needed a new body more than I needed friends.

And so it was settled. We needed to get inside Verena's compound. I knew Evelina would help us, but only if there was something in it for her. When this was over, Wren and Anders would just have to learn what every good felon discovered at one time or another.

How to fend for themselves.

21

WHILE WREN AND ANDERS GATHERED BLASTERS AND OTHER supplies for our first trip into Rebrone's villages, Elio and I hunkered down in the lab under the guise of making a few tweaks to our VEDs. But before I could even think about doing that, I needed to get something else out of the way.

I held up my comm link like a mirror, using the glass display to desperately smooth my frizzy hair into a ponytail. I flashed my reflection a smile, checking for errant cheese puff dust in my teeth, before drying the sweat lining my forehead with my shirt collar. I felt like a mess, but I couldn't look like a mess, not if I wanted to convince my family this was a good idea and not a suicide mission.

Elio beeped beside me while I dialed in the familiar frequency on the touch screen, then ran away to clean the dusty bookcases once the call started to connect. I couldn't blame him. I didn't enjoy talking to them either, but I couldn't exactly ignore them any—

"Cora?"

I thought I'd called Evelina's comm, but it was my cousin Blair who answered, his gaunt face partially obscured by smoke from the pipe of moon dust that rarely left his person. He took a long drag, then gave me a broad, sardonic smile. Stars, he was so stoned. I guess it was good to see that not much had changed in the time that I'd been away.

"You," Blair said, blinking slowly, "are not worth as much money as the universe says you are."

"I appreciate the compliment, sweet cousin. Where's Evelina?"

"Around . . ." He looked behind him, and I could see our youngest cousin, Mina, swiftly counting a stack of money on the kitchen floor, sorting it into four large envelopes. Nothing like handling a wad of illegal cash to help a four-year-old learn math.

"Evelina left her comm on the counter," said Blair. "I'll bring it to her if you pay me—"

"Who's that?" Nana Rae shuffled behind him. Her puff of silver hair was tied up in a spotted headband, a fluffy pink robe hanging on her narrow shoulders. My heart swelled at the sight of her. Senile or not, my grandmother was the only person in the house other than Elio and Mina who marginally cared about my well-being.

"It's no one," Blair said to Nana Rae.

I scoffed. "It's Cora, Nana."

"*Who*?" She squinted at the comm from behind a pair of bug-eye glasses.

Blair smirked. "Exactly."

"Shut up, Blair," I said. "You know she can't hear. Nana, it's Cora—"

But she'd already turned away from the comm and was humming her favorite rendition of Condor's national anthem.

While I watched Nana prance around the kitchen and Blair puff on his pipe, I felt like I had never left home, had never dragged Elio to Vaotis, had never gotten thrown into Ironside, had never met Wren and Anders. Earlier, the thought of everything going back to the way it was had filled me with a sense of anticipation. Only now I realized maybe not all kinds of anticipation were good.

"Blair! I hear voices! I thought I told you to shut up!"

Stars, no. Definitely not happy anticipation. The sound of Evelina's voice, growing closer to the comm with each dissatisfied word, sent an icy blast of wind into the *Starchaser*'s stifling laboratory. I glanced behind me to the main corridor, tilting my comm down in case somebody heard my mother's angry voice and came to investigate. But the halls were still.

The patter of Evelina's heels on the kitchen floor snapped me back to attention. "Blair, why do you have my comm? If you don't want your father chucking you off the roof of this house, then you better—*oh, hello there.*" She'd finally spotted me. Evelina grabbed the comm, casting Blair back to the table beside Nana Rae, and smiled like a predator who was two seconds away from ripping into its latest meal. "You've caused quite the intergalactic stir, haven't you, dearest daughter?"

I pushed aside the intimidation and tilted my chin up. I had something she wanted. Or I would. For once, I had the upper hand.

"You crashed into my ship, Evelina." I raised an eyebrow, clenching my jaw to hide my nerves.

"I was simply curious to see if the rumors were true. You were right where they said you were; however, I didn't expect you to be flying something so . . . vintage." She smirked.

I frowned. The *Starchaser* was a mess, but it was *our* mess. Only we were allowed to insult it.

"Enlighten me, Cora," she continued, grin widening. "Where are you now?"

"Not on the same planet I'll be on in three days, so I don't see how that information is pertinent."

"Oh, sweetheart. You do have a backbone. I'm so proud," she drawled. Patronizingly.

"Tell me something, Evelina." I leaned closer to the screen of my comm. I was holding all the cards here—I had to remember that. "How would you like a second chance at robbing Empress Verena's compound?"

Her eyes glittered. Blair sat up in his chair, and in the doorway behind them, I noticed Cruz appear, head tilted in his trademark silent curiosity. Here in the laboratory, Elio dropped his dust cloth to the ground.

"What you are suggesting," Evelina hissed, "is not possible."

"Maybe not before. But now I have a crew, and you have a crew. Once we get inside, we have double the chance for success."

"But what's stopping me from following you to Verena's compound and capturing you there? I can turn you all in, collect the bounty. It's a far easier payday. Far less messy too. You know, the four of you are all anyone is talking about on the net screens."

"We're taking bets on which of you is going to die first," Blair stated, thumping his chest. "I'm the head bookie."

"Charming," I told him. "Put that on your résumé." I forced myself to stay calm, willed my breathing to even out.

Evelina directed the comm back to her face. "I admit I've placed a few bets myself. Your father and I agree that the Andillian's head is going to look lovely mounted above the mantelpiece."

Don't flinch. Don't react. It's what she wants. You *are in control.*

"So I should take it that you don't want in on the job?"

"No, Cora, I do not. We're already behind on our monthly shipments. We have a case of taaffeite to retrieve and sell to a jeweler on Venus in four days. Then we're giving the treasury job at Vaotis another go, and—"

"And you're so occupied with all of those *small* jobs," I interrupted, "which, don't get me wrong, have their uses and their payouts, albeit very minor. You're so wrapped up in ferrying illegal shipments and going after the minuscule fifty-thousand-ritle bounty on my head that you don't have time for anything larger, such as, oh I don't know, the endless riches that you'll acquire after finding the Four Keys of Teolia, for example. But of course, if you'd rather make nice with *another* jeweler—"

Evelina cut me off. "*What*?" Spit hit the lens of her comm. "What did you say?"

"The Four Keys of Teolia. You're familiar with them? I thought you mi—"

"Shut up, you insufferable child! I'm thinking." She paced the kitchen, muttering to herself. I could see Cruz rubbing his hands together, smiling. It was a look so rare on him that I caught myself smiling back. With a beep, Elio abandoned his attempt to clean the shelves and came to sit beside me.

After a minute, Evelina turned back to me. Her eyes narrowed, and for the first time in so many years she looked at me not as if I were a nuisance, but as if I mattered. As if I wasn't just one of her workers, but part of her family.

"Cora," she said sweetly, "what exactly are you after?"

I wrapped an arm around Elio's shoulders and prepared to tell her the whole sordid tale. "Something I'm hoping is going to make both of us very, very rich."

"Okay. It *has* to be this village. We've gone to six already." Wren cupped her hand over her eyes to block the rays of Rebrone's dual suns as we trudged across the desert. She'd found a floppy straw hat somewhere—stolen from the last set of huts we'd visited, most likely—and used it to fan herself.

"Actually, we've only gone to five," Anders corrected her, consulting the map on my comm. With the *Starchaser* out of commission, we only had so many options for villages to visit. An hour's walk in each direction of the ship was as far as we could manage without dying of heatstroke.

"*Five*?" Wren groaned. "Only *five*? It's official. I'm hallucinating. I'm probably dehydrated, and now I'm going to have to drink my own urine to revive myself."

"That's a myth," said Anders. He helped us over the crest of a dune as the sand turned to gravel and then to stone. Village number six appeared in the distance, in the valley of four sloping mountain ranges. It was larger than the others, a central marketplace filled with tents, surrounded by supply ships, civilian spacecraft, and several clusters of clay houses leaning so far to the side that they looked like a strong wind might topple them right over.

"What about drinking blood?" Wren asked as we made our way down a cart path that descended into the village. Our disguises flickered to life. Plain Earthan holograms from the visual enhancers for me and Wren, a robotic hologram from a third VED I'd quickly built for Elio, and a generic blond-haired, blue-eyed Earthan face for Anders, which he donned like a second skin.

He gave Wren a startled look. "Yes, that's a myth too. Why would you suggest something so vile?"

"Vile." She snorted. "The Andillian wants to talk about vile? Just kidding, you sweet little nugget, you."

"What about sucking on a rock?" I interrupted. "Isn't that supposed to help?"

"Indeed, if your goal is to choke to death." Anders shook his head. "Honestly, what kind of survival tactics were you two raised on?"

"Um . . ." Wren scratched her head. "We weren't?"

"That's absurd. Once we're done fighting for our lives I'm going to teach you everything that I know."

Wren smacked my arm. "Did you hear that, Cora? He's going to teach you *everything* he knows. Wink, wink. Nudge, nudge."

"You're so juvenile." And yet I caught myself blushing. Because . . . heatstroke. Definitely heatstroke. I couldn't be thinking about him—about either of them, really. We were due on Condor in two days. Evelina had agreed to get the family together and meet us at Verena's home. The plan was in motion. The final key was in sight.

I couldn't ruin this by suffering from humanity's greatest weakness: *emotions*.

Beep!

Anders turned. "Yeah? What do you think, Elio? Up for a survival lesson too?"

Beep-beep!

I patted Elio on the back, wincing at the high whine of the fan in his processor that was struggling to cool his body down in the heat. The VED I'd built for him had changed his appearance to that of a shinier, cleaner servant bot—one without his floppy ears and wire patches—but he still needed some shade so his frame wouldn't melt.

"How about in here?" Wren led us into the market, where an auction was underway, the tents filled with laughter and heated bartering. She plopped Elio down on a couch made from the blue hide of some type of scaly animal.

The woman tending the stall stood and shook a finger at us. "Pay! You pay for that!" Her Isolat was heavily accented, all round vowels and jumbled consonants. Anders muttered something in Rebrone's native language, holding out his hands to placate her.

After frying us with her gaze for a few moments longer, she relented, resuming her seat at the other side of her tent. "Fine. You *borrow*. But *me*"—she stabbed her finger into her chest—"is watching *you*." She stabbed her finger at the four of us, then picked up her comm and quickly became absorbed in something flashing on the screen.

"You're unnaturally good at languages," I told Anders while he scanned the market. "Is that another thing we can thank the Andilly military for?" Although what I *really* wanted was to clobber them with my blaster after what they had forced him to do.

He thought for a moment. "No thanks necessary. It's natural skill. As I told you before, I'm multitalented." He flashed me a mischievous grin before picking up a pointed contraption for sale on the woman's table. It looked like a cross between scissors and a blowtorch, decorated with two yellow puffballs on the handles. My mind instantly started running through dozens of ways to attach it to my blaster and weaponize it.

"Aw, cute!" Wren flicked one of the puffballs. She lowered her voice. "Andykins, ask your new friend if she knows anything about Teolia's keys."

"Odds are she does not." Every village we'd visited so far had given us, at best, confused frowns when we mentioned the keys.

"Ask anyway. We're running out of daylight and I'm running out of self-control. Do you know how many things I want to steal in this place? Target one: these puffballs."

Anders pointed across the tent. "There's a sign right over there that explicitly says '*Thieves will be prosecuted.*'"

"So? I can't read that language."

"I just told you what it said!"

"I still can't read it. Why should I listen?"

As usual, it was time for me to play the part of mediator. "You"—I shoved Anders—"go make a friend. And *you*"—I turned Wren toward the thriving center of the market—"I don't care what you do. Just don't get caught."

"What's the worst that can happen? I'll get thrown in Ironside?" She laughed. "I'm going to get you something. Any requests? A new blaster? A sense of humor?"

"Hey! I have a sense of humor!" I called after her as she weaved through a group of ranchers and vanished into the crowd. I flashed Elio a look. "I have a *great* sense of humor."

Beep!

"Oh, whatever." I sat down next to him, watching Anders communicate with the grumpy merchant. She was shaking her head. More of the same. I pulled out my comm to research the next closest village while she attempted to shoo him away. But then Anders pulled out a handful of ritles, and the old woman stilled.

Behold. The eternal power of money.

The woman cupped the coins in her hands like they were water and she was parched with thirst. Slowly, she counted out the ritles, dropping each into her cashbox with a *ping*. She raised one crooked finger and pointed, not at the mountain path we had descended to reach the market, but at the one directly across from us. The northern mountain.

She waved Anders closer and started talking. I could only recognize one word, said with a shiver and then a sneer: *Andilly*.

"Oh no." I ducked out of her tent and hurried up the market's central path, the crowd thickening the closer I got to the auction block. I could hear Elio beeping, following me, but all I could see was the massive ship perched above the valley at the top of the mountain, its tail stamped with a crest of a twelve-pointed star.

The last time we saw that ship, it had been shooting at us.

"That's not good." Wren appeared at my shoulder.

I whirled around. I hadn't even heard her approach. "Where did you come from?"

"Where do any of us come from? Here, I got you some spoons." She pressed a metal bundle into my hands.

"Why do I need these?"

"Why not? They're engraved with little sunbursts. They're cute."

"Did you pay for them?"

"Of course not."

Anders ran up the path toward us, the blond hair of his disguise flopping into his eyes. "We're outnumbered. We need to stay out of sight, wait them out."

"What's the point?" I brushed my fingers over my tracking chip. "If they're here, they already know where we are." Hiding in one of the tents would be useless, and we were an hour away from the *Starchaser*. Not that it mattered when we still couldn't fly.

"We can't just stand here," Wren said, jumping when the auction crowd erupted in cheers.

Just beyond the edge of the market, along the northern mountain's cart path, a cluster of the warden's guards was making their way toward us. Was it wishful thinking, or did they look less menacing than all the other guards we had encountered in Ironside? Anders said they were ex-military, like him, but they were pushing each other along the path like children, smacking each other jovially and whooping loud enough that I could hear them over the crowd around us. Maybe they were just really excited to kill us.

"Down! Get down!" Anders ushered us inside a low-lit spice tent as they neared. Elio took his order literally, tripping to the ground, and I dragged him backward, his heels leaving two long grooves in the soil.

"Don't mind us," Wren said to the merchant manning the stall. She pulled a handful of the tent's fabric around us, leaving a slit just large enough to peer through. "We're playing hide-and-seek. It's an Earthan thing."

He stared at us over the top of a spice rack, then shrugged and returned to his wares.

The guards entered the center of the market, their heavy boots and thick, dark jackets immediately marking them as foreigners in the desert heat. The crowd parted for them automatically, Andilly's reputation preceding them. I tracked them as they neared. Four men, two women—all six weighed down by weapons strapped to their waists and chests. Anders pulled out his blaster, his stance sure as he lined up his shot through the gap in the tent.

"Come on," he muttered. "A little closer."

But he didn't have a clear shot. The market was too full, the auction too rowdy. Digging into my pack, I removed a stun grenade and ran my thumb across the pin.

One of the guards tapped his friend on the shoulder and pointed ahead. They all started running in our direction, quicker, louder. Anders sighted down the barrel of his blaster. Wren raised hers. I dug my nail under the grenade's pin and started to pull. And then . . .

They blew right past us.

Wait. *What*?

"What just happened?" I brought my mouth close to Anders's ear. "Why aren't we dead?"

"I'm not sure. I—" He jerked his blaster up as one of the guards started to double back. A girl, not much older than us, smiling with exhilaration, red skin dotted with sweat.

She held up her comm and located us easily. As I'd suspected, they'd known where we were all along.

Wren tried tugging the tent flap down to conceal us, but it was too late. The guard's lips pulled open into a smile so sharp it felt like a blade was being shoved into my chest.

Pointing at Anders, she spoke a few words of Andillian. Then, with a wave, she turned and joined her friends as they ran around the bend in the path and vanished from sight.

Wren, Elio, and I stared at Anders. "What did she say to you?" Wren asked.

Anders's claws came out, shredding the edge of the tent flap. "She said, 'Thanks for the head start.'"

I sank to the ground. The sharp combination of spices in the tent made my head ache. "So that means . . ."

"They found the key," Wren finished. "It *was* here."

"And now it's with them," said Anders. "I should have taken the shot. But I couldn't." Ripples of shame surrounded him. "Not again."

Wren shook her head. "It wouldn't have made a difference either way."

"How? Please share."

"Because." She pushed aside the tent flap, and the four of us stumbled back into the sunlight. "If they have the key, they wouldn't carry it into the market knowing we were down here. No, it's hidden somewhere else."

She nodded toward the edge of the valley. "It's on the ship. So, in turn, *we* have to get on the ship." The cloud of colors around her lit up like a firework display when she smiled at me. "Can you unlock the doors?"

"Well, breaking and entering *is* my specialty. Shouldn't be too hard." The doors would be simple; it was any aura-less guards left behind that would be tough. "You think you can nab the key?"

"Cora, I once stole a three-hundred-pound manhole cover and used it as a wall hanging in my bedroom." And with that, she turned and took off for the north mountain.

NOW *THIS* WAS A SHIP.

Twelve levels tall, a pristine paint job, and not a speck of rust in sight. With no guards to be found, I had my comm link hacked into the ship's wireless interface, the security monitors off, and the bolt on the door cracked in under thirty seconds.

For a military ship, the Andillians sure did travel in style. We crept forward slowly, hyper-aware of any shift in the shadows that signaled an incoming threat, and entered the ship's circular atrium. Copper ramps and walkways connected dozens of balconies on each level, all of them overlooking the main floor, which contained lounge chairs, a juice bar, and a double-paned glass lift that shimmered like a waterfall. I stepped closer, my dusty boots mucking up the spotless mosaic floor. This thing wasn't a ship—it was a star-forsaken hotel with wings.

"They've really upgraded since they kicked me out," Anders said, studying a screen on the wall that pointed in the direction of the ship's fitness center, galley, cabins, and many other options for a key to hide. We needed to do this fast. The market could only occupy the guards for so long, and I had a strong suspicion that we weren't the only four in here.

Wren returned from the bar with a glass full of bubbling blue juice. "We need to split up."

Snatching my comm, Elio typed out: *Horor moovies say not to do that.*

"Sorry, little guy, but we need to cover more ground." Wren nodded at us. "Me and Cora, Anders and Elio?"

Beep!

"It's okay, Elio." I nudged him closer to Anders. "He'll protect you."

"Come on." Anders hoisted him up. "We'll take the bottom six levels. You two take the top. Crew lockers are usually found in the fitness wing and in every cabin. The bridge is a good place to search too. You have weapons?" We nodded. "Good. Comm me if you find anything."

As we watched him walk away, it struck me how much had changed in the short time I'd known him. When we met, I never would have left him alone with Elio, and I would have been worried he was using splitting up as an excuse to contact his fellow Andillians and send them after us. Now, I knew better.

The lift in the atrium launched off the ground like a rocket as soon as Wren and I boarded. I leaned against the side of the cabin, ignoring the floor falling away beneath us, as I monitored my comm link. There was no sign of motion on any of the levels I could see. Likely none I would be able to feel either. But that didn't mean no one was there.

"Let's start on level twelve," I said, quickly hacking into the ship's floor plan on my comm. "It looks like the bridge is at the end of the portside corridor. Starboard side is weapons training and waste management."

"Portside it is," said Wren as the doors slid open with a ding. In the silence of the ship, it sounded more like a blaster shot. We had just taken our first steps down the wide corridor when the sound of *real* blaster fire echoed from one of the levels below. I stopped dead. A scream carried through the atrium, followed by three large bangs, and then . . . silence.

Anders.

Elio.

Wren pulled at my wrist. "Come on. Quickly. The sooner we find the key, the better."

As we started to run, I sent a comm to Anders.

Are you okay?

His response took a minute, by which time we had reached the doorway into the bridge, and I had started to sweat.

Elio is fine. I would welcome a large bandage, but I'm mostly unharmed.

Mostly was about as good as we would get right now. I bent toward the door, ready to hack into the ship's interface and pop the lock, but Wren and I both paused when we noticed the door wasn't automatic like all the rest. There was no holopanel, no keypad, no sensors. A heavy bar was screwed into the door, attached to a deadbolt that required a physical *key* to open.

"What year do they think this is?" Wren groaned. "Twenty-twenty?" She examined the lock, pulling out a knife and trying to twist it inside. "Can you pick things manually?"

"It's been a while. I need two pins."

"I have two shoelaces. That's about all you'll get from me."

"Hang on." I pulled out my blaster as two more loud bangs sounded from below. After twisting apart the barrel, I extricated two sturdy wires to weave into the lock. I was now weaponless except for a handful of stun grenades. And the spoons Wren had gifted me, I guess.

Kneeling on the floor, I pressed my cheek to the door and listened to the tumblers in the lock turn. The first one clicked after a minute. Then the second. The third one was almost there . . .

The lift opened, stopping my progress.

Wren's head snapped up. "Anders?" she whispered, but when we heard another crash from below, we had our answer.

"Are we shooting or are we hiding?" she asked me. I could hear someone's heavy footsteps cross the walkway off the lift and head this way, although I couldn't sense them. Was that one set of boots hitting the floor or two?

"Just a second." I crouched at the door. Lock picking was a skill of finesse, and it was nearly impossible to do it when my adrenaline levels were spiking, causing my hands to shake. I twisted the wire in my left hand, scraping the one in my right down toward the ground. The third tumbler miraculously clicked into place. "Just one more . . ."

The footsteps stilled with a squeak.

". . . second," I finished dully. The electric buzz of multiple blasters hummed in the air. I had none. Wren had a blaster, but she hadn't powered it up for some reason. I turned toward her and—

Gone. She was *gone*.

"On your feet," the guard commanded. He turned to his partner, his voice a hiss. "I suppose we should feel honored to be robbed by a member of such an esteemed crime family. Although your mother would have been more impressive."

I sighed. "Yeah, I've heard that before." I didn't even have the brain capacity to feel offended. Where was Wren? I pushed out with my mind, seeing past the dead space of the two guards to find the colorful prickle of an aura. *There!* A lilac plume coming from . . . *Oh stars*.

"I said on your feet!" the guard yelled. He fired his blaster, aiming just above my head. The wall exploded in a burst of flaming metal, and I ducked. When the smoke cleared, I raised my own blaster, obviously out of commission with half the barrel missing, the wires inside swinging out like intestines. The guards barked out a laugh. I really hoped Wren knew what she was doing.

"*Pew-pew*!" I jabbed my sad excuse for a blaster at the guards. This was like distracting the porci on Cadrolla all over again. "*Pew*!"

The first guard turned to his friend. "What . . . is she doing?"

His friend shrugged.

Wren's aura was growing deeper. Whatever she was up to, she was almost ready.

"*Pew!*"

Guard Two frowned. "Why are you making that noise?"

"Why not? I can't shoot you, so I might as well pretend."

"I . . . you are a *horrible* thief."

"I'll admit I'm not the best. But . . ." The entire corridor filled with Wren's purple glow. It was time. "I'm really good at providing distractions. I'm surprised you don't know one when you see it."

Guard One doubled over, laughing. "A distraction from what?"

I smiled sweetly. "Her."

Wren swung down from the rafters, landing on the shoulders of the first guard. He spun, trying to throw her, but she responded by digging her fingers into his eyes. He howled, stumbling into the wall. Wren finally pushed off him when he was far enough down the corridor, and then she fired her blaster at the ceiling.

Tiles and plaster and metal beams rained down, knocking the guard to the floor and encasing him in a tomb of debris. He was either really, really unconscious or really, really dead.

His friend looked on, frozen in place, eyes bulging out of his head. I easily plucked the blaster from his limp fingers.

"How did you get up there?" I asked Wren when she stumbled back to the bridge door.

She shrugged. "There was a chair down the hall. I pulled myself up. Quick and painless. Well . . ." She looked at the buried guard. "Not painless for him."

Guard Two finally snapped out of it and ran to dig the barely breathing body of Guard One out of the wreckage. "You killed him!"

Wren rolled her eyes. "No I didn't. He'll live to be annoying another day, I promise."

"D-don't hurt me too! Take whatever you want!"

"Wow," I said to Wren. "The quality of soldiers on Andilly has seriously gone downhill since Anders left."

"Agreed. Hey, you! Guard boy! How about getting us through this door?"

He froze again. His friend slipped from his grasp and crashed back to the floor. "You can't go in there."

I crossed my arms. "Big words from someone who doesn't want to get buried alive." I raised my dismantled blaster, taunting, "*Pew-pew.*"

He hesitated for a breath. "Fine! Just don't shoot."

He plucked a key from the breast pocket of his jacket and then the door was swinging open, revealing a wide cockpit full of flashing screens and a panoramic view. A conference table took up the middle of the floor, covered in diagrams, a small model of the *Starchaser*, and an overturned glass spilling water.

"Where's Teolia's key?" I asked the guard. He may have been taller than us, but he was unarmed. Wren and I each jammed a blaster under his chin.

"I said don't shoot," he protested weakly.

"Tell me where the key is and we won't," I said.

"I don't know."

"Do your friends in the village know we're up here?"

"I don't know."

"When are they coming back?"

"I don't know."

"Can you say anything other than 'I don't know'?"

"I—yes, of course."

"Excellent. Okay, listen up." Tightening my finger on the trigger, I watched a few beads of sweat drip down the tattoos on the guard's forehead. "Either you tell us where the key is, or this one"—I nodded to Wren—"is going to rip your intestines out through your eyes."

"It's true," Wren said. "I'm really good at that."

"And then after that, we're going to drag your dead body to the warden so he can string your insides around his office like party streamers. Does that sound like fun?"

The guard's eyes narrowed, but still he shook with fear. "You cannot intimidate me—"

"BOO!" Wren screamed in his face. The guard jolted, whimpering. "Yeah, I think we can."

"You didn't answer my question," I said. "Does that sound like fun? Yes or no?"

"No! Obviously no!"

"A compromise, then? Grab your friend, grab the others on the floors below, and get off this ship. If you don't, then you should know I have a bunch of grenades in my pocket that I'm growing tired of carting around. I've blown up an entire outpost, so don't think I won't blow up this ship too. Leave us alone."

"But the key—"

"BOO!" Wren screamed again. The guard jumped almost a foot in the air, but miraculously he listened, leaving a trail of dust and debris as he dragged Guard One through the wreckage and around the corner. Wren shot after them once, missing on purpose. Guard Two yelped, picking up the pace. I didn't release the tension from my body until I heard the lift doors slide shut at the end of the corridor. Then I rushed to the viewport in the cockpit to watch.

As instructed, Guard Two was dragging Guard One and leading a group of three others from the ship, toward the cart path into the village. I knew we wouldn't have much time before he told the rest of his friends that the ship had been compromised.

"As fun as that was," said Wren, peering over my shoulder, "he didn't tell us where to find the key."

"No. I doubted he would." Sighing, I started tearing through drawers on the wall behind the captain's chair. "Should we try another floor? I don't know if it's in here."

A sudden crash from the corridor outside had us both powering up our blasters. But it was just Anders, clutching his ribs as they leaked blood around his fingertips. Elio flitted around him with a rag, trying to clean the mess.

I helped him into a seat at the conference table. "What happened to you?"

He winced. "They tried shoving us down the incinerator shaft. Elio was great though. He ran into the galley and started throwing cans of pon at their heads. I was able to knock one of them out. The others ran for the door once a group of their friends came through." He looked at me strangely, silently questioning what I had done to get our guards to leave us alone.

Oh, you know, just threatened to cause an explosion and rip out a man's large and small intestines. No big deal.

Elio pulled at my arm and showed me Anders's comm link. On it, he wrote: *I'm x-lent in a crisis.*

"Good job, friend." I patted him on the head before going to the wall where Wren was wrestling with the door of a massive safe.

"How do you *do* this?" She spun the dial and tapped a series of numbers on the keypad. A light flashed red, an alarm ringing out.

Pushing her aside, I quickly hacked into the safe, my fingers trembling as the door creaked open. Hiding the key directly behind the captain's chair was rather obvious, but most Andilly guards I'd encountered so far didn't exactly scream *evil geniuses*.

"*Hello*, money!" Wren scooped a handful of ritles into her bag. My chest deflated. There wasn't much else hidden in the safe. A few piles of paperwork, a gold watch (which Wren also stole), and a bowl of frozen red food that had Anders jumping from his seat, even with his injured ribs.

"That's pon!" He elbowed me out of the way. "Give it here!"

"It looks disgusting," I said.

"If by disgusting you mean delicious, then yes, it is quite revolting."

Beep! Elio screeched. He pulled my hand, dragging me back to the viewport. *Beep-beep-beep*! He thrust his finger at the glass.

Incoming.

I'd hoped they would stay away a bit longer. The warden's guards were running up the mountain path. Only this time they weren't alone. The *entire market* was following them. Word must have gotten out about who we really were.

Anders appeared behind us, leaning heavily against me as he sucked an injured breath through his teeth. "We can't leave. The weapons facility is on the other side of this floor. The key could be there. Or in the cabins. Or—"

"Or it could be right in front of you," said a new voice from the doorway.

This time, Anders didn't hesitate. He fired his blaster toward the door, but his injury caused his aim to go wide, missing the boy that stood on the opposite end of the conference table. But . . . why would there be an Earthan kid on an Andilly ship?

The boy took a step forward into the cockpit. He had brown skin and kind eyes, though they were currently pinched at the corners with fear. A simple gold key swung from a chain around his neck.

"W-why are you in my ship?" he asked. He had a small pocket-knife clutched in his fist.

"This isn't your ship," I told the boy. Unless they were holding him hostage here and it was his prison.

"It is," he insisted. "This is my bridge, and you . . . you're one of them." He shrank back at the sight of Anders's red scales. "You're the ones they're looking for. You—all of you." The boy's eyes cut to the safe against the wall. "*Wren*?"

She took a step into the light, blaster propped against her shoulder, forgotten. "*Marcus*?"

"Yeah." His voice cracked, warmth filling his eyes.

"How are you—? I thought you—?" She glared at Anders. "Put

your gun down!" Then she rushed forward and tackled the boy with the fiercest hug I'd ever seen. Marcus. Her *brother*.

Of all the places for the lost boy to be, how had he landed himself on an Andilly warship?

"I pilot the ship," he told Wren when she questioned him. "Most people from Andilly aren't good flyers." He glanced at Anders, who scowled back. "The pay isn't great, and sometimes they don't remember to feed me, but I'm still alive. How are Mom and Dad?"

Anders interrupted him. "Your heart-wrenching family reunion is over. We have bigger problems." He pointed out the viewport. The guards had almost reached the top of the mountain. Most people from the marketplace had given up trailing them and boarded their own spacecraft, which were hovering in a buzzing cloud above the valley. Tunerth all over again.

Marcus rushed forward to look outside. "What"—he swallowed hard—"is that?"

"That," I answered, "is all the people who want our heads. Wave hello. I'm sure they'll introduce themselves later."

"That's why we need this key." Wren made a grab for the chain around Marcus's neck, but he ducked. "We have to get out of here."

"No!" He clutched the chain at his chest. "They gave it to me. They said if anything happened to it, they would kill me, Wren!"

Anders hurried to block his path when he ran for the door. "If you don't think they'll kill you anyway once you're no longer useful to them, then you're out of your mind. Give me the key. Don't make me force you."

"No! Wren! Don't let them hurt me, please!"

"I . . ." She looked so torn. I elbowed her and pointed out the viewport. The guards were at the door. I'd used my comm to lock down all the entrances, but they wouldn't hold forever.

Wren held out her hand. "Give us the key, Marcus. We'll keep you safe."

"I can't!"

And that was when I noticed it. A spot just below Marcus's left ear, gleaming like it was covered in blood. But then—it vanished.

Wren saw it too. She gasped, and the relief that had filled her eyes upon first seeing her brother turned cold and hard. "Kill him."

"No!" Marcus yelled, but Anders lunged forward, shooting his blaster at the boy's knee. Marcus hit the ground, and Anders knocked him unconscious with a strike to his temple.

It wasn't until his eyes slid shut that the change occurred. His skin rippled, turning red, growing scales. His jaw filled out, and the familiar swirl of Andilly military tattoos covered his flesh as "Marcus" transformed back into one of the warden's guards.

Elio darted forward and plucked the key from the chain around the guard's neck. He confirmed it was real with a beep.

"He was stalling until the others could get back to the ship," Wren said quietly. She looked nothing short of devastated.

"My father must have known about your brother," said Anders. "Maybe at one time he really was here—"

"Well, he's not here now, Anders! He's gone! Lost or dead or—or something!" She braced her hands on the control panel, staring at the freighters and cruisers dotting the sky over the desert, her shoulders heaving. "I'm stealing this ship."

I blinked at her. "You're crazy."

"Yes," she agreed. "But I'm still stealing this ship. Unless you have a better idea of how we can get out of here."

I didn't. The guards were trying in earnest to bust down the doors. I held up my comm, repeatedly scrambling their servers, but they were fighting back with their own tech and my grasp on the locks was slipping.

Gulping, Anders nodded and buckled himself into a jump seat beside the conference table. "Steal the ship, then." He gave her a shaky smile. "Captain."

Wren started up the engines while Elio and I strapped in. Off in the distance, the waiting ships flew forward, like they thought they could stop us. They were merely specks of dust compared to the size of the Andilly military craft.

The ground fell away under the rumble of the engines. The guards were blown back as we gained altitude, tumbling and rolling across the sand as the other ships surged toward us. Wren stared out the viewport, adjusting her grips on the controls.

She noticed a silver knob on the display in front of her. "Excellent! It has an invisibility shield. This thing is sweet." And yet, her enthusiasm sounded forced.

She zipped around two cruisers and a cargo ship as our hull shimmered, metal panels sliding out to reflect the terrain around us. Our ship vanished completely.

Sapphire light spilled off Wren in waves. It didn't let up, even as we traveled mile after mile away from the village and toward the *Starchaser*. The aura around her was more than just a simple burst of sadness.

I'd never seen anyone so utterly heartbroken.

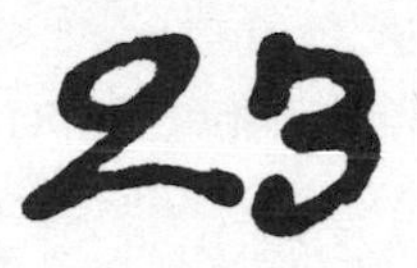

WE DUMPED THE DECOY GUARD IN THE MIDDLE OF THE desert. No one really felt bad about it. I mean, it wasn't like we had killed him or anything. And after what he'd done to Wren, he would have deserved it if we had.

Wren retracted the invisibility shield once we landed beside the *Starchaser*, dwarfing the old ship instantly. "This thing purrs like a kitten." She patted the control panel. "What did I do to deserve something so beautiful?" She was laughing, but I could see the murky blue cloud still floating around her, like she was trapped underwater and had forgotten how to swim. She caught my eye for a moment, then frowned and shook her head slightly. I got the message. *Shut up, Cora.*

The *Starchaser*'s engines were still useless, so after grabbing our belongings, we sadly agreed to leave the ship where it was and continue on in the Andilly military craft. With only a day and a half to get to Condor, we couldn't afford to waste any more time.

"Farewell, old friend," Anders said as the *Starchaser* faded from view. I was weirdly sad to see it go. It hadn't been flashy, but it had been dependable. The dinky, rusty ship had been there for us, and leaving it behind, watching it get covered with sand as the desert winds blew, felt like I was chopping off one of my limbs.

Bye, bye, Elio wrote on my comm and held it up to the viewport. But our trusty ship was already gone.

"Let's go over what's going to happen on Condor," Wren said. She shifted the ship into autopilot after we broke through Rebrone's atmosphere and sat at the conference table. "I mean, besides Cora giving us an awesome tour of her home planet. Hey, wait!" she called when I pushed out of my chair. "Where are you going?"

To distance myself so I don't grow more attached to you, I thought. *To find some magical way to turn my heart into a block of lead. To run and hide because I'm a coward.*

"I'm taking a walk."

"Oh, okay." For a second she looked puzzled, but the expression quickly cleared. "Hurry back. I'm going to raid the galley. We might as well eat like royalty before we charge headfirst into disaster again."

I flashed her a thumbs-up. "Got it. I won't be long."

She caught my arm before I could leave. "Hey. You're okay, right?"

"Are you?"

"That's not fair."

Nothing in this universe was fair. "Who has the key?"

Wren pointed to Elio, and he tapped a storage compartment in his arm. Good. He was carrying a key and I was carrying a key. Only one more to go.

"Yeah, Wren. I'm perfectly fine." I pulled my arm back. Hers fell limp at her side. "Why wouldn't I be?"

She didn't answer, and I thought I was in the clear. But I was gravely mistaken when Anders chased after me and pulled me to a stop after I crossed the bridge, emerging into the main atrium.

"Where are you going?"

"For a walk. Stars, is that a crime now?"

He stepped back, holding up his hands. "Not in the slightest. Would you . . . well, would you perhaps like company on this walk you're taking that is most certainly not a crime?"

Yes. "No thanks. I mean, I'm tired so . . . ," I lied when his face started to fall. He quickly replaced the frown with an easy smile.

"Oh. Right. Of course. Better rest up before the big day. Are you excited to be back on your planet?"

I didn't have to lie this time. "Not at all."

"I understand completely. I wouldn't want to return to Andilly either. I'm wondering if I'll ever go back once we're pardoned."

"Really? Where will you go?" Or not go, because his freedom was currently up for debate.

"I liked Rebrone a lot. Andillians are made for warm climates." He rubbed a hand over the lizard-like scales on his forehead. "What about you? Will you stay on Condor?"

"I . . . don't know." With my cut of the profits, I would likely have enough to travel the universe, even after I purchased Elio his new body. But Evelina would never allow it. She would want me home, available for any jobs that came our way.

"Ah. Well, you still have time to think about it, right? Oh!" He smiled sheepishly. "Sorry, I'm keeping you from resting, aren't I?" He started back to the bridge, but then he pivoted, offering me his hand with his palm facing outward. Just like a—

"Five high?" He winked.

"Actually, it's called a—"

"I know what it's called, Cora."

A spark of electricity rattled me to the core when his fingers curled gently around mine. Barely a breath of time passed, but it was long enough to make me wish I'd never stopped to talk to him. I shouldn't have talked to either of them. *Ever*. I put myself in this position.

"Five high," I whispered as Anders pulled back and walked away. He looked over his shoulder once. Then he disappeared through the door at the end of the hall, and I was left only with my thoughts.

Condor was dark. *Shocker*.

High noon in the middle of the city meant nothing. The sky remained inky black. Disguises in place, we left the ship in one of the landing bays beneath the city center and boarded an express tube out to the coast. The train was packed, full of people making the trek for the New Moon festival. Even if they didn't have invitations to get into the party at the mansion, there were always floats and dancing in the streets, the crowds so densely packed it was almost impossible to forge a path through them. You could only go where they took you, riding the masses like a wave until you were able to push your way out the other side.

In the privacy of our cabin, the four of us watched the city lights of Condor fade away, replaced by dozens of smaller coastal towns. The air outside the tube was swampy, as it always was on this side of the planet, and Wren traced her fingers through a path of condensation on the window. "Do you and Elio live out this way, Cora?"

"No, we're on the opposite side of the city. Manufacturing district. We don't have nearly as much open space there."

Wren hummed. "I like it here. I might stay. Will we get to meet the rest of your family while we're here?"

I cast a quick glance at Elio, who was playing some type of dice game with Anders that the two of them had picked up back at the tube station. He felt me watching and gave me a shrug and a beep.

"They're probably pretty busy at the moment," I told Wren. "But you might see them. You never know."

What Wren wasn't aware of was that I had been messaging Blair ever since our ship touched down in the landing bay. The whole family was en route to Verena's compound and was lying low, waiting for my signal. The last comm I'd received from him read: *Nana Rae won't stop singing, and I'm way too sober to listen.*

Why are you sober? I asked him.

You aren't the only one taking this job seriously.

In a way, he was right. Out of all of us, I was probably taking today the most seriously. But everyone in this cabin had something at stake, not just me. And that was why, when Anders tapped me on the arm and motioned for me to join him and Elio in their game, I shook my head.

I also believed I had the most to lose.

Wren and I climbed the steep ivory ramp to the front of the mansion. The cobblestone roads behind us were more crowded than I'd predicted, filled with men, women, and children carrying multicolored sparklers, dancing to heavy brass bands that had popped up on every street corner. Wren adjusted her long beaded veil, and I smoothed out a fold in my silk dress, pressing my VED more firmly against my chest. I was Earthan tonight, demure and unassuming. And every good thief knew it was the most unassuming criminals who were the most dangerous.

We were two groups away from the mansion doors. The black mist that shrouded Verena's compound settled over our shoulders, while the jagged cliffs connected to her home pointed down at us like knives.

Wren reached under her veil and squeezed my hand. "Together we will accomplish great, but possibly not legal, things," she whispered.

Against my better judgment, I squeezed back. "Aye aye, Captain."

The group in front of us stepped away. We were next. Gulping, Wren wrenched her hand away and clapped it over her chest. "*I've heard*," she started in a loud voice, "that Verena's table settings are worth more than one hundred thousand ritles *each*! Hey, you there!" She elbowed me. "What would you do with one hundred thousand ritles?"

I turned my nose up to the black sky, playing along. "I'd have enough to start a campaign to knock Verena right off her throne, that's what. But the table settings are child's play. What you should really go after are the *candelabra*. Word on the net is that each one is made of palladium from Planet Nine—"

Wren gasped dramatically. "Planet Nine! A myth, surely!"

"Definitely not! It's the wealthiest planet in the Milky Way Galaxy, and what Verena doesn't want anyone to know is that she has plenty of its priceless artifacts right inside her very—"

"*Excuse me.*" The shadow of an android guard fell over us. A red laser from his right eye roved over our faces, but not even it could see through the illusion of the VEDs. "What is the meaning of this commotion?"

"Well, excuse *me*. No, excuse *you*." Wren got right up in the guard's face, pretending to sway drunkenly. "I don't believe this . . . *commotion*, as you say, is any of your concern."

She ran her fingers over the android's metal arm before gripping his wrist and attempting to twist it behind his back. I could feel the crowd behind us pressing forward, impatient. Hopefully they were listening in as well.

In an instant, the guard had Wren on her knees. But he was careless. He'd turned away from me, leaving his blaster partially exposed on his belt. I dived for it, but I was attacked by a second guard who emerged from the mansion doors, throwing me down. My head hit the ground with a crack. The crowd gasped. Chest constricting as the guard pressed his boot firmly against my spine, I looked up at Wren through the tears in my eyes.

Accomplish illegal things? Certainly. Great things, however—that was yet to be determined.

The pressure on my back increased. Stars, it was going to snap. *Where was*—

Then, like something out of a net drama, the mansion doors swept open with a creak.

Finally.

The buzz of a fully powered blaster accompanied two leisurely sets of footsteps. The first set belonged to another, smaller android. The next set belonged to a Condor guard, his shiny black boots the only part of him I could see until he crouched down in front of me. Bright white skin, sharp ears, glowing eyes. He raised my chin with his weapon.

"You weren't thinking of robbing the empress." He exchanged his gun for his fingernails, which dug two long scratches into my cheeks. "Were you?"

"Of course not," I answered. "We're no criminals."

The guard hummed. He studied the others as a hush fell over the crowd. The New Moon was a time of celebration, but I doubted the citizens of Condor would object to an arrest or an execution. Anything for entertainment.

The Condor guard—the guard commander, judging by the insignia lining the shoulders of his uniform jacket—lifted me off the ground by my throat. I tried fighting him, but he dug his thumb into a pressure point in my neck, and my legs turned to rubber. The android who had accompanied him outside dragged Wren to her feet.

"You're both coming with me," the commander said.

"Sir!" The first android guard rushed forward to object.

"I don't want to hear it. Keep an eye on these doors. Ensure there are no further disruptions."

"But—sir! We should alert the security station in town, have them put these perpetrators under arrest. They were conspiring against the empress! They assaulted me!"

"Assaulted you?" The guard's lips widened into a smirk. "In that case, I suggest you hang up your blaster and return home to lick your wounds, you pathetic excuse for an enforcement officer. You couldn't even detain two unarmed Earthans on your own. Look at them." He squished his fingers into my cheeks. "They're harmless."

The commander's android partner pushed Wren toward the

mansion doors. Her shoulder clipped the doorframe, and she hissed in pain. The commander wheeled me around, prodding his blaster into the center of my back. "Inside. Move. *I'm not a slow walker.*"

I couldn't help but smile.

"Wait! Sir!" The android tried one final time. "You're locking them in the labyrinth? If Verena finds out we're letting them stay here—"

The pressure of the blaster left my back as the commander fired it into the air. The burst of light disappeared almost immediately into the smog above the compound, but it had the right effect. The crowd below hung on his every word. And behind us, just inside the doors, more guards—android and human alike—had come to investigate the source of the commotion.

"Verena won't find out," the commander snarled. "Imagine how she would feel knowing that her celebration has been tainted by criminal filth. Imagine what she would do to the guard who brought such ignominious news to her attention."

"I—I'm not sure what that word means . . ."

"Invest in a dictionary. And if you value your life, don't breathe a word of this scuffle to Verena." The guard poked me in the back. "I didn't tell you to stop walking!"

Blaster still at my back, I crossed the threshold of Empress Verena's mansion and entered a grand foyer trimmed with red curtains and black-and-white tiles. The room was full of guests milling around hors d'oeuvre stations and champagne fountains, and they all turned to stare while Wren and I were led through the center of the throng. Their finery—velvet coats and jewel-encrusted gowns—made my silk dress, which had suffered a long rip from my ankles to my knees after the tussle outside, feel like a flimsy nightgown. I held my head high anyway, ignoring the buzz of the guard's blaster that cut through the silence like a swarm of angry insects.

The commander and his android sidekick led us underneath a row of chandeliers dripping strings of pearls and between two elegant moonstone ramps to a side door built into a wooden panel on the wall. The staff hallway we entered, with its concrete floors and dirt-streaked walls, was freezing cold.

"Here. Take this." The commander immediately shrugged out of his jacket and draped it across my shoulders. His skin started to bubble, like it was boiling right off his bones. Then his face and body morphed back into the familiar form of Anders. He reached for me, nimble fingers grazing my cheeks. "Stars, I got you good, didn't I? I'm sorry, Cora."

"Don't worry about it. I knew it was coming." I dabbed at my skin, wiping away a smudge of blood.

Wren watched us with a scowl. "I'm cold too. Don't I get a coat?"

"Ask Elio. Although his might be rather small." Anders nodded at the android, whose appearance was flickering and shifting into the round body of a generic servant bot while Elio adjusted the VED stuck to his chest.

Rolling her eyes, Wren tossed us each new bundles of clothes that she had hidden under her skirt. We changed our outfits and then our appearances in silence, listening for the patter of footsteps from approaching mansion staff. Outside the doors, it sounded like the party had returned to normal. Hopefully the real mansion guards thought that their "commander" had neutralized the only threat they would see all evening.

But if the crowd had been listening before Wren and I were detained, then at least a few of them would heed our advice and try to swipe a few of Verena's valuables for themselves. The perfect diversion. Verena's guards would ideally be so occupied with preventing those robberies that the path beneath the compound would be left completely clear.

I pulled out my comm from a pocket in my new lace jumpsuit. Not only would the labyrinth be clear for us, but after all the guards ran to the front doors to see what all the fuss had been about, it would be left unobstructed for my family too. And according to Blair's latest message, they were down there right now, waiting.

"Does everyone have their flash bombs?" Wren asked. Her white hair from her VED illusion matched the white skirt hanging low on her hips.

Anders tugged on a suit coat, pulled a flask from his pocket, and used the liquid inside to slick back his hair. When I gave him a weird stare, he just shrugged, looking at me from behind a fresh Earthan face. "Of course. They're ready to detonate at the first sign of trouble. Here's to hoping we won't need them."

Beep! said Elio. He scurried forward and handed me a blaster, my phaser, and two fresh flash bombs.

I thanked him, offered Wren the phaser—my family was bringing my spare with them—and shoved the rest in my pockets. My comm was buzzing out of control. Multiple messages from Blair asking where I was, one from my uncle Alfie telling me to hurry up, and one from Nana Rae wondering if the food in the mansion was as good as rumor claimed. None from Cruz. Especially none from Evelina.

"We should split up," I told the others. "You two take the eastern passages in the labyrinth. Elio and I will handle the western. We can meet back up in an hour." The lie tasted sharp on my tongue. If things went according to plan—the *real* plan, not the one I'd fed them aboard our stolen Andilly ship—then this could very well be the last time I ever saw them.

I forced down the sudden wave of emotion that prickled at the back of my eyes. Crying now would be too suspicious.

Maybe . . . just *maybe* I could persuade Evelina to help hide Wren and Anders from the warden too, once we handed over the keys. But I knew she would never. She didn't aid anyone outside our family. If it weren't for the money, she wouldn't have even come here today to help me and Elio.

"I don't know if we should split up," Wren said, looking nervously at Anders. "We ran into trouble last time."

"Where's your sense of adventure?" I countered. "We are strong, independent, terrifying outlaws, and the universe apparently thinks we're worth something, so let's act like it and make the warden wish he'd picked some other group of misfits to mess with. Deal?"

Elio punched his fists in the air and beeped.

Wren started to laugh. "Did you make that speech up yourself?"

"No, I clipped it off one of your cereal boxes." I rolled my eyes. "*Yes*, I made it up myself."

Her smile grew, but she still didn't look totally convinced. Deep in my pocket, my comm continued buzzing. *Okay, I get it. You're all here.* This was the most my family cared to talk to me in, well, *ever*.

Anders seemed to weigh the pros and cons. "We can do this, Wren. We're better prepared this time. Comm each other if we run into trouble and we'll activate the explosives. That goes for finding the key as well. Alert the others and get out as quickly as possible. We'll all meet back at the tube station."

I nodded. "Perfect."

Elio beeped in agreement.

"And if the key isn't here?" Wren asked. "If we're wrong?"

"We're not," I insisted. "It's here. Somewhere. But if we can't find it, well, at least there's a lot of good food in this house."

She nodded adamantly, steeling herself. "You're right. Of course you're right. Sorry. Just got a little nervous there." For the second time that night, she reached for my hand. "I trust you, Cora."

Don't.

Instead of answering, I pulled up the blueprint of the compound on my comm and studied the network of tunnels running beneath the building. Evelina said all of Verena's most valuable artifacts were housed down there. The entrance to the western side of the labyrinth, where I'd agreed to meet my family, could be accessed from a door at the end of this hallway. The eastern tunnels were on the other side of the mansion, beneath the kitchens.

Hands on their blasters, Wren and Anders headed off in the opposite direction. But before they had taken more than a few steps, Anders hurried back.

"Cora, um . . . you . . . I . . ." Finally, he gave up and rested his palm against my cheek.

I wanted to pull away.

I wanted to pull him closer.

After everything we've been through, this could be the final time.

I settled for placing my palm on top of his. *Stupid.* So stupid of me to care this much. But he was more than a big red Andilly jerk. More than a murderer. More than a boy trapped in a prison cell. He was my teammate. And he was my friend. He didn't deserve this.

Neither of them did.

I let my hand fall. "Stay safe, Andy."

His fingers brushed the corner of my mouth as he backed away. "Stay safe, Cora."

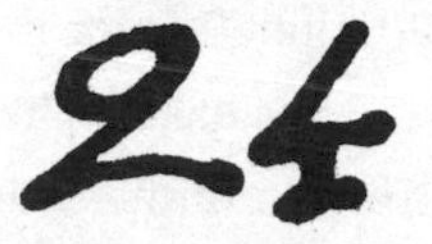

I FOUND MY FAMILY CROWDED AROUND A SEWAGE GRATE IN the tunnels. The location was strangely befitting.

"Took you long enough," Blair said, frowning at me and Elio after we removed the illusions from our VEDs.

I brushed right past him, my gaze focused on Evelina and the way she was almost grinning, as if admitting she didn't hate me anymore for botching the treasury job on Vaotis two weeks ago. As I neared, she and Cruz glanced at each other, then pulled me in for a hug so painful I felt like I was being smothered with a blanket. I guess they were a little out of practice in that department.

Once they released me, Evelina motioned for me and Elio to take the lead into the depths of the labyrinth. Relinquishing control of a job wasn't Evelina's style, but she did so without complaint and, *stars*, I would be lying if I said it didn't feel good.

Almost good enough to make me forget how horrible I was being to two people who considered me their friend.

I nearly stumbled as we rounded a bend in the tunnel. Nope. I couldn't let my mind go there. The rest of my family couldn't read auras as well as me, but they would still notice if my emotions didn't quite make sense. We were steps away from endless riches, steps away from getting Elio a body that wouldn't deteriorate. I had no reason to be anything other than thrilled.

But just as Evelina looked down at me and winked, Elio gripped my hand and squeezed. He nodded at me, then gazed sadly over his shoulder, back the way we came. Back to Anders and Wren.

"They'll be okay," I told him. "It's for the best."

"What's for the best?" Evelina asked. She was checking her comm for hidden rooms located in the tunnels, but at the moment all we could see was flickering halogen lights and an unbroken stretch of brick walls, curving around us like we were creeping through the throat of a gigantic beast.

"I was saying it's best if we get in and out quickly. We drew the guards to the front of the compound, but there's no telling how long they'll stay away."

"They don't traditionally patrol down here," Cruz said. "Or at least they didn't before . . ." He looked at his wife. *Before Evelina tried raiding the labyrinth.* But reminding her of a failure was likely to get him slapped.

Evelina chuckled. "Happy to be home, Cora dearest?"

I forced my emotions to remain calm. "Always."

We walked on, encountering nothing but a few rats. I studied my comm. I knew there was more down here, vaults and hidden passageways. But the longer I looked at the blueprint on my screen, the more the tunnels seemed to twist and blur together. Surely that was what Verena wanted. To confuse us.

After nearly twenty minutes, my comm vibrated and the screen brought up a magnified view of the bend ahead. I couldn't tell exactly what I was looking at, but my device's heat and motion sensors were flying off the charts.

"There's something up there," I said. "In an annex on the right side of the tunnel."

We passed beneath an archway covered in cobwebs that led into a circular room. Once again, Evelina suggested Elio and I head in first to investigate. Blair was then pushed in behind us against his will.

I spun around in the empty space. The walls and floor were made of rock, sprinkled with a thin layer of sand. Where had the heat signature come from? The ceiling was high, almost fifty feet above our heads. I couldn't see anything up there; I couldn't hear anything either.

"Let's keep moving," I said.

Evelina shook her head from beneath the arch. "No. That wasn't a false reading. If it's a possibility that the key is hidden—"

She never had a chance to finish her thought. With a screech of grinding metal, a door slid down from above the arch. It hit the floor with a clang, leaving my family trapped in the tunnels.

And me, Elio, and Blair isolated inside the annex.

"Mom! Dad!" Blair rushed the steel door, pounding with his fists. It had no lock, no internal interface that my comm could hack into to raise it. In a strange way, it seemed like our presence alone had triggered the door to fall.

"You brought my phaser with you, didn't you?" I asked Blair. I examined the door, searching for openings while Elio walked the perimeter of the room.

Blair scowled. "I didn't. Your mother probably has it."

Well, if she did, why wasn't she using it? I shouldn't have given my spare to Wren. I'd done it as a parting gift, a final show of solidarity, but now my kindness was stabbing me in the back.

"Was the battery dead?" I rammed my shoulder into the door, sending a shooting pain down my arm. Blair joined me, pushing and kicking at the metal.

"How should I know, Cora? I didn't build the cursed thing. Daddy! Mommy!"

"*Mommy*?" I snorted, sweat covering my brow. "At least try to act like you're part of an infamous crime family."

"Shut up. Just because you've seen the inside of a prison cell doesn't mean you're suddenly tough." He pulled at the collar of his T-shirt. "Why is it so hot in here?"

"No air circulation. We probably shouldn't exert ourselves so—"

Beep! Beep! Beep!

"I think your robot is broken," Blair said, watching Elio jump and spin in the center of the floor. Elio's eyes flashed with panic as he pointed high above us to the ceiling. There was a gap between the rocks up there, extending around the circumference of the room. Something inside it was shimmering, glowing red.

The heat signature I'd picked up on.

"Is the roof dripping . . ." Blair squinted. "Lava?"

Oh stars.

I pounded harder on the door. "Evelina! Cruz! Let us out!"

I swore I felt a thump come from the other side. Like they were shooting with their blasters, trying to break down the door.

"Hurry!" I shouted, backing away to get out of their line of fire. Cracks had formed on the walls and the ceiling, orange bubbles of lava squeezing through, dripping down toward us. We crowded into the center of the room to avoid them as they hissed and peppered the rocks around us. The temperature spiked, the heat dizzying. Elio clutched my leg, beeping.

Blair pushed his sweat-drenched hair out of his eyes. "This doesn't make sense. Verena booby-trapped an empty room?" A glob of lava fell inches from his shoes, and he jumped back, screaming.

"You're right. As much as I hate to admit that. There has to be something here . . ." Something worth protecting. Something worth killing us over. As more lava dripped down the walls, the floor shook. Fissures formed in the rocks. The ground tilted, the room splitting into two halves, forcing us apart. The rocks in the center shot up at a sharp angle, while the ones on the outside of the room lowered, forming a steep ramp declining toward the lava-covered walls.

"Cora! I swear I'm not going to die like this!" Blair hooked his arms over the top of the rocks on his side, while Elio and I did the same on ours. Our legs dangled down toward the lava, scrambling for purchase as the rocks shifted and shook as if alive. What was Verena protecting down here? It had to be the key.

I peered over the top of the rocks. A great chasm stretched out below us. A steaming rush of more lava ran like a river into a dark passageway. No way out. No way to safety. But then—the molten rocks bubbled, exposing for barely a second . . . a treasure chest.

"There!" I pointed as the lava rushed over the chest and the rocks continued to shake. "It's down there!"

"I don't see anything!" Blair called back.

The rocks shifted, pushing me and Elio even higher. They jerked to a halt. Fell again.

The sudden change in momentum forced Elio to lose his grip on the stones he was clutching. His tiny body flew into the air. Over the top of the rocks, above the chasm.

With nothing but the lava below to break his fall.

"NO! Elio!" I lunged over the edge to grab him, my fingers just barely hooking around his.

Beeeeeep!

"Hang on! I got you!"

But he was too heavy. I was halfway over the rocks as it was; if I moved so much as an inch to pull him up, I was going to lose my balance, and we would both fall. The weight of his body pulled my shoulders from their sockets.

Beep! Beep! Beep!

I couldn't lose him. Not like this. Not when we were *so close.*

Lava dripped from the ceiling, great globs of it landing with a hiss right next to me. The rocks rumbled on Blair's side, almost forcing him to fall. Then they shook on my side again, directly beneath me, pitching me up with the force of a rocket launch.

I lost my grip on Elio's hands.

A primal scream ripped out of me as I watched him tumble head over heels toward the river. He reached up just once, fingers splayed in a silent plea to help him. I couldn't watch. I couldn't look away. Despite the heat surrounding me, my body had turned completely numb.

He hit the river and—

And passed right through.

"What the—?" The lava was dense enough to support his weight. And yet, Elio had merely vanished.

As if the lava hadn't been there at all.

I wrenched a large rock off the wall beside me and hurled it down. It fell toward the river and then, right when it should have made contact, it disappeared too.

I looked up at Blair. "We have to jump."

"Are you crazy? I know you loved that bot, but self-sacrifice isn't the answer!"

"No, idiot! The lava is a hologram!"

The stuff sliding down the walls around us, causing the stifling heat, was undoubtedly real, but the river below was a mirage. It made me think of the treasure chest I'd seen. Was that real too, or another illusion?

I supposed it was time to find out. I hoisted one leg over the edge of the rock tower. Blair followed, looking sick to his stomach. Then, right as the real lava from the ceiling started gushing like a waterfall in a final attempt to kill us, I let go, tumbling through the air to reunite with Elio on the other side.

25

UP CLOSE, THE LAVA HOLOGRAM LOOKED LIKE A LINE OF orange static. The illusion rippled as Blair and I made contact, and then the rumbling rocks faded as we were thrown down a steel chute into the bowels of Verena's compound. We crashed into each other as the chute curved sharply in a frenetic spiral, his foot accidentally kicking me in the back of the head, my fist *not* accidentally hitting him between the shoulder blades. The darkness pressed in on my eyes like a blanket. I had been correct—the glimmering chest I'd seen for a split second had been fake too.

The chute spun in two more tight circles before spitting us out into an open room. I flew through the air, smacking the wall while my eyes struggled to adjust to the bright lights surrounding us. Blair smashed into my back before falling to the ground with a groan. Behind us, a door slammed shut.

I whirled around. We were in a wine cellar. I'd heard a door, but I didn't see one—just an expanse of shelves along the wall filled with old bottles. Were those more holograms? I touched them, finding them solid and real with no hint of a secret door behind them. Whatever passageway we had been shot through had somehow closed itself off.

"Elio?" I called out. He wasn't down here. But—he should have been. He should have been alive and safe, as we were.

"There might be multiple chutes out of the lava room," Blair said. "He probably got thrown out somewhere else." He pointed to a ramp leading upward and we climbed it, exiting into the kitchens. The eastern tunnels into the labyrinth where Wren and Anders had ventured were supposed to be beneath this very room—in the wine cellar. But I hadn't seen an entry down there. Wherever they were, hopefully they hadn't run into their own room full of lava. Or something more sinister.

Blair swiped a tea sandwich off a tray, weaving through a line of mansion employees as we exited the kitchen and emerged into one of the staff corridors. For the first time since entering the labyrinth, I looked down at my clothes. The lace on my jumpsuit was shredded along my ribs and caked with dirt. No longer good attire for Verena's fancy party, but I guess I should've just been glad the whole thing hadn't burned to ash.

"Where do you think Elio is?" I asked. We pushed through a door and entered the back side of a music room packed with guests. I attempted to activate my VED only to find it dead, along with my comm and Blair's too. Must have been all the heat from that room. I hoped Elio made it out okay.

"I don't see why you care so much about that little thing," he said. We backed into an alcove in the wood paneling where no one would see us.

"He's my best friend," I growled. "Which I know means nothing to you, so let me explain it in a way that you might actually care about: Elio is holding one of Teolia's keys."

Blair's skin paled even more than normal. "He's *what*?"

"The key we took from the Andillians. He has it stashed in a locked compartment in his arm. Even if we find the last key and the treasure chest, we're screwed without him. The warden still has key number four in his office in Ironside, but it's pointless for us to break in there and take it if we don't have the rest of them."

Blair tilted his head. "Evelina stole that from the warden yesterday."

"What? No, she said she was going to wait."

"I don't know. I'm just going off what she said. She posed as a ship mechanic or something. I saw the key. It's half the length of my arm, looks like a hook, has some sparkly things glued to it. Ringing any bells?"

"Several." I clenched my teeth. Why had Evelina deviated from the plan I'd given her? I supposed it didn't matter. A key was a key, no matter who stole it.

"So your robot actually has some use after all," Blair mused. "And here I thought he was only good for setting the kitchen on fire. When we find him, we get all the keys, correct?"

"When we find *all* the keys, then you get all the keys. Until then, they're safer with Elio."

"Okay, fine," Blair conceded. He stood on his toes to scan the room. "Too bad he's so short. Kinda gets lost in a crowd. What about those friends of yours? The ones everyone is looking for?"

"What about them?"

"I'm guessing they don't know that you're double-crossing them. What will happen to them without the keys? Will they get arrested again? Executed?"

I shoved him back against the wall. "Does it matter?"

"Not to me." He reached out and tweaked my nose. I had the sudden urge to bite his fingers off, but just thinking about what might become of Anders and Wren without the treasure took the fight right out of me.

"Looks like you're finally fitting into this family after all, Cora. You're ruthless." He stepped out of the alcove, swiping a glass of champagne off a server's tray before merging into the crowd. "I'll find the others and tell them about Elio. You keep looking for him. Meet us outside in an hour. Oh, and one more thing . . ."

"What?"

Blair nodded at the alcove next to ours. "Tell your friends the Saros family says hello."

"What are you talking about?" But he was gone.

The stretch of panels near us was totally empty . . .

Except for Wren.

She was using my phaser, standing half in and half out of the wall. Her clothes were just as dirty and ripped as mine from wherever she and Anders had gone; judging by the lack of a hologram surrounding her, her VED was broken as well. But that didn't matter. All I could see was the look of stunned betrayal hardening her eyes as an amethyst cloud of anguish spread out around her.

She'd heard everything.

"Wren!" I rushed toward her, but she stepped back and deactivated the phaser, sealing the wall shut. *Saturn's rings, not now. Not this.*

Blair had known she was there. When he scanned the room, he had seen her. I was sure of it. With the phaser in her possession, she could have disappeared to anywhere in the mansion. I had to find her. I had to find Elio. And I had to do both without the hundreds of people in this house recognizing me.

Head low, I pushed through the crowd back into the foyer. My fingers itched to pull the pins on my flash bombs. But if I forced everyone outside, it would be that much harder to get back in and find the key. No, I had to stay here. I had to find a way to work this out.

Elio couldn't have made it far on such tiny legs. I searched the entryway, looking along the walls and underneath the shadow of the chandeliers. The partiers had multiplied since the last time I came through. I could hardly take a step without accidentally standing on someone's toes.

I was edging across the room to the ramps leading up to the higher floors when the front doors blew open and slammed against the wall.

"FIND THEM!" a voice bellowed. I ducked on instinct. I knew that voice. It gave me shivers up my spine. *The warden*.

An army of guards spread out around him like a tidal wave. Verena's own guards didn't seem to know what to do about them. They retreated into the corners as the Andillians invaded the crowd, causing guests to scream and cower against the walls.

The warden tapped his comm, projecting our photos into the air. "We are not here to harm you," he said to the revelers. "We're searching for a few escaped convicts. Help us find them, and you will be rewarded. Stand in our way . . . and you will suffer the same fate as them. Any questions?"

No one dared to object. Groups rushed across the foyer, excitedly discussing their potential reward. That was the thing about rich people: they loved to get even richer. Those who decided not to partake cleared the way for the warden and his guards. They crossed the foyer, heading for one of the doors leading to the staff corridors.

"Their trackers are glitching," the warden said to a woman at his side. "I can't get a good read on their location, but they're definitely in here somewhere. Evelina said that whole blasted family would be here."

They passed right by my hiding spot at the foot of the ramps and disappeared from view. Legs shaking, I stumbled to my feet. Blair said Evelina robbed the warden yesterday, not that she had *spoken* with him. What was going on?

I started climbing the main ramp to the second level when voices rang out behind me. "There's one!" an android guard of Verena's shouted.

"Get her!" screamed an Earthan woman.

But I was already moving, pulling out both flash bombs and yanking the pins. The grenades hit the wall above the front door, exploding in a stream of light, shaking the mansion, knocking paintings from walls, food from trays, and guests from their feet.

I fell to my knees on the second floor, crawling into a staff corridor as my pursuers screamed and ducked. But this hallway was still crowded, some people running up a level to reach higher ground, while others pushed downstream to get to the front doors and the safety of the streets outside. I pulled my hair forward to hide my face just as another group of searchers rounded the bend.

And then I felt a hand clamp across my mouth and pull.

"Easy there! Easy!" The figure held me against the wall as I struggled. "It's just me." Anders's skin flashed from his Earthan disguise to red scales, then flashed back.

"Yoostangningtonmyfoo," I garbled beneath the pressure of his fingers. Anders removed his hand, flushing pink.

"Say again?"

"You're standing on my foot."

"Oh! Right. So sorry." He hopped back. "You look like a mess, Cora."

"Thanks. You look terrible too." His dress shirt was shredded to tatters, his hair knotted and filled with brambles.

"Verena is keeping some awful critters in the labyrinth's eastern tunnels. The giant hungry spiders did this." He gestured to his clothes. "What about you?"

"Molten lava waterfall."

"Delightful. No sign of the key?"

"None. You?"

He shook his head. This didn't make sense. Why fill rooms with lava and man-eating arachnids if you weren't protecting anything inside?

"Have you seen Elio?" I asked him. "We got separated."

"I haven't seen him since we split up," said Anders. "But he'll be fine. He's tough."

"Normally I would agree with you, but not today. Your father is here."

Anders's skin flickered, briefly turning red with anger. "Here? *Now*?"

"And a group of guards." I filled him in on our trackers glitching and the warden announcing our bounty to Verena's entire party. "And my VED is broken and Elio is gone and . . . and . . ." My chest and my mind filled with so much panic I couldn't even remember how to breathe. "I can't do this anymore, Anders." Tears welled in my eyes. "I can't. I—has Wren talked to you?"

"Not since we escaped the tunnels. Why?"

"Because I—"

Another blast shook the mansion. Screams echoed off the walls. Anders pulled me around the corner to another upward-sloping ramp. Servant bots rolled past us, following human staff who ran for cover just as a cluster of the warden's guards entered the hall.

They were nearly on top of us, shouting orders to each other in harsh Andillian.

"Come here," Anders said. "We have to hide you." He pressed me against the wall, blocking me with his Earthan disguise. But even though he looked inconspicuous, surely the guards would find it strange if they turned the bend and saw the two of us just standing here staring at each other.

"May I?" Anders asked me.

"May you what?"

"Sorry, we don't have time. Slap me later if this offends you."

Then he leaned down, blocking my face just as the guards appeared in my peripheral, and kissed me.

I didn't know what I had been expecting, but it wasn't *this*. The heat of his body pressed into mine, my fingers slipping through his hair, his lips crushing but also so gentle—warm and urgent and wanting. There were too many words to describe the sensation, like the endless stars in the sky, the endless galaxies in the universe. Even when we pulled apart, I knew I would carry this moment, this brief little flash of existence where time and space held still and there was us—only us—with me for infinity.

I vaguely heard the guards grumbling something about Earthans and their sick need for public displays of affection before they continued down the corridor, leaving me and Anders completely alone.

He leaned his forehead against mine. Our chests heaved, bumping into each other. "We don't kiss on Andilly," he said. "I've never done that before. I . . ." He wet his lips. "I think it gave me heartburn."

I laughed. "I think that's how you're supposed to feel."

"Truly? In that case, perhaps we should try it again. In the interest of science, of course. Just to make sure that I don't have some type of underlying medical condition . . ."

He pulled me closer, and I didn't protest, and I felt like the most selfish person in the universe because of it. He ran his hands over my hips, fingers skimming the tears in the sides of my jumpsuit. I lifted my arm to brush a strand of hair from his eyes, and then—

I was suddenly met with the cold pressure of his blaster against my temple.

In a blur of motion, he ripped my own blaster from my hip and slammed my arms against the wall above my head.

His skin bubbled, his true form rippling back into view. And, *stars*, he looked mad.

"Wren told me. *Everything*. She found me before the first explosion went off. I lied."

"I can explain—"

"Can you?" His claws came out and punctured the wall, caging my wrists. "Are you going to feed me more lies? That's apparently all you've been doing since we met!"

"It's not—"

"No." His finger tightened on the trigger of his blaster. "It is. Were you ever going to tell us the truth? Or were you just going to give the keys to your family and then disappear forever?"

I didn't answer, but that was all the confirmation he needed.

"I could kill you right now," he snarled. "You know I could."

"It that why you just kissed me? Wanted to get it out of your system before committing one more murder? That's sick."

"What's sick is that you were going to abandon us to the warden! I *trusted* you. We both did. No matter what you thought about us, we trusted that you were on our side."

"But she's not." The wall next to me blurred and Wren stepped through, phaser in hand. Her eyes filled with tears. "How could you do it, Cora?"

"Listen, Wren. You wanted to be part of my family? Well, here's your great big welcome. We aren't good people. We will lie to you and stab you in the back just to get what we want. Isn't this what you asked for?"

"To be a *distraction*, like you?" she choked out.

That word, that horrible word. *Distraction*. It stole the breath from my lungs.

"What are you talking about?"

"A distraction. That's what your mother called you. She's using you to get the keys, if you haven't figured it out. I heard her talking to the warden. They're going to split the profits of the treasure. Then she's going to hand you over to him, and he's going to drag all of us back to Andilly and make an example of us. I don't know how, but I'm sure you can use your imagination."

"But Evelina wouldn't . . ." I had to stop myself. Of course she would. Of course she would sacrifice me to get what she wanted. Every time she looked at me like she cared, it had been a lie. She only cared about the money.

"Well, we can stop them—"

"*We* aren't doing anything ever again." She nodded to Anders. "We're leaving. As long as our trackers keep malfunctioning, they won't be able to follow. Do what you want with the key. Give it to your mother and get screwed, swallow the star-forsaken thing. I don't care. Just tell Elio that I'm sorry it had to end like this."

They both turned and started down the corridor. Wren didn't look back. Anders did for less than a second, his face expressionless, his aura pulled as deep down inside as the day I met him. He still had my blaster clutched in his fist.

This had all been for nothing. I couldn't give Elio Wren's message because I didn't know where he was. Evelina probably already found him. We would both be handed back to the warden. He would never get a new body, never get a second chance at life.

And I would have to sit in a cell in Ironside while I watched him fade away.

No. I wouldn't do it. To hell with Evelina. To hell with my whole star-forsaken family. I was a Saros too. I could play their game.

And I would win.

"Wren! Anders! Wait!"

They didn't. I sprinted to catch up with them and blocked their path. "Hey, wait a second."

Wren scowled. "Go back to your family, Cora."

"I will. If you help me." She scoffed and they both started walking again. I wriggled between them and pushed them back against the wall. "Hey. Look, I feel bad about what I did, but I can't apologize. Not where Elio is concerned. And until recently, I honestly didn't even like you guys that much."

"Wow, thanks," said Wren.

Anders shrugged. "Honestly, I didn't like you guys much either."

Wren rolled her eyes. "No, *really*?"

"Listen," I said. "I get that you may never want to look at me again after tonight, but if we're going to leave here hating each other, then we may as well also leave being really, really rich. Agreed?"

"I mean . . ." Wren sniffed and crossed her arms. And then I knew I had her. "I like money . . ."

"Well, what if I told you there might be a way to take down the warden, take down my family, and ensure that we end up with the treasure *and* our freedom?"

Anders's aura flared. "I'm listening . . ."

"First, we need to break into Verena's chambers."

Wren started laughing. "That is the worst idea I've ever heard."

"So you're opposed?"

"No, I'm just saying it's the worst idea I've ever heard." She pulled my blaster away from Anders, presenting it to me with a mocking bow. "When do we start?"

"WREN, FIND VERENA'S CHAMBERS AND FIGURE OUT HOW heavily they're guarded. Anders, I'm going to need copper wire, as many glass fragments as you can find, and some of those meatball kebabs they were serving in the ballroom." I held up my broken VED. "I'm going to attempt to fix this."

"Why the kebabs?" he asked. "Are we using the skewers as weapons? Oh! Don't tell me! You're going to isolate the protein in the meat and use its energy to power the—"

"Oh, no, no!" I shrugged. "I just wanted them because I'm hungry. Creative idea though."

He blinked at me.

I waved them both toward the end of the corridor. "I'm serious about the kebabs. Go! We need to work fast!"

"But—"

"Go! And if either of you see Elio, tackle him and drag him back with you. Do *not* let my family touch him."

"Let's go, team!" Wren clapped her hands. "Andy, bring me back a few of those kebabs too. I'm famished."

"So am I." He scowled. "Unfortunately for you, I know of an Earthan who looks particularly delicious—"

"Team!" I yelled. "Move!"

Anders lumbered off, grumbling obscenities the whole way down the hall. Wren nudged my arm. "I was going to suggest we come up with a cheer for some team spirit, but I think if I did, he really *would* eat me."

"Nah. His soul is too gentle, remember?"

"Of course." She sighed. "You know, this doesn't mean that I forgive you."

"I can live with that."

She fingered the barrel of her blaster, jaw working like she wanted to say something else. After a moment, she gave me a tiny smile. "I'll be back as soon as I can."

Once the echo of her footsteps faded away, I slumped against the wall and let out the universe's shakiest sigh. "Here goes nothing."

I was still struggling with the last few pieces of my visual enhancer while the three of us raced down a lavishly decorated hallway on the fourth floor west wing. "Are you certain this is the right room?" I asked Wren.

"Of course," she replied. "I know how to do recon. A guard comes and leaves this hall at the top of every hour, always heavily armed. You want to know why they switch shifts so often? I'll tell you why. It's so they can always stay alert, because they're protecting something or some*one*—"

"Who's very important," I finished. "Good job."

She visibly deflated. "You ruined my big finish. I was even thinking about doing jazz hands. Anyway, how do we want to do this? Shoot down the door? Crawl through an air duct?"

"We're going to walk right in like we belong." I pushed Anders in front of me. He was disguised as a Condorian, and while he walked he brushed dirt from the shoulders of his guard uniform. The real guard that he'd stolen it from was lying naked and unconscious in a closet somewhere on the ground floor.

As we neared the bend in the hall right before Verena's chambers,

I took a second to read the woman standing statuesque outside the door.

"Okay, she's starving and bored out of her mind. She's also strangely distraught about something. Use that to your advantage." Nudging Anders around the corner, I grabbed Wren and the two of us ducked behind a velvet curtain covering a bay window.

The guard at Verena's door groaned when Anders approached. "You're late."

"Sorry. I brought you some snacks." I heard a rustle, and could only assume he'd pulled out a bag of extra kebabs.

"You're still late," the guard snapped.

"Look, I said I was sorry. And really, I am." His voice softened and his aura rippled, like comforting autumn leaves floating around the hall. "I heard what happened. If there's anything I can do . . ."

He couldn't have been any vaguer about the guard's situation, but she ate it up. Wren and I edged around the curtain. In front of golden double doors, a girl about our age dropped her head into her hands. Anders stood beside her, awkwardly patting her on the back while she sniffled.

"You're the first one who's said anything." She shoved two kebabs in her mouth before wiping her eyes. "Thank you. No one else has bothered."

Anders tipped his head toward her. "Anytime. It's important we stick together, right?"

"Right." Heaving a sigh, she quickly checked the lock on the doors behind her, then switched spots with him. My heart leaped. It was working! She was leaving!

Then the sadness around her blossomed into suspicion, and then to anger.

My knees went weak at the sound of her blaster powering up. "I never told anyone what Verena said to me yesterday." She studied him for a moment. "There's no way you could have known. What's going on? Why are there two more people hiding down the hall? I can feel them."

Crap. I thought Wren and I were far enough away that she couldn't read our auras, but her skills must have been better than I'd assumed.

Wren looked at me, eyes wide. Down the hall, it seemed like Anders had forgotten how to speak. He was clutching the empty bag of kebabs, mouth agape, but then he did the only thing that made sense in his warrior's mind.

He raised his blaster and started shooting.

The guard ducked behind a pillar, firing back. Anders blew half her shield to dust with two quick shots. A chunk of marble broke off from the pillar and torpedoed down the hall toward me and Wren.

We hit the floor, crawling out from behind the curtain. "We wanted discreet!" I yelled, shooting my own blaster once the girl spotted us. "This is *not discreet*!"

Shots peppered the hallway, exploding vases of flowers on accent tables, leaving charred holes in portraits hung along the walls. Shouts filled the corridors not too far from us. More guards. Right now it was three against one, but I knew I wouldn't like the odds so much once the girl's friends showed up.

Wren shoved me down when a stream of light from the guard's blaster flew dangerously close to my head. I smelled the tips of my hair burning as it whizzed by and smashed into the wall. The floor shook, the chandelier hanging above us quaking as Wren fired back, each of her shots missing the girl, who hid behind the pillar again.

Anders caught my gaze from the other side of the hall and nodded at the ceiling. I signaled to Wren, and this time when the girl ducked out from her hiding spot to attack, all three of us shot at the chandelier. It detached with a ferocious groan, tumbling down as wires sparked and glass bulbs popped. The girl covered her head just before it hit the floor. She didn't notice Anders creeping up on her, his aura nonexistent. He struck a pressure point in her neck, and she crumpled instantly.

"She's not dead," he assured us when Wren and I hopped over the wreckage and joined him at Verena's double doors. As if he thought he still needed to convince us that he wasn't the monster his father had made him be.

"I know she's not," I said. I studied the doors. I hadn't counted on them being locked, and without a working comm, I had no way to hack into the interface and open them electronically. The voices down the corridor were growing closer, so I raised my blaster and blew the lock to smithereens. Being discreet was pointless now.

We ducked inside. Anders reached for the first thing he saw—a velvet chaise—and dragged it in front of the doors to block them.

Spinning around, we took in the room before us.

Whoa.

Billowing teal draperies hung over the windows of a massive sitting room. Everything was covered in gold—the light fixtures, the furniture, the fireplace. A diamond as big as my fist gleamed from a shelf against the wall, just *sitting there*, out in the open for anyone to touch. And Wren did touch it. She stuffed the gemstone in her pocket with zero remorse.

To the left of the sitting room, a door hung open, revealing a two-story library, dusty books spilling onto the floor. To the right, a net screen blared from a bedroom dominated by a four-poster bed. Wren looked at me right as a laugh track rang out from some kind of comedy program, her eyebrows raised so high that they almost got lost in her hairline. Secretive Empress Verena didn't seem the giggly type.

We peeked around the doorframe as more laughter echoed through the chambers. The drapes were drawn, shadowing the room, but I could make out the shape of someone in the middle of the bed.

As soon as my eyes adjusted to the darkness, my heart lurched, relief and confusion swirling into a dizzying mess in my head. *How . . . ?*

Elio was sitting on Verena's bed.

Elio. Here. *Safe.*

I stared at him, dumbstruck. All I could manage in my state of utter disbelief was, "You didn't think to unlock the door for us?"

Beep!

"We've been busy chatting," another voice croaked from beside the bed. "My apologies."

Wren's breath hitched. Anders stepped protectively in front of us, but it was unnecessary. The woman stepping out of the shadows sounded old, maybe even older than Nana Rae. Harmless. Or I hoped.

"Your android tells me the four of you have an interest in a certain key."

Empress Verena.

Even after seventeen years of living on Condor, I'd only caught glimpses of her—just a few news streams on the net screens, her face always obscured. Even now, as she took languid steps across the bedroom, I could barely see her. She was short, covered in a thick cloak despite the warmth in the mansion, and she pulled on her hood as she looked up into my eyes.

"Well. Out with it. Tell me what you want."

I knew now was the time to beg for the key, because *duh*, that's why we were here, but instead I found myself brushing past the mysterious empress and rushing to Elio's side. "Are you okay? How did you get here?"

He reached for a comm on the bedside table. *Folloed sent a foood*, he typed, pointing out a tray next to him, covered in a few scraps of meat and fruit.

"You followed the scent of the food?"

"I thought he couldn't smell," said Anders.

"Your android is very . . . human." Verena appeared behind me, making me jump. "I understand that he is not well."

"Not well is an understatement." Wren shook her head. "Hey, Empress? You aren't going to sic your guards on us, are you?"

Verena's head tilted beneath her hood.

"What she intends to say is that we mean you no harm," Anders assured her. Then he nodded at me. "Cora? Is there something you'd like to ask?"

"Oh, right. Verena—uh, *Empress* Verena . . ." I wondered if I should curtsy. "Not to be pushy, but we were hoping you could tell us about Teolia's key."

"It exists," she stated dryly.

"Of course. But *where* exactly does it exist? We need to find it. For Elio. And for the rest of us. It's critical—"

"I highly doubt that." She yanked off her hood, revealing a row of scars crisscrossing puckered cheeks. Just as the rumors claimed. After sitting, she shoved a few meat scraps from the tray beside her bed into her mouth.

"You're desperate. I can read it all over you." She turned to Wren. "And you." Her eyes roved over Anders. "But not you. You're Andillian, then? Interesting . . ."

"Verena." Stars, maybe I *should* curtsy. "Teolia's treasure—"

"A treasure of that magnitude brings with it only grief. If you are close to reuniting all the keys, as your Elio claims, then it must be destroyed."

"No! Verena, it's not that simple!" I quickly explained what Elio needed, and Evelina and the warden's plans for the elixir. Elio beeped, shaking his fists when he learned of Evelina's intentions to betray us. Anders and Wren stood by the door while I spit out the entire story, both their auras thickening with nerves.

"Eternal life is a gift that no one needs," Verena stated firmly. She turned up the volume on her net screen, attempting to end the conversation. Hoping she wouldn't have me exiled, I grabbed the remote from her and powered the program off.

"Miss Saros, my drama starts in three minutes. Today's episode reveals whether or not Carter is cheating on Marci."

"I don't care about your net drama! You can help us, Verena!"

She acted like she didn't even hear me. "How is your grandmother?"

I jerked back. "Nana Rae? She's . . . fine. Why?"

"Hmm . . ."

"Wait, do you know her?" Nana Rae had never said anything, but Nana Rae never said much that made sense anyway.

"Our paths have crossed. Is she here tonight?"

"Yes . . ."

Joints creaking, breathing heavily, Verena pushed herself out of her chair. "I am reconsidering your request—"

"Excellent!" said Wren.

"*However*, if I tell you where to locate the elixir, I still demand it be destroyed once you unlock the chest."

Shaking my head, I begged her to understand. "I need the money from the treasure for Elio."

"You need *money*. You have no need for the treasure. No one does. If you do as I ask and destroy Teolia's elixir, then I assure you, you will be compensated. It's up to you, Cora Saros, what exactly that reward will be."

My mind reached out, reading her. She was calm, telling the truth. Furthermore, she had gone from not caring about us at all to being eager to help. I glanced at Elio, who had turned the net screen back on and was watching the drama with rapt attention. A reward. That's what we needed. That, and to bring Evelina to her knees.

"How easy is the treasure to retrieve?" I asked.

Verena chuckled. "How easy do you think? It's in a pit underneath the mansion."

"Not the pit of spiders?" Anders shivered.

"No, nothing that fun. Does this mean you accept my offer?"

I looked at Wren and Anders. A silent conversation passed between us, but I knew how I would answer Verena. I'd known even before I stepped foot in her bedroom.

"We accept."

Verena loaned us fresh comms. As we left her to her net drama and hurried back through the staff corridors, I couldn't resist mulling over what she'd said about Nana Rae. Or what she hadn't said. Whatever had happened between them, it was enough to force her to help us, and that was more than I could have asked for. After tonight, Elio would have a new body. The warden would be gone. Evelina would never call me a distraction again.

The four of us split up on the ground floor. Wren and Elio returned to the labyrinth, while Anders and I made a few more tweaks to my new VED. Just before they headed back into the tunnel to hell, I reached for Wren's arm.

I nodded to Elio. "Take care of him."

Elio beeped, as if to say he could take care of himself just fine.

"Take care of each other," I amended.

"Don't worry, Cora," Wren said. "We'll be back in no time."

Once they left, Anders and I crept through the floors of the mansion, avoiding Verena's guards, even though she assured us they wouldn't touch us. We ducked into shadowed alcoves and empty rooms whenever we heard the sound of approaching footsteps, our bodies pressed too tightly for comfort. Not even two hours ago, we had been in the same position and he kissed me. But we had both been lying then.

. . . Right?

After about thirty minutes, once we passed through three floors and successfully avoided half a dozen groups of guests who were determined to collect the bounty on our heads, we found our mark.

The warden was pacing a gallery on the fourth floor, surrounded by party guests, a drink in his hand and a scowl on his lips. Miraculously, only one guard accompanied him, and he was so busy guzzling his own drink that I doubted he could even fire a blaster straight.

Anders's aura blazed like an inferno. "Can't I just kill him instead?"

"Sure," I replied. "If you think that will satisfy you."

He reined in his aura, grabbed the VED from me, and his skin started to bubble as he transformed into one of the Condorian banquet servers. "It won't."

After taking a tray of hors d'oeuvres, he milled around the gallery until he was close enough to reach the warden.

I ducked behind a pillar, held my comm up to block my face, and peeked around the glass. Anders was serving a group of elderly women whose dresses were molting bright yellow feathers. Once they were finished, he took a step back, spun on his heel . . . and crashed right into the warden's back.

"YOU IMBECILE!" the warden bellowed as the tray of hors d'oeuvres went flying. He'd spilled his drink all over his pants and shoes. Anders frantically tried to help him clean it.

"So sorry, sir. So very sorry." Anders blew out a flustered breath, steadying himself against the warden's arm while he juggled his tray, the ruined food, and pieces of broken glass.

"Don't touch me!" The warden pushed him off. "I'll have you fired!"

"You can certainly try. But somehow I think I might be one of the empress's new favorite employees." Even from across the gallery, I could see Anders's eyes narrow. He shifted the bundle in his arms, and then it just so happened to slip . . . crashing down on the warden's feet.

The warden howled. The room was bathed in a black cloud of his fury, but Anders only shrugged. "Sorry, sir. Looks like you have a little something on your shoes." He patted the warden on the back, right between his shoulder blades. As Anders dashed from the room, he turned in my direction, giving me an almost imperceptible nod.

I tapped the screen of my comm, slipping the device into my pocket before stepping out of the shadows. The guard was hunting down another drink, and he didn't even notice when I approached the warden, who was still dabbing his pants with a napkin, and tapped him on the back.

"Hiya," I greeted. "Fancy seeing you here."

"Cora Saros," he growled. His aura glistened with triumph as he looked down his nose at me. "At last, you—"

"Oh! You there! Hi!" I called to the warden's guard, who was weaving back through the crowd, fresh drink in hand. When the man spotted me, he dropped his glass. It shattered on the floor.

He raised his blaster, and the party around us ground to a halt.

Sighing theatrically, I offered the guard my hands, waiting for his biting cold shackles to clamp around my wrists.

"I guess you win," I said. "You can arrest me now."

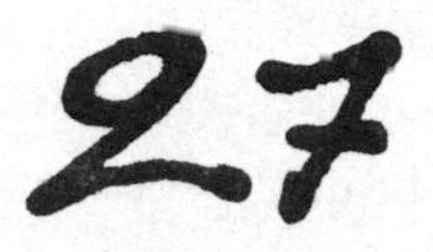

SURRENDERING WENT AGAINST EVERY INSTINCT I POSSESSED.

"Anders is in position. How did it go down there?" I whispered to Wren once the guards pulled her from the labyrinth. I'd told them exactly where to find her. The partygoers jeered as we were paraded, handcuffed, through Verena's foyer.

Wren's only response was a timid squeak.

"What's wrong? Did something happen to Elio?"

"No. He's right where he's supposed to be. But . . . we hit a snag."

"What snag? No snags. Wren, we don't have time for snags!"

Wren gulped. "The chest was at the bottom of a well. Right where Verena said. But when we pulled it up . . . the key wasn't with it."

"*What*?" I winced when the guard behind me, a brawny Andilly woman, shoved me up the ramp leading to the upper floors. Every step was one closer to Evelina. And if Wren was correct, we were about to face her while still missing the last piece of the puzzle.

"It's okay. It's fine," I muttered. "We don't need the last key. We can just blast the chest open."

"Tried that already," Wren said. "Didn't work."

"Silence!" The guards cuffed both of us on the backs of our heads.

"This is bad." My chest throbbed, my mind foggy. "This is really, really bad."

If we couldn't open the chest, Verena wouldn't get what she

wanted. And if Verena didn't get what she wanted, I wouldn't get what *I* wanted.

"We rushed into this. And just *why* did I tell everyone to meet us on the roof? I mean, I guess every good showdown takes place on a roof, but like, what's up with that?"

"You're nervous babbling," Wren hissed. "Stop it."

"I said *silence*!" The guards smacked us again.

As the screams of the crowd faded away, I was finally able to think over what Wren said. What Verena had said. She told us the chest was in the labyrinth . . . not the key. And yet, it had to be in the mansion somewhere. Surely she would have told us if it wasn't, if our plan was useless, if . . .

Oh stars.

Verena's hoarse voice filled my mind.

How is your grandmother?

Our paths have crossed.

The key was in the mansion. But it wasn't with the treasure chest.

"Wren," I gasped, "the last key is with—"

"SILENCE!" shouted the guards. They shoved us forward, hard enough to make us stumble. The door on the top floor of the mansion was thrust open, shadows from the cliffs around us flooding the air like spilled ink.

Evelina couldn't even do me the courtesy of looking at me. She glanced up from the far side of the roof, which dropped off sharply above an angry sea, and had eyes for only Wren.

"Where is it?" she hissed, hurrying forward. Our side of the tile roof sloped down gently toward the mansion gardens and the crowd celebrating in the streets. I peered over my guard's shoulder, wondering if they could all see us up here.

Evelina clenched Wren's arm. "They said you found the final key. Where is it? *Where*?"

"At least say please." Wren motioned for the guards to remove the key from the chain around her neck. The fake key I had created in the *Starchaser*'s laboratory.

Blair elbowed his mother and father. "We're going to be so rich."

Nana Rae just looked out over the ocean and smiled.

Cruz said nothing. That hurt the most. I expected Evelina's selfishness, was even shocked during those rare moments when she treated me as a human instead of a cog in the family's crime machine, but Cruz . . . he could have at least done something, one way or the other. I could feel his guilt, but if he still refused to act on it, then to me that was even worse.

Evelina snatched the key as the guards behind me and Wren shoved us to our knees beside Anders. His hands were bound, which I'd expected.

"Did they hurt you?"

He just looked at me, then looked at the ground.

Evelina's voice carried across the roof, over the roar of the wind off the ocean. "This is it, correct?"

The group of Andilly guards she was standing next to parted, revealing the warden in all of his revolting, red-faced glory. He took the key, running his fingers over the edges, sniffing the metal, poking it with his tongue.

"Appears to be a true key of Teolia." He removed a second key from an inside pocket in his coat, the gemstones sparkling even in the darkness. "This makes two. We agreed upon all four, Evelina." All twelve of his guards pointed their blasters in my family's direction. They actually looked nervous. They must have been disarmed before Wren and I reached the rooftop.

"You *will* have all four keys," Evelina insisted. "One is with my daughter. The other is with that pitiful servant bot that she drags around. Once we find it—"

"You'll do what, exactly?"

Blair cleared his throat. "We'll, uh, we'll rip it apart! Yeah. We'll throw its gears and wires in the ocean and take the key, and . . ." He trailed off under the warden's scrutinizing gaze.

"How cutthroat. But messy. I was under the impression you trained your employees better, Evelina."

She shrugged. "Blair is young."

What? She never granted me the same excuse, but I'd promised myself I would remain impassive until the right moment. But I didn't hate her any less.

"As I've told Cora," the warden said, "I expected a bit more from your family. Did you not attempt to infiltrate the treasury on Vaotis? Did you not pillage every planet in this galaxy and numerous others?"

Evelina held her head high. "Of course we did. I assure you, we are professionals. You agreed to overlook our transgressions if we located the keys."

He nodded. "So I did. The issue is that the last key is not here." He stepped away from her, kneeling down beside me and ripping the chain and the key from around my neck. Anders made a sound in the back of his throat at the sight of his father, but the warden paid him no attention. He grabbed my face instead.

"Tell me more about the impressive things your family has done, Cora Saros. If I were to take a transport across Condor to your home right now, what would I find?"

"Keep quiet!" Evelina snapped, but the warden held up a hand, silently ordering his guards to close in on her.

"You've run out of options, Miss Saros. Answer my questions honestly, and perhaps I won't kill you once we return to Andilly. Perhaps I'll only dismember two of your limbs. I'm feeling generous today."

I looked up—at Evelina, who was fuming at the line of blasters aimed at her head. At Cruz, who still said nothing. At my aunt, uncle, and cousins, who finally seemed to realize this meeting was not going according to plan.

Speaking would incriminate all of them. My family. But that was

Just a word, really. A bond made by blood. There were other kinds of families. The ones you laughed with. The ones you got sloppy drunk in a bar with and crashed a spacecraft with and walked away still breathing with. The ones who vowed to help you even after you proved you weren't worthy of their friendship. The boy and girl next to me—they were family. That group cornered by guards across the roof—they were just a bunch of people whose bad day was about to get a whole lot worse.

"If you visited my house in the manufacturing district," I told the warden, "it would look completely innocuous from the outside. But on the *inside* you would find millions of ritles, most of which were earned by ransoming a group of toddlers on Viicury about two years ago. Evelina bragged about that accomplishment for months. Let's see, what else? You would find priceless gems, all acquired illegally, typically ferried to elite jewelers throughout the universe. Ancient artifacts from Earth and Condor and everywhere in between. Blasters without proper registration. Badminton rackets and a whole crate of something from Earth called *parachute pants*, neither of which are crimes, but it does prove that Evelina has, at best, questionable taste."

Wren snorted.

"You would also find an entire family of people who are cruel to androids and humans alike, including but not limited to all the times they attacked my bot, Elio, and the time they tried to drown me in a pool to teach me how to swim—"

"We didn't drown you!" Evelina yelled. "You floated fine!"

"See? No remorse. I can see why you get along with her. I'd also like to add to the record that Evelina has tried and failed to rob Empress Verena's fine mansion once before."

The warden looked over to Evelina. "Interesting. Do you deny it?"

She huffed, exasperated. "No, I don't deny it. What is this, a trial? For as much dirt as you have on me, I have just as much on you. You sent the entire universe to hunt down a group of children for your own enjoyment. You put a bounty on their heads, but they didn't escape your prison. You let them walk right out the door!"

The warden grinned, finally releasing me. "I didn't do that," he said, standing. "Actually, what I mean to say is that *someone* here did, but it certainly wasn't me." He pointed down at Anders. "It was him."

Wren let out a theatrical gasp. "No!"

I frowned at her. "Work on your acting."

The warden stepped back. His skin started to bubble, the scar on his face replaced by several on his neck. His features shifted, turning younger, softer. A goofy grin full of life formed on his lips, a smile that I had certainly never seen the warden wear . . .

But one I had glimpsed on the face of his son several times.

After the transformation was complete, Anders—the real Anders—uncuffed my arms and Wren's, and helped us to our feet. "I never enjoyed pageantry, but that was quite fun."

"You didn't do a villainous monologue," I said. "I'm disappointed."

"Maybe next time."

"*What is going on*?" Evelina demanded. I could barely hear her over the confused mutterings of my family. Minus Nana Rae.

"What's going on," said Anders, "is a concept the Earthans refer to as *payback*." He nodded to his double, who writhed on the ground, screaming through his gag as three guards held him down. Anders pulled a comm from his pocket and tapped the screen.

In a blink, the warden appeared at our feet, seething mad.

"How's this for a villainous monologue?" Anders ripped my VED from the warden's back. "While he was fuming over getting a tray of food dumped on him, I stuck this to his jacket. His guards didn't even notice. By the time he realized he was wearing an illusion, they thought he was me and they took him into custody." He patted the warden on the cheek. "Enjoy your time in Ironside, Father. I tried my best to keep my cell warm for you."

The warden finally managed to remove his gag. "Release me!" he screamed at the guards. "As the warden of Ironside prison, I command that you release me at once!"

"They don't listen to you anymore," said Wren. "They listen to the highest bidder, who at the moment is our new friend Empress Verena of Condor." She turned toward the door leading back into the mansion.

Evelina's jaw dropped when Verena stepped out of the shadows, pushing back the hood of her cloak, and took frail steps across the roof. Her lips turned down in anger, but it shockingly wasn't because she had a group of criminals standing on top of her house.

"Carter *did* cheat on Marci," she said. "She was about to poison his dinner in revenge, but I had to turn it off to come up here and deal with all of you scoundrels!" She winked at my grandmother. "Hello, Rae-Rae."

On the other side of the roof, Nana Rae gasped. "*V*? Is it really you?" She turned to the rest of us and tried to whisper (but Nana Rae was never capable of whispering anything). "We went to the university together. We decided to just be friends, but really . . . we wanted to be *more*."

"You go, Nana," Wren cheered under her breath.

"Mother, what—" Evelina started.

"Quiet," Verena snapped. "I'll deal with you later." She held up her comm. "I was watching inside on the cameras that Miss Cora set up. And I believe I'm not the only one."

"*What*?" Evelina shrieked.

I leaned over the edge of the roof. Down below in the streets, net screens flashed, all the revelers glued to feeds from Verena's rooftop security cameras that I had rigged to broadcast into every festival tent. There would be no mistaking what happened here tonight. Verena knew the truth, and now all of Condor did too. My family and Anders's father would finally answer for their crimes.

Grinning like a maniac, Wren pulled three orange lollipops from her pocket, handing them out to me and Anders.

"The tangy taste of justice. Oh, how the tables have turned."

Verena cleared her throat. "As long-standing empress of the nation of Condor, planet nineteen in the Andromeda Galaxy, I hereby condemn the Saros family—with the exception of their daughter Cora, her grandmother Rae, and any other children under the legal age—to report to Ironside maximum security prison immediately to await formal sentencing. The same goes for Ironside's *former* warden."

"*No*!" Anders's father screamed, thrashing against the guards' hold.

"You are all being held on numerous counts of conspiracy, theft, intergalactic smuggling, trespassing, possession of illegal weapons, and murder. You are also a loathsome group of people, which technically isn't a crime, but I think it bears mentioning."

"But what about her!" Evelina started toward me, but she was held back. "Cora and her band of idiots destroyed an entire outpost! They stole a ship! Any illegal weapons I own, *she* built!"

Verena shrugged. "Their crimes are pardoned in exchange for your arrest. I am also taking into account that they brought Teolia's treasure to me. Painstaking work, which deserves to be rewarded."

"Where is the treasure?" the warden screamed. "Where is the elixir? I demand to see it!"

Beep-beep!

The door flew open again. Anders, Wren, and I ran to help Elio, who was struggling to lug an iron chest through the doorway and onto the roof. His body was dripping wet, twitching with what looked like the aftermath of a glitch, but he wrapped his arms around the chest, hugging it like a trophy.

Saturn's rings, it's really real.

The chest felt like one of the mirages in Rebrone's desert, liable to vanish if I tore my eyes away for even a second.

"Um, Nana Rae?" I said. "I think you have something we need."

"*What*?" Evelina screeched again. Stars, I wished she had a *mute* button.

Nana Rae dug through the folds of her jacket. A collective hush fell over the roof when she extracted a key—thick and brass and covered in moss—and presented it to Verena.

"I kept it safe for you, V. Just like you asked."

Wren gathered up all four keys, kneeling over the chest as she inserted each into a lock. The four of us stood behind them, turning them simultaneously.

The lid flew open with a puff of smoke.

Inside on a purple cushion lay the elixir.

Elio plucked it out, presenting it to the crowd. This was it. His salvation. All contained in a small glass vial.

Evelina lunged forward. "NO! I am not rotting in a cell while the rest of you claim my treasure! It was supposed to be mine—"

"*Ours*," interjected the warden.

"Oh shut up, you pathetic man. All of you *shut up*!"

Cruz looked at me over Evelina's head and shrugged. He seemed unperturbed to be surrounded by so many guards. Blair and his parents punched and kicked at the guards before being thrown to the ground.

Evelina bit at a man's hand before he struck her in the temple. He tried to snap cuffs around her wrists, but she ducked under his arm, spinning with the grace of a dancer. Of a thief who didn't know the meaning of getting caught. She ripped his blaster from his belt. Then, faster than I could process what was happening, she aimed her weapon at the chest.

No—she aimed her weapon at the four of us, standing behind it.

Anders and I reached for our blasters, but Evelina had already pulled her trigger. Her shot soared across the roof, an arch of cracking blue energy aimed right at Wren's heart—

I lunged to grab her, but I was too slow.

Elio leaped into the air to protect her—his friend—and the shot hit him instead.

"ELIO!"

I screamed as he shoved Wren out of harm's way—right before the blast threw him backward off the highest point of the roof.

With only the cliffs below to break his fall.

I rushed to the edge. The blaster's glow fizzled around him, ripping through his weak body, tearing apart every panel and gear and wire I loved so much.

We weren't in Verena's labyrinth anymore. There was no hologram at the bottom to disappear through. No chute to carry him away to safety. Nothing.

He collided with a cliff halfway down, his body splintering in two.

Then he hit the ocean and vanished beneath the waves.

I RAN THROUGH THE MANSION SO FAST I DIDN'T EVEN FEEL my feet hit the floor.

"*Cora*!" Anders chased after me, but I didn't respond.

I sprinted all the way down to the water's edge, where I finally sank to my knees in the sand. The tide was high, soaking me up to my hips. I wasn't afraid of it this time; I wasn't worried about drowning, not when Elio was already gone. Elio plucked it out, presenting it to the crowd. This was it. His salvation. All contained in a small glass vial, but destroying it didn't matter now. Nothing did.

"I can go out there," Anders said, pulling at the buttons on his shirt. "I'm a good swimmer. I can pull him out."

What was even left to pull out?

I fisted my hands in the sand, feeling a clump of seaweed curl around my wrists. Footsteps sounded on the beach behind us. Wren had caught up, followed by Nana Rae, Verena, and a small cluster of her guards. No sight of Cruz or Evelina or Blair or the warden. Good. I hoped they all got ripped to shreds in Ironside.

Anders paced the shoreline, squinting at the waves. "There has to be something we can—*Cora, look*!"

"What?"

"There! About five yards out."

I stood to get a better view as the tide rolled around us. Something was gleaming in the water. A piece of metal . . .

A hand.

The tide pushed it against my legs, and I picked it up. Elio's hand, full of holes, wires dangling out. And around us, more pieces of him dragged in by the tide. A leg, an ear, one of the sensors from his eyes. All that was left of my best friend.

Anders collected the parts as I choked back a sob. "I'm so sorry, Cora," he murmured. "I wish . . ."

I blocked him out. His apologies, Wren's frantic murmurs to Verena on the beach. None of them were here. It was just me and Elio. Like life used to be before everything got so messed up.

And then . . . an idea struck me.

My thoughts were moving too fast for me to reason with them. I ripped off my shoes and dived into the waves.

"*CORA*!" Wren and Anders yelled.

The water was cold enough to freeze the air in my lungs. I heard a splash behind me, more yelling, but I ignored them. A wave crashed over my head. I was thrown under. Upside down. Right side up. I couldn't tell.

My arms flailed, searching, but the water was too dark. I pushed myself toward what I thought might be the seabed, lungs screaming for air. Everything on this star-forsaken planet was too dark, and Elio was dead, and—

A blue light blazed around me.

I spun around, a stream of bubbles escaping my mouth in shock. A shape hovered in the water with me, holding a blaster. The figure shot again, and the glow illuminated Anders's face.

He shot a third time before pointing to the ocean floor.

Using the beam from the blaster as a searchlight, I could finally see just how much of Elio there was to sort through. Gears and bolts and sensors and chips. But it was a large panel, wedged between two rocks, that caught my attention. I reached for it, wrapped my fingers around its edges, pushing through the fog pressing on my mind.

My chest was on fire. My head was on fire. I was breaking apart, just like Elio . . .

With a fierce *yunk*, I was sucked backward and dragged toward the surface. As soon as my face hit the air, I hacked up a mouthful of water—spitting it directly into Anders's eyes.

Grimacing, he let the waves push us back to shore, refusing to release me until we washed up on the beach and Wren dragged us across the sand.

"Did you—did you get it?" he asked between coughs. "Whatever *it* is?"

I nodded, throat burning, salt water stinging my eyes. I showed them the square panel I'd freed from the ocean's grip.

"What's that?" Wren asked.

Heart throbbing, I pushed aside wires running back and forth into various ports, searching for a watertight compartment. If there was any chance it survived, any chance Evelina's blaster hadn't fried it completely . . .

My nails hit home. I dug them into the little box beside Elio's auditory interface and pulled the latch open.

"It's his memory core." Under the moonlight, a small glass cube twinkled, frosted as if it were covered in ice. "And it's still whole."

"So if we get him another body," Wren said, "could you transfer his memories—?"

"Yes," I breathed. I dug my fingers into their arms. "Yes, yes, yes!"

Elio was still here, his entire life sitting in the palm of my hand, and as soon as I got a new bot I would bring him back.

"Excuse me? Miss Saros?" In my excitement, I hadn't noticed Verena creep up behind us. Nana Rae watched us all with concern from the edge of the beach.

"Miss Saros, was the elixir lost in Elio's fall?"

We all nodded.

"Good." Verena smiled. "Thank you."

"Don't thank us quite yet." I laughed. "You should see all the property damage we did in order to get here."

"Nonetheless. I believe I owe you a reward." She nodded to the cube cupped in my hands. "You need only ask."

Wren let out a happy squeal, squeezing my shoulders. "Go ahead, Cora. Ask."

"I . . ."

Anders had gotten revenge on his father. I'd given Evelina what she deserved. I still had Elio. I didn't need Verena's reward. I already got exactly what I wanted.

But what did Wren get? She wanted friends, and she stood by me even when it was the last thing I deserved. Her heart was so much bigger than mine, and when Elio was here he had seen it too. He could wait a little longer for his new body. No matter what, he would want her to be happy.

"Actually, Empress Verena . . ." Turning to Wren, I watched with glee as her eyes went wide. "If you have the resources, Wren has a lost brother who needs finding."

"Can someone tell me what this is?" Wren yelled from the closet in Evelina's foyer. Well, I guess it was now Nana Rae's foyer—and sometimes Verena's foyer, whenever she came over for a visit. "Is this a magic hammer or something?"

I looked down the hall to see what she was holding up. "That's a croquet mallet."

"A cricket mallet?"

"No, a *croquet*—wait, aren't you supposed to know this stuff? You're Earthan."

She tossed the mallet back in the closet and slammed the door.

"Doesn't mean I've ever had a cricket mallet. Your parents have a lot of weird stuff in here."

If weird was synonymous with *way too much*, then yes, it was plenty weird. I'd spent the weeks following the New Moon trying to clean it up, selling the more expensive items. Most of the stolen artwork was returned to the same galleries that Cruz and Evelina had taken it from. Occasionally, the curators gave me a finder's fee, more out of pity than anything, but I wasn't complaining. Nana Rae helped when she had time, and day by day the floors of the house grew tidier, emptier—especially with significantly fewer people dumping their stolen treasures throughout its halls.

"What are we having for dinner?" Wren scrolled through her comm. "I heard that porci puffs are on special at that deli down the street, but somehow eating one feels wrong. Is fried jellyfish any good?"

I shrugged from my spot at the kitchen table. "Order anything you want. I'm almost done here."

"I'm putting in a vote for pon," Anders mumbled around the lollipop in his mouth. He dropped his hand on top of mine. He was doing that a lot lately—the hand-holding thing. We hadn't done anything else, not after everything that happened at Verena's party, but it was still nice to know he cared.

Picking up the pliers on the table, I gave the wires in front of me two final twists before snapping the control panel shut. "Wren! You better get enough food for four."

"Wait, wait, wait!" The floor shook as she ran down the hall and skidded into the kitchen. "Did I miss it?"

"You're just in time," said Anders.

"Thank the stars!" She looked down at her comm. "Marcus, I gotta go. What? Yes, of course I'm flying out to meet you for Christmas! Condor doesn't celebrate, so I'm not staying here. No, I'm not giving you a venomous shrub from Cadrolla as a gift! Are you insane?"

Anders and I looked at each other, snickering. Ever since Verena sent out her personal team of investigators to locate Wren's brother, she hadn't gone more than a few hours without comming him to chat. They'd found the boy on an outpost in the central Milky Way, ferrying aristocratic businessmen and women on a loop from Uranus to Mars in order to work off a debt he owed to the warden. Anders's father had given him money for a new spacecraft, but he'd been too ashamed to tell his family the truth of where it had come from. Now that the warden was behind bars, Marcus was raking in the cash, so Wren couldn't exactly be angry with him. Just because she was now making a conscious effort not to steal (as often) didn't mean she no longer appreciated his huge stacks of money.

"Okay, okay! I'll *try* to get you the venomous shrub. Marcus, I have to go!" Wren disconnected her comm with a beep, then wiped her brow. "Kids, right? Sheesh!" She looked at the table, a huge grin spreading across her face. "Is he ready?"

I nodded. "He should be waking up in three . . . two . . . one . . ."

Beeeeep!

The three of us huddled around the bot lying on the table as he squeezed his hands into fists, slowly turning his head from side to side. He hadn't opened his eyes yet, and I held my breath, afraid that something would be different. That a fancier body would somehow change the friend I had known all my life.

After a minute, he sat up, feet swinging toward the floor, eyes fluttering open. They weren't as large as the sensors on his old body. His eyes looked more human, as did his ears, which were small and round instead of flopping onto his shoulders. He was taller now, too. All the new models were taller, and I'd used every ritle I'd saved up recently from purging the house to buy Elio the nicest, tallest body I could find.

The fan in his central processor whirred while he stretched his arms, no wire patches or dents in sight. His mouth popped open in awe, and then, after what felt like the longest moment of my life, he looked at me and smiled.

"I hope you brought me a milkshake to smell."

"Elio!" I threw my arms around him, squeezing him to my chest. Finally, after enduring so much, he was here. He was safe.

"I missed you too," he mumbled into my hair. "I fell off a building."

"I know you did. I know."

"It really hurt."

"I'm sure it did." I pulled back. "Here, I didn't get you a milkshake, but I got you something else." I grabbed a strip of brown fluff off the counter.

"A mustache! You remembered!" Elio ripped off the adhesive and slapped it on his face. "Friends, how do I look?"

"Very dignified," Anders said.

"Very human," Wren added.

Elio pumped his arms in the air. "*Yes*!" He looked around at all of us. "So . . . what happened after I . . . ?"

"Died?" Anders finished. I punched his arm.

"You're so insensitive!"

"You said I had a gentle soul!"

I ignored him. "Cruz, Evelina, and the warden are gone. They're in Ironside. Evelina has tried comming me and Nana a few times, but we keep ignoring her."

"That's what the wicked witch deserves," Elio said.

Squealing, Wren held out her hand for a high five. "Elio! Babycakes! I've seen that net drama too!"

Anders pushed her out of the way. "They all ended up in the same cell we did, if you can believe it. I visited the prison the other day to make sure they're being shackled properly. They seem pretty happy, actually. If they knew how many times I pissed in the corner of that cell, they'd feel differently, but I'm not planning on telling them."

"There's our Andilly warrior," said Wren. "Classy to the max."

Anders pushed out a claw and waved it in her face.

"Hmmm . . . what else has been going on?" Wren tapped her chin. "Oh! I have news! I just got a new ship!"

My jaw fell open. "You did? Wait, when you say 'got a ship,' did you steal it or did you—?"

"No, I *bought* it. Ye of little faith." She showed us a photo on her comm. The ship was sleek, painted as black as the Condor sky. Most importantly, it wasn't hideous.

"I have a name all picked out. Ready? It's so good. I'm calling it . . . the *Disaster*."

I laughed so hard that I started snorting, which just made all of us laugh even harder. "That's ironic."

"I know! But wait, there's more. This is colossally big." Eyes alight, she leaned forward. "I heard from my brother, who heard from his mechanic, who heard from her cousin's boyfriend's sister's bartender that there's another one of those dangerous, life-altering treasures lurking around in the Sombrero Galaxy." Wren leaned back in her chair, legs crossed. "Supposedly, it's some magic rock that can create alternate dimensions, shift the fabric of reality. I've even heard it has the potential to clone an army of humans. How scary is that?"

Anders frowned. "Sounds like it would be detrimental in the wrong hands, certainly."

"I was going to say it would sell for billions of ritles on the black market, but sure, that too. I just want to find the star-forsaken thing." She looked around at all of us, then her gaze dropped to the floor, suddenly shy. "I, uh, I was hoping maybe you all would want to find it with me?"

Elio gasped. "As long as I get to bring snacks, I'm in."

"Done! Chef Elio is onboard! Andykins? Cora? C'mon, you can't let us go without you."

Anders nudged me in the shoulder just before his hand tangled up with mine again. "I have nothing else on my agenda," he said. "If you buy me four blasters and two bags of lollipops, then I'll consider coming."

"Two blasters and one bag," Wren countered.

"Three blasters and three bags. And I get to insult all your stupid ideas as much as I want."

"You do that anyway!"

"So it shouldn't be a problem." He squeezed my hand again. "Cora? What do you want? Her guard is down, so now's the time to make your demands."

Laughing, I shook my head. I didn't have demands. Spending time with them, sitting in my kitchen taking jabs at one another, was more than I had ever wanted.

I'd never considered this house my home. I still didn't. Home was always wherever Elio was. And now, it was with Wren and Anders too. There was nothing for me on Condor. Nana Rae didn't need me to stay. She had Verena. And I had my own family now.

"You know . . . ," I said, rubbing my hands together. "We're probably the best idiots for this job . . ."

Wren's grin flared. "We're the *only* idiots for this job."

"Thank goodness we don't have competition," Elio added with an excited beep.

Anders groaned. "Can we please rephrase this so it doesn't sound so derogatory?"

"Certainly." Wren cleared her throat. "*Anders* is the best idiot for the job. Now you have bragging rights."

"I can't believe I'm getting back on a ship with you imbeciles."

"Now who's being derogatory?" Elio puffed out his chest. "At least we're the best imbeciles."

All of us laughed, even Anders. After Wren sobered up and wiped the tears from her eyes, she nudged my leg with her boot. "Are we doing this or what?"

I thought about it, even though I already knew what to say. When we were on Tunerth, Wren had called us the start of a really bad joke. *An Earthan, two aliens, and a robot walk into a bar . . .* But today's joke was far more satisfying.

An Earthan, two aliens, and a robot board a ship and take on the universe . . .

That treasure wouldn't know what hit it.

Kicking up my legs into Anders's lap, I reached for Elio's shiny new hand. Turning to Wren, I smiled and then asked her, "So, Captain . . . when do we take off?"

ACKNOWLEDGMENTS

Somehow, I naively thought I would be the exception to the *writing a second book is really super hard* rule. Yeah. That didn't happen. Now that I'm no longer pounding my laptop keyboard at four in the morning, I can finally collect my thoughts long enough to say THANK YOU!

It truly takes a village to create a book, and this story could not have grown without a tremendous amount of help from the following people:

Emily Settle: I am so grateful to have an editor who appreciates and encourages all the weird jokes I make in my manuscripts. (And also one who christens my characters "the cinnamon roll," "the burnt cinnamon roll," etc.) Thank you for your kind critiques when I'm writing something super weird and wrong, and for your enthusiasm when I'm writing something (still) super weird but at least funny. I appreciate you SO MUCH!

Jean Feiwel, Lauren Scobell, Liz Dresner, Brittany Pearlman, Kelsey Marrujo, Teresa Ferraiolo, and everyone at Swoon Reads and Macmillan who works so hard to bring these books into your hands: you are all rock stars! Thank you! And thanks for letting me stick around to write a second book for you. (Hehehe!)

Markia Jenai: thank you for creating the zany mugshot cover of my dreams!!! You nailed it! It's safe to say that I'll be fangirling over it for a *long* time. Anah Tillar: thank you for your help reviewing Wren's character. I appreciate your time and your insight so much!

Readers, booksellers, librarians, teachers, bloggers, and bookstagrammers: Thank you for your support, your reviews, your tweets, and your gorgeous photos that always leave me squealing at my phone in glee. Books are nothing without the people who read them. Thank you from the bottom of my heart for supporting mine.

The Swoon Squad (aka the coolest group of writers on the whole gosh darn internet): thank you for the love, the support, and for always *getting it* when it seems like no one else does. Stay awesome, friends!

Big thanks to the pool deck at Disney's All-Star Movies Resort, where I did chapters seven through ten of my line edits. If I could work there all the time, then I suspect I would be a million times more productive.

My amazing friends: I'm so sorry for all the times I told you, "I'd like to grab dinner, but I literally can't leave my computer this weekend." I'm not sure I deserve your support, but I'm so thankful to have it.

And last, but certainly not least, Mom and Dad (and Coop!): thank you for your love and unwavering support, for passing out bookmarks to the entirety of Giant Eagle every "Happy Wednesday," for helping me through my plethora of anxiety attacks, and for always ensuring I'm not starving in a ditch somewhere. I love you. I promise I'm working on getting more sleep!!!